AH

THE LIVERPOOL MATCHGIRL

Liverpool, 1901. The Tempest family is all but destitute, barely able to put food on the table. When Florrie falls ill with pneumonia and Arthur is imprisoned after a drunken fight, their thirteen-year-old daughter Lizzie finds herself parentless, desperate and alone. Despite her young age, Lizzie has spirit and determination, and she knows that she must find work to keep herself off the streets. In a stroke of luck, she gets a job in the match factory, and foreman George Rutherford takes her under his wing. But will her new home with the Rutherfords shield her from trouble ahead?

THE LIVERPOOL MATCHGIRL

THE LIVERPOOL MATCHGIRL

by

Lyn Andrews

Magna Large Print Books
Gargrave, North Yorkshire,
BD23 3SE, England.

British Library Cataloguing in Publication Data.

A catalogue record of this book is
available from the British Library

ISBN   978-0-7505-4728-4

First published in Great Britain in 2018 by
Headline Publishing Group

Published in Large Print 2019 by arrangement with
Headline Publishing Group Ltd.

Magna Large Print is an imprint of Library Magna Books Ltd.

Printed and bound in Great Britain by
T.J. (International) Ltd., Cornwall, PL28 8RW

For Alice and Jill Bennett, not forgetting Bob Bennett (of England World Cricket Management fame), who enjoy my books and with whom we have spent so many happy Sunday lunch times and strolls along the Promenade at Peel.

As Lynda Ormesher and Alice Ormerod we both had down-to-earth, no-nonsense Lancashire upbringings, which is probably why as Lyn Andrews and Alice Bennett we get on so well together. Alice, you're a star!

My very special thanks go to Jill Bennett, without whose kindness and generosity this book might never have made it to publication so soon. After falling and fracturing my right shoulder (and I'm right-handed) it looked as if publication would be delayed for an indefinite period, but thanks to Jill who valiantly stepped in and typed up the notes I dictated (quite an experience for both of us!) we got it to Headline and hence my readers.

Lyn Andrews
Isle of Man 2017

Part One

Chapter One

Liverpool
1901

Lizzie, wake up! Wake up! Come on, luv, you have to get up *now!*'

The urgency of the words gradually penetrated Lizzie's sleep-clogged mind but she wriggled further down in the bed. She didn't want to wake up – and she certainly didn't want to get out of her warm bed.

'Lizzie, there's no time to be tardy! Get up!' Florrie Tempest shook her daughter, her face taut with anxiety. She wished she could let the girl sleep on, but she couldn't.

Reluctantly Lizzie rubbed her eyes and struggled to sit up. 'Oh, Mam! It's the middle of the night and its cold!' she protested, shivering as she clutched the thin blanket tightly to her.

'I know, Lizzie, but ... but we've got to ... *go!*'

Lizzie's eyes opened wider, her heart sank and she pulled a face. How many times before in her life had she heard those words? Too many, and she knew from bitter experience just what her mam was telling her. 'Oh, not *again*, Mam! Where are we going this time?'

Florrie allowed herself the luxury of sitting down on the edge of the flock mattress. 'Bootle ... to Bennett Street your da said we're to go. I'm afraid it's going to be a long walk, luv.'

Lizzie nodded as she swung her legs over the edge of the bed, curling her toes against the icy cold of the bare flagged floor, knowing her mam was right. It was a long way to walk. She had no idea what time it was, but she was certain there would be no trams or omnibuses running – even if they'd been able to afford the fare, which they decidedly could not. They were embarking on yet another 'moonlight flit' because, obviously, her da hadn't paid the rent in weeks.

Over the years they'd had to move from one dilapidated, dismal, damp room to the next in every slum area of the city. Her da must owe pounds in unpaid rent to numerous landlords but she now realised that things had obviously become so bad that they were having to 'flit' even further away. To Bootle which, although adjacent to Liverpool, was not a suburb or a borough but a totally separate town. It had its own town hall, Mayor and Corporation, hospitals, churches and schools, trams and – more to the point – its own police force.

She shivered and frowned, remembering that her da and her eldest brother, Billy, were well known to the scuffers in Liverpool. In fact, eighteen-year-old Billy was currently serving time with hard labour in Walton Jail for theft. Her da too had spent time in the cells in the Bridewell and had gained something of a reputation as a persistent troublemaker, which was why he could seldom get any work. Her other brother, Edward – or Ned, as he was known – had declared when he was fifteen that he'd had enough of the 'Pool'

14

and had gone to try to find work somewhere else, and they'd not heard from him since. She didn't even know if he was alive or dead, and she knew her mam worried about him.

If she was truthful, she didn't miss Billy at all; he'd never paid her much attention – she being five years younger – and had viewed her as something of a nuisance. She did miss Ned, though, for he'd always been more open, more affectionate and more cheerful than Billy. He'd been the one who had picked her up when she'd fallen over as a small child; he'd taken her side when she'd been teased and tormented by kids in the street. He'd tried to cheer her up when they were both hungry and cold and had been forced to move on – again. But even if, by some remote chance, he'd written to them, they moved so often that they never received any mail.

'Have you got all our bits together, Mam?' she asked as she began to search around in the dark for her boots and her shawl. She knew her mother dared not light the stump of a candle in case it alerted someone to the fact they were up and about. They never used the gaslight; there was never the penny to spare for it. She'd slept in her clothes for the bit of added warmth they provided, so at least she didn't have to get dressed.

Florrie got up, pulling her own shawl tightly around her thin shoulders as she sighed heavily. There wasn't much to 'get together'; what little they did have she'd already tied up in a bundle. 'Our things are by the door, luv,' she replied heavily. The last thing she wanted was to move yet again. She was sick and tired of it all, but she'd long ago realised that Arthur Tempest – or 'Art', as he was known to his disreputable so-called 'mates' – would spend whatever he managed to get his hands on buying beer before he'd pay the rent, putting them constantly at risk of eviction and leaving very little for food or other basic necessities. She shook her head sadly, thinking things hadn't always been like this – not in the first couple of years of her marriage, anyway.

She'd been a plump, pretty girl then, with light blonde hair and vivid blue eyes, and Art had been a well-built, handsome lad with a shock of thick black curls and brown eyes that had always held a twinkle. They'd had high hopes of one day living in a decent house – a whole house and not just a room – with enough money for food and clothes and fuel to keep the place warm in winter, and maybe the occasional night at the music hall as a treat. But those hopes had all faded when she'd had to give up her factory job after Billy was born, and then Ned. And then they'd died completely as Art had become disillusioned and increasingly bitter, while they'd sunk deeper and deeper into grinding poverty. Eventually he'd turned to drink to try to get through the depressing days and months and years. Now, she knew she looked old beyond her years; she was painfully thin, her hair was lank and streaked with grey, and constant worry and fear had etched deep lines on her face. Art's hair too was turning grey, and drink had coarsened his features and soured an already volatile temper.

She sighed as she put her arm around Lizzie's thin shoulders. With decent food and clothes

Lizzie would be a pretty girl; she'd inherited her father's thick, dark curling hair and her mother's lively blue eyes. At least she'd managed to rear Lizzie to the age of thirteen. She'd lost both Lily and Sarah when they'd been barely toddlers. Babies and children had a hard time surviving the slums of Liverpool.

'Come on, luv, we'd better get going,' she urged, trying to put a brave face on the situation.

'Where's Da?' Lizzie asked, still filled with bitter resentment at their predicament.

'He's going to meet us at Miller's Bridge. He said it's not far from there. He ... he hopes he'll have a better chance of getting work on the Bootle docks – you know he's never had much luck on the docks up here.'

Lizzie didn't reply, but she didn't feel very optimistic about his chances. She knew her da had been marked out for years as a habitual drunkard and troublemaker, so he seldom got taken on anywhere. Maybe he'd stay out of the pubs in Bootle. She took some comfort from the fact that he wouldn't have the money to be coming back here regularly to visit his 'mates' – he certainly wouldn't walk all that way and back. Things just might improve. Her mam seemed to have accepted the way things were, but she herself found it hard; she'd noted that other people's lives, although far from easy, didn't seem as desperately bad as theirs. If only her da could get steady work and not waste his wages, she was sure life would become a lot easier for them all.

Picking up the bundle, Florrie cautiously opened the door, knowing the hinges creaked from lack of oil, and wincing as they did so. She was terrified the noise would wake someone up, but the house remained silent. She urged Lizzie to follow her out into the dark, narrow lobby and they groped their way along the wall to the front door, which was never locked – after all, the occupants had nothing worth stealing. Both were relieved when they were at last out in the street.

The January night was bitterly cold. Frost sparkled on the cobbles and had etched delicate patterns on the darkened windowpanes of the surrounding houses, and the water in the gutters was frozen solid. The sky was dark but the moon was very bright; thousands of stars were visible, but it was quiet and there was no one in sight.

'Well, I'm not sorry to be leaving this place,' Lizzie whispered as they made their way as quickly but as carefully as they could towards the end of the street. 'Maybe this new one will be better, Mam. Did Da say anything about it?'

Florrie shrugged. She didn't have the girl's optimism. 'Not really. He just said it was a "decent enough" room with a few pieces of furniture and isn't going to cost much to rent.'

Lizzie wondered about how decent it would really be, but she was glad that there would be furniture, for they had none at all of their own; their few pieces had been pawned or sold long ago. They didn't even have any pans or plates or mugs, just a battered old kettle and one small blackened pot. Not that there was any need for such luxuries as pans and plates. There was hardly ever anything other than bread and a bit of dripping to eat. They used salvaged empty jam jars to drink the weak,

18

unsweetened tea which was their only beverage, besides water from the standpipe in the street – and folk said that wasn't safe to drink.

As they trudged on, through the silent and deserted streets, Lizzie felt her fingers and toes becoming numb. She had no stockings, and her thin dress and shawl did little to combat the bitter cold. She began to shiver uncontrollably and prayed they wouldn't be confronted by a copper on his beat, for they had no plausible reason to be out at this time of night in such weather and could be arrested as vagrants. She also prayed that her da would indeed be waiting for them when they reached Miller's Bridge, not sleeping off a bellyful of ale in some dosshouse. If he wasn't, how would they find Bennett Street on their own? she thought fearfully. There was no one about to ask, and they couldn't go banging on doors at this hour.

'Is it much further, Mam?' They seemed to having been walking for ages now, and she was tired, cold and hungry.

'I don't think so, Lizzie. I noticed that this road is called Brasenose Road, and your da said Miller's Bridge Road crosses it. So we must be nearly there by now,' Florrie replied thankfully. She too felt she could not go much further. She was feeling sick and dizzy with exhaustion and lack of food.

They both halted as they reached the cross-roads and stood peering into the darkness of the deserted streets, which was alleviated a little by the few gaslights that still burned. Down to their left Lizzie could just make out the looming bulk of the huge warehouses that bounded the docks, and she knew that the river lay beyond. But then, to her profound relief, she caught sight of a familiar figure emerging from a doorway.

'Well, youse two certainly took yer time about getting here! Me feet feel like two blocks of flaming ice!' Art Tempest muttered belligerently.

Both Lizzie and Florrie smiled, despite the far from cheerful greeting.

'It's a long way to walk, Da, and we're freezing cold too,' Lizzie reminded him.

'Well, we're here now, so let's go and find this house in Bennett Street. I'm fair dropping, I'm that tired,' Florrie urged, handing the bundle containing their possessions over to her husband. He did smell of beer but, thankfully, he wasn't drunk – he must have managed to pay at least a week's rent on this new place.

Lizzie tagged along behind, also relieved at her da's presence, but wondering just how squalid the new room would be. It was always the same, she mused sadly. Da would never change, he was just ... Da. Well, she'd try to get a job, she vowed to herself. Any kind of a job would do, as long as she could earn a few shillings. She knew she was officially too young to be employed, but maybe if she said she was fourteen she'd find something. True, she had virtually no education, for she'd often been unable to go to school – she'd had no boots to wear, let alone a decent dress or pinafore, so she'd stayed at home. And they'd moved so frequently that she'd learned very little in the numerous schools she'd attended – the School Board hadn't bothered much about the likes of her and her lack of attendance. She'd never stayed long enough in one place to make any real friends, either. She was small, even for thirteen, so she didn't hold out much hope of passing for fourteen, but she had to try. She was fed up being forever hungry, cold, dirty and poorly dressed. Like her brother Ned, she was sick of the 'Pool'. So maybe Bootle would prove to be a turning point in her short life – and one for the better.

Suddenly she remembered that they were just one year into the new century. Was that a good omen? she wondered. Everyone in their old street had seemed to think so, and that provided a glimmer of optimism; maybe they'd left the bad old days behind. That thought buoyed her up as she trudged the last few yards behind her parents.

When her father had lit the candle that stood in a battered tin holder on the mantel over the range, Lizzie looked around curiously. From what she could see this was indeed a far better room than the one they'd left. There was a big iron-framed bed taking up most of the space, but it had a mattress over which was spread a faded patchwork quilt. There was a small table and two straight-backed wooden chairs, a mesh-fronted food press and a chest of drawers. There was even a bit of a rag rug, set before the range, over which the previous tenants had rigged up a line, obviously to dry clothes.

'Well?' Art demanded, sitting down in one of the chairs and rubbing his cold hands together.

'This will do us just fine, Art. You did well to find it, it's much better than Fulton Street,' Florrie replied gratefully. But she couldn't help

21

wondering how long it would be before the chest of drawers and the table would have to be chopped up for firewood. They seldom had money for coal, and it was one of Lizzie's jobs to scour the streets for anything that would burn. There were no curtains at the window – but then, it had been years since she'd last had a pair of curtains. 'I'll get the bundle unpacked, it will seem more like home with our bits and pieces around us.'

Lizzie smiled tiredly at her mam; she knew Florrie was exhausted, but she was trying to make the best of things. All Lizzie wanted to do was climb into that bed and pull the quilt around her and sleep, but she doubted she would be very comfortable. They would all have to share the bed, but that didn't bother her. She was always so exhausted that she slept soundly all night – but her da would take up most of the space, as usual.

'I don't suppose there's anything ter eat in that bundle of stuff?' Art queried, taking off his boots.

Florrie shook her head. 'Sorry, luv, there isn't. But first thing, I'll go and find a shop that might give us some bread and tea – on the slate, like.'

Lizzie watched her father climb into the bed and pull the quilt over him. As she'd assumed, he took up most of the space; she'd have to make do with a few inches on the edge, as would her mam. Her belly rumbled emptily but she tried to ignore it. She'd go with her mam when it got light to find a shop, and just pray that the shopkeeper would take pity on them. Then she'd try to get her bearings in this new area and see what chances it offered of a job for her. Surely there must be a way out of all this?

Chapter Two

She'd slept fitfully until she was woken by the dismal grey light of the winter morning that crept in through the curtainless window. For a few seconds she couldn't remember where she was. But taking in the few pieces of old, scarred furniture, she remembered and sat up. She was surprised to see that both her parents were already up. Her da was pulling on his old jacket and wrapping a grubby muffler around his neck, and her mam was trying to get a small fire lit in the range with the aid of some bits of wood and an old newspaper that she'd found in a corner of the room.

'Maybe you'll have some luck today at the docks, Art,' Florrie said hopefully, blowing on the tiny flame.

'I'll give the Brocklebank dock a go first, as it's the nearest. A feller I met in a pub opposite the dock gate said the blockerman there isn't a bad bloke,' he informed her.

Florrie nodded, picturing the foreman – or 'blockerman' – in his bowler hat. Maybe her husband would indeed manage to get at least half a day's work, but how long would it be before he got into an argument with someone – probably the blockerman? 'Good luck, then,' she nodded, trying to sound encouraging.

'I wonder what the neighbours are like, Mam?' Lizzie ventured after her father had left. She had no idea how many other people lived in this small terraced house. As they'd arrived in the middle of the night, it would be obvious to everyone that they'd left their last place in a hurry.

'I suppose we'll find out today, Lizzie. Oh, this fire is going to die on me, I just know it! The paper's damp – and so are these bits of kindling.'

'Maybe we'll find some good bits of wood and thick cardboard while we're out, Mam,' Lizzie said hopefully. There was nothing at all for breakfast, so the first thing they had to do was go out and find a shop.

As soon as they went out of the front door Lizzie realised the narrow street of terraced houses ran from Derby Road at its bottom end to the canal at the top end. She could see that there would be no shops up there and was about to remark on this fact to her mother when a woman emerged from the doorway behind them.

'You look a bit lost, missus. Are you the ones who moved in late last night? I'm Nellie Gibbons,' the woman greeted them affably.

Lizzie studied her as Florrie nodded. She looked to be about her mam's age but she was better dressed, with a heavy, lined shawl over a flannel blouse and thick worsted skirt. Lizzie also noticed that she had good stout boots. A hemp shopping bag was over one arm and she clutched a battered purse in the other hand.

'I'm Florrie Tempest and this here is our Lizzie. Me husband's gone to see iffen he can get any work.'

'What does he do then, luv?' Nellie asked.

'He's a docker – a "holdsman",' explained Florrie. 'Things haven't been good lately, not for Art – on the Liverpool docks, at least. We're hoping it will be better down here.'

The other woman nodded her understanding. It was a familiar story; work was hard to find for unskilled labourers but, not having met the man, she couldn't judge if there was another reason why things had obviously gone very wrong for this family. Both her new neighbour and the girl looked half-starved, and it was obvious they'd had to do a 'flit' – something she too had had to undertake once or twice in her married life, although not for years now, thankfully. But she had taken a liking to them both for, despite their obvious plight, Florrie hadn't made a meal of her situation – and the child looked bright enough.

'Well, Florrie, I hope you're right. I'm just off down to see Sadie Morgan at the shop on the corner of the dock road. Why don't the pair of you come with me and I'll introduce you, like? I don't suppose you know this area at all?'

Florrie nodded gratefully. If Nellie Gibbons was prepared to 'introduce' her to the woman who had the corner shop, she stood a better chance of getting a few things on tick.

As they walked the two women chatted amiably, and Lizzie listened while taking in her new surroundings. They really didn't seem very different at all to the area they'd just left, she mused. Same rows of old terraced houses all blackened with soot, same dirty narrow cobbled streets, same number of pubs and warehouses. She learned that Nellie's husband usually managed to get work helping one or other of the carters who ferried goods by horse and cart from the docks to various parts of the city, as he was known to be reliable; but it also helped that she had two daughters who both had factory jobs locally and so contributed to the household budget. That there were factories in the area employing women and girls made Lizzie feel far more optimistic about the chance of a job for herself. She also learned that the Gibbons family rented two rooms and that there were two other tenants in the house, both of whom were unmarried men with regular work who tended to keep themselves to themselves, although it wasn't unknown for Mr Herbert to go for a pint or two with Ernie Gibbons on occasion.

Morgan's corner shop was the usual small, rather dark premises crammed with goods of all descriptions from tea, sugar, flour, oatmeal, bacon, lard, molasses and treacle to small bundles of kindling known as 'chips', washing soda, starch, carbolic soap, small bags of coal and even mop heads. There were already two other women purchasing groceries when Lizzie, her mam and their neighbour entered.

'Mornin', Nellie, I'll be with you in a minute,' the woman who was serving called out as Lizzie looked around, feeling hunger gnaw at her belly as she sniffed the tantalising smells which permeated the small cluttered space.

'No rush, Sadie. I've brought you a new customer. Me new neighbour, Florrie Tempest, and this is their Lizzie,' Nellie replied genially.

Three pairs of eyes were immediately turned on Lizzie and her mother, and Lizzie looked down, embarrassed by her dirty, creased clothes, untidy

26

hair and grubby face.

'Shouldn't you be in school, girl?' Sadie asked pointedly as she deftly weighed out two ounces of sugar, poured it into a small blue paper bag and twisted up the corners.

Lizzie said nothing; this wasn't what she wanted to hear, not if she hoped to find work.

'Oh, she'll be going in a day or two, I suppose. We've only just moved into Bennett Street, you see, and we're new to Bootle too,' Florrie supplied.

'Then it'll be St John's Church School for you, Lizzie, and I have to say that Mr Fletcher – the headmaster, like – doesn't stand no nonsense,' Sadie informed her.

Lizzie determined, there and then, that she was not going to set foot in St John's school; she wanted a job. Maybe later on in the day she might get to meet Nellie Gibbons' daughters and find out where they worked – and if there was any chance at all that she might get a job. Factory work was unskilled; you didn't need an education for that, and she could write her name and read a bit.

At last it was her mam's turn to be served and, after some initial hesitation on Sadie Morgan's part, it was agreed that a couple of shillings' worth of credit could be extended. 'But I insist on being paid prompt on Friday evening, Florrie, after your feller gets his wages. If not, then I'm afraid that's it – no more tick!' she stated firmly.

Florrie nodded, praying that Art would have earned enough by Friday to cover her purchases, for it was now Wednesday and they'd need food for today and tomorrow too. More to the point, she prayed he wouldn't spend the lot in the pub on the way home on Friday. These people were being kind to her, helping her, trusting her, and she knew she would be utterly humiliated if she had to let them down.

As they made the return journey to Bennett Street Lizzie kept her eyes peeled for bits of wood, cardboard, paper, even vegetable skins that could be used as fuel. But she felt warmed by the fact that her mam had been able to purchase a couple of ounces of tea, a loaf, a small tin of condensed milk, half a pound of dripping and a few pounds of potatoes. All of which were now being transported home in Nellie's hemp bag. With a bit of luck there would be a slice of bread and dripping, and tea, when they got in, and then boiled potatoes when Da got home, later on – providing she could find enough stuff to keep the fire going to cook them.

Just as they were nearing the house the bell from St John's Church began to toll. The mournful sound echoed down the street, partly drowning out the traffic noise, and both women stopped and looked at each other in some consternation.

'What's wrong, Mam? What is it?' Lizzie asked, frowning and tugging at the edge of Florrie's shawl.

'That's the tocsin bell. Someone's died,' Nellie pronounced grimly.

Lizzie didn't understand. People were always dying – there were funerals nearly every day – so why was the church bell tolling?

'Must be someone important. They don't usually ring the bell unless it's Sunday, and it never sounds like *that* then. It's probably been announced in the morning paper, but we missed it,' Nellie added.

Lizzie looked around and realised that doors were opening, up and down the street, and people were gathering in twos and threes, all looking very sombre and concerned.

Nellie took it upon herself to find out what had happened, calling over to an old man who was standing with two women, all shaking their heads. 'Mr Peabody, what's up? What's happened? Who's dead?'

'It's Queen Victoria, she ... she died late yesterday, God rest her,' he called back.

Florrie gasped, as did Nellie.

'God 'ave mercy on her soul! It's a sad, dark day, Florrie. I can't remember a time when she wasn't Queen – and neither can anyone else.'

Florrie nodded her agreement. She could remember the Golden Jubilee back in 1887, and even Lizzie had been able to enjoy the celebrations four years ago for the Diamond Jubilee. No one had ever reigned for so long before – it seemed that Victoria had always been there on the throne, and now it was hard to imagine that she'd ... gone.

'You'd best come on in with me and we'll have a cup of tea, for the shock, like. I might even have a bit of soda bread left too,' Nellie urged.

Lizzie's mind was partly diverted from the momentous news by the thought of soda bread. Of course it was very sad that the Queen had died – but after all, she'd been very, very old. Lizzie had seen pictures of her: a dumpy, little old lady with grey hair pulled severely back under a white lace cap, and always wearing widow's black. She'd looked rather grim, as if she never smiled or laughed. But perhaps you were not supposed to if you were such an important person as a Queen Empress? No doubt there would be a very grand funeral, down in London, in the near future – not that that would make any difference to their lives up here. Still, she was glad that Nellie Gibbons had asked them into her rooms for tea, and maybe something to eat, and hopefully there would be a good fire too. Some good things looked likely to come from the morning's sad news.

Chapter Three

Nellie Gibbons' small kitchen, which clearly doubled as a living room, was the most luxurious Lizzie had ever been in. It was warm, for a good fire burned in the hearth. There were faded patchwork cushions on the chairs, equally faded rag rugs on the floor, curtains that had seen better days but still kept out the draughts, a glass shade over the gas jet, dishes on the dresser and even a few ornaments on the mantelpiece. It looked so cosy and comfortable that, by comparison, their one room was terribly bare, cold and cheerless.

She'd sat happily on the rug on the floor, as near to the warmth of the fire as she could possibly get, her hands cupped around a mug of sweet tea, which she'd sipped appreciatively after quickly devouring the thick slice of soda bread Nellie had given her. Nellie and her mam had reminisced about their lives, their families and what they called the 'good old days' – and, of course, the dead Queen and her large family. They had then speculated about what kind of a king Edward, who was known to be a 'bit of a one' for the ladies, would turn out to be and whether times would get better, as everyone hoped they would. The war in South Africa was over, it was a new century and now they'd have a new King.

She'd been quite content to just sit and let it all wash over her and had begun to doze, having slept little last night. But at length her mam had reluctantly said they'd have to go, that she was sure Nellie had chores to do and she wouldn't take up any more of her time. 'I'll have to try and get that room into some kind of order for when Art gets home,' Florrie said briskly, getting to her feet and earning an approving nod from Nellie.

Lizzie too got up from her place by the fire, stretching her cramped limbs and wondering just what her mam could do to get their room into any kind of 'order'.

'Well, when you've all had your tea tonight, why don't you come on in and you can meet Ernie and the girls – that's if your feller isn't too tired,' Nellie suggested as she showed them out. After all, they would be living in close proximity to this new family and it was a good idea to see if they all got on.

Florrie nodded gratefully, although she doubted Art would be very interested in meeting their new neighbours. The thought cheered Lizzie up, though, for she realised it would be the perfect opportunity to meet Nellie's daughters.

Lizzie spent the rest of the day wandering the surrounding streets and collecting fuel for the fire, promising to be back before it got dark, which thankfully was fairly early these winter afternoons. Their few bits of food had been placed in the press, and then the bed straightened. Her mam had borrowed a brush and a mop and bucket from Nellie and set about trying to make their room a bit cleaner, at least. Although there wasn't much else she could do to improve it, she'd remarked downheartedly.

While she was out, Lizzie had taken note of the various factories in the neighbourhood and where they were situated, as well as the types of shops and businesses that might offer employment, noticing that many were already displaying symbols of national mourning. Windows were draped in black crêpe; pictures of the old Queen were prominently displayed and edged in black; blinds were respectfully lowered. It was all everyone seemed to be talking about too, Lizzie realised.

At last, as the January dusk began to descend, she made her way back to Bennett Street, her arms full of what to most people would appear to be rubbish, but which would ensure that they had a fire on which to cook and heat the place up a bit. She was hungry again, and cold, but she was looking forward to getting home and to the first hot meal she'd had in days.

'I was beginning to get worried about you, Lizzie,' Florrie greeted her.

'I did get a bit lost, but I managed to find some good stuff near the docks, Mam. Even some pieces of wood from a broken packing crate,' she answered as she dumped everything down on the floor in front of the range and began to feed the best bits into the fire.

'That's great, luv. I've washed the spuds and they're already in the pot. With a decent fire they'll be ready for when your da gets in.'

Lizzie nodded and spread her cold fingers out to the increasing warmth emanating from the fire. 'Do you think Da will come with us to meet the rest of the Gibbons family?'

Her mother shrugged. 'I don't know, Lizzie. He might well be too tired. It's hard work, you know, heaving cargo around by hand, and ... well ... he's not used to it ... now.'

She could understand her father's reluctance, Lizzie thought, as she watched the water begin to bubble in the pot. But it would look rather ungrateful, and decidedly unfriendly, if her da refused. Still, whatever he decided, she was looking forward to the evening.

When Art finally arrived home it was fully dark and Florrie had lit the single candle. With the glow from the fire, it made the place at least look a bit more welcoming, she thought. Added to that, her new neighbour had lent her a couple of tin plates, which she'd placed on the table, and the potatoes were cooked. There was nothing else to go with them, except bread, but at least it was a hot meal on a cold winter night.

'How did you get on, then?' Florrie asked hopefully as her husband pulled off the heavy piece of sacking he wore around his shoulders. It served as a sort of protection from both the weather and the cargo he had to manhandle, saving more wear and tear on his already old jacket.

'Managed to get a full day, but I'm fair done in! Don't know about tomorrow, though, and don't know if I'll be able for it, either,' he replied, sinking down gratefully on to a chair.

Lizzie rushed to help him off with his boots. 'Well, it's just great you got a whole day, Da! And there's a hot meal ready too,' she added, hoping he would get more work tomorrow and find the energy to carry it out.

'Just boiled potatoes, Art, but if you get work tomorrow we might be able to afford scouse at the weekend. That Mrs Morgan down at the shop gave me a few shillings' tick, but I'll have to pay up on Friday,' Florrie informed him. 'Isn't it sad about the Queen? Did you hear?' she asked to steer the subject away from their lack of money.

'I've 'eard nothin' else all day! I don't know what everyone's getting upset about, she did precious little fer the likes of us! What would she know – or care – about 'ow we has ter live, down there in 'er grand palaces, waited on 'and an' foot all 'er life!'

Florrie shook her head but didn't reply, only too aware of her husband's anti-royalist opinions, which frequently caused offence and, on occasion, outrage.

'Mrs Gibbons from down the hall showed us where the shop was, and she's asked us all in after we've eaten to meet the rest of her family,' Lizzie said brightly, hoping to divert her father's mind.

'Well, yer can count me out of that! I'm not in

the mood for being sociable, I'm too flaming tired. When I've 'ad me tea, I'm going ter bed,' her father replied before attacking the three large potatoes on his plate.

Lizzie frowned but didn't reply, while Florrie cut a slice of bread and handed it with a jar of tea to her husband. She hoped he'd be taken on again tomorrow – and indeed Friday. That would mean he'd have at least ten shillings due in wages. She'd try to make sure the rent was paid, she'd pay Sadie what she owed, and then she'd have half a crown left for food for next week. Two shillings and sixpence meant food, candles and maybe even a bit of coal. It was a lot. She couldn't help feeling a little disappointed that he had no wish to take up Nellie's invitation, but she understood. The main thing was he had a day's wage in his pocket.

After blowing out the candle, they left him snoring noisily and went down the lobby to meet the rest of Nellie's family.

A girl of about seventeen opened the door to them. Her brown hair was piled on top of her head and she wore a calico apron over her dark dress which, both Lizzie and her mother noted, was quite fashionably cut – even though, like most women's dresses round there, it was made of 'shoddy', a material manufactured from what was basically rags. Recycled clothing that was just too badly worn to be serviceable.

'Mam, it's the neighbours!' she called over her shoulder, ushering them into a room that already appeared crowded.

'Come on in, Florrie. Your 'usband not with

you, then?' Nellie remarked, pushing the kettle on to the hob.

'No, he got a full day in and he's wore out, so he's gone to bed,' Florrie replied rather apologetically.

'Lena girl, move up on that bench and let Lizzie sit down! Florrie, sit yerself down by the fire.' She rattled off the introductions. 'This is me 'usband, Ernie ... our Peggy let you in ... and this 'ere is our Lena.'

A little hesitantly Lizzie sat down on the wooden bench by the table beside the girl called Lena, noticing that, like her sister, she wore a plain but serviceable dress and her hair was twisted into a knot on the top of her head.

'Nice to meet you, Lizzie. How old are you?' Lena asked, as Florrie shook hands with Ernie. He had risen to his feet and then nodded amiably to Peggy before sitting down by the hearth, while Nellie busied herself making a pot of tea.

'Nearly fourteen,' Lizzie lied stoutly, ignoring the glance her mother shot at her. Well, she would be fourteen in a few months' time.

'I'm fifteen and our Peggy's seventeen,' Lena supplied.

'I'll be eighteen next month – and I'm "walking out"!' Peggy corrected her sharply.

Lena grimaced. 'Don't we all know it,' she muttered to Lizzie under the buzz of the conversation that was going on between her parents and Lizzie's mother.

'I take it Lizzie is short for Elizabeth?' Lena queried. 'Mam decided to call me Helena' – she rolled her eyes – 'but it's a bit fancy for around

36

'ere, like, so I'm Lena for short. Where did you live before, Lizzie?'

'In Fulton Street – by the docks, in Liverpool – but me da decided we'd be better off moving here, and he actually got a whole day's work today, so it looks like he was right.'

Lena nodded her agreement. 'I suppose you'll be going to St John's, then?'

Lizzie shrugged. 'I don't think it's really worth it for a few months. I'd be better off getting a job of some kind. Where do you work, Lena?'

'Both Peggy and me work at the match factory in Linacre Lane. It was bought by some American outfit called the Diamond Match Company but it's still Bryant an' May's, like. It's not bad, but you just 'ave to be careful you don't pick up "phossy jaw" from the stuff they use for the match heads. It's not as bad as it used ter be, though, is it, Peg?'

Peggy shrugged as she untied her apron and hung it on the back of the door. 'Bad enough if yer do get it. Rots right through to yer jawbone, it does – and there's no cure.'

Lizzie looked taken aback and she shuddered; she'd never heard of this 'phossy jaw' but it didn't sound very pleasant at all. 'How much do they pay?'

Peggy raised her eyebrows and frowned at her younger sister. She hadn't taken to this skinny, grubby-looking girl at all, and she considered the question a bit hard-faced. After all, Lizzie Tempest hardly knew them; she'd only moved in last night. She sniffed. Next thing she'd be asking how much rent they paid.

37

'It's long hours on yer feet, like, but that's usual in all factories, and we do get a couple of breaks. Cos I'm only fifteen I get five shillin's a week. The older girls get eight,' Lena replied, ignoring the look her sister shot at her. In her opinion Lizzie was only being curious – and besides, their wages were common knowledge, not some big secret. But Peggy was like that, a bit prone to making a drama out of everything.

Lizzie nodded slowly, thinking that if she could earn a whole five shillings a week she'd consider it a small fortune. It would help her mam no end with the housekeeping, and she might even get some decent clothes – in time. She'd be prepared to take her chances with this 'phossy jaw' for all that. 'Do you think they'd take me on?' she asked Lena. 'I'd work really hard.'

'They'd not take you until you're fourteen,' Peggy informed her bluntly.

'I could say I'm nearly fourteen,' Lizzie said hopefully.

'You don't even look thirteen – more like twelve – so you've no chance,' Peggy said derisively.

'Well, there are other places you could try, Lizzie. Shops or the tannery, like; they're not as fussy about age. Just to tide you over until you're old enough,' Lena suggested, having seen the flicker of hope die in Lizzie's eyes.

'Maybe I'll try them, then.' She lowered her voice. 'You see, we ... we desperately need money, we ... we've got nothing!'

Lena looked at her sympathetically. 'You'll get something, Lizzie. I know you will.'

Lizzie managed a smile. She liked Lena, but she

38

wasn't too sure about Peggy, and it seemed obvious that the older girl didn't like her. Well, she wouldn't let that bother her. Tomorrow she'd go and try her luck at the tannery, if she could find it.

Chapter Four

It was starting to snow as Lizzie trudged wearily home on a Saturday afternoon, the flakes quickly sticking to her shawl and adding to her mood of deepening depression. She knew that the state funeral for Queen Victoria had taken place earlier that February day, in London, for she'd caught sight of the newspaper headlines. But beyond thinking that it was a thoroughly miserable day for such an occasion her own problems had taken precedence in her mind.

Over the last ten days she'd tried numerous factories, businesses and shops in the area but no one was prepared to offer her work of any kind. She'd almost been laughed at when she'd tried the tannery, she remembered bitterly, and at one factory they'd told her to come back when she'd grown up. She'd gone home these last couple of nights close to tears. She'd had such hopes of being able to earn money of her own, but no one would give her a chance. At least, so far, her da had managed to get work on a fairly regular basis. Although he'd gone to the pub most evenings, he'd limited himself to a couple of pints so her mam had been able to purchase food, candles and a bit of coal from Morgan's. They'd not gone hungry, and Sadie Morgan now considered them 'reliable' customers.

She clutched her shawl tightly to her and tried to hurry her steps, for the snow was getting heavier, driven by an increasingly strong wind, and it was getting more difficult to see where she was going. She was cold, wet, tired and dispirited, and the snow was now seeping through the thin soles of her boots. She just wanted to get home, and so it was with relief that she pushed open the front door and hurried through the lobby.

'Lizzie, you're soaked through. Come over here to the fire, luv!' Florrie greeted her daughter.

Lizzie shook the snow from her shawl, put it over the back of a chair and went to stand by the range, holding out her hands to the warmth. 'It's getting really thick out there now, Mam.'

Florrie nodded – she'd watched with concern for the past half-hour as the thick, heavy flakes swirled past the window, almost obliterating the light from the street lamp.

'And I had no luck again today!' Lizzie added gloomily.

'Never mind, Lizzie, luv. You'll spend the rest of your life working – one way or another – so don't get too downhearted just yet. There's blind scouse for tea, that'll warm you up, and Nellie showed me how to make soda bread, so there's some of that too. And there's always next week – although, if this weather lasts, folk will find it hard to even get to their work,' she added.

'Is Da not in yet?' Lizzie asked.

Florrie shook her head. 'He said that when he'd finished he was going to see Tommy Marshall and his other mates, as he's not seen them since we moved. I'd hoped he'd be back by now, especially with the weather turning nasty, like.'

Lizzie didn't reply, wondering how much of his wages her da had kept back for himself. He obviously wouldn't have walked to Liverpool, and he'd have wanted money for beer. If the snow got heavier, then the trams would stop running – so maybe he wouldn't get back at all tonight. 'Will we have our meal now, Mam? I'm starving,' she suggested hopefully.

Florrie frowned. She hadn't wanted Art to go back to Liverpool but it would have been useless to say so. He'd take no notice, his mind was set on it, and he'd only given her enough money for the rent and to pay what she owed Sadie. He had money in his pocket, which he was obviously determined to spend. She hoped he'd get work next week, but it didn't look likely with this weather. 'Give him a bit longer, he might be on his way now,' she said.

The room was growing chillier and the candle was burning down, and still there was no sign of her da. Mother and daughter had both had a thick slice of the soda bread and a bowlful of the meatless stew, the remains of which Florrie left simmering gently on the fire which was now dying.

Mam didn't look well, Lizzie realised, but maybe she was worrying about what state her husband would be in when he got home – if he got home in this snow. 'Are you all right, Mam?

You look a bit flushed, like?'

Florrie nodded. 'I'm fine, Lizzie, although I do feel a bit sort of ... feverish. It's probably just a bit of a cold.'

'Shall I put the last of the coal on the fire?' Lizzie asked.

'No, luv, we'd best save that for tomorrow, we'll need it.'

Before Lizzie could comment there was a knock on the door and Nellie's voice was heard from the lobby.

'Come on in, Nellie,' Florrie called, wondering what her neighbour wanted.

'I just came to see if Lizzie got 'ome safe. Our Peggy and Lena were late in from work. It's shockin' out there now, we'll be snowed in if it carries on like this all night,' Florrie pronounced grimly.

'Thanks, Mrs Gibbons, I've been home a while now,' Lizzie replied, getting up while Florrie gestured to the older woman to sit down in the chair her daughter had vacated.

'I'd hoped that Art would have been home by now too, Nellie. He's gone to Liverpool to see his mates. Are the trams still running?'

Nellie frowned. 'I don't think so. Our Peggy said they had to wait ages and then the driver said they were only goin' as far as the depot, as it was gettin' too bad, so they had to walk the rest of the way 'ome.'

Florrie bit her lip and looked anxious.

'I wouldn't worry too much, luv. 'E's big enough an' daft enough to take care of himself!' Nellie said, thinking Arthur Tempest was indeed daft to go traipsing all the way up there to a pub when, if

42

he wanted a drink, there were plenty of alehouses nearby. On the two occasions when she'd actually spoken to him she'd decided she didn't particularly like him. He was what she termed a 'waster' – and glancing around the bare room, she also thought he was a selfish fool to go spending hard-earned money on ale when Florrie couldn't even afford to heat the place properly, let alone buy enough groceries to put a decent meal on the table.

'At least the weather didn't interfere with the old Queen's funeral,' she continued, trying to take Florrie's mind off her errant husband. 'The girls brought a copy of the late edition of the *Echo* in with them an' I've been reading all about it. Bye, it was a grand affair by all accounts. There were kings, queens, princes an' princesses from countries far an' wide, and most of them were all related to her. The "Grandmother of Europe" they're callin' 'er now, isn't that something...?' Nellie's words trailed off abruptly as Florrie put a hand to her forehead. 'Are yer all right, Florrie?'

'I don't think she's well, Mrs Gibbons,' Lizzie put in worriedly.

Nellie got up and placed her hand on her neighbour's forehead and tutted. 'Florrie, you're burnin' up, luv! There's a lot of that "influenzey" goin' around, so I heard. You'd best get to bed,' she urged.

Florrie didn't feel well at all, although she was struggling to protest, when suddenly, to her consternation, some sort of commotion seemed to erupt in the lobby outside.

'What's goin' on out there? What the hell is all

43

that noise about?' Nellie cried, going to the door and flinging it open.

Ernie Gibbons was standing outside doing his best to hold at arm's length a soaking wet, belligerently noisy and obviously very drunk Art Tempest.

'God, I'm 'aving a right time with 'im!' he pronounced. 'All I was tryin' ter do was get 'im in out of the cold an' wet, and doesn't 'e turn on me, like! I'm amazed 'e managed to find 'is way 'ome at all, the state 'e's in!'

'Well, I wouldn't 'ave bothered, Ernie!' Nellie snapped, her eyes narrowing as she took in Florrie's husband. Oh, her Ernie liked a pint – and she didn't begrudge him a drink, either – but she'd have killed him had he come home like this, especially as Florrie so clearly needed the money he'd obviously wasted.

'Gerroff me! I don't need yer bloody 'elp!' Art roared, shaking off Ernie's grip and staggering towards the bed.

'Oh, Art, don't yell at Mr Gibbons! Look at the state of you!' Florrie cried, struggling to her feet. 'You'll get pneumonia!' She was upset that he had drunk himself into a near stupor, as well as feeling humiliated that her neighbours should see him in this condition.

'I'd say he's got enough drink inside 'im to keep out the cold!' Ernie commented grimly.

'I'd have bloody well left 'im outside to freeze, Ernie!' Nellie retorted angrily to her husband, thinking that poor sick Florrie certainly didn't deserve to have to contend with a drunken bully. However, she didn't intend to leave her to cope with him alone. 'Well, I suppose we'd better 'elp you get him to bed, Florrie, luv. Let him sleep it off, like. An' I hope he has one almighty hangover termorrow!' she added venomously.

Lizzie said nothing, but as she watched the combined efforts of Ernie and Nellie Gibbons and her mam to get her father out of his wet clothes and into bed she felt a sense of dread creep over her. No doubt he would indeed have a hangover tomorrow, which didn't bode well for either herself or her mam – nothing they did would be right – and she was worried that her mother wasn't well. Neither of them would get much sleep tonight; and the chance of him getting work on Monday seemed remote, because of the weather, which meant money would be scarce next week. But at least he'd stopped yelling and cursing, she noted.

'I'll sleep in the chair tonight, Mrs Gibbons,' she said quietly as she picked up her da's clothes and draped them over the line above the rapidly cooling range.

'I'll come in in the morning to see how she is, luv,' Nellie promised. She glanced over at the now snoring figure of Art Tempest with a look of disgust. 'Will yer be all right, Lizzie?'

Lizzie looked miserable. 'I'm used to ... it ... him.'

Nellie patted her on the shoulder. 'Well, if he wakes up an' ... starts ... just knock on the wall.'

Lizzie nodded. She should have known things wouldn't change, that moving here wouldn't change her da. She'd hoped they would, she thought bitterly, and she'd hoped to get a job; but perhaps she'd better give up hoping for ... *anything*.

Chapter Five

By Monday morning most of the snow had gone, leaving just a few patches of dirty grey slush in the gutters and in the corners of the pavement below the front steps. Lizzie was thankful as she prepared to walk down to the corner shop to see what Sadie Morgan would let her have in the way of food. She was seriously worried about her mother, for Florrie had spent most of yesterday in bed, barely able to raise her head and complaining of aches in all her joints. She was still feverish. True to her word, Nellie had come in to check on her neighbour. Studiously ignoring a deathly-looking Art, she had shaken her head and told Lizzie to keep her mam warm and give her plenty to drink, hot tea if possible.

'She really should see a doctor, Lizzie, but I don't know one who offers 'is services free, and I know there's no money to spare,' she'd said grimly, shooting a malevolent glance at Florrie's husband who, she thought, seemed more annoyed than concerned about his wife's illness.

Lizzie had done her best but there'd been barely enough coal or wood left to keep the fire going all day. At least this morning her da had reluctantly taken himself off to try to get work, while she'd have to stay at home to see to her mam.

She waited her turn patiently as Sadie gossiped with her customers about the weather and the

46

Queen's funeral and speculated about when the Coronation would be.

'Come by yourself this mornin', Lizzie,' Sadie remarked when she finally turned to serve her.

'Mam's not at all well, Mrs Morgan.'

'What's up with her, luv?' Sadie enquired with genuine concern. She'd come to like Florrie for her quiet, uncomplaining manner in the face of the hardships she endured – an attitude few of her customers shared.

'She's feverish and says she aches all over, especially her head,' Lizzie supplied.

Sadie nodded. 'I'll give yer a drop of vinegar, Lizzie. Soak a bit of cloth in it and put it on her forehead; that sometimes helps.'

'Mrs Gibbons said I've to make sure she keeps warm and has plenty of hot drinks, so could I please have some things ... on the slate, like?'

Sadie nodded, although she stared intently at the girl. 'Yer da got work this week, then?'

'He's gone off this morning down to the Brocklebank; he's been lucky, so far, and I'm just glad all the snow has gone.'

'Aye, the kids are the only ones who are disappointed about that, Lizzie,' Sadie replied. She'd heard about the state Art Tempest had come home in on Saturday night, so he obviously wasn't as 'reliable' as Florrie had implied. Of course, he wasn't the only one who staggered home on a Friday or Saturday night around here, but she certainly didn't envy poor Florrie. 'Now, luv, what do you need? I'll see what I can do.'

As she walked home with her few purchases Lizzie kept her eyes peeled for stuff they could

47

use for extra fuel, knowing the small bag of coal wouldn't last long. She was desperate to do all she could for her mam. Maybe by tomorrow mam would be over the worst, she thought, and maybe the vinegar would help. As she turned into Bennett Street she saw, with dismay, that her da was walking slowly up the street ahead of her. Obviously he'd had no luck this morning.

'Nothing then, Da?' she ventured as she caught up with him.

He shrugged. 'What did yer get, girl? Me belly thinks me throat's been cut!'

'Tea, bread, dripping and some coal,' she replied gloomily. She'd wanted to get more coal – and perhaps some vegetables and pearl barley with which to make soup – but she'd not dared to put more money on the slate, and now she was glad.

'Is that all?'

'I ... I didn't want to spend too much, Da, in case...'

He said nothing as he pushed open the front door and Lizzie followed him down the lobby.

The room was cold and felt damp. After putting the few groceries down on the table, Lizzie went over to see how her mam was while Art busied himself getting the fire going again, muttering that it was warmer out in the street than it was in here.

Lizzie was a little relieved to see that Florrie didn't seem to look quite as flushed. 'How are you feeling now, Mam? You look a bit better, and I've got some tea and things. Does your head still ache?'

Florrie attempted to nod but the movement made her wince. 'It ... it's still bad,' she murmured.

48

Lizzie bent over her. 'Mrs Morgan gave me a drop of vinegar, Mam. She said I've to put it on a bit of cloth and bathe your forehead with it.'

Florrie tried to smile at Sadie's thoughtfulness.

'We'll soon have the place warmed up, Mam. I got coal and ... and Da's making up the fire.' Then she bit her lip as she saw her mother's expression change. She raised her voice and looked pointedly at her father's hunched back and shoulders as he knelt before the range. 'He's going to go down again this afternoon, aren't you, Da?'

'I suppose so. Now get that kettle on, girl, and make us all a cuppa,' he instructed her bluntly.

Lizzie busied herself with the vinegar and a piece of an old tea towel she'd begged from Nellie, wrinkling her nose at the smell. But at least it did seem to help Mam a bit, she thought.

Thankfully, her da went out after having a couple of slices of bread and dripping and some tea. At least she knew he had no money for beer, so he wouldn't be tempted to go into a pub. Nellie had remarked that the landlords in the pubs around here refused to give drink on credit; if they did, they'd be out on the street themselves within a few weeks.

She desperately hoped her da would get taken on this afternoon, for she was worried about what she would do if her mam's condition worsened.

He returned at six o'clock looking a good deal brighter. 'It seems as if yer mam's not the only one who's gone down with this 'ere "influenzey". The blockerman said 'e might well 'ave work for me for the rest of the week, there's so many of 'is regulars gone sick.'

49

Lizzie smiled at him. 'Oh, that's great news, Da! Well, for us … not those who are sick, it's not. We'll be able to afford more coal.'

'And a proper flamin' meal. I'm sick of livin' off bread and scrape! A good bowl of oxtail would go down a treat.'

'I'll see what Mrs Morgan will give me … and Da … if … if Mam doesn't get any better, do you think we could afford a dispensary doctor and some medicine? Mrs Gibbons said they only charge sixpence for a visit and sixpence for a bottle of medicine, and I'm really worried about her,' she pleaded.

'I thought yer said she looked better? We 'aven't got money to spare fer flamin' doctors, Lizzie! An' she'd 'ave to go to the dispensary, 'e wouldn't come 'ere,' he replied curtly. Florrie would get over whatever was wrong with her after a few days' rest, food and warmth. He was the one who would have to go out in the cold and damp, working out in the open with the biting wind from the river cutting through to his very bones – and all for a few shillings, a miserable pittance. A man would need a drink after that.

Lizzie turned away from him, biting her lip. She knew she would have to fight tooth and nail to make him give her enough money to keep them going next week, and with almost a full week's wages in his pocket he'd go off on a bender again; she knew it. They had nothing left that could be pawned to pay the shilling for a doctor and medicine for her mam; she'd just have to pray that her mother got a little better each day.

50

As the days wore on Lizzie's fears for her mam increased. Florrie had seemed to improve a little on Tuesday, but then she got worse by the day.

'What am I going to do, Mrs Gibbons? She's getting no better ... she can't seem to breathe properly now!' Lizzie pleaded when, on Friday lunchtime, Nellie came in to enquire about Florrie's health, as usual.

When Nellie saw for herself that what Lizzie said was true she deduced, grimly, that what had been influenza had now turned into the dreaded pneumonia; after years of never having enough to eat, Florrie had no stamina. 'She really does need a doctor and medicine, Lizzie; she's not strong enough to fight off this illness,' she said, grave worry sounding in her voice.

'But I've no money until Da gets home,' Lizzie cried, frantic now for her mother. At least her father had had work that week but, coming in exhausted every night, he'd shown little concern for his wife.

Nellie pursed her lips as she thought about Lizzie's dilemma. 'Go down to the dock gate, Lizzie, and wait for him to finish. He'll have been paid. Get a shillin' off him before he can go into a pub, and then go straight to the dispensary and tell them how bad yer mam is. If they won't come to see her, then ask if they can give yer something for her. Go on, I'll sit with her, luv, so don't you worry too much about her while you're out. But first I'll have to go back 'ome and bring in some wood for the fire; she needs to be kept warm. Thank God, Ernie managed to cadge some wood yesterday from Webster's timber yard. Offcuts, or something, he said they are.'

As soon as Nellie returned, bringing with her a pillow and the wood to make up the fire, Lizzie pulled her shawl around her and went out into the bitterly cold February afternoon. It wouldn't be long before the lamplighter would be doing his rounds, lighting the gas jets of the street lamps, she thought, shivering. She hated this time of year, when she was permanently cold and hungry, but today seemed to be far, far worse than usual, for a deep sense of anxiety was added to her woes.

When she'd crossed Derby Road and reached the dock she walked slowly up and down outside the stark, high walls that bounded it, trying to keep her feet and fingers from becoming completely numb with cold. She was also trying to stay out of sight of the policeman on the dock gate, who might well chase her away – although she was almost sure he wouldn't venture out of his hut, as he at least had the luxury of a brazier in there to keep him warm. She visualised the glowing fire, enviously, as she paced.

As the time passed she noticed that she wasn't alone; she'd been joined by two other women, both as anxious, thin and poorly dressed as herself and just as furtive. They were obviously here for the same reason she was; to try to get some money off their menfolk before it was spent in the nearest pub.

As the winter dusk deepened, at last the men began to start leaving the dock, some walking with shoulders hunched against the cold under thin, shabby jackets and caps, a few exchanging chat with their mates, but all looking cold and exhausted. Slowly she edged her way forward, searching the gaunt, tired faces for that of her father.

A man of about her da's age, but better dressed than the rest and wearing the bowler hat of his rank, took pity on her and stopped. 'Are you looking for anyone in particular, girl?'

'Yes. Arthur – Art – Tempest. He's me da.'

The man frowned. 'Well, you'll not find him here. Said he was feeling too sick to go on working so he was paid what was owed and went off home at dinner time,' he informed her, although he'd had his doubts about that being the truth. There was a lot of sickness going around but Art Tempest hadn't looked ill.

Lizzie stared at him in confusion. 'Dinner time! But ... but that was hours ago and ... and he didn't come home! And ... and it's me mam who's sick, not him. She's really bad, sir, that's why I came down here. To try to get a shilling off him to go to the dispensary for her.'

He shook his head, looking grim. He hadn't particularly liked the man – he'd found him sullen and occasionally argumentative – but he'd not been a bad worker, and with so many men absent from work he'd kept him on. 'Then I suggest you start looking in the pubs, girl. And good luck, I hope your mam gets better.'

Lizzie stared bleakly after him as he walked away, panic beginning to rise within her. Where should she start? What if they wouldn't let her over the doorstep? She was far too young to go into licensed premises. And when she found him, what sort of a state would he be in? Would he give

53

her the money? And all that would take up precious time, time in which her poor mam might get worse. What if she didn't find him at all? If he'd been paid off hours ago, then what if he'd decided to go back to Liverpool to see his mates, like he'd done last weekend?

She stood there, biting her lip, and tears pricked her eyes; the long, cold hours of waiting were forgotten now as she tried to think what to do next. Should she go back home, tell Nellie what had happened and ask her advice? Should she just go straight to the dispensary and beg and plead for some help? Or should she do as the blockerman suggested and try the pubs? She quickened her steps and decided to start with the alehouses she had to pass on her way home, and also to ask anyone she saw on the way if they'd seen him. If she couldn't find him, she'd go back home. Because the more she thought about it, the more she suspected her da had taken a tram to Liverpool.

Chapter Six

She'd tried at least four pubs and been roared at to get out by one landlord who bawled he didn't intend to lose his licence over a little slummy like her. Scarlet with humiliation, she'd run out. Each pub had seemed to be full of dockworkers, but there had been no sign of her father. Then, just as she was about to push open the door of the Knowsley Arms, a man who, judging by his clothes, was no docker, came striding out. He almost collided with her, and she braced herself for the inevitable curses that would follow. But when she looked up at his face, she saw that he was quite young – a rather more grown-up version of her brother Ned – and she dared to hope that, like Ned, he might be willing to show her some kindness.

'Oh, please, sir, can you help me?' she begged, before he could berate her.

He looked down at her pale, pinched face with its huge, worried blue eyes, and stopped. 'What's the matter, lass?'

'I ... I'm trying to find me da, but I can't go inside. I'm not old enough.'

He nodded his understanding; unfortunately, this wasn't an unusual occurrence. 'What's his name?'

He saw the flash of relief that crossed her face, and he felt sorry for her. How old was she? he wondered. She looked to be about twelve – or thirteen, at the most – and despite her untidy, dark curly hair, poor clothes and obvious distress, she was a pretty girl.

'Arthur – Art – Tempest, sir. He ... he's a docker, but the blockerman told me he'd been paid off at dinner time, and I need to find him to get the money for the dispensary doctor! Me ... me mam's really sick, sir!'

He nodded again. 'I'll go and ask, then. Wait here, I won't be long.'

Lizzie waited outside, clutching her shawl tightly to her and praying her da was indeed inside and that the gentleman could persuade him to come out. She didn't care what he thought of her, or her da; all she wanted was the money.

After a few minutes he came out shaking his head. 'I'm sorry, he's not in there – and Jem Hicks, the landlord, said he's not seen him at all this week. Have you tried the Prince of Wales?'

Tears welled up in Lizzie's eyes as she shook her head. 'There's no time left now... I ... I'll just have to go ... home.'

He frowned; she was obviously very upset and concerned about her mother and, judging by her appearance, the family must be virtually destitute. He was aware that it cost upwards of two shillings and sixpence for a doctor's consultation. In fact, he'd paid exactly that only last week for his wife's visit to the surgery. 'How much do you need for the dispensary doctor, lass?'

Lizzie gazed up at him through her tears, wondering if she'd heard him correctly. 'Sixpence for the medicine, sir,' she faltered as she dashed her hand across her eyes.

He delved into the pocket of his overcoat. 'Here, take this and go and get what you need,' he instructed, pressing a silver shilling into her hand.

Lizzie was so overcome that she couldn't speak; she just grabbed his hand and shook it before turning away and breaking into a trot.

The man, who wasn't really a regular in the Knowsley Arms but sometimes called in after work on a Friday, stood and watched her as she hurried off down the road. Poor little lass, he thought. If her mother was as ill as she seemed to think, then he doubted that a shilling would be much use. As a senior factory foreman, George

56

Rutherford enjoyed a fairly decent standard of living. A shilling wouldn't break the bank, he thought, and obviously her need was greater than his. He and Eileen rented a house in Olivia Street – a quieter, more respectable part of Bootle. In the ten years they'd been married they'd not been blessed with a family, even though they'd married young and had expected children to follow quickly, and so Eileen, a seamstress, continued to do a little work from home. Although she had, like quite a number of people recently, succumbed to influenza, thankfully she was now recovering. He hoped the young girl's mother might pull through too.

He turned the collar of his overcoat up against the biting east wind as he turned to walk to the tram stop. He and his wife were fortunate in their circumstances. He hoped his shilling would help.

Lizzie arrived at the small, shabby building that housed the local dispensary, flushed and gasping for breath. When the nurse on duty had calmed her down sufficiently, she managed to inform the woman of her mother's condition. She was told to wait while the nurse went off to see if a doctor was available. Lizzie looked around nervously; it was the first time she'd been here, and she noted that there were a couple of other women sitting on a wooden bench, both looking pale and ill. At last the nurse reappeared with a tired-looking, middle-aged man.

'Your mother is running a temperature, I'm told?'

Lizzie nodded vigorously. 'She's very feverish,

sir, she's too sick to get up and ... and when I left she could 'ardly breathe! She's been getting worse each day.'

'How long has she been ill?'

'She took bad last weekend, sir. I ... we ... thought ... hoped she'd get better but...' Tears threatened to overcome Lizzie.

He shook his head, knowing he should have been called sooner, but judging by the girl's appearance, there had been no money, he surmised. And if he was right, they no doubt had poor lodgings, scant heating and very little in the way of nourishing food. He'd seen far too many such cases in his working life. Sometimes he wondered if the poor souls would have been better off in the workhouse; at least there they would get plain but regular meals, and proper medical care when they were ill. But he also knew of the fear with which such institutions were viewed. They were a last resort.

'Please, sir, will you give me some medicine for her?' Lizzie begged, holding out the shilling. 'I've got the money.'

'I'd better come and see her, child.'

'I can pay for that too, sir!' Lizzie urged.

'Give me a minute to fetch my bag and my coat. Where do you live?'

'In Bennett Street, sir. Near St John's Church, it's not far,' she informed him, relief evident in her voice.

As they hurried through the dark and now mainly deserted streets he asked her name, how old she was, and if she had any siblings at home, trying not only to judge the family's circumstances but also to alleviate her concern. 'So there are just three of you at home, then?'

Lizzie nodded her agreement.

'Does your father work, at all?'

'Yes, he's a docker, and he's been lucky this week, sir, but ... but I don't know just where he is ... right now. I did try to find him, but...'

He frowned but made no reply. It was Friday evening, so the man would have been paid – and he'd probably been handed his wage packet in one of the pubs nearby. It was a common practice, but one he deplored; it offered far too much temptation to spend money on drink – money that could be ill afforded, in his opinion – to the detriment of both the man himself and his family.

When they arrived at the house the family's obvious poverty shocked him. He'd expected them to have very little, but not to be virtually destitute, and it saddened and angered him. At least the room was reasonably warm, he thought, as Lizzie ushered him in.

'Oh, Lizzie, you're back at last!' Nellie cried in relief, getting to her feet.

'You are?' the doctor enquired.

'Mrs Gibbons, sir. I live along the lobby. I've been sitting with 'er. She's not good, sir. Not good at all.'

Both Lizzie and Nellie watched anxiously as the doctor examined Florrie.

'Where's yer da?' Nellie demanded in a whisper – she'd expected Art to accompany Lizzie home.

'I don't know. He was paid off at dinner time, said he was sick, so...'

Nellie uttered a sharp, disapproving sound.

Sick! Sick of work, more like! she thought angrily.

'Is there ... anything you can give her, sir?' Lizzie ventured, biting her lip, for the doctor was looking very grave.

'I'm afraid she's going to have to go to hospital, child – and don't be worrying about the cost, there will be no charge. It's pneumonia and there's little I can do to help her ... here.'

'Oh, dear God!' Nellie cried. She had a terror of hospitals, as did most people she knew; they were places you seldom came out of alive.

Lizzie began to cry softly and so Nellie put her arm around her and tried to suppress her own trepidation. 'It'll be for the best, won't it, sir? They ... they'll take care of her.'

'They will indeed. She'll have a far better chance of recovery in hospital, Mrs Gibbons. I'll go and call an ambulance to take her to Bootle General, that's the nearest.' The poor woman had a very slim chance of recovery, in his opinion; she was too weak, undernourished and exhausted by the grinding poverty she'd endured for the Lord alone knew how many years.

'Can I ... can I go with ... her?' Lizzie begged.

He shook his head. 'I'm afraid not, they're very strict. But I'll accompany her, so try not to worry too much,' he replied kindly.

Although very upset and desperately worried, Lizzie held out the silver shilling. 'Thank you, sir.'

He shook his head; he felt so desperately sorry for her. 'There's no charge, I've done very little. Keep it, child, you'll need it.'

After he'd gone to find a public telephone box, Nellie went over to the bedside and looked anxiously down at her neighbour. 'You'll be fine now, Florrie. You'll get proper ... care.'

As Lizzie came and stood beside her she could see that her mam didn't appear to have heard Nellie's words; her eyes were closed and her breathing very laboured. She tugged at the older woman's arm. 'Is she ... can she...?'

'Don't fret, luv. She's just ... sick and worn out. They'll take good care of her in there.'

Lizzie tried to take comfort from her reassurances, but her mam looked so old and very frail.

When Florrie had been taken away in the ambulance, Nellie ushered the pale, subdued girl into her own rooms. Quite obviously, Art Tempest had no intention of returning home until he'd spent his wages, and she didn't want to leave the poor lass on her own until he fell in at some ungodly hour – and probably in a deplorable condition.

'They've taken poor Florrie to Bootle General, so I've brought Lizzie in 'ere,' she announced to her husband and daughters. 'I couldn't leave her on her own, and he's gone missing!' she finished in a loud whisper.

'Come and sit here, Lizzie, by the fire,' Lena instantly urged, guiding Lizzie to a chair. 'Have you had anything to eat?'

Lizzie shook her head, but strangely she no longer felt hungry.

'We've had our meal, Mam, but there's scouse left over, enough for you and Lizzie,' Lena informed her mother. 'Our Peggy's gone out,' she added.

Nellie nodded. 'Is there any tea in that pot,

61

Lena? I'm parched, and I'm fair worn out with worry too.'

'Will Lizzie be able to go and see her mam tomorrow?' Lena asked.

Nellie nodded. 'I expect so. I'll go with her too, when we've found out about the visiting times.'

Feeling relieved at Nellie's words, Lizzie gratefully took the mug of tea Lena handed her, and sipped it.

'Did yer say your da was paid off at dinner time, Lizzie?' Nellie asked, suddenly wondering where the girl had got the shilling from.

'The blockerman said he was. Da had told him he was ill and that he was going home, but...'

Nellie exchanged a scornful glance with her husband. 'A likely tale!'

'I tried four pubs but he ... he wasn't in any of them. I ... I think he's gone up to Liverpool – again.'

'Well, iffen 'e comes 'ome in the same state as last week, 'e can just sleep in the flamin' street! I'm not goin' to try ter 'elp 'im in!' Ernie stated bluntly.

'I met a gentleman coming out of the Knowsley and he was really kind to me,' Lizzie informed them. 'He went back into see if Da was in there, but he wasn't and I ... I got upset and ... and he gave me the money for the dispensary.'

Nellie raised her eyebrows. 'Well, you don't often meet folk like that coming out of a pub around here!'

'He didn't look like someone from around here, Mrs Gibbons. He had a really good overcoat on, and a bowler hat too.'

'A foreman I suppose he was,' Nellie deduced.

'Did he say what 'is name was, Lizzie?' Ernie enquired. He knew most of the foremen on the local docks but none who would be as generous to a waif like Lizzie; she was a complete stranger with a sob story which, for all they knew, might or might not be true.

'No, and I was so upset and ... taken aback ... that I didn't ask, but I was so grateful to him.'

Nellie got to her feet and started to ladle out what remained of the stew into two bowls. 'Come and get this down you, Lizzie. You can stay here tonight, if you like, luv. It'll be a bit of a squash, but we'll manage, and you've had a horrible day.'

Lizzie felt a surge of relief wash over her. She hadn't been looking forward to staying on her own in their room, waiting for her da to get home and then having to try to make him understand that her mam was so ill that she'd been taken to hospital. 'Thanks, Mrs Gibbons, I'd like that.'

Nellie handed her a slice of bread to dip into the stew, and smiled tiredly. 'Once you've had a decent night's sleep, things will look better in the morning, Lizzie, they always do.'

Lizzie smiled back, feeling relieved and ravenous. Nellie was right; things wouldn't look half as bleak tomorrow, and she still had the shilling the gentleman had given her.

Chapter Seven

Despite the cramped conditions Lizzie had slept well, for she'd been utterly exhausted. She was used to sharing a bed, so Lena and Peggy's presence hadn't bothered her, and there were blankets and a quilt to cover them, so she'd been warm. As she rubbed the sleep from her eyes and struggled to sit up, she thought that she did feel better, less worried. Nellie was right; things didn't look so bad this morning.

When she went into the kitchen cum living room, Nellie was already up and she realised that Ernie, Lena and Peggy had already left for work, so it must be after eight o'clock.

'I let you sleep on, Lizzie. You were worn out. Now, here, have this tea and I'll cut you a slice of bread.'

Lizzie nodded her thanks and sat down on the bench by the table. 'Did ... did Da get home all right, do you know?'

Nellie put down the bread knife and looked candidly at the girl, hands on hips. 'I don't know and I don't flaming well care, Lizzie, an' that's the truth! Iffen he'd had any ... feelings for yer mam, he wouldn't have gone off on a bender in the first place. He's downright selfish to the bone, in my opinion, so I wouldn't be worrying about him, luv!' She resumed slicing the loaf. 'Mr Herbert from upstairs said the visiting time at the hospital is from two to three o'clock this afternoon. He's a porter there, that's why I asked him. We'll go up there then, and I'm sure that after a night in the warmth an' being looked after, yer Mam will be a bit ... better.'

Lizzie nodded, encouraged by the woman's optimism. She finished her breakfast in silence, thinking about Nellie's cutting remarks regarding her father. In her heart of hearts she knew Nellie Gibbons was right but, all the same, she'd go and see if he had come home. He usually managed to – although, on occasions, he'd not made it home until the following day.

When she went in later that morning and glanced around the cold, bare room, she wasn't surprised to see that he wasn't there; nor was there any sign of him having come back earlier. He'd have very little – if anything – left of his wages, she surmised bitterly, so how was she going to pay the rent and what they owed Sadie? She didn't know, but of one thing she was certain: he wasn't going to get the shilling the gentleman had given her. She was going to give that to Nellie who was feeding her, letting her stay and was going to accompany her to the hospital.

Her father still hadn't arrived home by the time they left for the hospital but Nellie didn't comment on the fact as they walked through the streets, busy with weekend shoppers and workers who had finished for the day. Lizzie hoped that it would be warmer in the hospital for, once again, it looked like snow; dull, leaden clouds were massing thickly overhead, and it was bitterly cold.

They stood with all the other people waiting that raw February afternoon to be admitted to the wards of the hospital, but at last they were ushered inside. After some enquiries they were directed to the women's general medical ward.

Nellie shivered involuntarily and sniffed. 'I hate the smell in these places!' she muttered.

Lizzie nodded her agreement. It smelled of carbolic soap and something else she couldn't put her finger on. But it was at least warm, for there was a stove in the centre of the large ward. They both stood and stared around them, taking in the half-tiled white walls against which were lined up narrow, iron-framed beds in regimented rows – all of them occupied. The bedclothes were neat and spotlessly clean, as was the floor, and high windows let in shafts of cold, grey daylight. It was what she would call 'orderly', Nellie thought, but there was nothing remotely cheerful about the place, not even a few flowers to brighten it up.

'We're lookin' for Mrs Florrie Tempest,' Nellie informed the nursing sister, who sat at her desk to one side of the stove, writing notes in a file in a meticulous script.

She looked up. 'And you are?' came the rather brusque question.

'This 'ere is Lizzie, her daughter, and I'm her ... sister,' Nellie lied. Maurice Herbert had told her they were very strict about visitors – usually it was family members only.

'Fourth bed on the right, but please don't disturb her too much. She's very poorly but we're hoping that with rest, warmth and nourishment she'll be able to fight the infection.'

66

Lizzie bit her lip and Nellie looked grave. 'She's no better, then?' she enquired.

Sister shook her head. 'She's very weak but, as she is also very undernourished, that's only to be expected. Her constitution has been undermined by lack of a substantial diet.'

Nellie nodded sadly as she ushered Lizzie down the ward, knowing Florrie was likely to have frequently gone without food for the sake of her children in the past.

'She ... she doesn't look any better, Mrs Gibbons, does she?' Lizzie whispered, trying not to disturb her mother, who looked much as she had last evening, although the bed looked comfortable and clean. She'd desperately hoped she'd see some signs of improvement.

Nellie didn't reply but bent closer to her neighbour. 'Florrie, love, can you hear me? It's Nellie, and I've brought Lizzie with me.'

Florrie slowly opened her eyes and tried to smile. She was aware she seemed to be sleeping a lot, and sometimes she really didn't know exactly where she was, except that she was warm and being cared for. And now Lizzie and Nellie were here.

'Mam, do you feel any better, maybe just a little bit?' Lizzie begged.

There was a slight movement of Florrie's head and Lizzie looked up at Nellie and smiled. 'Perhaps we were expecting too much, like? Maybe it ... it's going to take some time.'

Nellie nodded. 'You might well be right, Lizzie. She'll need to gain some strength. It's like that sister said, she's not been eatin' properly, but she'll get well looked after in here.'

Florrie seemed to drift back to sleep, so Nellie and Lizzie just sat in silence, watching her, until the bell sounded to announce that visiting time was over. Lizzie felt a little more relieved and hopeful that with rest, warmth, medicine and nourishing food, her mam would get better. She didn't want to even think about what would happen if she didn't.

'Come on, Lizzie, luv. We'll come back to-morrow afternoon, and there's bound to be an improvement in her by then,' Nellie urged confidently, far more confidently than she felt. She couldn't see poor Florrie improving any time soon, but at least she was in the best place, and she didn't want to increase the girl's anxiety.

As they turned out on to Derby Road again, Nellie turned to Lizzie. 'She's obviously going to be in hospital for quite a while, so when we get back home we'll have to sort some things out with yer da,' she said firmly.

'I know. The rent has got to be paid ... and Mrs Morgan too and...'

'He'll just have to face up to his responsibilities. Cut out the booze and try to get regular work,' Nellie said grimly, thinking that most of the blame for poor Florrie's condition could be laid at the feet of Art Tempest. 'And he's responsible for seeing that you don't go hungry, Lizzie.'

'I know, but I just wish I could get some kind of a job, Mrs Gibbons, then I wouldn't have to rely on Da. I ... I don't know what I would have done without ... you. I ... I'd have had nothing to eat and no fire,' Lizzie replied with a sob in her voice.

At least she had given Nellie the shilling, so she didn't feel too beholden, but the older woman had also given her advice and comfort, for which she was immeasurably grateful.

'Well, it was the least I could do, Lizzie. Now let's get home and get things sorted out.'

When they reached Bennett Street Nellie was furious to find that there was still no sign of Art Tempest.

'Where the hell is he?' she demanded of Ernie.

He shrugged. ''Ow do I know, Nellie?'

Lizzie bit her lip. 'Perhaps he's had an ... accident?'

Nellie shoved the kettle on to the hob as she took off her shawl. 'Accident my foot! The closest he'll 'ave come to that is getting into a fight! He's probably still dead drunk in a gutter somewhere! Well, this is a fine to do, I must say!'

Ernie frowned. The responsibility for both Florrie and Lizzie didn't lie with them. It was totally Art's concern, even though he seemed oblivious to that fact.

'I suppose all we can do is wait until he flaming well turns up!' Nellie pronounced as she made the tea. 'Then, he'll have to just face up to things!'

'How was Mrs Tempest, Mam?' Lena asked tentatively, for poor Lizzie looked upset and was biting her lip.

'Not much better, Lena, I have to say, but she's being well looked after. We'll go in again tomorrow. Maybe he'll have turned up by then.'

Lena smiled sympathetically at Lizzie; she'd been trying to think of something to take Lizzie's mind off her worries. 'Would you like me to put your hair up, Lizzie? We'll have the bedroom to ourselves once our Peggy's gone out. It might help cheer you up, like. Make you look a bit older too.'

Lizzie smiled back at her. She couldn't remember when she'd last brushed her hair. She'd been too preoccupied – and besides, she had no hairbrush, just a bit of an almost toothless comb.

Nellie smiled too. 'Aye, that's a good idea, Lena. Make her look a bit more ... presentable for when she sees her mam tomorrow.'

Lizzie shared the evening meal with them and then, after Peggy had gone out, resplendent in a second-hand but still fashionable jacket and wide-brimmed hat, she went into the bedroom they all shared and sat on the edge of one of the two beds.

Carefully Lena brushed out the tangled dark curls. 'You've got lovely hair, Lizzie. I wish mine was as thick, and that it curled like yours. Now, you hold these pins for me,' she instructed.

When she'd finished she handed Lizzie a small mirror that belonged to Peggy. 'How does that look? Do you like it?'

Lizzie gazed at her reflection in astonishment. It didn't look like her at all, she thought. Lena had piled her hair up on top of her head but had teased a few curls to fall across her forehead. It did make her look older, and her eyes appeared to be much larger. 'Oh, it's ... gorgeous, Lena! It... I don't look like ... me, at all!'

Lena laughed. 'Your mam will 'ardly recognise you, Lizzie!'

Lizzie grinned at her but then looked serious. 'Oh, I just hope she'll be a bit better, Lena, I really do, and I wish ... I wish me da would come home. At least he should know she's in hospital ... and ... I don't know what we're going to do about the rent and things for next week.'

Lena put her arm around her. 'Try not to worry too much, Lizzie. 'E'll come 'ome, and there'll be plenty of time to sort everything out,' she urged. 'Come on, let's show Mam how pretty you look.'

Nellie looked up as the two girls came back into the room. 'Bye, you look ... different, Lizzie! It suits you like that. Our Lena's got a real knack with hair.'

'I'll do it up for you again tomorrow, Lizzie,' Lena promised, before turning to address her mother. 'But ... but she's still frettin' over her da, Mam.'

Nellie sighed. 'I suppose it's only to be expected, but the Devil looks after 'is own, is what I say. He'll turn up eventually. And no doubt he'll be skint, so he'll have to take himself to the docks on Monday. Let's hope that the blockerman will have forgotten about 'im skiving off early yesterday and is charitable enough to take him on.'

Lizzie didn't look convinced, so Nellie smiled. 'Don't you go worrying, Lizzie. I'll have a word with Sadie, she'll understand. Things will be getting back to normal by next weekend, luv, you mark my words.'

Lizzie tried to find some comfort in Nellie's words, but she really didn't hold out much hope. When all was said and done, what was 'normal' for her family was pretty dire to contemplate when compared to the Gibbons family. Her hand strayed to the curls on her forehead. Perhaps if she'd had her hair done like this these last few weeks, she might have been able to get a job. But it wouldn't do her much good now, she thought. How could she concentrate on anything when her poor mam was so ill and her da had gone missing?

Chapter Eight

When Nellie and Lizzie set out for the hospital that Sunday afternoon, Art Tempest still had not returned. True to her word, Lena had done Lizzie's hair. She'd even let the girl borrow the jacket she usually wore for Sunday best, since she wasn't going out that Sunday, although Nellie had remarked that a good thick shawl would be more serviceable and infinitely warmer.

'But she looks so much more grown up, Mam. It might cheer her mam up to see her looking so ... well,' Lena had urged.

Nellie hadn't replied, but before they left she'd had a quiet word with Ernie.

'While we're out, an' if *he's* still not back, you'd best go up to the police station, Ernie. Just to see if somethin' *has* happened to him. If Florrie's feeling better, she's bound to ask about that useless husband of hers, and I know Lizzie is frettin' over him.'

Ernie had nodded, although he was loath to go into any police station enquiring after the likes of

Art Tempest.

Lizzie shivered a little as they walked to the hospital – whether from the cold or apprehension, she wasn't sure. Lena's jacket, although smart, was very thin. She'd never owned anything like it, and she was very grateful to Lena, but she couldn't help thinking that Nellie had been right about the shawl.

There was the usual crowd of relatives waiting at the hospital gates, but Lizzie was relieved that they didn't have to stand in the cold for long.

'I know they has to have their rules, but honestly, you'd think that in this weather they'd be a bit less strict, like. They could at least let us stand inside,' Nellie grumbled.

When they eventually arrived on the ward, both she and Lizzie were relieved to see that Florrie did look a little better.

'Lizzie, what have you done to yourself, luv? You look ... different,' Florrie murmured as Lizzie took her hand.

'It was all Lena's idea, Mam. She did my hair and lent me the jacket.'

'She'd have been better off with our Lena's shawl; it's bitter out there, so you're in the best place. And I can see you're feeling better, Florrie,' Nellie added.

Florrie nodded, although she was still weak and realised that she was very ill. In fact, there had been a time during the night when she'd been very afraid that she was going to die. She'd got upset, found herself sobbing with fear and weakness, anxious about what would happen to her poor Lizzie, wondering if she would ever see either of her sons again. The sister had tried to calm her, but a doctor had been called and she'd been given more laudanum, after which she'd at last drifted off to sleep.

'Don't you go worrying over ... anything,' Nellie said firmly, wondering what she was going to say if Florrie asked why Art hadn't come to visit her.

'Mrs Gibbons has been very good to me, Mam. I ... I've been staying with her,' Lizzie added, flooded with happiness that her mother could at least speak to her today. But then she could have bitten her tongue, for Florrie was frowning and there was puzzlement in her eyes.

'Art...?'

'He's fine, Florrie! Don't you be getting all upset about him now!' Nellie lied stoutly.

'Why ... why ... hasn't...?' Florrie was getting agitated and began to gasp for breath.

'He didn't want to ... tire you, luv,' Nellie interrupted hastily. It was the only thing she could think of on the spur of the moment, and she looked across anxiously at the ward sister who immediately got to her feet and came over to them.

'She's getting a bit flustered, like, Sister,' Nellie informed her.

The woman glared at her. 'I would have expected you to show a bit more consideration, seeing how poorly she is. What did you say to upset her?'

'She ... she was asking about her husband, Sister.'

'I see – the absent Mr Tempest,' was the abrupt retort.

74

Lizzie held her mother's hand and tried to calm her while Nellie took the sister to one side and explained. Sister listened in grim silence, then nodded.

'I think it best if you leave her to rest now, Mrs Gibbons. A doctor had to attend her during the night, and he has prescribed some medicine which should help. If her husband happens to turn up, I would ask you to strongly dissuade him from coming in. It sounds as if he might even prove ... disruptive. And I can't have that!'

Nellie nodded. 'She will be all right, Sister? She did seem a bit better today, at first.'

'We can only take things one day at a time, Mrs Gibbons. She is not on the road to recovery yet.'

Outside again, Lizzie shivered as the bitter wind cut through her but she'd heard the sister's remarks. 'What are we going to do, Mrs Gibbons, if me da insists on going in to see Mam?'

Nellie frowned and pulled her shawl more tightly to her as protection against the icy blast. 'There's not much we *can* do, Lizzie. Mind you, they won't stand any nonsense out of him – and you can bet that sister will warn him not to go upsetting her patient. If the truth be told, she's only going to go on worrying about him if she doesn't see him. And we can't go on making excuses.'

Lizzie nodded, thinking that she too would impress upon her da that it was important that he didn't upset her mam.

As they walked into the kitchen Lena instantly pushed the kettle on to the hob. She could see that both her mother and Lizzie were cold and

75

looked dispirited. She glanced quickly at her father, who had put down his newspaper.

'So, how was she today?' Ernie asked.

'She seemed a bit better – at least she was, until she started asking where *he* was,' Nellie replied, sitting down beside the range and holding out her hands to the welcome warmth.

Lena made the tea, handed out the mugs and smiled at Lizzie, wondering how both her mam and her friend were going to take the latest news.

'Well, luv, I went up to the police station–' Ernie announced.

'And what did you find out?' Nellie interrupted.

Ernie shook his head. 'Well, 'e hasn't been involved in any kind of ... accident, they were sure of that.'

'Oh, that's such a relief, Mr Gibbons,' Lizzie cried, her hands tightly cupping her mug of tea.

'So, where the hell is he, then?' Nellie demanded. 'Or didn't they know?'

Ernie looked grim. 'Oh, they knew all right. Someone from Liverpool City Police 'ad been in touch, because of the address 'e gave, an' it's not good news, luv. 'E ... 'e's in jail.'

'What!' Nellie cried.

Lena glanced at Lizzie and saw that she was on the verge of tears.

'What ... what's he done?' Lizzie asked shakily. It was the worst news possible, and the one thing she had least expected.

''E got into a fight outside a pub on the dock road and then, when the scuffers arrived ter break it up, like, he started on them,' Ernie replied, shaking his head at the sheer stupidity of Art

Tempest's behaviour. 'So they carted 'im off to the Bridewell in Dale Street and 'e was up before the Magistrate on Saturday mornin'. You know they come down 'ard on violence against the police.'

Nellie nodded, her lips pursed tightly in disapproval, for she shared her husband's opinion of their neighbour's actions. 'So, what was 'e charged with?'

'Drunk an' Disorderly, Causin' an Affray, Breach of the Peace, Resistin' Arrest an' Grievous Bodily 'Arm,' Ernie informed them.

'So they threw the book at him! Well, I can't say I blame them; they're there to keep the streets safe. Nor do they have to put up with getting a hiding from the likes of *him!*' Nellie replied scathingly.

Ernie nodded. ''E'll be in Walton Jail for a couple of months now.'

Lizzie looked at him, her eyes wide with shock and fear. 'Oh, what ... what am I going to do now?' she pleaded, panic rising in her. Without her da's wages she'd have no money for ... anything. And what effect this news would have on her poor mam, she didn't know.

Lena put her arm around the girl's shoulders. 'Don't get upset, Lizzie, we'll ... we'll think of something, won't we, Mam?'

Nellie nodded slowly, for her thoughts had been running along the same lines as Lizzie's. She couldn't give two hoots what happened to Art Tempest, but of one thing she was certain: she wasn't going to let Lizzie go into the workhouse. Then she wondered how on earth she was going to break the news to Florrie. 'Next time we go into the hospital, Lizzie, I'll have a word with that sister, she seemed a sensible woman. I ... I don't know if yer mam should be told...'

Lizzie nodded. 'Sister'd know best, wouldn't she? But ... but what am I going to do now?'

'You'll stay with us, Lizzie. I'll not see you without a roof over your head – and there's no way I'd let you go into the workhouse, even for the couple of months he'll be inside! It would kill yer mam if ... if she thought...'

Lizzie burst into tears as she realised the desperate position her father had left her in. 'I ... I'll get a job, Mrs Gibbons, I *will!* I'll need to give you ... something, you can't afford to keep me for ... nothing,' she sobbed.

'I'll see what I can do to help, Lizzie. I'll ask at our factory tomorrow, there might be something,' Lena promised, only too aware that Lizzie was right. Money was scarce in their family too, but at least Lizzie wouldn't have to go into the workhouse – that didn't bear thinking about.

Nellie took the situation in hand. 'Dry yer eyes, Lizzie. Let's take one thing at a time. It would help if you could get something, but don't go fretting about it for the time being. There's nothing we can do about yer da – until 'e gets out.'

Lizzie nodded. 'There's something ... something Mam didn't tell you,' she blurted out.

Nellie stared at her hard. 'What, luv?'

'Me brother ... our Billy! He ... he's in Walton too,' Lizzie sobbed.

Nellie cast her eyes to the ceiling. 'What's he in for?'

'Theft,' Lizzie replied. 'I ... I can't remember when he is due out...' She paused. 'Me other brother – Ned – he ... he left to find work, and he's not like our Billy. He's ... honest, I know he is.'

Nellie tutted as she exchanged a glance with her husband, a little surprised by the fact that Florrie had two sons who had not been mentioned, until now. 'So, Billy takes after yer da, then? Well, the pair of them are not worth gettin' upset about, Lizzie, and I don't think we should go worrying yer mam with all this ... trouble,' she advised. She was determined that this information would not be bandied about the neighbourhood; she wasn't having the women of the Tempest family tarred with the same brush as the men, even though Lizzie swore Ned had never been in trouble.

Lizzie nodded, feeling a little relieved that she had at last told Nellie about her brothers. She dashed away her tears with the back of her hand and looked up at Lena. 'Will you ask for me tomorrow, Lena? I've got to get work now. I've just *got* to.'

'I promise, Lizzie,' Lena replied firmly. She'd go and see Mr Rutherford; he was the senior foreman in their department, although she didn't know him very well. But he was a decent enough man and very fair, so Peggy always said. She'd explain about poor Lizzie's circumstances – well, some of them.

Lizzie managed a watery smile. She'd do as Nellie suggested and take one thing – one anxiety – at a time. Her priorities were her mam and finding work. She wouldn't worry about her da or her brothers. Sadly, she realised that Billy was indeed like her father. He thought only of himself and she knew that, even if he had been released, he wouldn't come looking for them; he wouldn't care. She didn't know where Ned was, either – so she couldn't contact him. Now she had to just think of herself and her mother.

Chapter Nine

By the end of the following morning Lizzie felt a little more hopeful. Before she'd left for the factory Lena had made a point of promising to see if there was any work available, while Nellie kept the girl busy helping with the chores to keep her mind off her worries.

Nellie had also been down to Morgan's corner shop and informed Sadie of the events of the past few days.

'And yer say she was a bit better yesterday then, Nellie?' Sadie said as she weighed out the loose tea Nellie had asked for.

'She was at first, poor soul. Oh, I know none of us has had it easy, Sadie, but she's had a terribly hard life these past years because of *him*.' She lowered her voice. 'And her eldest lad is in Walton too, so Lizzie told me yesterday, but I know I can trust you to keep that to yourself.'

'You can,' Sadie promised.

'There's another lad too, but Lizzie says he's honest. He left Liverpool to look for work and they haven't heard from him since.'

Sadie shook her head sadly. 'You're right, she's not had it easy, Nellie. So, even if ... when ... she's well enough to come out of there, what's she going to do? How will she manage with him inside and no money coming in?' she asked grimly.

Nellie leaned on the counter as she shook her head. 'I don't know, Sadie, and that's the honest truth. She's not strong enough to even take in washing – and besides, there's no facilities in that room to do it. And she won't be fit enough to go out cleaning offices in the evenings or get a job cleaning at the Immigrant House. Although that's pretty desperate,' she added, referring to the big building where the Cunard Line housed steerage passengers before they boarded one of the many ships and made the crossing to a new life in America.

'Then it's all down to Lizzie getting a job. I have to say, Nellie, the girl doesn't look old enough to work, she's that slight and skinny.'

'I know, an' she *has* already tried to get work, Sadie, and not got anything. But our Lena is going to see if there's anything at the match factory, even if it's only brushing the floor, like. Sometimes it helps if someone will say a word in the right ear. We can only hope.'

Sadie tutted. 'Nellie, the girl hasn't even got a decent rag to her back, let alone something fit for an "interview". And even if she does get taken on, whatever she can earn won't keep the pair of them.'

'Oh, I know that, Sadie, but you know what the only alternative is.'

The other woman nodded grimly. 'The workhouse – God help them!'

Nellie began to pack her purchases into her bag.

'Let's just pray it doesn't come to that, Sadie. We're going in to see Florrie again this afternoon, and I'm going to have a chat with the sister about *him*. With a bit of luck,' she finished resolutely, 'our Lena will have some good news.' But privately she didn't hold out much hope.

Nellie was still out, and Lizzie had gone out into the yard to empty the ashes she'd raked out of the range into the communal ash can. But on her return she was surprised to find a man knocking on the door to their room.

'Is there anyone in there, or are they just ignoring me?' he demanded of her.

'There's ... there's no one there,' Lizzie replied hesitantly. 'Do you need to speak to them?'

'What I need, girl, is this week's rent!'

Lizzie's heart dropped. 'But ... but it's not due until Friday.'

'They're new here and, until I've reason to believe they're reliable, I like to collect the money early.'

Panic was beginning to rise up in her. What should she do? What should she say? She had no money, and he didn't look like a very sympathetic person.

'Who are you? Do you know when they'll be back? *If* they'll be back at all!'

'I ... I'm staying with Mrs Gibbons and ... and they've not gone, but I don't know when they'll be in,' she stammered.

His frown deepened. 'Then I'll just have to come back again until I catch someone in. Which, believe me, I *will* – eventually.'

To her intense relief he turned away down the lobby. She scurried into Nellie's kitchen and closed the door behind her, leaning against it. She'd have to tell Nellie that he'd called; she hoped she would be able to get him to understand their plight, but his visit had shaken her.

The ward sister listened in grim silence that afternoon as Nellie told her of Art Tempest's recent incarceration, and then took the decision Nellie had hoped for.

'Mrs Tempest is still very poorly indeed, and I don't think it would help one iota for her to learn of her husband's situation. However, I will take advice from matron, who will have the final word on the matter. In the meantime, try not to mention him at all.'

Nellie nodded, thinking that might be easier said than done. However, when they reached Florrie's bedside she seemed to be in a restless sleep.

'I don't think we should disturb her, Lizzie, luv,' she whispered. 'Rest is the best thing for her, and then we won't need to mention yer da at all,' she added.

Lizzie nodded silently but bit her lip; Mam didn't seem to be getting any better at all. As she sat watching her mother's laboured breathing she prayed that Lena might come home with some hopeful news; then perhaps tomorrow when she came to visit Mam she would at least have something good to tell her.

Nellie patted Lizzie's hand as she sat at her mother's bedside. The poor girl had been in such a state that morning, after the rent collector called. It had taken all Nellie's patience and good sense to calm her down and reassure her that they would find some way to pacify the man when he returned on Friday.

Florrie seemed barely aware of their presence. As they prepared to leave at the end of visiting hours, the sister delivered matron's decision that the truth should be kept from Florrie. No good would come of her learning about her husband's latest brush with the law.

As they trudged home, Nellie reflected that this decision was the right one. At least until Florrie got better, which she now realised was going to take quite a while. But she still wondered what kind of excuse she could give Florrie for Art's continued absence. It was all very worrying, and she determined to discuss it with Ernie later that evening. Perhaps he could come up with something plausible.

When Peggy and Lena finally arrived home that evening Lizzie could hardly contain herself, she was so anxious.

'Did ... did you ask about a job for me, Lena?' she begged.

Peggy looked slightly annoyed as she hung her heavy shawl on the peg behind the door. 'We've barely set foot over the doorstep,' she muttered but didn't continue, as she caught the look her mother shot at her.

Lena grinned. 'I did, Lizzie and it's good news! I told Mr Rutherford all about you and ... your mam, and he said if you go in to see him tomorrow he'll see if he can offer you something. He didn't promise, mind – just said he would ... see.'

'Oh, Lena, thanks! I'm so grateful...' Lizzie cried, relief surging through her.

'Don't go getting your hopes up too high, Lizzie,' Nellie warned cautiously, although she too was pleased that Lena had at least managed to get the man to listen. And as both girls worked in the packing room, the work wasn't heavy, which would benefit Lizzie.

'You'd better make an effort to tidy yourself up before you go,' Peggy advised tartly.

'You can borrow my jacket again, Lizzie, and I'll show you how to do your hair. You can practise after we've eaten,' Lena offered, glaring at her sister who just shrugged. 'How was your mam today?' she enquired, to change the subject.

While Nellie busied herself with the meal, and Lena and Lizzie set the table, Lizzie imparted what news there was on her mother's condition.

'Well, you might have some good news for her soon, Lizzie. That should cheer her up,' Lena said confidently.

'What time did he say? Where will I go? Should I ask for him by name?' Lizzie asked.

Lena nodded. 'He said to go in at four o'clock; he has his break then, so he'll have time to speak to you without being interrupted. Go to the main gate and tell them you've an appointment to see Mr Rutherford; they'll direct you up to his office.'

Lizzie nodded, beginning to feel nervous already. So much depended upon seeing this Mr Rutherford tomorrow – her entire future, in fact – and she'd have to impress upon him just how much she needed the job and that she would work so hard. She realised that she would have to leave the hospital early. Hopefully, her mam would be awake when she arrived and would understand when she explained. Then she wondered if she should even mention it to her mother – in case she didn't get a job at all. But she had to get one; she just *had* to.

Lizzie hoped she looked tidy – and even quite smart – as she left the house in Bennett Street with Nellie the following afternoon, once again in the borrowed jacket and with her hair pinned up, although she didn't think it looked as neat as when Lena had done it. She was so nervous that she didn't even feel the cold of the winter's afternoon; she just prayed that by the time she got back to Bennett Street she would have a job and that her mam would have improved a little.

Sister was waiting for them at the entrance to the ward, which Nellie thought was unusual and rather disturbing. 'Is there something ... wrong, Sister?'

'Is Mam ... worse?' Lizzie could hardly get the words out. Her heart seemed to have dropped like a stone and there was a lump in her throat.

Sister ushered them into a small room off the main ward, and Nellie's anxiety deepened.

'I'm terribly sorry to have to tell you that ... that poor Mrs Tempest passed away early this morning. She ... she just didn't have the strength to overcome the illness.'

Nellie groaned and shook her head sadly. 'Oh, poor, poor Florrie. God rest her!'

Lizzie just stood, white-faced, staring at the

sister, unable to take in her words. But at Nellie's exclamation of grief she gave a heartrending cry. 'No! No! She can't have ... she was getting better!'

Nellie put her arms around her. 'No, luv, she wasn't. You told us she was very poorly yesterday, didn't you, Sister?'

The sister nodded. 'I did, Mrs Gibbons. We ... we hoped she would pull through, we did everything possible. I'm so sorry.'

Lizzie felt sobs choking her and she just couldn't believe that her mam was ... gone. She'd never hear her voice again; never feel her arms around her, comforting her. Mam had been her rock, given her the only love she'd ever known. She'd not even had the chance to say goodbye. Her world was crumbling around her and she clung desperately to Nellie.

'I'm sorry to have to mention this, Mrs Gibbons, but ... arrangements will have to be made,' the sister said quietly.

Nellie nodded. 'There ... there's no money, I'm afraid.'

Sister had assumed as much. 'I understand. You can leave matters in the hands of the almoner. You will be contacted about the ... arrangements.'

Lizzie wasn't listening to the conversation; she was too shocked and confused in her grief-stricken state.

Again Nellie nodded. This was the final indignity for poor Florrie. There would be no flowers, no service, no proper funeral at all. She would be buried in an unmarked pauper's grave.

'I'll leave you both to ... compose yourselves,' the sister said sympathetically before she left.

After a few minutes, Nellie pulled herself together. 'Come on, Lizzie. There's nothing for us to stay here for now. Let's go home, luv,' she urged gently, guiding the sobbing girl towards the door. There wasn't any point in remaining. Florrie's body would have been taken to the hospital mortuary, and there were no belongings to collect. She'd not even had a wedding ring – that had long since been sold.

Nellie's heart went out to Lizzie; she was now effectively an orphan. She supposed someone would have to inform Art Tempest, but it wasn't going to be her. As far as she was concerned, he could rot in jail, she thought venomously, for in her opinion he'd been the cause of poor Florrie's demise.

As they left the hospital she remembered suddenly that Lizzie was to go to the match factory at four. How on earth could she be expected to keep the appointment now? she wondered distractedly. Should she go instead and try to explain? That would mean leaving the poor girl alone – but now, more than ever, Lizzie needed a job. She came to a decision. 'Lizzie, luv, we'll go home and have a cup of tea for the ... shock and then I ... I'll come with you to Bryant & May's.'

Lizzie looked up at her, her eyes red and swollen. The interview had been wiped from her mind. 'I ... I can't go!'

Nellie bit her lip. However dire the circumstances, it wouldn't look good if the girl just didn't turn up – and it would reflect badly on Lena too. 'Shall I go and ... explain?'

Lizzie nodded dumbly. She couldn't think about the future, not now. But through the mist that clogged her brain came the thought that she needed a job desperately. There was no one now to provide for her. She was on her own, at least until her da got out of jail – and what then? Would he have mended his ways? She doubted that. Even with a job she couldn't pay the rent and keep herself, let alone both of them. Where would they live and ... how? It was all too much for her to think of now. 'Maybe ... I should go,' she said, fighting down her sobs.

Nellie looked concerned. 'We'll think about it, Lizzie. After we've had a cup of tea and you've calmed down a bit. It might be best if I go and explain. I'll ask if you can go tomorrow.'

'I ... I think I could manage it ... tomorrow,' Lizzie replied. She couldn't even think straight today; she felt as if her heart had turned to stone and her senses were numb. Maybe tomorrow she would feel better, although she doubted it.

They had a cup of tea when they got home. Nellie stoked the range to try and impart some warmth into the chill of the day. Lizzie sipped the comforting brew, sitting in numbed silence, and then Nellie went off to the match factory as she'd promised.

She returned to inform a still quietly sobbing Lizzie that she was to go and see Mr Rutherford tomorrow; he had seemed a very decent man, even expressing his condolences for Lizzie's loss. It all hardly registered with Lizzie – and nor did the remaining events of the day. She was dimly aware of Nellie discussing the situation with Ernie when he returned from work. They both agreed that, desperately sad though things were, there was no chance of the money being found for a funeral for poor Florrie. Nellie was hard put to find the penny a week they each needed for their own burial funds.

'It just can't be 'elped, luv,' Ernie stated. 'We've done all we can for both Florrie and Lizzie, and I don't suppose 'e will care where she's buried.' But he promised to go back to the police station and ask for the news of Florrie's demise to be passed on to Art Tempest in Walton Jail – and Billy Tempest too, if he was still in there. They also agreed that Lizzie should stay with them until her da got out.

'It's not the ideal situation for her, but she's got no one else now,' Nellie concluded. The girl was Art Tempest's responsibility but, until he got out of jail, she would be theirs.

Chapter Ten

At four o'clock the next day Lizzie duly presented herself at the main entrance to the match factory. She had pulled herself together sufficiently to realise that she had to somehow make a favourable impression on this Mr Rutherford. She was trying hard to concentrate and appear composed; trying hard too not to think of her poor mam and the days that lay ahead without her. But it was so hard, and she felt it keenly that there would be no decent funeral. She promised herself that if ever, in the future, she had enough money, she would find her mam's grave and have a stone erected and take flowers every week.

She took little notice of her surroundings as she walked towards the imposing brick building she'd been directed to. She pushed open the door, which led into a bare, brick-lined and dimly lit corridor, and was instantly aware of the odour that seemed to pervade the building. It was the smell you sometimes experienced after you'd struck a match, she realised.

As instructed, she climbed the narrow stone stairs. Ahead of her was a set of big double doors bearing the words 'Packing Room'. Hesitantly, she pushed them open and peered inside. Beyond lay a cavernous room, seemingly packed with fearsome-looking machinery and numerous people, nearly all women and girls. The noise was deafening and that smell seemed to catch the back of her throat. It was the first time she had ever been in a factory of any kind, and it was rather daunting. As she gazed around, feeling overwhelmed and very nervous, her attention was drawn to a man who had emerged from behind one bank of machines and was walking purposefully towards her. He wore a buff-coloured overall over a suit, shirt and tie, and his wavy brown hair looked a little dishevelled. She surmised that this must be the senior foreman Lena had spoken of – Mr Rutherford.

She tried to steady herself and calm the butterflies in her stomach, and her hand went instinctively to her hair to make sure it was tidy. But as the foreman drew closer her eyes widened in astonishment and she forgot her nerves as a frisson of relief passed through her. She recognised him; he was the gentleman who'd given her the shilling for the dispensary doctor. He'd been so kind to her then, so maybe now...?

'You're Miss Lizzie Tempest, I take it?' he said, ushering her into a tiny room to the side.

Lizzie had nodded and now glanced around tentatively. The room was crammed with a desk, two chairs and four tall cabinets. As stacks of paper covered most of the surfaces, she assumed it was his office. She felt completely out of her depth.

He indicated that she should sit down and then he stared hard at her, a puzzled frown creasing his brow. 'Don't I know you?'

She nodded. 'I ... I met you coming out of the Knowsley Arms. You were very good to me, sir. You gave me a shilling ... for the dispensary doctor,' she reminded him quietly.

'Now I remember you,' he stated, smiling. She'd been looking for her father, as her mother was ill. He looked more closely at her, and with some concern. So, sadly her mother had died – and only yesterday, in Bootle General. She seemed to be bearing up well enough, although it must have been a terrible blow for one so young. She looked different now to that previous occasion: cleaner, tidier and even a little older. 'I was very sorry to hear about your mother,' he said in a rather formal tone.

Tears pricked Lizzie's eyes. 'Thank you ... sir.'

'Did you find your father?' he asked rather more gently.

She shook her head. 'No, at least not that night.

It was the dispensary doctor who said Mam had to go to hospital and sent for the ambulance.'

'I see.' He leaned back in the chair. 'Well, Miss Lena Gibbons has informed me that your circumstances are – how shall we say? – rather desperate, and that you need a job.'

'Oh, I do, sir! You see, I ... I'm living with them now. Mrs Gibbons wouldn't see me go into the workhouse, but I need to give her money for my keep. I've no one else to turn to.'

He frowned at the mention of the dreaded workhouse, trying to work out why she was living with neighbours. 'What about your father? Does he not have work? Is he not able to provide for you?'

Lizzie bit her lip and felt her cheeks burning with shame. She really didn't want to have to tell him the truth, but what else could she say? 'He ... he's in jail, sir. He got into a fight on the night Mam went into hospital and ... and ended up going to prison.'

George Rutherford let out a long, slow breath; he could see how humiliated the girl was at having to tell him this. On top of losing her mother she had quite obviously been left in a terrible predicament. 'I see. Have you any brothers or sisters?'

Lizzie shook her head. 'My sisters died when they were very little, and my brother Ned left a year ago to find work and we ... I ... haven't heard from him since, sir. I don't know where he is.' She definitely wasn't going to mention Billy; she'd been shamed enough.

So, she had no one, poor lass, he mused. He assumed that, whenever her father was released, his parental responsibilities would be far from what

93

he himself would consider satisfactory. 'How old are you, Miss Tempest?'

Lizzie looked at him hopefully. 'I'm nearly fourteen. I know I'm a bit ... young, and I know I don't look my age, but I've always been slight. But I'll work hard and I'll do ... anything, anything at all, sir,' she pleaded, twisting her hands nervously together in her lap.

He felt sorry for her. She really was in a dreadful predicament; she'd obviously had a very hard life so far, and it must be an ordeal for her to come seeking work the day after her mother's death. He leaned forward and nodded. 'Well, I think I can offer you a position as a packer here, in this part of the building, and we'll see how you get on with that. The work isn't very interesting, I'm afraid – in fact, it's rather dull and repetitive, and you'll have to learn to be very quick at it – but the pay is five shillings a week, and it's a much ... better part of the factory to work in. How soon can you start?'

Lizzie was so relieved that she was finding it hard not to be overcome by her emotions. 'Oh, thank you, sir! Thank you! I ... I can start tomorrow, if that's all right?'

He smiled kindly at her. 'That will definitely be all right.' Maybe it would even be for the best; take her mind off her present situation, he thought.

She managed a smile. 'I'll come along with Lena and Peggy Gibbons in the morning, then.'

'Of course, and then if you report to Miss Woods – she's in charge of that end of the production line – she'll set you to work, show you what's required of you.' He got to his feet to indicate that the interview was over.

Lizzie rose too. 'Thanks again, sir. I'll never be late, and I'll work ever so hard at whatever Miss Woods tells me, I promise. It ... it's the best thing that's happened to me in weeks, sir. I really mean that,' she added shyly.

Noting the sincerity and relief in her voice, he nodded. It wasn't much, he mused, five shillings a week for working nine long hours a day at a boring and repetitive job, with the added hazard of inhaling the white phosphorous used for the match heads, which could result in the dreaded 'phossy jaw'. Yet she was obviously so very grateful. She wasn't quite fourteen – the required age – but in the circumstances it wouldn't hurt to bend the rules slightly. She had to survive on her own until her father was released, although he wondered if that would make any difference at all to the way she had to live. He doubted it. The girl would have to stand on her own two feet, and he was glad to give her the chance to do so. But this was the second time their paths had crossed, and he wondered fleetingly if Providence had played a part in it.

When Lizzie returned home, Nellie could see by her expression that she'd been successful. 'Come and sit here by the fire, Lizzie, and tell me all about it,' she urged, for although the girl looked a little happier she also looked pinched with cold.

'I'm to start tomorrow. Oh, I'm that relieved! I know it's long hours and he said it was a bit boring, but I'll be paid the same as Lena, and ... and what was best was I knew him! I actually *knew* him. He was the same gentleman who gave me the shilling for the dispensary.'

Nellie looked astonished. 'Well, wasn't that a bit of good luck? You'll be all right now, Lizzie.'

'I will, and I'll work hard so as not to let him down, and I'll be able to give you the same money as Lena does.'

Nellie smiled at her. 'I'll not take it all off you, Lizzie. You'll have two shillings for yourself, like Lena does.'

Lizzie stared at her in some astonishment; she hadn't expected this, for Nellie would be giving her a home and feeding her too. Two whole shillings to herself! She'd never had any money of her own in her entire life. Instantly she made a decision. 'I'll give it to you to save for me, and then – when I've got enough – I'll buy some ... clothes!' The thought lifted her spirits. All her life she seemed to have worn little more than rags – third- or fourth-hand cut-downs, already well worn and shabby. But now she'd be able to buy her own clothes, even if they weren't brand new, to actually choose them and look decent – even fashionable – in them!

Nellie nodded, smiling. 'That's very sensible, Lizzie. So, you see, it's not been such a bad day, after all, has it?'

Lizzie smiled back. The ache in her heart had lessened a little, and she was actually looking forward to tomorrow. She could hardly bear to think about her mam, but she knew she would be proud of her. It hadn't been easy to go out and find a job, but she'd done it. Oh, the work might be boring, but at least it would be something to take her mind off her troubles – and she'd have the company of the other girls and women too. She was certain the time wouldn't drag heavily.

It wasn't long before Lena and Peggy arrived home, chattering about the events of the day. Lena was delighted by Lizzie's news, happy that she'd played a small part in facilitating her friend's good fortune, although Peggy's enthusiasm was a bit more restrained. She nodded knowingly when she found out that Mr Rutherford was the benefactor who had given Lizzie the shilling. 'So, it was only to be expected then that he'd give you a job. He'd taken pity on you once and he took pity on you again.'

Lena turned on her angrily. 'Why do you always have to be so ... nasty to Lizzie? What's Lizzie ever done to you?'

Peggy shrugged but Nellie quickly diffused the situation. 'Well, he did, so that's all that matters, and that's the end of it! She'll be going in with you two in the morning.'

Nothing further was said on the matter, but later, when the girls were chatting after tea, Lizzie confided her delight to Lena that she could save up and, in the not-too-distant future, be able to buy some nearly-new things.

'I'll take you along to the Strand,' she offered. 'There are lots of shops there that sell things second-hand – some good stuff too. That's where I got me jacket.'

'Thanks,' Lizzie replied, thinking that when spring arrived, and the weather got warmer, she would have saved enough to look clean, neat and smart for the first time in her life. It was quite an uplifting thought.

Later that evening, Nellie was dozing contentedly before the range while Ernie read his newspaper. Peggy had gone to see a friend who lived two doors down, and Lena and Lizzie were sitting at the kitchen table, Lena explaining in detail what Lizzie's job would entail, when they were all disturbed by a furious pounding on the front door.

Shaking herself, Nellie frowned. 'Ernie, go and see who that is, luv. No one ever knocks on the front door. Everyone knows who lives here, and any callers go straight to the door they want.'

Reluctantly Ernie got to his feet, feeling as uneasy as his wife. He returned a few seconds later, accompanied by a tall, burly police constable, both men looking grim.

'Dear God in heaven! What's wrong now?' Nellie exclaimed, getting to her feet. She'd never known the police to come to this house – or any other house in the street, for that matter – unless it was ... trouble.

'He ... he's come with bad news, Nellie, I'm afraid,' Ernie replied, glancing with concern at Lizzie.

'This was the address given by one Arthur Tempest to the Liverpool City Police...' the constable began, glancing at his notebook.

'Now what's he flaming well done?' Nellie demanded.

The constable looked even grimmer. 'Got into an argument with a prison officer and lashed out at him, causing quite a serious injury.'

Nellie looked pityingly at Lizzie. Hadn't the

poor girl had enough to contend with lately?

'The bloody fool! So, what'll happen to 'im?' Ernie asked.

'His sentence has been increased to five years' hard labour, and he's been moved to another prison,' was the curt reply.

Lizzie found her voice. 'I ... I'm his daughter. Where has he been sent?'

'Manchester, miss. I'm sorry. It's standard procedure, and it's our duty to inform you of these things.'

Nellie put her arm around Lizzie as she addressed the unwelcome visitor. 'Well, you've done that so now ... if you'd leave, please? This poor girl has just lost her mam, and now ... this.'

The officer nodded, replacing the notebook in his pocket before Ernie showed him out.

Lizzie sat down, looking dazed. The slight sense of relief she'd begun to feel these past few hours was draining away. Her da wouldn't be out in a matter of weeks; now it would be five more years. She ... she'd be nearly nineteen – grown up – and Manchester ... it might as well be the moon. How would he get back to Liverpool then, with no money and absolutely no chance of work? Would he even try?

A sense of despair began to wash over her as she realised that she was truly alone now, for she knew that when Art Tempest got out of prison, the last person he would think of was his daughter.

George Rutherford couldn't get Lizzie's plight out of his mind, and when he finally got home to

Olivia Street that evening his wife could see that something was disturbing him – their relationship was close and loving, and she could always tell when he was upset.

'Is everything all right at the factory, dear?' Eileen asked, taking his hat and kissing him on the cheek, as she did every night.

He put his arm around her; he hated her to worry about anything, as she still looked rather frail to him after her illness. She'd never been what people called a 'classical' beauty but he'd always thought that, with her soft brown curls and clear grey eyes, she was a very attractive girl. 'Everything is fine. In fact, production is up this month, or so I was informed today.'

'Then why were you frowning, George? It's not like you,' she persisted, drawing him down on to the sofa beside her.

It was useless to try to hide anything from her, he thought fondly. She knew him too well. 'A young girl came to see me today, looking for work. Oh, there's nothing unusual in that, but ... her case was different.'

'Why?' she asked quietly.

He told her about how he'd first encountered Lizzie Tempest and detailed her life's grim and tragic events since that night, while Eileen listened in compassionate silence. When he'd finished, she nodded. 'Poor child, but at least you were able to help her.'

'Yes ... and, ever since, I've had the feeling that Providence played a part in putting her in my path.'

Eileen nodded again. They had both been

brought up as Baptists; that was how they had met. They'd both attended the Providence Chapel and had been married there too. George attended chapel infrequently, these days, and did not adhere as strictly to the tenets of their religion as he had formerly done, but he still had a deeply ingrained sense of God's will working through the events and people He put in their way.

'You mean that you really feel you were meant to meet and help this poor unfortunate girl?'

He nodded. 'I do, Eileen. And I wonder if there is anything more I … we can do to help her?'

She looked thoughtful. 'Such as?'

'I don't know. She is living with neighbours now, at least until her father is released, and she does now have work, but–'

'But you feel that, even after he's released, her life won't improve, she'll be no better off? Perhaps finding herself in an even worse predicament?'

'I do. It's almost impossible for someone like her father to get work, and he might demand her wages and then continue to neglect her. She hasn't had much of a chance in life up to now, and I'm beginning to feel that perhaps Providence meant us to … help her.'

Eileen thought about it all in silence and, at last, decided that maybe her husband was right. After all, surely it wasn't just a coincidence that George had met the girl searching the pubs for her father and then she'd come to him seeking work? She could easily have gone to another factory; she could easily have been outside a different pub that night – there were certainly enough of them in that area. She nodded. 'Perhaps you're right, George.'

101

He smiled at her. 'Let's see how she gets on at work. I'll have more opportunity to get to know her and her circumstances much better, and then perhaps we...?'

'Could offer her a home, here with us?' It was a constant sorrow to her that they'd never been blessed with children, and it wasn't for the want of trying.

He put his arm around her and drew her closer. 'You are a very generous and kind-hearted woman, Eileen, and I love you for it. But let's see how things ... progress before we make a decision about that.'

She smiled up at him. 'I think we'd have to find her another job too, George. A matchgirl being taken in by her boss ... the other girls would make her life very uncomfortable, and I don't think your superiors would take too kindly to it, either.'

'You're right, but we'll sort that out in the future,' he replied. 'Of course, everything would depend upon you liking Lizzie Tempest and feeling happy to give her a home. If you don't, then I wouldn't press it upon you, you know that.'

'Of course, but I trust your judgement, George. I always have.'

He nodded, feeling increasingly convinced now that Providence had deemed that they should help little Lizzie Tempest.

Chapter Eleven

Her mam was always in Lizzie's thoughts. Not a day went by that she didn't think of Florrie and hope that, wherever she was, she was looking down on her with approval. Lizzie thought of her now as she walked to work with Lena and Peggy one Monday morning in April. She seldom gave a thought to her da, or to Billy, but she did hope that Ned was faring well and that maybe, one day, he would get in touch.

She'd settled down to living with Nellie and her family, and even Peggy's attitude towards her had thawed lately, but she put that down to the fact that Peggy was now engaged and was delighted with herself. Even Ernie seemed to approve of her more than he had done when she'd first come to live with the Gibbons family. She assumed it was due to the fact that she'd got a job and had proved herself to be a hard worker. For the first time in more years than she could remember, she had a secure and far more comfortable home than she'd previously been accustomed to. She no longer went cold and hungry, and she never listened warily for the heavy, unsteady footsteps and slurred curses that used to herald her da's return home from the pub. She now had a plain, serviceable dress, heavy shawl, stockings and decent boots for work – all second hand, but better than the rags she'd worn when she lived next door. She helped Nellie and Lena with the chores as much as she could, to try to show how grateful she was for their kindness, and of course she had her job and money of her own, which she religiously handed to Nellie each week. Nellie then put it into an old tin on the mantel over the range.

She enjoyed the company of the girls and women she worked with, although some of their talk she either didn't understand or it made her blush. At first she had been teased about being 'the gaffer's favourite', but the redoubtable Miss Mabel Woods had soon put a stop to that; she'd had a word with one or two of the girls she considered 'bold and brassy' and warned them to watch their tongues as Mr Rutherford was a decent Christian man who frowned upon 'unseemly' behaviour and idle gossip. In fact, some of the girls speculated about why Miss Woods was still single: had she never been asked out, had she been jilted, did she have aged parents to look after? Lizzie listened to the gossip but seldom joined in.

The weather was definitely getting warmer now, Lizzie mused, as they neared the factory. Mornings were lighter, and the evenings were drawing out. On Saturday she'd asked Nellie for her carefully saved money and had gone shopping down the Strand with Lena. She hugged the memory of those happy hours to her now. Oh, the sheer joy and novelty of being able to pick out garments that took her eye and try them on! She'd felt such a sense of pride and satisfaction as she'd paid for the skirt, blouse and jacket she'd finally settled on, none of them new but, well ... almost ... and they were the most stylish clothes she'd ever had. And then there was the hat. She'd never owned or worn a hat in her entire life, nor had she ever seen her poor mam wear one, but Lena had insisted that she spend her last one shilling and three-pence on the large-brimmed, pale blue straw decorated with a bow of black ribbon.

'You're a grown-up girl with a decent job now, Lizzie! You're not a kid any more; you *have* to have a hat to go out in!'

'But I don't really go ... *anywhere!*' she'd protested; it seemed somehow very extravagant, not to say irresponsible, to leave herself with no money at all until the next pay day.

'But we will! We'll be going out on Sundays, Lizzie, now the weather is getting better. There's no point going out in winter – it's just plain miserable, and we don't have money to spare to go to the music hall – but now we can go for walks in the parks in Liverpool or Bootle, there's a great palm house in Stanley Park. The Pier Head is always busy, so there's always something to see. Or we can go for a sail across the river and back, or even take a trip on the overhead railway to see all the ships in the docks – both only cost pennies,' Lena had urged enthusiastically.

She'd nodded in reply, and once the hat was placed at an attractive angle on her head by Lena, and she'd viewed the effect in the mirror the shopkeeper had handed her, she *had* felt grown up and ... different. Mam would barely recognise her now, she'd thought wistfully. Little Lizzie in a hat!

When they reached the factory both she and Lena

took off their shawls and hung them on the pegs provided, and Peggy joined her friends and went off towards her own workplace on the other side of the room. Lizzie immediately sought out the woman who supervised her work. She was still a little in awe of her, for Mabel Woods was in her late twenties, an attractive woman in a restrained sort of way, and neatly and more soberly dressed than many of the girls, who seemed to go in for bright – even garish – colours for work. She was also better educated, and considerably more refined than the women and girls under her.

That first morning she had explained in detail the production process and what would be expected of Lizzie in the packing room. 'We are quite fortunate being up here, away from the really noisy procedures and unhealthy atmosphere. In the workshops where the wood is sliced into lengths and then into small pieces by machines, the men do all the work. Then those pieces are attached to large frames which go to the clipping room, where they're dipped into the phosphorus paste. That's a really messy and dangerous job. Then these "splits", as they are called, are removed and cut into "singles" ready for drying. At that stage they're finally proper "matches", and they come up here to be packed.'

Lizzie had nodded her understanding of the somewhat complicated procedures. 'Do many people get "phossy jaw", miss? Or is it only those who work in the dipping room?'

Mabel Woods had looked thoughtful. 'Unfortunately, those working with phosphorus paste are indeed at risk, but it's quite prevalent in other parts of the factory too – less so up here, where there is good ventilation.'

Lizzie had looked very apprehensive but the supervisor had smiled at her. 'But Mr Rutherford – and many others in management too, these days – thinks that one of the main reasons for the condition is poor teeth. If teeth have cavities – holes – in them, then the phosphorus seeps in.' She'd smiled briefly at Lizzie's rather bemused expression. 'But things are much improved now, and as long as you have sound teeth there's nothing to fret about.' She had become business-like. 'So, Lizzie, this is what your job entails,' she'd instructed, rapidly taking a box from one conveyor belt with her right hand and, with the left, grabbing a handful of matches from the other belt and cramming them neatly into the box. 'Be careful not to overfill the boxes, Lizzie, or they will combust – flare up. Then that box will be wasted – and it could be a hazard not only to yourself but to the other workers.'

Lizzie had nodded slowly, thinking it sounded dangerous – she doubted she'd ever be able to fill a box as quickly as the older woman had. And she was still worried about the dreaded 'phossy jaw'.

As the days had passed, she'd become very proficient at her job. Mabel Woods had been impressed by the speed with which she could fill the boxes. 'I think it's because you have small hands and slender fingers and good coordination, Lizzie. That seems to help a great deal,' she'd remarked.

Lizzie had smiled happily at her supervisor. 'Thank you, Miss Woods, I'll try to keep it up and perhaps even improve as time goes on.'

Mabel had returned the smile as she'd walked away and, to Lizzie's astonishment and pleasure, two weeks later she'd been promoted, if it could be termed that, to the other end of the line with the older and more experienced girls.

'I see you've got your feet firmly under the table then, Lizzie!' Peggy had remarked cuttingly.

'I didn't ask to be moved up. Miss Woods recommended it and Mr Rutherford agreed,' Lizzie had replied, making sure that she kept working as quickly and as deftly as the older girl.

'Well, he would, wouldn't he? Quite the gaffer's little favourite, you are!' had come the tersely mocking reply.

Lizzie had been stung to annoyance. 'I'm not, Peggy Gibbons! I was just lucky enough to be able to pick the job up quickly.'

'You'd better watch out, Peg, she'll be able to fill more boxes in a day than you can,' Lily Birtles, one of Peggy's mates, had joked, knowing Peggy prided herself on her abilities.

This had only served to annoy Peggy even more. 'Then I'll have to warn Miss Woods to look out for *her* job! I wouldn't put it past you, Lizzie Tempest, to be thinking you could be a supervisor and go bossing us all around!'

Lizzie had bitten back the words of outraged denial. That was utterly unfair; she had no ambitions to rise to such a position, she'd thought angrily. But she had begun to wonder how Mabel Woods had managed to gain such a responsible position. She knew that the woman had started like herself, as a packer, but that it had only been a couple of years before she'd been promoted to her present position. Obviously, someone had noticed that she had qualities the others did not possess. Could she ever rise in the same way, she'd wondered idly as she carried on deftly filling the boxes? She'd earn more money, she'd be looked up to, if not exactly liked, and it might even give her a bit of control over her own life and future. They were heady thoughts, but then reality had taken over; she'd only been here a very short time, she'd told herself. She'd have to work long years before she had any hopes at all of her life changing.

Mabel Woods was smiling at her. 'Good morning, Lizzie. Make sure that mop of hair of yours is firmly pinned up out of harm's way – we don't want any accidents, do we?' she instructed.

Lizzie grinned at her. Miss Woods said the same thing every morning to all the girls, but she dutifully tucked the few dark curls that had become loose tidily behind her ears and went to take her place on the packing line beside Lena – who had also been moved up – as the machinery cranked and rattled into life. The work was indeed repetitious, but not hard – more 'fiddly' than anything else – but she was as quick and deft as Peggy and Lily now, and she gave little thought to the pervasive smell of phosphorous or its dangers.

There was the usual chatter about the events of the weekend – all conducted in near shouting mode, because of the noise of the machines – and Lizzie was asked to describe in great detail all her purchases, which were then debated at length, much to her satisfaction. By break time she was looking forward excitedly to wearing her new outfit at the end of this week, when Lena had said they would take a tram to one of Liverpool's parks, weather permitting.

She was surprised when Mabel Woods approached her, just as she was leaving her place in the line, to inform her that Mr Rutherford wanted to see her. He often spoke to her – in fact, he had done so since the day she had first started work here hence the fact she'd been teased. He usually enquired how she was, how she was finding the work, if she found life easier now that she was living with Mrs Gibbons and her family, but thankfully he never mentioned her father. At first she'd been rather in awe of him, but gradually she'd become easier in his company; but he'd never actually sent for her before.

'What does he want to see me for? Have I done something wrong, Miss Woods?' she asked, fearful that she had.

The older woman shrugged. 'Not that I know of, Lizzie. Best get along to his office and find out.'

Lizzie frowned as she walked quickly towards the little office, feeling decidedly uneasy. 'What if he was going to tell her that he couldn't keep her on? That someone had told his superiors that she still wasn't of the required age to be employed? Oh, she desperately hoped it wasn't that, for she knew she had little chance of getting another job. She tried to push the thought away as she knocked on the half-open door.

'Come in, Lizzie,' he greeted her affably, 'and close the door behind you or we'll not be able to hear ourselves speak.'

Thankfully, he was smiling, she noticed, while she did as she was bidden. He didn't look as if he had bad news or anything serious to impart.

'Sit down,' he instructed her. 'There's nothing to be worried about,' he added, taking in her expression and the blue eyes, wide with anxiety.

'You've done well in the time you've been here. Miss Woods is pleased with your work, and I've been taking a close interest in your progress...' He started slowly, thinking how much she'd changed from the half-starved, distraught little waif he'd taken on back in January.

Over the months he had indeed taken an interest in Lizzie and her welfare. He'd known about the terrible hardships she'd suffered in her short life – and her life now was still no bed of roses – but he admired her determination to try to overcome all that had happened to her. She was bright and intelligent, which was rare in one so young, and he'd become more certain that she deserved better than this poorly paid, unskilled, mundane job, and life in an overcrowded house in a slum. He'd conveyed his observations and feelings to Eileen, and they had reached a decision. They would take the girl in, give her a decent home and teach her how it should be managed – depending, of course, upon Eileen's approval of Lizzie. Bearing in mind her husband's position, she had suggested that perhaps Lizzie could learn the skills of a seamstress, if she had the ability, for that was a trade at which she could earn a respectable living in the future. George had agreed; he'd also impressed upon his wife that he felt she herself had not yet fully recovered from the effects of the influenza and that help in the house would surely be beneficial.

Lizzie was waiting with bated breath, for she was sure Mr Rutherford hadn't summoned her just to tell her she was doing well at her job.

'There's something I want to suggest to you, Lizzie, and I'd like you to think hard about it before you give me your answer.' He leaned across the desk, pressing the tips of his fingers together and choosing his words carefully.

Lizzie stared at him hard, not knowing what to expect.

'I have been discussing your ... future with my wife, Lizzie, and we've come to a decision. We have a decent-sized house in Olivia Street, much bigger than we actually require – we have no children – although Mrs Rutherford does see clients at home; she's a seamstress. She caught the influenza before Christmas and isn't fully recovered and, well ... we ... we would like you to come and live with us, Lizzie.' He delivered the last piece of information a little hurriedly, as he remembered that her mother had not recovered at all. 'Eileen will happily teach you all about cooking and house-keeping ... things like that ... and if you wish, will also teach you how to sew. Of course we'll keep you, and we'll also give you a small allowance in return for your help in the house. I strongly believe that I was meant to meet you that night you were looking for your father, and I ... we think you deserve a better chance in life and the opportunity to learn a trade, Lizzie,' he finished.

Lizzie's eyes widened – she was speechless. Had she understood him correctly? He and his wife were offering her a ... home and the chance to learn a trade, which would give her a much better quality of life and remove her from all the dangers of the match factory! She could hardly believe it! Finally, she gathered her scattered wits. 'You mean ... you want me to come and ... live and work...?'

He nodded. 'We do, Lizzie. You'll have your own room, the work won't be overtaxing, and you'll be quite free to come and go as you please, as long as Mrs Rutherford knows where you are going and what time you'll be back. It will be a fresh start, Lizzie, a new life and a new home. Will you think carefully about it?'

She nodded her agreement, still stunned and not knowing what to think, although a tiny bubble of excitement was rising within her.

'Oh, and Lizzie, can I ask that you don't tell your workmates – just yet?'

Again she nodded, but then she thought of Nellie. 'But what about Mrs Gibbons, sir?'

'Of course you'll have to discuss it with her; in fact, I'm quite prepared to come and see her, in case she has any misgivings. And I'd like you to come and meet Mrs Rutherford.'

Lizzie got to her feet, her heart beating oddly in her chest. 'I ... I'll do as you ask.'

He smiled at her, knowing she was stunned and confused, but hoping that she wouldn't be persuaded to turn down the offer.

When Lizzie returned to the production line, Lena immediately noticed her preoccupation. 'What's up? What did he want you for?'

'I'll tell you on the way home, I promise. But it wasn't anything ... bad,' she replied as they went back to their work.

Lena frowned; she was filled with curiosity, but seeing the determined set of Lizzie's mouth, she knew it would do no good to pester her. She'd just have to be patient.

'So, what's the big secret, then?' Lena demanded as soon as they were outside the factory gates and had detached themselves from the group of girls they usually walked with.

'I still can't believe it, Lena! All afternoon I've been wondering if I heard him right, or did I make a mistake?'

'Believe *what*? Lizzie Tempest, stop being so maddeningly ... secretive!' Lena cried exasperatedly.

'He and his wife want me to go and live with ... them. They live in Olivia Street and they've no kids. She'll teach me to cook and keep house, and even to sew – she's a seamstress! I ... I could learn a proper trade, Lena! And they'll give me an allowance, and he wants me to go and meet her!'

Lena caught her arm and stared at her in astonishment. 'Are you kidding me, Lizzie?'

'No! It's the truth. I've got to discuss it with your mam and then meet Mrs Rutherford.'

Lena shook her head in amazement; she'd never heard of anyone ever doing such a thing before. At least, not taking in a girl who was absolutely no relation to them and who was definitely of a lower class – and whose father and brother were both in jail, although maybe Mr Rutherford didn't know that. 'So, what will you do?' she finally asked.

Lizzie smiled at her friend. 'Just what he says –

114

talk to your mam about it.'

'You'd be mad not to take a chance like that, Lizzie,' Lena conceded. 'But I'll miss you,' she added.

A little of the excitement faded as Lizzie realised for the first time that she would have no companions of her own age in that house in Olivia Street, though perhaps as churchgoers the Rutherfords would have young people amongst their friends. And then she reminded herself of all the benefits she would gain. As Lena had said, she'd be mad not to seize this opportunity.

Chapter Twelve

Nellie was as astonished as her daughter when Lizzie imparted the news on their arrival home.

'He's deadly serious? There's no chance you've got the wrong end of the stick, Lizzie?'

Lizzie shook her head. 'No, he asked me to think about it, to talk to you about it and then ... meet his wife.'

Nellie wiped her hands on her apron and sat down at the table, her preparations for the meal forgotten. 'Well, luv, I don't know what ter say, I mean it's all a bit ... sudden, like! I'll admit that 'e's been good to yer in the past, but we none of us really *know* 'im, nor his wife. An' what if she doesn't take a shine ter you?'

'I've got to know him better since I started work,' Lizzie said thoughtfully.

'I suppose you have, Lizzie. But it's really nothing to do with me. I'm not yer legal guardian, or anything, but naturally I'm concerned for yer well-being. I suppose it's really down to yer da, but ... well, under the circumstances...' She frowned. 'Does he know about yer da?'

Lizzie nodded. 'I told him when I went for my interview. I had to, but ... but I didn't mention our Billy.'

'That I can understand – having to admit to one jailbird in the family is more than enough. Well, Lizzie, have you given it any thought?'

'I've thought of nothing else all afternoon, and sometimes I'm ... excited and delighted and really can't believe it's true, and sometimes, I ... I just don't know. It will all be so *different!* I've never lived anywhere like that before, or with people like them, and he said I'd have a room of my own – and that's something I've never, ever had. He said that they'd provide for me and I could come and go as I please, as long as I tell her where I'm going and when I'll be back, so they obviously *care* about me. She'll teach me to cook and everything I'll need to know about running a house – a whole house! And they'll give me what he called a "small allowance" for helping. But best of all, he said she'll teach me how to sew. She'll teach me her trade.'

Nellie thought about all this. On the surface it seemed a heaven-sent opportunity, particularly for a half-educated waif like Lizzie, and this Mr Rutherford had proved to be considerate and generous towards her in the past. But as she'd mentioned, they didn't know the Rutherfords; it all sounded too good to be true and, in her ex-

116

perience, that usually meant it was. The last thing she wanted was for the girl to be used as a drudge and a skivvy. Working in the match factory wasn't a great job but, in her opinion at least, it was better than that.

'She'd be mad to turn it down, Mam!' Lena put in.

'You keep your nose out of it, miss!' Nellie instructed.

'What do you think I should do, Mrs Gibbons?' Lizzie asked, a little perturbed by Nellie's doubtful expression.

Nellie sighed and made up her mind. 'I think Lena's right, luv. I don't see how you can afford to turn it down. At least give it a try, and if Mrs Rutherford decides she can't take to you, then you can always come back to us.'

'Mam, she wouldn't want to come back here, not after having a room of her own and all,' Lena protested.

Nellie glared at her. 'What did I just tell you, Lena!'

'He said he'd be prepared to come and talk to you, if you had any ... misgivings,' Lizzie informed her.

Nellie raised her eyebrows. 'Did he? Well, I think I just might take 'im up on that offer, just to be easy in my mind that it's the right thing for you, luv.'

'I'll tell him that tomorrow,' Lizzie replied, feeling happier.

'Tell 'im that if it's convenient, he can call on Friday evening,' Nellie suggested, thinking that that would give her time to make sure the place was clean and tidy, and also that Lizzie would have a week's wages in her pocket to give her a bit of financial security, although she would miss the girl's contribution to the household budget.

Lizzie hadn't been able to sleep much, contemplating the new life that had been offered to her but also wondering how she would get on with Mrs Rutherford, for she'd never met her. She wondered if she was as agreeable as he was to taking her in, but she'd assured herself that if the woman was as thoughtful and generous as her husband, she'd have nothing to worry about. She'd asked Nellie what the houses in Olivia Street were like, for she'd not ventured into that area of Bootle.

'Well, it's a much quieter neighbourhood. Most people seem to have steady jobs – and they'd need to, as the rents are more than any of us in Bennett Street can afford to pay. The 'ouses are a fairly decent size too. They're bigger than this house, anyway, and they're better looked after – for a start, there's usually only one family to a house. They even have a bit of a garden in front, if I remember right,' Nellie had informed her.

It would seem strange at first, she'd thought, for she'd never lived in a house occupied by just one family. In fact, there would only be three people living in that entire house, and that would be no small novelty. Compared to the rooms she'd lived in when her mam had been alive, Nellie's rooms had seemed the epitome of comfort. She was finding it hard to envisage having the run of a whole house – and, no doubt, one far better furnished and with more modern amenities than this one.

As soon as she arrived at the factory that morning, Lizzie duly imparted Nellie's message.

George Rutherford nodded his agreement. 'I understand. Tell Mrs Gibbons I'll call at eight o'clock on Friday evening, Lizzie. And did you come to any kind of decision?'

She nodded. 'If ... if after she's talked to you, she thinks it's best for me, and Mrs Rutherford is happy too, then I'll be ... delighted, sir,' she replied a little shyly.

'Good! I don't think you'll regret it,' he smiled. 'And Lizzie, you'll have to stop calling me "sir".'

She frowned, a little perturbed. 'What should I call you?' she asked, knowing there was no way she could bring herself to call him by his given Christian name.

'Mr Rutherford?' he suggested, realising her dilemma.

She nodded. 'And shall I call your wife "ma'am" or Mrs Rutherford?'

'Mrs Rutherford, I think. "Ma'am" is far too formal, and you won't be a domestic servant, Lizzie.'

Feeling more content now that such formalities had been cleared up, Lizzie dutifully went back to her workplace, where Lena winked at her conspiratorially. They'd agreed to say nothing to anyone else about Lizzie's proposed change of circumstances. Lizzie would simply hand in her notice and leave. Although excited and happy for her friend, Lena was both saddened and a little envious. She would miss Lizzie's company, both at work and at home, but then she cheered herself up with the thought that Lizzie would come and visit quite often; she'd have lots to tell her about her new life, and she might even be able to invite her to see her new home.

Nellie had spent the entire day cleaning and polishing everything in her small cramped kitchen, but she still felt a bit apprehensive when Mr Rutherford arrived punctually on Friday evening.

'I don't know why you're getting into such a state, Mam. He'll only be here for about ten minutes and probably won't even notice if the place is tidy or not,' Peggy had remarked rather caustically as she'd adjusted her hat, preparing to go out to spend the evening with her fiancé. 'You never made such a fuss when Bertie's mam and da came round to see you when we got the ring. And if you ask me, Lizzie Tempest seems to lead a charmed life. Landing herself a position like that when she's just a matchgirl like the rest of us!'

'Not exactly like the rest of you, Peggy! At least you and our Lena have always 'ad a good home and respectable, hardworking parents. Oh, I know we 'aven't got much, compared to the likes of Mr and Mrs Rutherford, but I like to think that this is the only decent home Lizzie's ever had, no matter how hard poor Florrie tried to provide one,' Nellie replied bluntly. 'So, don't you go begrudging her, miss!' she finished.

Peggy had just shrugged. But it was she who actually opened the door to their visitor on her way out, giving him a polite smile, for he was still her boss, when all was said and done.

'Mrs Gibbons, it's very good of you to see me,' George Rutherford greeted her. 'I hope this visit is not inconvenient.'

'Not at all. Sit down, sir. Lena, take the gentleman's hat,' she instructed before she introduced Ernie, who had been informed of the reason for this visit but would be relieved when it was over.

'Lizzie's told us all about this here ... er ... position you and your wife have offered her,' Nellie started, a little hesitantly. She wanted to be sure the offer was genuine and that Lizzie would have a secure future, and yet, because he was of a more affluent class, she was a little in awe of him. He was a good-looking man of about thirty, she judged, with light brown curly hair, neatly cut, and hazel eyes that seemed frank and honest. He was well dressed, as she'd expected, and quietly spoken, with good manners.

'As you know, Mrs Gibbons, I'm fully acquainted with Lizzie's background and I think you'll agree that life hasn't dealt kindly with her at all up to now. I strongly feel she deserves ... more.' He turned and smiled at Lizzie before resuming. 'Eileen and I are prepared to give Lizzie a good home. We are both respectable, hard-working people and will look after her. And Eileen will teach Lizzie her trade, if that's what Lizzie wishes.'

Nellie nodded slowly. 'It ... it's very generous of you both–'

'But? I can see there is something bothering you, Mrs Gibbons,' he interrupted.

'She'll be cooking and cleaning and helping to run the house too?'

He nodded as understanding began to dawn on him. 'But I can assure you that we won't expect Lizzie to do everything. She'll not be treated as a servant – a maid of all work – more a ... companion for my wife. Lizzie tragically lost her mother as a result of that epidemic of influenza, and my wife caught it too. It's left her ... weakened. She tires easily and she'll be glad of Lizzie's help, but please rest assured that Lizzie will be well treated and certainly not put upon, Mrs Gibbons. I give you my word.'

Nellie glanced quickly at Ernie and then finally smiled. 'Then I'll be quite happy for her to go, sir, even though it's not really my place to decide. You're right, she's had a rotten life up to now, she deserves this chance, and I know her poor mam would say the same if she were 'ere.'

He looked across enquiringly at Ernie. 'Do you think we should inform her father?'

Ernie didn't reply, but Nellie raised her eyes to the ceiling. 'If you feel it's the right thing to do, sir, but being honest, I wouldn't bother. Art Tempest never gave a second thought to what would happen to Lizzie! You first met 'er when she was scouring the pubs lookin' for 'im, and poor Florrie so ill! All 'e was interested in was 'imself, and probably always has been, and when they finally let 'im out, I doubt we'll see 'im around 'ere again. No, he won't care where Lizzie is, or what she's doing.'

George Rutherford nodded, then got to his feet and turned to Lizzie, smiling. 'Well, I think that tomorrow afternoon I should take you and introduce you to my wife, Lizzie. And if all goes well,

122

then perhaps a week on Sunday you can bring your things and move into your new home with us?'

Lizzie smiled back at him, feeling both relieved and excited now that Nellie seemed satisfied. 'I'd like that, Mr Rutherford, and I haven't really got that much stuff to bring.'

'I'll collect you at three tomorrow afternoon, then. Good evening, Mrs Gibbons and Mr Gibbons. Thank you for your time.'

Lizzie showed him out, noticing now how shabby and dilapidated the lobby looked in the evening sunlight with its peeling paintwork, bare floorboards and damp patches on the wall by the door. 'It really is very ... good of you ... both, and you won't regret it.'

He looked down at her earnest little face and smiled before bidding her goodbye. 'No, I don't think we will, Lizzie, and neither will you.' He hadn't failed to notice the difference between his own home and Nellie Gibbons' kitchen, which obviously served as a living room too, and this dilapidated hallway. Lizzie's days of living in an overcrowded slum house were almost over. 'I'll see you tomorrow,' he said as he turned away, feeling that they had made the right decision, guided by Providence.

'Are you nervous at all about meeting ... her?' Lena asked as Lizzie came back into the room.

Now that she felt she could relax, Nellie put the kettle on.

'A bit; I hope she'll ... like me,' Lizzie replied.

'What is there not to like about you?' Lena demanded.

123

'She might think I'm a bit ... common. I mean I'm not used to any of the things she's used to,' Lizzie confided.

Nellie put down the tea caddy and turned to her. 'Get that idea right out of your head, Lizzie Tempest! You're a good girl, you can't help the way things were ... or how you were brought up. Your poor mam did her best, God rest her. You've nothing at all to be ashamed of. You just do your best, learn everything you can, and things will work out just fine.'

Lizzie smiled at her. 'I think I'll still wear my new clothes and be on my best behaviour tomorrow, though. I don't want to let anyone down, least of all myself.'

'You'll not do that, Lizzie. You'll see, luv, things will really start looking up for you now,' Nellie said firmly, spooning the loose tea into the big brown pot.

Chapter Thirteen

Lizzie was ready by two o'clock on Saturday. She'd dressed carefully in her newly acquired cornflower-blue ankle-length skirt and short jacket, nipped in at the waist, over a plain white cotton blouse that Nellie had starched. With its high neck and pin-tucked front, the blouse looked stylish under the neat jacket. Nellie didn't possess a full-length mirror but both she and Lena – and even Peggy – said Lizzie looked very well, and after Lena had done her hair and secured the blue hat with a long pin, Lizzie felt very grown up. But try as she might, she couldn't suppress the butterflies that were doing a manic dance in her stomach.

'You'll get along fine, Lizzie, just wait and see. I bet she's really, really nice,' Lena said to bolster her friend's spirits.

Mr Rutherford arrived again punctually at three. 'Goodness, Lizzie, I hardly recognised you! You look very ... smart,' he greeted her, somewhat taken aback by her appearance.

Lizzie blushed at the praise. 'Thank you. I ... I've been saving up for ages for some nice clothes.'

Nellie beamed her approval. 'You look very presentable, Lizzie. Now, off you go, luv,' she urged.

The closer to her new home they got, the more nervous Lizzie became, although George Rutherford kept up a lively conversation on the short tram journey, sensing her apprehension. Nellie had been right, she mused, as they walked the short distance from the tram stop to Olivia Street in the warm sunlight of the late April afternoon. This neighbourhood was quieter and more affluent than Bennett Street, being further away from the docks and warehouses and factories, and the houses were indeed bigger and in much better condition. They were built of red brick which, over time, had acquired a coating of soot like every other building in the city. And Nellie had been right about the gardens; there was a small patch of grass enclosed by a low wall in front of each house. Three broad stone steps led up to the Rutherfords' front door, which was painted a dark green and adorned with a well-polished brass knocker. She noted that the steps themselves were neither worn nor chipped and seemed to have been scrubbed and whitened with what was known locally as 'donkey stone'. A square bay window was set to the right of the front door, and the white cotton lace curtains were pristine.

Lizzie waited patiently behind George Rutherford as he inserted his key into the lock and opened the front door before ushering her inside. She glanced quickly around, noting the polished linoleum, the runner of carpet on the floor, the plain cream-coloured walls and varnished paintwork. It smelled much fresher than the house in Bennett Street too; there were no lingering odours of damp, cooking, coal fires and communal living, and she thought she detected a hint of furniture polish ... mixed with the scent of flowers perhaps. She could feel waves of excited anticipation rushing through her and she clasped her hands tightly together, feeling very nervous as she was ushered into a room which was the largest, lightest and most comfortably furnished room she'd ever seen. It was obviously a parlour, bigger than Nellie's kitchen, and filled with the sunlight that streamed in from the bay window.

George Rutherford propelled her gently towards the woman who was sitting on the chintz-covered sofa opposite the cast-iron fireplace embellished with decorative tiles. 'Eileen, my dear, this is Lizzie. Lizzie Tempest.'

Lizzie managed a shy smile as the woman rose to greet her. She was surprised to see that Mrs

126

Rutherford didn't look as old as she'd somehow imagined she would be; she'd envisaged a slightly younger version of Nellie. This woman looked much younger, slim – not to say quite thin – and she did look rather pale and washed out. Her hair was a very light brown, but fashionably dressed, and the deep rose-coloured skirt and pale pink and cream blouse were of good-quality material. She had very pale grey eyes that seemed to reflect the light, but Lizzie was very relieved to see that she was smiling.

'So, you are Lizzie. George has told me all about you. Things haven't been good for you up to now, have they?' She indicated that Lizzie should sit beside her as she studied the girl more closely.

'No, not really, and I'm very grateful to you, Mrs Rutherford,' Lizzie replied, sitting gingerly on the edge of the sofa and noticing that the cool grey eyes were taking in every aspect of her appearance.

'You're nearly fourteen, I believe.' Eileen looked across at her husband for confirmation, and smiled as he nodded.

'I'll be fourteen in July,' Lizzie informed her, beginning to feel a little more at ease and notic- ing that there were some delicate china orna- ments on the mantelpiece – things both her poor mam and Nellie had only ever dreamed of possessing. Oh, this was the grandest house she'd ever been inside; everything was clean, well cared for and bright.

'I have to say, you look older than I'd imagined,' Eileen Rutherford remarked, casting another look in her husband's direction. She'd imagined the girl would be a small, undernourished waif, virtually an orphan, who was legally too young to be employed in the match works. She really had felt sorry for the child's plight, and George's descriptions of Lizzie's character had strengthened her belief that she was doing the right thing in giving the child a chance, but now she was not quite so sure. For now she was faced not with a childish waif but with a girl who would soon undoubtedly grow into a beauty, with all the problems that could generate.

Lizzie smiled shyly at her. 'I expect it's because I'm ... sort of dressed up. Mr Rutherford has only ever seen me in rags and the dress I have for working in the factory. I've only just saved up enough to buy this outfit, and I thought I'd better wear it to look ... decent, seeing as I was coming to meet you, like. I felt it was important that I should make an effort. I hope you like it?'

Eileen Rutherford nodded, smiling. 'I do, and it suits you, Lizzie.' She got to her feet, thinking that the girl had an open, honest and natural charm. 'Now, I expect you'd like to see your room and the rest of the house? I think it's been agreed that you'll be moving in a week tomorrow?'

'If you don't mind, that is,' Lizzie replied as she followed her hostess back out into the hall, leaving George Rutherford to pick up his newspaper.

Eileen Rutherford led the way up the carpeted stairs to a narrow landing.

'I hope you'll be comfortable here, Lizzie,' she said as she ushered Lizzie into the smallest bedroom, which looked out on to the street.

Lizzie's eyes filled with tears as she looked

around her in amazement. 'Oh! Oh, it … it's beautiful! I … I never expected anything like *this*, Mrs Rutherford!' She clasped her hands together as she turned to the woman, tears falling unashamedly down her cheeks. 'You see, I've never, *ever* had a room all to myself, most of the time we only ever had one room for … everyone and everything. I've never even had a bed to myself!' She was quite astounded by the sight of the single bed with its clean blue-and-white patchwork quilt and pristine white pillows, the deep blue rug on the floor beside it and the pale blue curtains at the window. There were even pictures on the walls, a frosted glass shade over the gas jet, and a small dressing table complete with a mirror on a stand. There was a wardrobe and a chest of drawers – and it was all just for … *her!*

Eileen couldn't help feeling touched at Lizzie's reaction, and any doubts she'd had melted; it was obvious the girl was utterly unused to even such simple comforts. God knows what kind of places she'd had to call home, up to now. She put her arm around the girl's shoulders. 'I'm glad you like it, Lizzie. Now, dry your eyes and I'll show you the rest of the house and then, while George is engrossed in his paper, we can have a chat about your future here and whether you have any aptitude for sewing. Then you can help me make some sandwiches and we'll have tea before you go back to Bennett Street.'

Lizzie sniffed as she took the proffered handkerchief and dabbed at her eyes. 'Oh, I'd really like that – I'll work hard and do everything you ask me to do,' she promised eagerly.

Eileen nodded, thinking that even if the girl had no aptitude for sewing she would at least prove very useful in the house, once she'd been taught the way things should be done properly – for judging by the type of home she'd come from, she would have no idea of that at all.

Lizzie was amazed by the other rooms in the house. All were so clean and bright and well furnished. The kitchen was neat and functional, and obviously not used for living in too. It boasted a gas cooker, a sink with hot and cold running water, shelves on which the pans and crockery were displayed, and there was even a separate pantry.

Eileen instructed her on which dishes to use, and Lizzie confided that Nellie didn't have as many cups, saucers, plates, jugs and bowls as this, nor of such fine quality, and that her mam hadn't even had mugs for the tea. She was shown how to cut the crusts off the sandwiches – which, privately, she thought was a terrible waste of the expensive, soft white bread. She then had to arrange the sandwiches on a plate after first covering it with a paper lace doily. Milk was poured into a jug and the sugar cubes – a commodity that she'd seldom been able to afford – were presented in a bowl accompanied by tongs.

'There's so much to remember, and that's just for making tea and sandwiches,' she exclaimed, keenly aware now of how lacking her upbringing had been. Learning to cook using all these different pans and utensils would be quite a daunting task. 'But you see, Mrs Rutherford,' she explained, 'we never had enough money for food, never mind these other ... things. I don't think I've ever tasted butter – and I've never even seen a butter dish before!'

Eileen smiled wryly. She could foresee quite a few trials and tribulations ahead, but she was sure it would all be worthwhile. She was determined that she would make a silk purse out of this little sow's ear.

When Lizzie arrived back in Bennett Street, Lena and Nellie were all agog to hear about the house that was to be her new home.

'There's actually six rooms! For just three people?' Lena marvelled.

Lizzie nodded. 'And the kitchen is just for cooking and preparing things in – and I've never seen so many dishes or pans in my life!'

Nellie shook her head, thinking she'd give her right arm for a kitchen like that. 'I suppose that's what you can expect if your man's got a good, steady job with a decent wage. They're very fortunate – and so are you, Lizzie.'

'I know I am. I ... I actually couldn't stop myself from filling up when she showed me my room. Oh, Lena, it's just ... gorgeous! I think I'll be happy there, but there is so much to learn, so much I'll have to get used to. And that's before I even think about learning to sew. It ... it's a whole new world for me!'

'Of course it is, luv, and you just make sure you take advantage of everything,' Nellie urged.

'So, you'll be handing in your notice on Monday, then,' Lena added.

'I suppose he'll have already taken that for

granted, him being my boss,' Lizzie replied.

'Well, I wouldn't go announcing it to all and sundry, Lizzie. There's a lot of those girls who would make more of it than there is – and neither you nor Mr Rutherford deserve to be gossiped about,' Nellie advised, thinking there would be a great deal of jealousy amongst Lizzie's work-mates, which might be vented in spiteful and malicious speculation.

Lizzie nodded, although she was a little perturbed by Nellie's words.

'Well, where shall we go tomorrow, Lizzie? It's going to be your last Sunday here,' Lena asked.

'I think I'd like to go and see that palm house you were telling me about, Lena,' Lizzie suggested, thinking it would be nice to spend her last Sunday with her friend. If she was going up in the world, she would have to get used to things like palm houses!

Chapter Fourteen

They'd spent a pleasant Sunday afternoon in Stanley Park, off Walton Lane, which boasted a boating lake and a bowling green. As the weather was warm and sunny, the park was quite crowded. Lizzie had marvelled at all the exotic shrubs and plants in the huge glass-domed palm house – although she was glad it wasn't too sunny, as it was already hot and sticky inside. She and Lena had been happy to go back outside into the fresher air and walk beside the lake.

They had decided that Lena would accompany Lizzie to her new home the following Sunday, for nothing had been mentioned about Mr Rutherford coming to collect her, and she'd confided to her friend that she didn't want to go alone – the thought was a bit daunting.

'I'm going to feel a bit sort of ... sad, leaving you all,' Lizzie had admitted.

Lena could understand that, for she knew she would miss her friend too. 'You're bound to, Lizzie. But you'll soon get used to everything – and you'll be visiting us,' she urged.

'I haven't got much to take with me, but it will be a good opportunity for you to come and see everything,' Lizzie had added.

'I expect we'd better ask Mam what she thinks,' Lena advised, hoping her mam would agree. She was filled with curiosity about this house in Olivia Street and had hoped to actually see it for herself.

Nellie had voiced no objection to the plan, thinking it might help Lizzie to have Lena's company. Although it was a great opportunity, it was a whole new world that Lizzie was facing now, and she might well find it overwhelming. Ernie agreed that Lena should accompany Lizzie, and Peggy for once kept her opinions to herself. No one made any mention of the fact that Lizzie would be leaving the match works on Friday. Nellie had thought it best not to; there would be time enough for that next week, she'd stated firmly.

Lizzie herself had suppressed any qualms when she left work on Friday evening. Saturday had seemed to pass in a blur of anxious anticipation until, at last, on Sunday morning Lena had helped her pack what few things she possessed into a brown paper parcel which they tied with string.

Nellie checked both girls' appearances before they left. 'You'll do, both of you. Now, Lena, you mind yer manners an' don't go "Oohing" and "Aahing" or picking up the ornaments and things,' she instructed firmly.

'Oh, Mam! As if I would!' Lena protested.

Nellie's expression softened and she smiled at Lizzie. 'Good luck, Lizzie. Do everything Mrs Rutherford asks, mind yer manners, and you'll not go far wrong, luv.' She hugged the girl to her, thinking how she'd miss her. But how could she begrudge her the opportunities that were being afforded her? She just wished she could give her girls a life like that.

'I'll miss everyone, I really will, but thank you for ... everything. I don't know what I'd have done without you. I'd be in the workhouse now, if it wasn't for you and Mr Gibbons,' Lizzie replied, close to tears now that the moment of her departure had finally arrived.

'Well, all that's behind you now, Lizzie. Off you go, but don't forget you're welcome here any time you want to visit,' Nellie reminded her.

Lizzie smiled. 'I know, and I *will* visit,' she promised.

'Just think, Lizzie, you won't have to spend another day in that factory with all the noise and the smelly phosphorous!' Lena reminded her as they alighted from the tram on the corner of the road.

'I wonder just what I will be doing instead?' Lizzie said, voicing her thoughts. After Mr Rutherford had gone off to work, she would be left alone with his wife all day. She was sure that she would be far from idle. Her time would be more than occupied – she had so much to learn – but it would be strange not to be joining the other girls and women in the factory tomorrow, gossiping about what they'd all done over the weekend.

'Here we are,' she announced, stopping in front of the house.

Lena looked up and nodded. It certainly was a cut above Bennett Street.

Lizzie knocked and the door was opened by George Rutherford himself.

'Welcome, Lizzie, come on in,' he greeted her, smiling. 'And I see you've brought Lena to help you ... er ... unpack,' he added, a little surprised to see the other girl.

'I hope it's all right?' Lizzie queried as he ushered them both inside.

Eileen appeared from the kitchen, a crisp white cotton apron covering her best, dark green skirt. 'I didn't expect you quite this early, Lizzie, and ... who is this?' she asked, catching sight of Lena.

'This is Helena – Lena – Gibbons, she's my friend. I live ... lived,' she amended, 'with her family, if you remember, Mrs Rutherford.'

'I see. Of course,' Eileen replied, rather caught off guard by this unexpected visitor. 'I'll just finish in the kitchen, if you'd ... both ... like to go up and unpack your things,' she suggested, shooting a startled look at her husband who just shrugged and returned to the parlour.

135

Lena went into raptures when Lizzie showed her into her room. 'Oh, Lizzie, you're *so* lucky!'

Lizzie smiled and nodded as she untied the string on the parcel and shook out her work dress. It wouldn't take her long to unpack, she mused ruefully, as she hung the dress in the wardrobe along with her shawl which, now that summer was on its way, she hoped she wouldn't have to wear much. Her few underclothes she placed in a drawer in the chest, and her brush and comb and hairpins she arranged neatly on the dressing table.

Lena was examining everything with interest and exclamations of delight.

'It will seem very ... strange, sleeping here on my own, Lena,' Lizzie confided, watching Lena trace the intricate pattern etched into the glass of the gas shade with the tip of her finger.

'I suppose it will – but just think! There'll be no one pulling the quilt off you, digging their elbows into you, or coughing and grunting to disturb you. This lovely bed all to yourself! Look, there's even a bit of lace edging on the pillowcase. Wait until I tell our Peggy and Mam that!'

Lizzie smiled at her. 'Well, that's my unpacking done. I suppose we'd better go down and see if there's anything Mrs Rutherford wants me to do.'

Lena followed her down the stairs, making a mental note of everything she saw to pass on to her mam. They arrived in the hallway just as Eileen Rutherford was coming out of the parlour. Lizzie thought she looked a little perturbed.

'There you both are! Come into the kitchen and we'll have a cup of tea before Helena goes home,' she instructed.

136

Again, Lena took in every detail of the room, particularly noting the fact that pans were simmering on top of the cooker and, judging from the appetising aroma, there was a joint of meat cooking in the oven. Obviously, Lizzie was going to be treated to the first proper Sunday dinner she'd ever had; she half wished she could stay too, for she knew there'd be no Sunday roast in their house.

Lizzie was quick to note that the tea was taken in the kitchen, unlike the last time she'd been here. There was no mention of them joining Mr Rutherford in the parlour, although a cup was taken in to him, and then Lena judged that it was time for her to go.

'Thank you for the tea, Mrs Rutherford. I'd best be off home now,' she said, glancing at Lizzie.

'Yes, I think that would be best, Helena. Lizzie and I have a great many things to sort out. And of course there's the lunch to see to, as well,' Eileen replied, rather curtly.

Lena hugged Lizzie. 'Bye, then. I'll ... I'll see you soon?'

Lizzie nodded, beginning to feel for the first time rather bereft.

'Why don't you see Helena out, Lizzie?' Eileen suggested, turning to the cooker.

'I don't think she was very pleased that I came too,' Lena whispered as Lizzie opened the front door, thinking that Eileen Rutherford didn't seem half as nice as her husband, and she truly hoped her friend would be happy here.

'I think she was just a bit surprised, that's all, Lena. I'll come and visit you on Saturday, if I can,' she promised as Lena went down the steps.

Lena turned to wave and then walked on as Lizzie closed the door and went back to the kitchen.

'The table is already set, the vegetables are nearly done and I've checked on the lamb, so we have about half an hour,' Eileen informed her new charge as Lizzie gathered up the dirty cups and took them to the sink.

'Leave those for now, Lizzie, and come upstairs with me. I have some things for you,' she instructed.

Lizzie followed her upstairs but waited on the landing as she disappeared into the third, unused bedroom, and was surprised when she was called inside. She'd not been in here and it was obvious that it was some sort of sewing room, for there was a treadle sewing machine set under the window, a long mirror against one wall, various lengths of material neatly folded on shelves, and a chest of drawers on top of which were reels of cotton, scissors and boxes of pins.

'I got these for you, Lizzie, but they'll need to be altered to fit you,' Eileen informed her, holding a small selection of garments over her arm. She had noted the small parcel Lizzie had brought with her and knew she'd been right in her assumption that the girl had few clothes and probably virtually nothing that would be acceptable for the life she was now to lead. 'Whatever you wore for the factory and in Bennett Street won't be suitable now.'

Lizzie was surprised; she'd not given a thought to what she'd wear each day. Here were two skirts and two blouses, a jacket, petticoats and chemises and stockings. All the clothes looked to be of good-quality material, but she doubted they were new; still, she now had more clothes than she'd ever had before in her life, and that pleased her and she felt grateful to the woman.

'If you try them on, I'll have time to pin them before lunch,' Eileen said, reaching for a box of pins. 'And, I have to explain this to you, people in this neighbourhood have certain ... standards, Lizzie. *I* have certain standards, and things like shawls have no place in Olivia Street. When you go out, you must always wear a jacket and a hat.' She nodded towards the plain straw boater that lay on the table beside the sewing machine. She considered it far more suitable than the hat Lizzie had worn earlier.

Lizzie nodded as she tried on the royal-blue-and-white striped skirt and the white blouse trimmed with blue braid, both of which were too big for her, and submitted to having them pinned to fit. Of course it was a much better neighbourhood, she mused.

'I'll get these sewn up this afternoon – you can watch me, it will give you an idea of how things are done – then you'll at least have a respectable outfit for tomorrow, for when we go for the groceries.' Eileen had no intention of letting the girl be seen by her neighbours, or by the staff in the shops she frequented, in the dreadful dress she'd brought with her and which, she'd noted, was now hanging in the wardrobe with the despised shawl.

'Will I go with you for the shopping, Mrs Rutherford?' Lizzie asked timidly, for she had an idea that it would not be a quick trip to a corner shop like Sadie's, and she doubted that anything would be bought on tick.

'Of course, Lizzie, how else are you to learn what we require and what can be bought for the budget?' came the rather indistinct reply, for Eileen was holding pins in her mouth.

'I ... I've got a lot to learn, I know that,' Lizzie admitted, but she was rather looking forward to the shopping trip, particularly as she would be wearing her new clothes.

Eileen sat back on her heels, having finished pinning up the hem of the skirt. 'You have, Lizzie, and no doubt it will take us ... both ... time to adjust. But I don't expect you to learn everything in a week or two. George tells me you are a bright girl, so you should pick things up quickly.'

Lizzie managed a smile at that, pleased that Mr Rutherford should think so highly of her.

'But I'd be obliged if you wouldn't invite your former ... friends to the house. You must understand, Lizzie, that my husband has a position to maintain and I can't have the girls who work for him at the factory calling to the house, it wouldn't do at all! Of course, you're quite at liberty to go and visit them, particularly Mrs Gibbons, as is proper. And I'm sure she will expect you to,' she added, seeing the girl's expression change and the slight flush that crept over her cheeks. 'Right, that's done. Now, when you've dressed we'll go down and see to the lunch,' she finished firmly, having got that matter settled.

As Lizzie took off the pinned garments she felt a little hurt. Clearly, Mrs Rutherford didn't consider

Lena good enough to come here. Did the woman view her in the same light? she wondered. Had she agreed to take her in only because Mr Rutherford had asked ... maybe insisted? Oh, she could understand that he wouldn't want a procession of matchgirls coming to visit his home, but still she felt that she hadn't really been welcomed here with open arms – at least, not by Eileen Rutherford. She was no longer to wear her shawl, a garment so comfortingly familiar and something her mam had always worn, but deep down she vowed that this was one edict she was not going to adhere to. She'd find the odd occasion to wear her shawl – after all, it proclaimed who she was.

Chapter Fifteen

In the days that followed Lizzie felt more and more that she was here under sufferance. Mrs Rutherford wasn't unkind; there were no cutting remarks about her lack of a proper upbringing and her ignorance of almost everything deemed necessary by society. But she sensed she wasn't entirely welcome as far as Eileen Rutherford, in whose company she spent most of her time, was concerned. George Rutherford was up promptly at six each morning and left for work at seven, not returning until at least six thirty in the evening, sometimes later. She'd become used to working with a lot of other people, as well as seeing him on the factory floor, where they'd often have brief conversations, and she found it difficult to get used to her new solitude.

She did quickly learn how to set a table correctly, the appropriate dishes and cutlery that should be used for each meal, and how to plan the meals for the week and keep the larder stocked. She had enjoyed the shopping trip too; it had been an enlightening experience and she'd been amazed at the choice of goods that were now affordable. They had taken the tram on Monday morning to the shops Eileen patronised – and not just one shop but the grocer's, butcher's, fishmonger's, greengrocer's, ironmonger's and even a florist's. She had been introduced to everyone as 'Miss Lizzie Tempest, my new young companion and hopefully apprentice', standing politely while Eileen had been served, noting that she was treated very deferentially, that her purchases were carefully wrapped and packed into her basket and that she paid for everything there and then.

She helped in the house with the cleaning, dusting and polishing. She learned that the washing was sent out to be done and, when it was returned, how and where it was put away. On Friday afternoon she had even made a Victoria sponge cake for Saturday tea, under Eileen's supervision, and they had both laughed at her efforts at creaming the butter and sugar. But Eileen was a patient teacher, and Lizzie had been delighted with the result.

She'd noted that the older woman did seem to get tired as the day wore on. Eileen was content to let her clear away and wash up after the evening meal, while she sat with her husband and read or worked on some embroidery. Nor had she much of an appetite, while Lizzie herself ate everything put before her, relishing all the new dishes, flavours and previously unheard-of treats, such as puddings with jam, custard or cream.

If she was truthful, she had to admit that she did enjoy having a room of her own, a far more comfortable life with better and more varied meals – which included many things she had never tasted before – fashionable clothes and even a few shillings in her purse. But the house was so *quiet;* her life now seemed devoid of any chatter or companionship. She really didn't have anything in common with her new mistress, apart from household tasks, and there wasn't the easy familiarity she had experienced living at Nellie's. Mrs Rutherford seldom asked her about her previous life or what family she still had – although, remembering her da and Billy, she was glad of that. But she had begun to feel that she didn't quite belong here; she just didn't fit in.

Mrs Rutherford had also hinted that perhaps, in a week or two, she might start to learn the basics of needlework, for she couldn't even do a simple, straight seam. She had watched as her clothes had been expertly and quickly altered, but it had all seemed so complicated, and she had viewed the sewing machine very warily indeed.

'It's not nearly as difficult as you might think, Lizzie. Oh, starting a new garment completely from scratch is something that does have to be learned, and that takes time and experience, especially with regard to tailoring for jackets and coats, but things like sewing on buttons, taking up hems or putting in darts are not hard,' she'd urged.

Lizzie had nodded but had still been rather doubtful.

'Of course, it's been possible to buy Vogue paper patterns for years. They do make things easier, and the instructions are fairly straight-forward, but adjustments are still needed for a perfect fit, and care needs to be taken in placing the pattern pieces so as to match any pattern in the fabric,' Eileen had continued.

'Instructions?' Lizzie had repeated, puzzled.

'Yes, they're printed on sheets of paper,' had been the reply.

'I ... I don't think I could manage to under-stand them,' she'd confided hesitantly.

Eileen had looked up from the hem she was tacking, frowning slightly. 'Why ever not? They're in simple, easy-to-understand language.'

'I'm ... I'm not great at reading, you see,' she'd replied, her cheeks flushing with embarrassment at having to admit this. 'We ... we moved around a lot from place to place, so I never went to school ... much.'

Eileen had sighed and nodded; she should have known. The girl had virtually no knowledge of a decent, orderly lifestyle so it stood to reason that she was lacking in a basic education too. 'Well, we'll have to remedy that, Lizzie. To get on in life you must at least be literate. I'll speak to George about it,' she'd promised.

Lizzie's colour had deepened; what did Eileen Rutherford think of her now, and what would her husband think of her? That she really was noth-ing but an ignorant slum girl, possibly only fit to work in a match factory? It had all made her feel even more ill at ease and out of place.

George Rutherford brought the subject up the following evening, after they'd eaten, but as considerately as possible.

'Eileen tells me that due to your ... circumstances, Lizzie, you didn't receive much of an education.'

She nodded. 'No, we were always moving, so there was never time for me to learn much,' she replied, feeling her cheeks flush. 'I can write my name and read ... a bit,' she added.

He nodded. Her lack of education wasn't unusual, considering her background; plenty of her former workmates were also virtually illiterate. He smiled at her, seeing her humiliation. 'Well, we'll have to see if we can improve on that, Lizzie. You're a bright girl; you'll soon pick it up.'

'I won't have to go back to school, will I?' she asked fearfully.

'No, of course not! I'll help you. We can make a start at the weekend. I'll go into Liverpool on Saturday afternoon after work and buy some suitable books, then we'll make a start on Sunday. Once you can read fluently, Lizzie, I'm sure you'll find you enjoy it, and then you can learn so many other things too,' he said confidently.

He was quite willing to give up some of his time to help her, for he'd promised her a better life, and being literate was one of the basic things she would need to master. It would open up another world to her and give her the confidence in herself she lacked, for he could see she was still not entirely at ease living here, although Eileen

145

had assured him she was settling down.

Lizzie had asked permission to go and visit Nellie and Lena on Saturday afternoon, and Eileen had agreed. She had promised to be back in time for 'supper', as she was now to call the evening meal, having done her chores and helped to make the meat pie and tidy the kitchen. She had changed into the royal-blue-and-white striped skirt and white blouse, which was the nicest of her outfits, securing the straw boater to which a band of blue ribbon had been added and pulling on the short white cotton gloves she'd purchased on her last shopping trip. Mrs Rutherford had stated that a lady always wore gloves, and although Lizzie didn't aspire to that description at all, she'd bought a pair, just the same, to placate her. Besides, her hands still bore all the signs of factory work – not something Mrs Rutherford would want her flaunting.

'Heavens, Lizzie! You look ... different, even after just a week living there!' Nellie greeted her. She'd never seen her looking so neat and tidy, and she looked far healthier.

'You look like a proper lady!' Lena added, noting Lizzie's new outfit and especially the gloves.

'You've really come up in the world, Lizzie. It's a wonder you can be bothered to come and visit us at all,' Peggy remarked scathingly, jealous of Lizzie's clothes. She couldn't help noting she was a far more attractive girl than either herself or her sister.

'That'll do from you, miss!' Nellie rebuked her daughter. 'Now, come and sit down and tell us

146

how you've been getting on,' she urged Lizzie.

While Lizzie informed them of her progress, Nellie made a pot of tea. Lena showed her the new blouse she'd bought, and Peggy took herself off to get ready to go and visit her future mother-in-law; Bertie had gone with his father and Ernie to the match, and they wouldn't be back until at least six o'clock.

'Well, it sounds as if you've really fallen on yer feet, luv, and I have ter say, yer looking well on it,' Nellie pronounced when she'd finished.

'I'm not ... ungrateful,' Lizzie said hesitantly, 'but, but I miss you all, I really do ... and I miss the girls I worked with. It's so quiet in that house all day, I hardly see anyone apart from her; he goes out early, and isn't home until supper time. There's no one for me to chat to, have a giggle or a gossip with. The only other people I see are the assistants in the shops we go to.'

'Doesn't she bother with the neighbours, then?' Nellie queried, for relationships with the neighbours – good or bad – had always been the mainstay of life in the likes of Bennett Street, and it was inconceivable to her that they were kept at arm's length, or perhaps even ignored.

'Not really, and she doesn't seem to have any friends, either. Well, no one has ever called to see her, so far.'

'Doesn't she have people coming to have things made?' Nellie pressed.

Lizzie nodded. 'I suppose so. I know she's got some work in hand, but no one's called yet...' She paused, frowning. 'She wants me to start learning to sew soon, and she was telling me about things called "paper patterns" that had printed instructions on them, and I had to say ... that I'm not great at reading.'

Nellie too frowned – she wasn't good at reading herself, and she'd never even heard of these 'patterns'.

'That all sounds dead ... complicated, Lizzie,' Lena remarked, refilling her mother's cup.

'Of course, she told him and now he's gone into Liverpool to buy some books; he's going to teach me himself, starting tomorrow. They seem to think it's terribly important.'

Nellie nodded. For people of their class she supposed it was.

'Oh, I'd hoped we could go for a walk tomorrow,' Lena confided, a little disappointed. Seeing that her friend had come to visit, she'd thought Lizzie would be free.

Lizzie smiled ruefully. 'I'd have liked that, Lena, but I can't say I'm going out. Not after he's gone to the trouble and expense of buying the books. Maybe next week?'

Lena consoled herself by trying on the new blouse, at Lizzie's instigation, and they chatted on, the way they'd always done, with Lizzie becoming more and more relaxed and much happier, and not noticing the time slipping past until Nellie at last said that she'd have to make a start on the tea. Ernie and Bertie would be in soon from the match, a local derby between Everton and Liverpool football clubs. It was always well attended, and they'd probably go for a pint afterwards – either to celebrate or drown their sorrows, depending on the result.

Lizzie reluctantly got to her feet and put on her hat and gloves, realising that it must be after six. She'd lost track of the time; she had promised to be back for supper and was now beginning to feel anxious, hoping that the trams wouldn't be packed with football supporters.

'I'll come and see you next week,' she promised as she took her leave and hastened towards the tram stop.

To her dismay she had to wait for a long time before she managed to board a tram. Quite a few had passed by but all were full to capacity and hadn't even stopped. She was beginning to think that she would have to walk back to Olivia Street, and that would make her terribly late.

When she alighted from the tram she hastened her steps, not daring to break into a run, for she was sure that Mrs Rutherford wouldn't approve, and she was flushed and a little out of breath when she at last reached home.

Eileen opened the door to her, looking worried. 'Lizzie, where on earth have you been?' she greeted her. 'Do you realise what time it is? You should have been back an hour ago.'

'Oh, I'm sorry! Really I am! I stayed too long, I'd forgotten about the match, and then I couldn't get a tram, they were all full of supporters,' she gasped, following Eileen into the hall.

'We've had supper already; if we'd have waited, that pie would have been utterly ruined! What were you thinking of? We were worried about you! George knew there was a big game on, and we didn't want you to get caught up in the crowds. Those matches can cause quite a lot of trouble between the rival supporters – which, as you know, can lead to ... violence! Really, Lizzie, you've been very thoughtless.'

'I'm sorry. I didn't realise,' Lizzie reiterated as she took off her hat and gloves.

Eileen tutted. 'If we can't trust you to be back on time, Lizzie, I'm afraid you'll have to curtail your visiting,' she stated, with obvious annoyance.

Lizzie bit her lip. All the enjoyment she'd felt that afternoon and evening drained away. She'd promised she would visit again next week, and she'd hoped that she and Lena would go on an outing together. If she wasn't to be allowed out on her own, life was beginning to look miserable indeed. Lizzie realised that she still had some way to go before she would really win Eileen's trust and enjoy some freedom to see her friends.

Chapter Sixteen

Nothing more was said about Lizzie being late home. The following day, after lunch had been served and she and Eileen had cleared away, Lizzie sat at the table with George Rutherford, struggling with the reading book he'd bought, having laboriously copied the letters from another book, as her new teacher had suggested. She was grateful for his patience but knew it was going to be an uphill struggle before she was halfway proficient in reading, let alone writing.

After an hour and a half she felt exhausted, her

head had begun to ache and it was obvious to them both that she was struggling.

'I think that's enough for today, Lizzie. Shall we have a cup of tea now?' George suggested, realising just how much of an effort it had all been for her, and not wishing to overtax her.

She nodded thankfully. 'I know I've got to master it, but it's ... hard. I think it will be almost as hard as learning to sew,' she confided, for Eileen had gone up to her workroom half an hour ago.

He smiled at her. 'Everything must seem ... difficult for you, Lizzie, but don't give up. It will be worth it.'

'There's just so *much* I've got to learn about ... everything!'

'I know, but look how quickly you picked up what to do at the factory.'

She managed a wry smile. 'But that was easy. I didn't have to worry about things like hems and darts and tacking stitches. I had the other girls to help me along and cover for me when I messed things up, and Miss Woods was always very considerate to me.'

'And I'm sure Eileen will help you all she can too...' He paused, frowning thoughtfully. Life for Lizzie must seem to be a constant round of mastering difficult tasks. 'Is there anything you really like to do, Lizzie, that's not what you'd call "work"? Drawing or painting, maybe?'

She looked puzzled, not really knowing what he meant.

'I mean as a sort of ... hobby?'

She shook her head. 'I don't think so. I ... I've never tried anything like that. People like me just

151

don't ... didn't ... have time for hobbies,' she replied.

He nodded, thinking ruefully that she'd had enough to do keeping body and soul together in the past, so there'd never been even the remotest opportunity for such pastimes. They were completely alien to her. 'It was just a thought, but maybe if you think there is something you might like to try, you could do so? The public library has all kinds of books – and they have pictures in them,' he added quickly, seeing the flash of consternation in her eyes at the mention of the word 'books'. 'We could go together and I could help you find something that might interest you?' he suggested. The girl had to have some pleasure and interests in life, he thought; everything really must seem like work to her at the moment, and that wasn't good. He didn't want her to be unhappy; he wanted her to enjoy her new life.

'I ... I'll think about that,' she promised before going to the kitchen to make the tea, though she couldn't see how she would ever have the time for such pursuits.

George mentioned it to his wife later that evening, after Lizzie had gone to bed. 'At the moment life must seem like all work and no play to her,' he concluded, after he'd told her about his suggestion of the library.

'Do you really think you should be putting such ideas into her head, George?' Eileen asked.

'We don't want her to view life now as a never-ending uphill struggle. That's a recipe for misery – and surely that's not what we want for her?'

'No, of course not ... but maybe after she's

become more used to us, when she can do things automatically, without having to think about such things as which plates or knives and forks to use. It's very early days yet, George,' she reminded him. It wasn't that she would begrudge the girl a hobby, but she considered it best for Lizzie to get used to doing what work she could undertake competently before encouraging her to go down other roads. It would only confuse the girl.

He sighed. 'Maybe you're right, dear. When she's reached a good standard of reading, she could go to the library herself, if she's interested.'

She nodded her agreement and determined that tomorrow she would start Lizzie on the very basics of sewing.

By the time Lizzie went to visit Nellie the following Saturday, she had indeed mastered a few things, and though her fingers bore many pin-pricks, she felt quite proud of herself.

'I really can't be late back this week, Mrs Rutherford was so cross and crabby last week,' she confided to Lena.

Lena rolled her eyes, but Nellie nodded. 'I suppose she was only worried about yer, luv. What with the derby match, an' all – and some of those fellers are right 'ooligans, so Ernie tells me.'

Lizzie nodded and placed a small brown paper bag on the table. 'I brought you these, for a bit of a treat. I bought them myself when we went to the shops yesterday.' The idea had occurred to her when she'd been with Eileen in the Home & Colonial Stores. The older woman had looked a little taken aback but had said nothing when she'd asked if she could purchase something too – using money of her own, of course.

'Biscuits! And with chocolate on them too! This certainly is a treat, Lizzie!' Nellie exclaimed. 'And we're not going to scoff them all at once, either!' she added, casting meaningful glances at both her daughters.

'So, what have you been doing this week, luv, apart from going to the shops and buying us biscuits?' Nellie asked, folding the corners of the bag tightly; they would have just one each with a cup of tea later, she decided.

Lizzie laughed, sitting down on the bench at the table beside Lena. 'All the usual stuff ... house-work and learning to cook ... but at least now I know how to sew buttons on, turn up a hem and sew a straight seam. Although she won't trust me with the sewing machine yet, and I'm not sure I want to even try it.'

Both Lena and Peggy looked impressed, for such simple tasks were beyond them too.

'Do you think you'll be able to make things to wear – for yourself, I mean – eventually?' Lena asked, proud that her friend seemed to have learned so much in just a week.

Lizzie shrugged. 'It'll probably take me years before I can make something that's fit to be worn.'

'I bet it won't!' Lena said firmly. Lizzie appeared to have learned so much about all kinds of things since she went to live in Olivia Street, and she had great faith in her friend's abilities.

'How's the reading coming on, Lizzie?' Nellie enquired.

Lizzie grimaced. 'Slowly. Very slowly. Oh, Mr

154

Rutherford's really patient with me and goes over everything, time and again, and explains things, and he sits with me while I do half an hour each night after supper.'

'Aren't you the lucky one?' Peggy remarked, rather cuttingly.

'Take no notice of her, Lizzie!' Lena hissed, glaring at her sister. 'She and all her mates are dead jealous of you! It caused quite a stir when she told them you'd left and gone to live with the Rutherfords. And you'll soon get the hang of it, if you do a bit each night and he's helping you.'

Lizzie smiled at her. 'I hope so.'

Lena turned her attention to her sister. 'And when she can make dresses, you might well be singing a different tune, our Peggy!'

'What do you mean by that?' Peggy demanded.

'Well, when you finally marry Bertie you'll be wanting a special dress for the occasion, won't you?' Lena pointed out sweetly.

The older girl frowned. She hadn't thought that far ahead but realised that Lena was right and indeed, by then, Lizzie might be able to actually make a dress.

'Oh, Lena, I couldn't possibly make a wedding dress!' Lizzie cried, horrified at the thought of what her friend was implying.

'Why not?' Lena demanded. 'Lizzie, you can do anything you put your mind to now, and she won't be able to afford anything really fancy.'

'But they're so ... complicated, Lena. You've just no idea...'

'Wouldn't she – Mrs Rutherford – be able to help you?' Lena pressed.

Lizzie shrugged helplessly. She didn't think Eileen Rutherford would be very well disposed towards helping her make Peggy a dress, for she charged quite highly for her services. People were paying for her years of experience and expertise, she'd impressed upon Lizzie when she'd looked astonished at Eileen's list of charges.

'Lena, leave Lizzie alone! Stop putting her on the spot like that! Our Peggy's got to save up for her bottom drawer yet, before she can go thinking about dresses and the like. Now, let's have a cup of tea and one of them gorgeous biscuits each, and then why don't you two girls go out for a walk? It's a lovely day, it'd be a shame to waste it stuck in here,' Nellie urged, thinking Lena was getting carried away with Lizzie's capabilities, and putting ideas into Peggy's head. Her elder daughter would find it hard enough to save up for a few basic household things, let alone any kind of a wedding dress, fancy or otherwise.

Remembering that she dare not be late back this week, Lizzie suggested they just go for a walk in the nearest local park. As they strolled in the sunshine, arms linked, Lena again brought up the subject of sewing.

'Our Peggy certainly altered her face when I mentioned a wedding dress,' she laughed.

Lizzie shook her head. 'I don't think I could ever make anything like that, Lena, honestly! It really does take years and years to learn to sew to Mrs Rutherford's standard – she can even make winter coats and tailored costumes – and your Peggy won't want to wait *that* long to get married!'

Lena pursed her lips. 'It gave her something to think about, though, didn't it? I bet she won't be so down on you now, because she certainly has been lately. She's always talking to her mates about you, saying you're just a dead common, ordinary girl like the rest of us. So why should he single you out? Why should you get to go and live with them in what's luxury, compared to what we have, and be taught a trade by his wife? And why is he so concerned about you that he's teaching you to read and write himself? She swears there's more to it, and Lily and the rest of them agree with her.'

Lizzie stopped walking and turned to her friend, frowning. 'What does she mean by that, Lena? "More to it"?'

Lena shrugged, fearing she had said too much and knowing that, if Lizzie repeated this to Nellie, there would be hell to pay for herself – and particularly for Peggy.

'Oh, come on, Lena, what exactly does your Peggy mean? You can't just drop the subject now!' Lizzie demanded.

Lena bit her lip and looked anxious. 'I think she means that he ... well, he sort of ... likes you, Lizzie. Likes you a lot more than just ... as a ... sort of friend,' Lena explained hesitantly.

Lizzie's eyes widened and she was utterly astounded. Such a thought had never occurred to her. 'What? He felt sorry for me, and yes, he's been ... kind to me, and so has she. But Lena, that's ridiculous ... he's old!'

'Oh, Lizzie, I should have kept my big mouth shut! I'm sorry I even mentioned it! Mam would absolutely kill me and our Peggy – and I've gone

157

and upset you too now,' Lena cried, clutching at Lizzie's arm, utterly repentant.

Lizzie managed a weak smile. 'I'm not really upset, Lena. Just a bit … taken aback – shocked, really – and anyway, it's just jealous gossip. He doesn't think of me like *that* at all!'

'You won't tell Mam?' Lena begged.

Lizzie shook her head. 'No. Just forget all about it, Lena. I'm going to,' she said firmly.

They walked on in silence but Lizzie felt that some of the joy had gone out of the sunny May afternoon. She was very grateful to George Rutherford; he was a kind, generous, considerate man, and she had become fond of him and tried hard to justify his faith in her. But that's all it was. She considered herself little more than a child – and an ignorant one, at that. In her eyes he had treated her as a brother or a father would; at least, a caring and concerned brother or father, unlike either her brother Billy or her da.

She would do as she'd told Lena – put it out of her mind completely. She had no intention of letting such malicious gossip spoil her new life or her relationship with the Rutherfords.

Chapter Seventeen

Over the next weeks Lizzie put her mind completely to all the tasks that she was given, working determinedly in both the house and sewing room and applying herself diligently to her studies in the evening, allowing herself no time at all in which to dwell on Peggy's nasty innuendoes. The weather continued fine and sunny and, as May turned into June, it became even warmer and so, when she visited Nellie, she and Lena spent as little time as possible in the cramped, stuffy rooms in Bennett Street – and, therefore, not in Peggy's company.

She had remained in the sewing room when Eileen's clients came for fittings, holding the pins, making herself useful and taking note of everything. She found using the sewing machine very hard to master and she was terrified that she would get her fingers impaled on the flying needle. Cutting out filled her with trepidation; she was happy enough to do the pinning, but the actual cutting of the material she undertook hesitantly, knowing that if she made a mistake, then it would be ruined – for, as the older woman said, there was no putting it back together again. But she was progressing, if slowly.

'In a few more weeks, Lizzie, you'll be able to put together a simple garment, and that's no mean achievement for someone who could barely thread a needle,' Eileen had praised her one afternoon, to Lizzie's delight.

She had now settled into the daily routine and barely gave a thought to the chores she'd once found unfamiliar and rather daunting, and she'd become accustomed to her comfortable lifestyle. Her reading had improved considerably and she was actually beginning to enjoy it, realising that George Rutherford had been right when he'd said there were so many other things she could now take an interest in and learn about. Writing she found more laborious; she was slow at it, but she persevered.

She did, however, also remember what he'd said about books that could be found in the library on hobbies and pastimes, and she determined that she would go and see just what was on offer. Now that the evenings were so much longer she found that she actually did have some time on her hands, time she didn't want to idle away, and she was curious about hobbies, never having considered them before. He'd never mentioned taking her to the local library again, and she wasn't going to bring the subject up, but late one afternoon she asked Eileen just where their local branch was.

'There's one up on the main road, Lizzie. It's not actually very far. Do you intend to join?'

Lizzie frowned. 'I don't know. I just thought I might go along and see what they've got there. Does it cost much to borrow a book?'

'No, it's free, Lizzie.'

She hadn't known that; having barely been able to read in the past, she'd not given books or libraries much thought at all, but she would now.

She found the building without much trouble, for she must have passed it numerous times since she'd lived in this part of Bootle, but had never noticed it.

She looked around curiously as she entered the building and was quite amazed; she'd never seen so many books before. But she wasn't alone, for there were other people browsing amongst the shelves, and it was very, very quiet. All she could

160

hear were the sounds of traffic and muted voices coming faintly from the street outside. She went to the polished wooden counter behind which a young woman was sitting, engaged in sorting through a pile of books.

'May I help you, miss?' she asked, looking up.

She looked friendly, so Lizzie decided to explain. 'I hope so ... you see, this is the first time I've ever been into a library as, up until now, I've not had time for ... reading, but the people I live with suggested that I come and have a look at some books on ... er ... pastimes.' She decided that sounded better than 'hobbies'.

'Do you have any particular pastimes in mind?'

'I'm not exactly sure...' she faltered, not knowing how to explain that she didn't have a clue what she was capable of – or indeed, what really interested her.

The young woman rose. 'If you'll follow me, we'll see what we can find. And then, if there is something you would like to borrow, we can sort out the necessary paperwork and I can issue you with your ticket.'

That sounded a bit complicated to Lizzie, and she felt a bit uneasy about the 'paperwork', but she duly followed the woman to a section towards the back of the building.

'There are lots of books on sketching, painting, sculpting, decoupage, needlecrafts, lace-making and all kinds of crafts. There are books on design too and, if you are interested, on the lives and works of the great artists of the past.'

Lizzie managed a smile, despite feeling rather overwhelmed. 'Thank you.'

'If you find something interesting, there is a table and chair in the corner where you can sit and browse. I'll leave you to have a look; take your time, we don't close for another hour yet.'

Lizzie smiled her thanks and began to walk slowly along the aisles, perusing the shelves. It was all a bit daunting, not least because she really didn't know what would interest her.

At length she selected a book on sketching, another on the basics of water-colour painting, and one on the designs of something entitled the 'Arts and Crafts Movement'. She settled herself at the table in the corner and began leafing through the book on painting but soon decided it was all too complicated for her. She would need to buy paints and brushes, and special paper which would need to be soaked in water and then left to dry, according to the text. But the other two books looked more promising. She'd never tried to draw anything in her life and doubted she was capable of reproducing anything like the illustrations, but they did show you how to do it, step by step, so she supposed she could at least *try*. The last book she found fascinating – the one on the designs of the Arts and Crafts Movement. The patterns, unlike any she'd ever seen before, intrigued her; particularly when she saw them used on fabrics, ceramics, furniture and soft furnishings, and even jewellery. They appealed to her practical nature. At last she decided she would like to learn more about design and so, after replacing the book on water-colour painting on the shelf, she made her way towards the young woman at the desk.

'Could I borrow these two, please?' she asked.

The librarian smiled. 'Of course. Now, let me fill in this form and then you can sign it and I'll make out your tickets.'

She was relieved that she was only asked for her full name, address and her date of birth, which the librarian filled in on the form. She duly signed her name at the bottom and then waited while two small buff-coloured cardboard tickets were written out. The books were stamped with the date by which they were to be returned and it was explained that, if they were late, there would be a fine imposed. Then she was handed her books; that's all there seemed to be to joining a library, and she wondered why she had been so apprehensive. She walked out into the warm, late afternoon sunlight feeling far more confident than when she'd left the house. She was looking forward now to getting home so she could study the books in more detail, maybe even try her hand at one or two of the simple sketches, if she could find some suitable paper.

When she arrived home, she showed the books to Eileen. 'I'm going to at least try to draw something. And if I'm no good at it, well, then at least I'll know.'

Eileen nodded. 'That's very true, Lizzie, it's best to give things a try. What's the other book about?'

'Designs and something called the Arts and Crafts Movement. It's really interesting.'

'Good,' Eileen said, peering at the book with genuine interest. 'The designs are simpler, less fussy and ostentatious than those of the last decades. I like them,' she added. 'And the goods are usually handmade, not mass produced in a factory, and so are better quality. There's another modern style coming to the fore now too – it's called Art Nouveau,' Eileen enthused.

Lizzie was surprised by her knowledge. 'I'd not heard of that one, but I like the way the designs can be used for all kinds of things, from furnishings to jewellery.' She settled down to look more closely at the illustrations and to slowly read the print, becoming increasingly absorbed in the book.

Eileen smiled at the serious expression on Lizzie's face, wondering if the girl had any kind of artistic flair. If so, she would be delighted to see Lizzie find something she enjoyed and was good at.

Two days later, Lizzie decided to return the books. She had surprised herself by finding, after a few attempts, that she could indeed manage simple sketches, but realised that she had her limitations. She definitely wasn't a talented artist, and never would be, but it was design that really interested her. She hoped there would be other books on the subject, particularly the designs of a Manx man called Archibald Knox whose intricate scrolls and knots appealed to her.

The same young woman greeted her, smiling. 'You got through those quickly, Miss Tempest. Were they not to your liking?'

Lizzie smiled back. 'Oh, I enjoyed this book so much, I was wondering if there are any other books like it – and on something called Art Nouveau?' she replied.

164

'Why don't you go and look? I'm pleased you found it so enlightening.'

Lizzie made her way to the appropriate section. She hadn't mentioned to George Rutherford that she'd joined the library, and obviously Eileen hadn't informed her husband either, for he'd made no mention of it but had praised her for the progress she was making with her handwriting. But she was going to tell him about her library visits this evening, for she'd had an idea yesterday when she'd been tidying the sewing room, and she wanted his advice.

It was Eileen's birthday next month – exactly six days before Lizzie's – and she'd been thinking about what to give her as a gift to mark the occasion. It seemed only right somehow to show her gratitude for everything she'd been taught so far, even though she didn't have much money. But while she was tidying up the small scraps of material left over from cutting out, she'd hit on the solution – one she could make herself. She found a book she liked, and as she left the library she realised that there were lots of things such designs could be used on, all practical things. She'd give it some thought, but first of all she had to see just what she could achieve. She was so deep in thought that she was a little startled to hear someone call her name.

'Oh, Miss Woods! I didn't notice you, I'm sorry,' Lizzie apologised.

Mabel was looking at her with some astonishment. 'I thought it was you, but goodness, Lizzie, how you've changed!'

Lizzie smiled at her former supervisor. 'Thank

you, Miss Woods.'

'And are you happy living with Mr and Mrs Rutherford? It was very, very generous of them to take you in. I have to say, I was extremely surprised when I heard about it ... and I wasn't the only one,' she confided. In fact, she'd been stunned when she'd heard – and Lizzie Tempest's newfound fortune had had the packing room in a turmoil for days.

'I am. They are very good to me. I've just been to the library and borrowed this book.' Lizzie turned the volume over in her hand.

The older woman looked at it with interest. She was surprised at the very fact that the girl could read. And her choice of book was intriguing. 'I wouldn't have thought you were in any way "artistic", Lizzie?' she remarked. She'd assumed Lizzie would have chosen a novella or some other form of 'light' reading.

'I didn't know I was, miss. But you see, it's Mrs Rutherford's birthday soon and I want to make her something special, and I like these Art Nouveau designs. She's teaching me to sew,' she added, seeing Mabel Woods' eyebrows rise slightly.

'That's very ... thoughtful. I wish you luck with it, Lizzie. Well, I'd better be going. I'm pleased I met you and that you're doing so ... well.'

Lizzie smiled at her; she'd always liked the woman. 'Thanks, it's nice to see you again, Miss Woods.'

Mabel marvelled to herself as she walked away. She was astonished the girl even knew words such as 'Art Nouveau'. There appeared to be more to Lizzie Tempest than she'd ever imagined.

Chapter Eighteen

After supper was over and they'd cleared away, Lizzie decided to broach the subject of her idea before she began her evening studies, for Eileen had gone up to the sewing room. She had two clients calling tomorrow morning and wanted to make sure everything was in order.

Lizzie and George were sitting together downstairs, ready to start her reading practice, when she produced her library book. 'My reading is much better now, so I took your advice and I've joined the library on the top road,' she informed him.

He was looking for the relevant page in the book she was currently reading, but he looked up with interest – although he was a little surprised, for he'd assumed she'd forgotten all about that conversation. 'That's ... good, Lizzie. Did you find it helpful? Did you find anything to your liking?'

She nodded. 'I did; I came across this book. I found it really interesting.' She leaned forward across the table after glancing towards to hall. 'I'd like to ask your advice about something, before Mrs Rutherford comes down.'

He leaned back in his chair, intrigued. 'Fire away, then.'

She handed him the library book. 'Well, I know it's her birthday next month, and I'd like to give her something. But I haven't got much money, so I thought ... well, you see, she's got lots of pin cushions but her needle case has seen better days, and I thought I'd make her a new one ... and matching cases for her cutting-out shears, pinking shears and scissors.'

He was touched. 'That's very thoughtful of you, Lizzie. I take it your sewing has improved to that extent?'

She nodded. 'I'd like to try to decorate them with designs like those in the book. I know she likes them – she told me so – and it would make them a bit more ... special. There are plenty of scraps of material and bits of braid and ribbon in the workroom that I can use.'

He opened the book and studied the Celtic knots and scrolls of Archibald Knox's work, and looked thoughtful. He doubted she would be able to replicate such intricate designs, but he didn't want to pass on those doubts and upset her. 'They're very intricate, Lizzie.'

'I know, but that's what makes them stand out. And I'll draw them first on the main pieces of fabric, and see how I get on...' She paused, looking a little abashed. 'I ... I've tried my hand at sketching too. The designs won't be exactly the same; I don't intend to copy them. They'll be more *my* designs, but in that style. But do you think she'll like the gifts? I know she'll find them useful, but I want her to ... admire them, and be pleased with them too,' she confided earnestly. It would be the first time she'd ever done anything like this, completely off her own bat, but she did want her efforts to be appreciated.

He looked into the wide blue eyes, filled with such eagerness, and smiled. He wasn't going to

168

say anything that would dim that enthusiasm. He couldn't do that to her; it would be cruel, and he could never do anything to deliberately hurt her. He was certain that she would struggle with such designs, but even if she made a complete mess of them, he wouldn't comment on the fact. He was sure his wife wouldn't do so, either; she'd realise the girl had spent so much time making them especially for her birthday.

'Lizzie, I'm sure she'll be delighted with them. She'll be touched you thought of her on her birthday.' He looked at her quizzically. 'How did you know when her birthday is? I've not mentioned it. Did she?'

She smiled and shook her head. 'I heard her mention it to Mrs Clements – one of her clients – last week in conversation. I remembered the date because it's my birthday six days later.'

He hadn't realised that. Of course, when she'd first come to the factory, she'd given her date of birth but he hadn't remembered it. 'Is it really? Well, we'll have to think what to do about that...'

Lizzie gasped aloud; she hadn't meant it to sound as if she was dropping hints. 'Oh, no! I ... I didn't mean...'

He laughed good-naturedly. 'Don't get all flustered, Lizzie! I've no such thoughts. Now, we'd better get on with your reading, for I think my wife is coming back downstairs – and we don't want to spoil the birthday surprise you've planned, do we?'

Lizzie worked hard on the designs, discarding quite a few of her sketches, but she was finally happy with what she had managed to produce.

She'd found it easier not to try to copy the illustrations in the book but to use her own imagination and let her drawings flow by themselves. And she'd also realised that there was quite a difference between Art Nouveau and Arts and Crafts, and that she could take elements from both styles and combine them.

She set about choosing the colours and fabrics, and then came the laborious task of the actual sewing, which she had to undertake in her own time and when Eileen was otherwise occupied. It was very fiddly work, needing tiny stitches that would have been far easier on the Singer sewing machine, but she was still wary of that contraption and hadn't quite got the knack of completely controlling its speed. And, of course, she would have had to ask Eileen's permission to use it, which would have ruined the surprise. But when the needle case was nearly finished she could see the beauty of the intricate design and was pleased with it. It was turning out far better than she'd expected. All she had to do now was put the finishing touches to the needle case and make the three cases for the scissors – she just hoped she'd have everything completed in time for Eileen's birthday.

Lizzie was a diligent worker, and two days later she'd completed the needle case. She was so pleased with her work that she decided to show it to George Rutherford to get his opinion on her efforts. She found the opportunity on Sunday afternoon, before she left for her visit to Nellie's. The weather had become oppressively hot, even for July, and Eileen had pleaded a headache and gone to lie down.

He'd opened the windows in the parlour and sat browsing through the Sunday papers when she came in, dressed in her lightest outfit for such a sultry afternoon – a white cotton dress printed with a pattern of tiny, pale pink flowers. The neck of the bodice and the leg-of-mutton sleeves were edged with pink ribbon. She'd also changed the ribbon on her straw boater from blue to pink.

'You do look lovely, Lizzie, and very cool. Are you off now to visit Mrs Gibbons?'

She sat down on the chair opposite him, took a small package from her bag and handed it to him rather shyly. 'Yes, but I wanted to show you this before I go – and before I give it to Mrs Rutherford. I've still got the scissors cases to do, but...'

He took it from her, feeling a little apprehensive but determined not to show it.

When he took out the needle case she'd made of a dark red felt, he was completely astounded. The design she had embossed on it was made of varying shades of yellow and green ribbon and braid, and was nothing short of a miniature work of art. 'Lizzie, you did this all by ... yourself?'

'I did. Do you think she'll like it?' she asked.

'It's ... it's wonderful, Lizzie! How could anyone not like it? Not think it ... beautiful? I certainly do! You're gifted.'

She felt the blood rush to her cheeks at such enthusiastic and genuine praise. 'I did try very hard.'

He handed it back to her and she replaced it carefully in her bag, then got to her feet. 'I hope I'll have the other pieces ready in time.'

He looked up at her and smiled. 'I'm sure you will, and they'll make a truly wonderful gift, Lizzie.'

She smiled back and took her leave, unaware that George Rutherford was staring after her in amazement. He'd never imagined her to be capable of making anything like that. If she managed to produce such fine work on the other things she intended to make for his wife, then she certainly had a remarkable talent. The design was intricate and had been executed with a real flair for colour. Lizzie Tempest was proving to be a very unusual girl indeed, he mused. He'd wanted to give her a better life – and a means of earning a decent living, in time – but he'd never envisaged that she might have such hidden talents. They might even provide her with more than just a living, given the opportunity and the right support. It was something he would think about, and maybe discuss with his wife; he was sure she would be of the same opinion as himself.

When Lizzie reached Bennett Street the door was wide open, as usual. She walked into the lobby and wrinkled her nose at the smells that seemed to have been intensified by the heat. As Lena ushered her into Nellie's kitchen she felt as if she'd walked into a furnace. Because the range was needed for cooking it was kept alight, even in weather such as this, and added to the discomfort.

'You look lovely and fresh and cool, Lizzie,' Nellie greeted her. 'I 'ate this weather! This house is as hot as the hobs of hell – but what can we do?'

Lizzie nodded as she took off her hat, noticing Peggy eyeing her dress with open envy. Lizzie ignored her.

'It's not much better at the factory, either,' Lena added. 'I do envy you, Lizzie, not having to work there now, with all the noise and in this heat.'

'Oh, aye, it's well for some!' Peggy muttered.

Again Lizzie ignored her, thinking that if Lena and Peggy were having to suffer the oppressive conditions in the factory, George Rutherford would be too. Yet he never complained.

'Where have you decided we should go this afternoon, Lena?' she asked.

'Somewhere where there'll be a bit of a breeze,' Nellie put in, struggling to force up the sash window that overlooked the yard at the back. 'We could do with a bit of air in here too.' It refused to budge and she turned to Ernie in exasperation. 'Well, don't just sit there, Ernie Gibbons, give me a hand.'

'It's no use, Nell. It's stuck fast. The wood's all warped an' has been fer years,' he replied wearily.

'Mam, leave it. You'll only be letting in the stink from the privies and the ash cans – and we can do without that,' Lena reminded her mother.

'And more flies! There's enough of them in here already. You'll have to get more fly papers tomorrow from Sadie's, Mam,' Peggy added.

Realising her daughters spoke the truth, Nellie gave it up as a bad job; they'd just have to put up with the stifling heat.

'Well, the Pier Head it is, then,' Lena announced. There was a constant breeze by the river, and there were always ships tied up and

173

crowds of people boarding them, some of them in very fashionable and expensive clothes too.

Lizzie opened her bag. 'Before we go, I'd like to show you what I've made for Mrs Rutherford's birthday next week. It took me ages, but ... but I showed it to Mr Rutherford, and he said he thought it was ... beautiful, and that I'm really gifted.'

Both Lena and Nellie looked intrigued, but Peggy narrowed her eyes thoughtfully.

'Oh, Lizzie ... it's gorgeous!' Lena exclaimed in awe, although looking a little puzzled at the same time. 'But what is it? What's it for, like?'

'It's for keeping sewing needles in – not that you'd know anything about that,' Nellie stated. 'And you made it, Lizzie? Bye, there's some work gone into this! I've never seen anything like it! Never seen anything so ... fine.'

Lizzie flushed with pleasure. 'The design on the front I drew myself; then I used the braid and ribbon for decoration. I got some books from the library that helped me. There are lots of different designs, and they can be applied to all sorts of useful things,' she told them.

Both Nellie and Lena nodded their approval, and even Peggy was curious enough to look over her mother's shoulder at what Lizzie had produced.

'You mean you actually did all that yourself?' Peggy asked, a note of suspicion in her voice, for she was finding it hard to believe that someone like Lizzie Tempest could have made something as delicate as that. 'I bet she helped you,' she added spitefully.

Her words deflated Lizzie's feelings of pride and pleasure, and she was stung. 'Don't be so stupid, Peggy! Why would I ask her to help me make a gift for her own birthday? That doesn't make any sense. I did this myself, and I'm ... proud of it.'

'And so you should be, Lizzie!' Nellie said firmly, glaring at her eldest daughter, yet understanding Peggy's jealousy. In the girl's eyes, Lizzie seemed to have everything Peggy did not. And now it was obvious that Lizzie had a special talent too.

Lena was annoyed by her sister's remark. 'You're just jealous, Peggy! You're envious of everything Lizzie has and does.'

Nellie took the situation in hand. 'Right, that's enough! Lizzie, luv, put this back in your bag so it doesn't come to any harm. Mrs Rutherford will be delighted with it, I'm sure. Lena, get your hat, and the pair of you take yourselves off out of this inferno of a kitchen. And Peggy, didn't you say you were going round to see Bertie's Mam?'

Still looking mutinous, Lena went for her hat as Peggy shrugged off her allegations and Lizzie carefully put the precious needle case back in her bag. She knew Lena was right – Peggy was deeply jealous of her, but there was little she could do about it. She had no intention of curtailing her visits because of Peggy's spitefulness. She would be glad when Peggy finally got married and moved out, but that wouldn't be for a good while yet. At least there had been no nasty remarks about her going to the library or discovering that she could produce designs people seemed to like. She supposed that was a small bonus.

175

Chapter Nineteen

To her relief Lizzie finished the other pieces in time for Eileen's birthday. The night before, she wrapped her gifts carefully in tissue paper and tied a ribbon around the little parcel. She'd bought a card from the stationer's earlier, and her writing had improved so much that she was quite proud of her inscription inside it.

She got up early in the morning and placed both the card and parcel beside the plate she'd set for Eileen at the breakfast table.

'You're up in good time, Lizzie,' George remarked when he came down to find her finishing the task.

'I wanted to put my card and gifts out ready for her,' she replied.

'So you got them completed on time?'

She nodded, before going out to the kitchen to put the kettle on and start to prepare breakfast. She heard Eileen come downstairs. It was only right, she thought, that she let Mr Rutherford have time to wish his wife a happy birthday, and perhaps give her his gift, before she went back in. But she felt a sense of excitement bubbling up in her as she wondered what Eileen would think of her gifts.

When she finally entered the room, bearing a tray with the teapot, toast rack and hot milk for the porridge, she noted that Eileen looked flushed and happy. She was examining a pair of gold and garnet earrings, obviously a gift from her husband.

'Happy birthday, Mrs Rutherford!' Lizzie said, smiling as she set down the tray on the sideboard.

Eileen put the earrings aside and got to her feet. 'Why thank you, Lizzie. I didn't realise you knew it was my birthday.'

'You sit down, I can manage. It's your special day,' Lizzie urged. 'And I ... I put something beside your plate,' she added.

Eileen smiled at her. 'Your writing has improved so much, Lizzie,' she remarked, opening the card first.

Lizzie caught George Rutherford's gaze across the table as she sat down, looking pleased with herself.

Eileen untied the ribbon carefully and unwrapped the tissue just as carefully. The little parcel was certainly a surprise, and what it contained was even more unexpected: the work was exquisite.

'Oh, Lizzie! They're beautiful, and so very useful too. You really shouldn't have spent so much money on what are obviously expensive items,' she enthused.

'I didn't, Mrs Rutherford. They weren't expensive at all. I ... I made them,' Lizzie replied proudly.

George Rutherford sat back and smiled at the expressions on both their faces. Lizzie's full of pride and satisfaction, and his wife's a picture of utter astonishment.

'You *made* them, Lizzie?'

'I did. I drew the design myself and used scraps from the workroom,' she replied, for she had used the same design on each piece. 'They're a sort of ... set.'

Eileen fingered them carefully. Hours of work had gone into them, but it was the intricacy of the design and the clever use of shades of the same colours that really astonished her. Lizzie had never shown any great aptitude in the making of garments, but obviously the girl had talent for design and a flair for colour. 'Lizzie, I've never seen anything quite like them. Did you take the design from those books?'

'Sort of, but I didn't actually copy anything.'

Eileen looked enquiringly across at her husband. 'They're really quite beautiful, George, don't you think?'

'I do, and I was as amazed as you are. Lizzie showed me the needle case first, for my opinion and advice as to whether or not you would like it. It seems as if she's found a talent she never realised she possessed, and neither did we.'

'I knew you liked the designs in the books, so I thought I'd try,' Lizzie explained.

Eileen smiled at her. 'I never realised that you could produce work like this, Lizzie, but you know it would have been much easier for you to have appliquéd the ribbon and braid using the sewing machine.'

Lizzie nodded. 'I thought that myself, but I'm not really comfortable using it yet.'

'It just takes practice, Lizzie.' Eileen looked thoughtful. 'Do you think you'll do more of this ... work?'

'I'd like to. I'd really like to,' she replied, flashing a hopeful glance across the table first to Eileen and then to her husband. 'It can be used on all sorts of useful things in the house to make them look ... more attractive.'

George leaned forward, looking interested. 'Like what, Lizzie?'

'Well, for a start, I could make covers for the matchboxes we use,' she suggested. 'We use a lot of matches to light the stove and the fire and the gas lights.'

'You could indeed, Lizzie,' Eileen agreed.

George laughed light-heartedly. 'It seems our little "matchgirl" could end up by designing some very fine vesta cases!'

Lizzie looked puzzled. 'What are "vesta" cases?'

He delved into his pocket and drew out the small metal case that contained matches. She'd seen him use it on numerous occasions but hadn't realised what it was called. 'This is one, Lizzie. This is only made of a base metal, but you can buy them in silver – gold, even – and they come in all kinds of shapes and sizes and are often decorated and enamelled.' He passed it over to her.

She examined it carefully; it was really little more than a metal box with a hinged lid and a strip on the bottom to strike the match on. But everyone used them, for a man who didn't smoke either a pipe or cigarettes was very rare indeed, and even some women smoked. She nodded; she could see his point. A case like this could be made to look much more expensive and decorative if it were embellished. 'Are they all made of metal?'

'Mainly, although some are made of bone or

ivory – but that's very expensive – in fact, any material that won't catch fire.'

Lizzie frowned. 'Then how could I decorate them?'

'That would have to be done by a craftsman, but you could create the designs, Lizzie,' he informed her, realising the implications.

Eileen thought he was putting ideas into the girl's head that were impossible for her to realise. 'That's all a bit ... complicated and involved, George. Lizzie, why not start with pretty covers for household matches? They would add a bit of "class" to any parlour and brighten up a kitchen,' she added, not wishing to put a damper on the ambition that had flashed across the girl's face.

'Maybe you could persuade some of the shops to sell them for you?' George added enthusiastically, realising his wife was right. It would take money to set up a business that involved making and decorating vesta cases – money they just didn't have to spare.

Lizzie beamed at them both. Suddenly she had found something she excelled at and which, hopefully, could earn her money. 'Do you really think I could?'

'You won't know until you try, Lizzie,' George encouraged her. It would be worth trying; perhaps it might prove to be the first small step towards something greater.

Lizzie embarked with enthusiasm on designing the cases for household matches, and it took her only a few days to complete the first ones. Both Eileen and George were pleased and very impressed by her dedication and evident skill. Lizzie invested the few shillings she had saved on buying the materials, and Eileen made up the shortfall, although Lizzie promised to pay her back when she could. Eileen also took the time to teach Lizzie how to use the sewing machine to greater advantage, and she felt proud of herself when she finally mastered it.

To Lizzie's delight the little pile of embellished cases began to grow. She had already made a mental list of the shops she would approach, starting with the local smaller haberdashers. And then, if that went well, she might even take some samples to the big department stores in Liverpool, an idea that both excited and daunted her. 'Don't go getting carried away with yourself, Lizzie Tempest!' she told herself firmly – yet she could dream, couldn't she?

She was so involved and busy with her new project that she had forgotten that it was her fourteenth birthday. On a bright, sunny July morning she came down to find a card and a small, neatly wrapped gift on the breakfast table.

'Happy birthday, Lizzie!' Eileen greeted her, smiling.

'Oh, Lord! I'd forgotten!' she exclaimed, pressing both hands to her cheeks.

'You're growing up, Lizzie. Now you are officially able to be employed – if you so wish,' George added, laughing.

'No! I'm quite happy – more than happy – to work for myself,' she replied. 'That's if I can sell my work,' she added.

They all sat down and Eileen poured the tea as

Lizzie opened the first birthday card she'd ever had in her life. It was so pretty, she thought, with its paper lace fan and tiny bow of pink ribbon and silver lettering. It was obviously expensive. She turned her attention to the little parcel.

'We hope you'll like it, Lizzie. I thought it was very appropriate, the minute I saw it,' Eileen Rutherford explained, smiling at the girl's transparent delight. She wondered if Lizzie's birthday had ever been marked, let alone celebrated, before.

When Lizzie opened the little box her eyes widened as she took in the small silver brooch set with tiny polished agates, resting on a cushion of black satin. She recognised the design instantly.

'Oh! Oh ... it's ... *beautiful!* Thank you! It's by Mr Knox, isn't it? I ... I've never, ever had anything like this before!' Her eyes filled with tears as she lifted the brooch out of the box. She'd never owned a single piece of jewellery; she'd never imagined she ever would, for there was never money enough for such luxuries. If she'd thought about it at all, she vaguely imagined she might one day have a wedding ring, as her Mam had – before it had been sold. No woman she'd ever known, apart from Eileen Rutherford, had ever owned anything like this. Peggy Gibbons didn't even have an engagement ring, just the promise of a wedding band. She was so very, very lucky – and the fact that it was a design by Archibald Knox made it even more special. It had obviously not been cheap.

'Not just a birthday gift, Lizzie, but hopefully a lucky token for a successful career,' George Rutherford added, touched by her obvious delight.

Lizzie couldn't contain herself, she was so filled with gratitude and pleasure. She jumped up, still clutching the little brooch, and threw her arms around Eileen and kissed her on the cheek. Then she turned to George, her eyes bright with tears of joy, and reached up to kiss him too. 'Thank you! You are both so ... good to me! I ... I can't believe how lucky I am! I never expected anything like this!'

Eileen smiled at Lizzie, touched by her gratitude. She realised that she had grown fond of the girl and also recognised how much Lizzie had changed since the day she'd first come to live with them.

George looked bemused. He could see that Lizzie was overcome and delighted, but her display of genuine and open affection had surprised him. He'd only ever thought of her as a girl who had had a rough start in life and deserved better. But now he wondered whether he had begun to see her in a different light. She was a young girl who was growing into a talented and confident young woman, and her modest and sincere delight in her newfound abilities couldn't fail to charm anyone who witnessed her enthusiasm. He caught his wife's gaze and smiled back at her.

Lizzie wiped her eyes and pulled herself together before pinning the brooch to her blouse. 'I'd better go and get your breakfast, Mr Rutherford, or you'll be late for work.'

George again looked at his wife and smiled. 'Lizzie, I think my wife will agree that it's now time you dropped the Mr and Mrs.'

Eileen nodded, while Lizzie looked from one to

the other questioningly.

'Do you think you can call me George?'

'And me Eileen?'

Lizzie smiled at them both. 'I ... I'll ... try,' she replied, feeling as if today she had not only reached fourteen – something of a milestone birthday – but that the past was firmly behind her and she had become part of this family. They'd both given her so much, invested so much time and effort on her behalf. Thanks to George, as she must now call him, she was now literate and had discovered she had a talent, and thanks to Eileen she'd learned the skills she needed. She now had a confidence in herself she'd never had before; she knew how to dress and speak and run a household. She'd become fond of them both and obviously they'd become just as fond of her. The beautiful little brooch seemed to have set the seal on it. She was sure it was indeed a token of luck that pointed towards a happy and successful future.

Part Two

Chapter Twenty

1905

The train was late, Lizzie realised, as it at last pulled into Lime Street Station but, glancing at the fob watch pinned to her jacket, she realised thankfully it was not so late that Lena would have had a long, tedious wait on the platform. With a juddering, grinding and grating of brakes, and with clouds of steam issuing from the engine and rising up towards the cavernous span of the glass-domed roof above, the train came to a halt. Gathering up her reticule, she got to her feet and made her way along the corridor towards the door of the carriage.

It was good to be home, she mused, as she stepped down on to the platform. It was the second time she'd been to London and, although she was a city girl born and bred, she had to admit that she'd found the capital city just too big, too busy and too noisy. But she did enjoy some of the hustle and bustle; it was a very vibrant city, she had to admit. Like last time, it had been only a short visit – just an overnight stay, really – and she was still not sure if it had been worth the trip. She certainly had plenty to tell her friend and, of course, both Eileen and George when she arrived back in Olivia Street.

As she made her way down the platform,

following the crowd of people who had also arrived at their destination, she at last caught sight of Lena who was scanning the mass of faces anxiously. She waved to attract her friend's attention.

Lena greeted her with a hug and a smile of relief. 'Oh, Lizzie, I thought the train was never going to arrive! How did it go? Were you a bag of nerves?'

Lizzie laughed, and they linked arms and walked towards the exit leading into Lime Street. They made an attractive pair, and quite a few heads turned in their direction, but the young women were seemingly unaware of the admiring glances. At eighteen, Lizzie was tall and still slender, and her damson-coloured wool crêpe travelling costume was the height of fashion, set off by the high-necked white lace blouse beneath it. Her thick, dark hair was piled high on top of her head and covered by a large-brimmed damson felt hat embellished with a big bow of white satin ribbon and two white artificial roses. Lena was now nineteen and, although not as tall and slim as Lizzie, she'd blossomed into an attractive, curvaceous and vivacious young woman. For some years now she had bought the material for her clothes and then Lizzie, sometimes with a little help from Eileen, had made them up for her. The royal-blue loose three-quarter coat with its wide sleeves and quilted collar, worn over a matching skirt and pale blue pin-tucked blouse, suited Lena's fair complexion. A large-brimmed, pale blue hat covered her light brown hair, and she carried a small black bag which she'd recently purchased.

The fact that Lena now had far more clothes and

was more stylishly dressed than her sister Peggy was a source of much bitterness between them. Peggy, now married, was still working but had little money to spare to spend on herself, for she and Bertie were renting two rooms and trying to furnish them. She resented the fact that her younger sister always looked smart and fashionable, and that it was mainly down to Lizzie's assistance. She'd not forgotten the fact that Lizzie hadn't made her a dress for her wedding, something that rankled deeply, and the animosity between them had certainly not diminished. In the months before the wedding Peggy had dropped numerous hints and made an effort to be as pleasant as she could towards Lizzie, but Lizzie had studiously ignored the matter. It had come to a head when Lizzie made her first dress for Lena, provoking a row of monumental proportions between Peggy and Lena. The altercation had severely tested Nellie's patience, and the sisters were still not fully reconciled.

'So, what did they finally say?' Lena asked as they emerged into the pale sunshine of the September afternoon and joined the crowds on the busy street outside.

'They were very nice about it. It ... it *was* all a bit daunting. It's a very grand shop, very modern, and they stock things that are much more ... exotic than anything I've ever seen before – different from anything we have here. You wouldn't believe the things they sell, Lena – I think a lot of their designs come from different parts of the Empire.'

'But did they give you an answer? Will they be

189

offering you a job designing for them?' Lena persisted.

'I don't know. They said they'd write and let me know,' Lizzie replied thoughtfully. Further down, and across the road, she caught sight of the ornate five-storeyed building of Lewis's – one of Liverpool's most prestigious department stores – and she marvelled at how successful she'd become these last few years. Sometimes she could still hardly believe it. Her initial covers for household matches had gone down very well – extremely well, in fact. Starting with the smaller local shops, she'd gone on to obtain orders from larger stores and finally, after submitting some samples, even from Lewis's.

Eileen had cut back on her own business to help Lizzie, and they had even enlisted the aid of Lena in the evenings to cut out, something her friend had proved adept at. As the workload had increased, and she had begun to earn more than she'd ever imagined she could, she'd bought a second sewing machine. She had discussed the situation with George and Eileen, and it had been decided that she should teach Lena how to use the Singer and employ her full time, if she agreed. Lena had jumped at the opportunity to leave the match factory and now earned a living from what had started as a very small business.

Lately, Lizzie had concentrated more on the design work, for she'd been encouraged to do so by the buyer at Lewis's, who was a very shrewd businessman. She learned that the designs Lewis's commissioned from her would be used for many of the things they sold. They commissioned a lot of their fabrics directly from the mills, and purchased other household and haberdashery items from the factories that made them, and so her designs could be incorporated at source and would be exclusive to Lewis's, which had proved to be a good selling point. The mass production wasn't true to the ideals of the Arts and Crafts Movement, but as she favoured Art Nouveau it was not a concern for her. She was now building a name and a reputation for herself, and earning far more than she'd ever imagined possible – and all for doing something she loved.

'If ... if they do offer you a job, Lizzie, will you have to go to live in London?' Lena asked.

Her words brought Lizzie back to reality. Moving to London was something she had given a great deal of thought to, and she still hadn't made up her mind. 'Probably, Lena, but nothing is certain yet. Liberty's might decide that they're not interested, that my work isn't really what they want, that I'm too ... provincial, or not an experienced enough designer.'

Lena didn't look convinced. She'd seen brochures of some of the things they sold, and Lizzie's designs looked as if they would be very suitable. She didn't want her friend to go and live in London. She'd miss her terribly, for they'd become very close these last few years; they were more like sisters, she mused, and she felt much closer to Lizzie than she'd ever been to Peggy.

Seeing her expression, Lizzie squeezed her arm. 'Oh, let's forget all about Liberty's and London for now. It's a lovely afternoon, so why don't we walk to the Pier Head for the tram? There's always something to see, and we can do some window-shopping on the way.'

Lena smiled at her friend and nodded. It *was* a lovely afternoon; it would be a shame to waste it, and there wouldn't be many more like it now that autumn was here. She could put aside her anxieties for a few hours.

They walked slowly along Church Street, stopping to admire the latest autumn fashions in the windows of such shops as the Bon Marché and Henderson's, and then continued up Lord Street and across Derby Square, where the building of a grand monument to the late Queen Victoria was well underway on the site of the old castle.

'Isn't that Mabel Woods?' Lizzie suddenly asked her friend, spotting the woman who'd once been their supervisor walking a little ahead of them.

Lena nodded. 'It is. I haven't seen her for ages, but she never seems to change.'

'I've seen her a couple of times in Lewis's, and she always stops to chat. But the last time, I got the feeling she thinks I've got a bit "above myself" these days,' Lizzie confided.

Lena shrugged. 'She probably thinks the same about me too. She'd be even more peeved if she knew about your interview with Liberty's.'

Lizzie frowned. 'Oh, I don't think she's jealous or anything, Lena. Just that perhaps I've done a bit too well for myself, considering I was once a matchgirl.'

'Well, she's gone round the corner, so at least we don't have to talk to her,' Lena remarked. She'd never viewed stuffy Mabel Woods in the same way Lizzie had. In her opinion, the older woman took her position far too seriously. She was, after all, only a female supervisor in a match factory, so she had no right to think Lizzie was getting above herself.

As they reached James Street the breeze seemed fresher, and from here, between the buildings, they could see the grey waters of the river capped with white wavelets that sparkled in the sunlight. Across the expanse of the waterfront known as Man Island, the warehouses of the Goree Piazza were flanked by the raised supporting pillars and the platform of the overhead railway, known locally as the 'dockers' umbrella'. As usual, there were crowds of people milling about. Further down, facing the landing stage, there was great construction work being undertaken on the site of the old George's Dock, where it was intended that three large, magnificent buildings would eventually rise to dominate the waterfront.

'Oh look, Lizzie! There's a Cunard liner at the landing stage,' Lena cried, forgetting all about Mabel Woods and pointing to the red-and-black funnel that towered above the buildings. Plumes of smoke were issuing from the mouth of the funnel, indicating that the ship was almost ready to depart, which always provided an entertaining sight.

They quickened their steps and, as they drew nearer, they could see the name *Saxonia* on her bows. The last gangway was being hauled up and the vessel's upper decks were already lined with people, most looking forward to a new life in America, others making the journey for business or personal reasons. As members of the crew moved between them, there was an almost festive atmosphere amongst the milling crowd.

'Wouldn't it be exciting to sail to America?' Lizzie wondered aloud, enthusiastically.

'It would, as long as I could come back,' Lena replied, more seriously. She'd never travelled outside Liverpool and had no wish to, either – that vast expanse of ocean was nothing short of frightening, she thought. A trip across the river on the ferry was quite enough for her.

They stood and watched as the ship slowly began to draw away from the landing stage, ready to be guided out into the river by the tugs. They both jumped with alarm and then laughed as three loud blasts of the ship's steam whistle sounded across the water, the traditional farewell to Liverpool. They turned away and began to make their way through the now dispersing crowds to the tram terminus. Suddenly, they were both jostled by a couple of urchins who appeared to be having some sort of scrap, pushing and shoving each other violently.

'Hey! Just watch where you're going!' Lizzie cried in annoyance as they broke apart and went in opposite directions. 'Honestly! A right pair of little hooligans!'

Lena gasped and uttered a cry. 'Lizzie, my bag! My bag! That bloody little thief has pinched my bag!' she yelled.

'Stop him! Stop that boy! Stop him, someone!' Lizzie cried, desperately trying to push her way after the boys, who were rapidly disappearing, while Lena followed her.

'Oh, it's no use, Lizzie, the pair of them are too damned quick and sly! We don't even know which one of them's got my bag.'

Lizzie realised her friend was right, but she could see that Lena was shaken, as she was herself. 'Oh, what a pair of fools we are to fall for a trick like that! Are you all right, Lena? Was there much in it?'

'About two shillings, and a comb, a handkerchief and some other bits and pieces. But it's not just that, Lizzie. I really liked that little bag; it's the best one I've ever owned. Oh, if I could get my hands on that little sod, I'd give him such a belt around the ears!'

Lizzie nodded. 'There's not much chance of that now. Oh, let's go home. It's just ruined the afternoon. I'm sorry, Lena. It's my fault; if we'd got a tram from Lime Street, instead of walking down here, it wouldn't have happened.'

Before Lena could reply, a commotion erupted a little way ahead of them and a young man pushed his way towards them, dragging one of the culprits by the ear. 'Miss! Miss, hold on a minute! I saw what happened and managed to grab this lad here. He's got your bag.'

'Oh, thanks! I thought I'd seen the last of that,' Lena cried out in delight.

The lad, who looked to be about eight or nine but was probably older, was doing his best to wriggle out of the painful grasp.

'Give the lady back her bag and say you're sorry, and I'll give you threepence and I won't drag you off and hand you over to the nearest scuffer,' the young man instructed the lad firmly.

'Yer won't? Honest? An' yer'll give me threepence?' the lad cried, full of suspicion, not quite believing he had heard correctly.

'I just said I would!'

The lad handed over the bag to Lena. 'Sorry, miss.'

Lena had recovered her speech. 'What are you giving him money for? He pinched my bag! He's a little thief!'

The young man had duly passed over three pennies, and the lad grabbed them and darted away, quickly lost in the crowd.

The young stranger turned to Lena. 'Aye, I'll give you that, miss. But look at him, he's barefoot, ragged and he's hungry. I can see myself ten years ago in the lad. I know what it's like to have to beg or steal just for a bit of food.'

Lena stared up at him in confusion, noting for the first time that he was a good-looking young man with a shock of curly black hair under his cap and dark, intelligent eyes. The whiteness of his shirt enhanced a face tanned by the sun and wind, and she noted his clothes were clean and well pressed. 'Oh, I see, but I still think you're mad. Well, thanks anyway for getting my bag back,' she said, but then continued. 'You don't look as if you were ever the same as *him*.'

He laughed good-naturedly. 'Maybe not, but, believe me, I was. I was lucky; I left some years ago, but I came back. I go away to sea on the passenger liners – with Cunard – but I'm on leave.'

The little crowd had drifted away, but Lena was loath to leave and turned to Lizzie who had remained silent during this conversation. She was startled to see her friend staring hard at the young man, her eyes wide as she shook her head slowly. 'Lizzie, what's wrong?'

Lizzie found her voice. 'No, it … it can't be! It can't be! Ned! Ned Tempest, is it really you?'

He looked startled and stared at her intently, but didn't recognise her. 'Aye, that's my name.'

'It's me, Ned. Lizzie! Lizzie Tempest! I'm your little sister – don't you remember me?'

Recognition slowly dawned on him, and he put his hands on her shoulders and began to smile. 'Lizzie! Little Lizzie! Dear God, I'd never have recognised you! You've grown up!'

Chapter Twenty-One

Lizzie stood staring at her long-lost brother in disbelief, but then slowly she began to smile as joyous laughter bubbled up in her. 'Ned! Oh, Ned, I never thought I'd see you again! Where have you been? What have you been doing? Why didn't you try to get in touch?' The questions tumbled out, one after another.

'I can't believe it! But hold on a minute, Lizzie! One thing at a time!' He looked around, a little perplexed. 'We can't stand here making a right spectacle of ourselves. Come on, let's go and find somewhere we can talk.'

'There's a tea room at the top of James Street,' Lena suggested helpfully. She was as astounded as Lizzie at the sudden appearance of Ned Tempest. Of course she'd known about him, although Lizzie seldom mentioned him nowadays,

197

and sadly she'd thought her friend had given up all hope of ever seeing her brother again.

Lizzie remembered her manners and introduced Lena. 'Oh, this is Helena – Lena – Gibbons, my greatest friend.'

'It's nice to meet you, Lena. I'm glad I was able to get your bag back for you. Come on, we'll walk up and find this tea room,' Ned urged. He'd been on his way to the lodging house when he'd stopped to watch the *Saxonia* leave, and now he was very glad he had. Lizzie was hanging on to his arm, and he glanced down at her and shook his head in amazement. The last time he'd seen her she'd been little more than a street waif – thin, grubby and in rags. Never in a million years would he have recognised her, for she'd grown up into a lovely young woman – quite a beauty. He glanced at Lena, thinking she was a pretty girl too. And both women were well dressed, so they obviously had decent jobs. Hundreds of questions were buzzing around in his mind, but they'd just have to wait a little while longer. He'd never dreamed he'd ever find Lizzie again, and he felt dazed at what the day had brought him.

The tea room wasn't far, and they managed to get a table near the back of the room. It was quite crowded; the mild and sunny Saturday afternoon had brought many people out to enjoy the weather. Lena ordered tea and tea cakes for them all, as Lizzie still seemed stunned.

'You said you go away to sea, Ned,' Lena reminded him, thinking someone had to start this conversation.

He nodded. 'I do. I'm just a deck hand, but I

hope one day to work my way up to be a steward or a waiter; they get tips on top of wages. I'm on the *Ivernia*, a sister ship to the one that's just sailed for Boston.'

Lizzie at last found her voice. 'I still can't believe it's really *you*. But why didn't you try to get in touch or try to find me, Ned? It's been so long. I've missed you, and I thought ... I thought I'd never see you again.'

He looked abashed. 'I didn't know where to even start looking for you, Lizzie. I was mad keen to get away and find work, and you were all living in that place by the docks in Liverpool when I left, but knowing me da...'

Lizzie nodded as Lena poured the tea and gave her an encouraging glance. 'Yes, we had to move on. We ... we moved to Bootle, to Bennett Street – another "flit" – but it wasn't any better.' She left her tea and cake untouched as, haltingly, she told him of what had happened to their mother and father, and of how Nellie had taken her in and then she'd got a job in the match factory.

Ned listened in grim silence, nodding occasionally, although when he learned of his mother's death, tears filled his eyes. 'What happened to da? Have you heard from him?' he asked eventually.

Lizzie shook her head. 'The authorities got word to me about eighteen months ago that he'd died in prison – of some kind of "contagion", they called it.'

'And our Billy?'

'God knows where he is – and, to be honest, Ned, I really don't care. He never had much time for me.'

Her brother nodded his agreement. 'He never had much time for anyone other than himself.' He wondered if it would be worth his while to try to trace his older brother – probably not.

Lena thought it best to try to lighten the atmosphere. 'But Lizzie doesn't work in the match factory now, and neither do I.'

Ned turned and smiled at her. 'I was going to say they must pay very high wages, judging by the style of the pair of you.'

Lizzie relaxed a little and managed to smile back at him. 'I actually work for Lewis's, Ned. I'm a designer, but Lena works for me too. It's a long story...'

He grinned at her. 'We've got the rest of the afternoon, Lizzie.'

Lena ordered more tea as Lizzie told Ned of how she'd gone to live with the Rutherfords, of how much they'd helped her, how she'd discovered she had a talent, and where it had led her.

'So, you see, maybe everything that happened when I was younger was for the best,' she concluded, still unable to take it in fully that she had found her brother after all these years. 'But I still miss Mam. I did try to find her grave, but ... but it just wasn't possible. When I enquired, they told me that, as it had been a pauper's funeral, she'd been buried in a mass grave. That really upset me, Ned; she doesn't even have a separate plot of her own. But I've had a nice little plaque made, and they let me have it attached to the cemetery wall, so she's not entirely forgotten. Now, where did you go? What did you do? When did you come back?'

He took a bite of the tea cake and looked thoughtful. 'I had big plans ... well, big hopes, at least for a far better life ... and I got as far as Ormskirk with the bit of money I had. But I was kidding myself, and soon found out it was no better. It's not just folk who live in towns that live in poverty; there's rural poverty too. I took whatever work there was to be had, not that there was much for someone like me. I was a city lad, and it's all countryside out there, but I managed for a while, just labouring here and there, sleeping in barns and the like, most of the time – which was all right, until the winter came. Then it all got too much for me ... the cold, the damp and all those fields, no lights, and all that ... quietness! I made my way back to Liverpool, although it took time as I had no money for any kind of transport, and barely enough for food. I got what work I could on the way and I was pretty desperate by the time I finally made it, but then my luck changed. I met a feller I knew from one of the schools I'd gone to...' He grinned ruefully at them both. 'One of the many. But he remembered me, and he works for Cunard now. So he urged me to try and sign on for a ship. He took me down to the "Pool" himself and, once again, I was lucky.

'So here I am. I've been going away to sea now for four years, and I like it. It's not a bad life; they feed you well but there's no strong drink allowed, there's a clean bunk in a mess with seven other blokes, a steady wage, and I get to see places I'd never have dreamed I'd see. We're not in port long, though, so that's probably why I've never bumped into you before.'

Lizzie leaned across the table, hardly able to tear her eyes from his face. 'Where do you stay when you're here, in port?' Now that she'd found him, she wanted to know more about his life. She'd missed him so much.

'In a lodging house in Great Howard Street; it's not great, but it's better than some. At least it's fairly clean, and the pair that run it are honest, which is more than can be said for many. They'll safely mind your pay for you, if you want them to. I look after my money myself, but there's some who can't wait to go out on the town and get blind drunk. Then they're easy prey for all the thieves and ruffians who hang around just looking for an easy mark, and they wake up with everything they owned gone. I just don't see the point in that at all; I work too hard for the few pounds I earn.'

Lizzie looked thoughtful, wondering how she could make sure she didn't lose contact with him again. 'Ned, will you come home with me to Olivia Street and meet George and Eileen?'

He considered her request. He would like to meet the people who had been so good to his sister, for they must be exceptionally kind and generous, but he frowned. 'Would they want to meet me, Lizzie? I mean ... I hardly did the right thing by you, running off and leaving you like that, and not even trying to find you again.'

'You didn't know Da would end up in jail, or that Mam would ... die.'

'But I didn't make any effort to find out, Lizzie, did I? Now I really do feel bad about that.'

'Ned, it's all in the past. I'd like you to meet

them, see where I live,' she urged.

'You can come and meet my mam and da too, if you like,' Lena added. 'We still live in Bennett Street.'

Ned grinned at them both. 'All right, then.'

Lizzie paid the bill and they all left to walk to the nearest tram stop, Ned with his sea bag slung over his shoulder. All the way to Bootle Lizzie kept marvelling that they'd only been a few miles away from each other, and yet hadn't known. Of course he was often away at sea; it was just sheer chance that they'd found each other again – and all because of a ragged street urchin, as Ned admitted he'd once been. Oh, they were both so fortunate now, she mused happily, all thoughts of her trip to London gone from her mind.

Eileen was very taken aback when Lizzie and Lena arrived with a young man in tow.

'Goodness! Lizzie, I ... I ... expected you earlier and ... who is ... this?'

Lizzie laughed. 'Eileen, don't get all flustered, this is my brother Ned! I haven't seen him for nearly six years, and we just sort of ... bumped into each other at the Pier Head.'

'I had my bag snatched, Mrs Rutherford, and he got it back for me. We didn't know who he was then,' Lena added.

Eileen had gathered her wits. 'Well, come on in and tell us all about it. George! George, Lizzie's back and she has a surprise!' she called down the hallway.

As George Rutherford emerged from the parlour, he too was a little disconcerted to see Lizzie clinging to the arm of a handsome young man – obviously a merchant seaman – smiling delightedly up at him. But as both young Lena and his wife were smiling too, he held his consternation in check while the situation was explained to him.

'George, this is my brother Ned,' Lizzie announced proudly.

Ned stepped forward, his hand extended. 'I'm very pleased to meet you, sir.'

George shook his hand and nodded. 'Lizzie has mentioned you in the past, but...'

Ned looked a little abashed. 'I haven't seen her for six years. I ... I was away.'

'Oh, let's all go into the parlour, and then Lizzie can tell us everything!' Eileen urged, ushering them towards the open doorway. Ned dropped his bag in the hall and followed them into the bright, well-furnished room. Lizzie certainly had a very comfortable home now, he thought, a little enviously. It was a far cry from the squalid rooms they'd lived in as children, and a step up from both his lodging house and the cramped crew mess on board the *Ivernia*.

He sat on the edge of the sofa, pressing his hands together, as both Lizzie and Lena recounted the events of the afternoon. The Rutherfords looked to be good people, and they were much younger than he'd imagined them to be, clearly not short of money, but probably not wealthy, he guessed. They obviously were very fond of his sister, but he had the feeling that George Rutherford was wary of him. Maybe he didn't approve of him, thinking he shouldn't have just abandoned his family the way he had. The man seemed very protective of Lizzie.

'...and now that I've found him again, I'm not going to let him escape!' Lizzie finished, laughing.

'When do you sail, Ned?' George asked. He could understand Lizzie's delight, but he wondered how often the lad had given his young sister a thought during the past years. He could at least have made some attempt to find her, knowing she was in the same city.

'Monday morning, early, because of the tide,' Ned informed him.

Lizzie was a little dismayed. 'Oh, so soon! I'd hoped we could spend some time together.'

He turned and smiled at her. 'Sorry, sis. If I don't turn up, I'll not get another chance. I'll not get another ship.'

She nodded her understanding. 'Well, at least there's tomorrow.'

'And now I know where to find you when I get back,' he reminded her.

'Ned, I'm afraid that we can't offer you a bed, but you must stay for supper. You haven't made other arrangements, have you?' Eileen asked.

'No, that's very ... good of you; I'd like that, Mrs Rutherford.'

Lizzie understood that there wasn't a spare room Eileen could offer Ned, and she certainly wouldn't countenance him sleeping on the sofa here in the parlour, but for the first time she wished she had the kind of home where she could invite her brother to stay.

'Should we make tomorrow a special occasion?' Lena asked tentatively, hoping that she would be

205

included in any plans Lizzie had; she'd taken a liking to her friend's brother, and it wasn't just because of the fact that he'd retrieved her bag.

'Yes, that's a great idea, Lena. Later on, we can discuss what we'll do, where we'll go,' Lizzie enthused.

'Whatever you decide to do, Lizzie, you must all come back here for supper, for Ned's last meal ashore – you too, Lena,' Eileen said firmly.

'Would you like to come and meet my mam and da, Ned?' Lena asked, a little shyly. 'I know they'd be happy to meet you, especially my mam – she was fond of your poor mam.'

Ned nodded as he got to his feet, feeling a little relieved to get away from George's scrutiny.

Lizzie got up too. 'We'll all go. I haven't seen your mam for two weeks, Lena.' She turned to Eileen. 'But we'll be back in time for me to help you get supper,' she promised.

After they'd gone, George looked at his wife and frowned. 'Well, that's a turn-up for the books, I have to say, Lizzie finding her brother again after all this time.'

'He seems a decent enough young man, and Lizzie is obviously delighted,' Eileen replied, before sighing. 'I suppose he's the only real family she has now.'

George's frown deepened. 'I like to think that she regards us as family, and don't forget he didn't even try to find out what had happened to her. She seems to have completely forgotten all about her trip to London. I'd have thought she would at least have told us how things had gone before she went rushing off to Bennett Street.'

206

'George, you can't blame her for being so totally wrapped up in her brother – don't forget, he's going away again on Monday. She'll no doubt tell us all about London, later on.'

He nodded. She was right, but he still thought that Lizzie could have mentioned how her interview at Liberty's had gone. It was a very prestigious store, and a position there would mean a great deal both to her future and her reputation. George was aware that, if he was honest, there was something else lurking beneath his concern for Lizzie's career as a fledgling designer. She was a lovely, unaffected young woman who wore her heart on her sleeve, and he would challenge any man who dared to betray her loyalty and affection. Ned Tempest had better look out.

Chapter Twenty-Two

Nellie was astonished and delighted when the two girls arrived with Ned and explained who he was and how they'd met.

'Well, I never thought I'd ever get to set eyes on you, lad,' she informed him, noticing he was a good-looking lad and quite like Lizzie – and of course Lizzie had grown up into a beautiful and talented girl. He looked well too, thanks to having a steady job at sea. Poor Florrie would have been proud of them both.

'I've already told him that. But it would have been almost impossible for him to find us, we were always moving,' Lizzie put in.

Nellie nodded as she busied herself putting the kettle on. 'So, you've done all right for yourself, Ned. It's a good company to work for. They're reliable – they seem to employ half of Liverpool – and there's that many people emigrating to America now, and only one way to get there, so they'll never go out of business. As long as you keep your nose clean, you'll always have a steady job and a regular wage.'

'I intend to do just that, Mrs Gibbons. I'm determined I'm not going to end up like me da, or our Billy. I'm not going to waste my life – and I'll not end up in jail, either,' Ned answered firmly.

'Aye, well I never had much time for your da – even before he got carted off to jail. He didn't seem to care much about what happened to your poor mam, just left her to struggle along as best she could; went off on the beer, and her so poorly. Neither did he care what happened to Lizzie; he gave no thought to how she was going to manage on her own. Of course, I've never set eyes on the other one, but it sounds as if he's of the same ilk as your da.'

'I don't know about our Billy, but with my da it was the drink, Mrs Gibbons. He couldn't leave it alone, no matter how often Mam begged him to,' Ned said flatly.

Nellie nodded her agreement, noticing for the first time that Lena seemed just as enthralled by the lad as Lizzie was. 'So, where do you stay when you're on leave?'

Ned informed her of the situation and she nodded, frowning. 'I just wish I could offer you a

208

bed, lad, but...'

'That's all right, Mrs Gibbons, I understand. I've been lodging there now for a couple of years. They know me, and I know them. I'm comfortable enough there ... and it's only ever for a couple of nights at a time.'

'We're thinking of going somewhere special tomorrow, as Ned's sailing again on Monday,' Lena informed her mother as she helped to pour out the tea.

'Trouble is, we need to think of somewhere that's not too far away and is better than the local parks or a trip on the ferry. That would be a bit like a busman's holiday for Ned.'

Nellie looked thoughtful. 'You could always go on one of those day excursions to North Wales, or across to the Isle of Man, but then I suppose that's a boat trip too.'

'I wouldn't mind that, I like being at sea,' Ned supplied.

'We'd not get back in time for supper, and Mrs Rutherford has invited both Ned and me to join them,' Lena informed her mother.

Nellie nodded. 'That was good of her. Well, you can't insult the woman by turning up late for that, so boat trips are out.'

'Shall we get the train to Southport? We could be back in time for supper then,' Lizzie suggested. 'And we've never been there, Lena. Have you, Ned?'

He shook his head. 'I know it's not all that far from Ormskirk, but I never went there. I had neither the time nor the money.'

'It's supposed to be very posh, and I've heard

they have lovely shops,' Lena enthused.

'Probably with very "lovely" high prices to match,' Nellie remarked caustically.

'It's Sunday, Mam. They'll be closed,' Lena reminded her. 'But we can window-shop,' she added.

Ned grinned and settled the matter. 'Then Southport it is. Do you know, I've been to the Back Bay area in Boston – which is "posh" – and the better areas of New York, yet I've not even been a few miles down the coast here.'

'Let's just hope that this good weather holds, then. Now, sit yourselves down and Lizzie can tell us how she got on down in London,' Nellie urged.

Lizzie had to repeat all the details of her London trip that night, once Ned had gone after supper, first apologising for not mentioning it earlier. 'I got so totally wrapped up in Ned that it went clean out of my mind,' she said regretfully.

George looked thoughtful. 'But it went well?'

Lizzie nodded. 'I think so.'

'But they didn't give you a definite answer?'

'No, they'll write and let me know their decision,' Lizzie replied. It had been a momentous and emotional day, and she was so looking forward to tomorrow that she'd hardly given much thought to what lay in the future.

'If they agree, Lizzie, will you be happy to go to London to live and work?' Eileen asked. She would worry about the girl; she was only eighteen, after all, and in her opinion far too young to be alone in a great city like London.

Lizzie frowned. 'I thought I would be, but now

... I'm not so sure. It's a big step to take, to leave everyone I know and go to live amongst strangers. And Ned is only home for a couple of days at a time, so I'd not see him ... and I've only...'

Eileen could understand how Lizzie felt and glanced across at her husband, looking for some support.

'But Lizzie, it's everything you've worked towards. It's a very prestigious store, at the very forefront of modern design and innovation – it's the chance of a lifetime!' George urged. 'Surely, you can't contemplate turning down such an offer?' He was so proud of her and of what she had achieved. He too would miss her and worry about her, but this was her future, one he'd helped her to make possible. It was her chance to become a well-known name and to have not just a job but a career, with a good salary and an equally good lifestyle.

'I ... I know all that, but ... but I'm ... confused,' Lizzie replied distractedly.

'It *is* all very confusing, Lizzie, and you are very young. You've had a tiring and emotional day, so why don't you go to bed? You want to be fresh to enjoy tomorrow,' Eileen urged, somewhat puzzled by George's attitude.

Thankfully, Lizzie nodded her agreement and went to bed. Eileen was right, she didn't want to have to start thinking about going to London – not yet.

When she'd gone, Eileen poured both herself and George a small sherry. 'I don't think we should put pressure on her over this decision. Oh, I understand that you only want what's best for her, and so do I. And it is a wonderful opportunity – if she's offered it – but she's very young, George. She's never been away from home...'

'I know, but don't forget she's resourceful and determined. She was virtually fending for herself when I first came across her.'

'But that was years ago! She's not used to living like that now.' Eileen sipped her sherry and looked thoughtfully at him. 'It ... it's as if you *want* her to leave us, George.'

'Of course I don't! I just want her to do well for herself, and with an opportunity like that she *will*,' he replied firmly.

'So do I, but I want her to be happy too. I can't bear to think of her being lonely and miserable. Life isn't all about ... work, George, and she's happy enough at Lewis's,' Eileen replied, just as firmly.

He didn't reply but finished his drink slowly. He wanted Lizzie to be happy, of course he did, and he half admitted to himself that he would miss her terribly if she went to live in London. He had grown accustomed to her lively presence around the house and looked forward to their conversations in the evenings, which acted as a breath of fresh air at the end of a tiring day at the factory. But she was being offered a rare chance, perhaps even of a successful career, and he would be wrong if he tried to hold her back. He was ambitious for Lizzie, and he didn't want her to turn down this opportunity just because Ned Tempest had suddenly appeared on the scene.

Lizzie was thankful when, next morning, she

awoke to find the sun shining and a mild breeze sending the few white clouds drifting across the pale azure sky. She had vowed nothing was going to spoil the day with Ned, the first full day she'd spent with her brother for so many years.

He was waiting for them outside Exchange Station as she and Lena, in their best outfits, got off the tram and walked to meet him.

'I'll be the envy of every feller on the train with two gorgeous girls on my arm,' he laughed as he offered them an arm each.

The station was busy, but Ned bought their tickets and they joined the other passengers on the train bound for the smart seaside resort some miles down the coast.

'Look, there's a couple of posters showing scenes of Southport,' Lena observed, indicating the coloured prints fixed above Ned's seat.

'One looks like a park and the other a promenade,' Lizzie surmised.

'I expect you're used to all this travelling around the country by train, Lizzie,' Ned joked.

'Not really, I've only been on two train journeys.'

Lena was keen to learn more about Ned's sea voyages. Travelling to London was nothing when compared to crossing the Atlantic to New York. 'Have there been times when the crossing was rough?' Lena asked.

Ned nodded and then regaled them with some of his experiences of the North Atlantic and its storms, which caused both girls to utter little gasps of mock horror, so he changed the subject to descriptions of the cities of both New York and

Boston. 'But I've never been to London, our own capital city, like you have, Lizzie,' he finished.

'It's very big and busy and crowded, but I know there are lots of lovely parks – and of course there are all the historic buildings and churches, though I didn't have time to go and see any of them. I had enough trouble finding my way to Liberty's in Regent Street,' Lizzie supplied, grimacing at the memory of how confused she'd been on her first visit.

Ned nodded. 'I suppose, in some ways, big cities are very similar, but in America they don't seem to have much in the way of historic buildings. Everything is so modern, and it's really exciting, not that we get much time to go sightseeing. It's mainly the dock areas we get to know best...' He paused and looked enquiringly at his sister. 'So, do you think you'll go and live there, Lizzie, if you get the job in this "posh" store? I'm still finding it hard to come to terms with the fact that my little sister is so ... talented. I don't know where you get it from, Lizzie. No one else could draw, let alone "design".'

She smiled at his last words, but then her expression changed. 'I don't know where I get it from either, Ned. As for going to London, I *know* it will be a really great opportunity for me. I can hardly believe that I've achieved so much already – me a scruffy little waif from the slums, a match-girl! But ... but I know I'll miss everyone ... and especially now that I've found you again...' Her words trailed off and she bit her lip.

'You can't let that stop you, Lizzie! I'll be away more often than I'm in Liverpool.'

'But you wouldn't have time to come to see me

214

in London,' she reminded him.

'Why not? If you can go down one day and come back the next, so can I. I'll find somewhere to stay overnight.'

'But what if I'm working, Ned? I might only be able to spend an hour or two with you.'

'That's better than nothing, Lizzie,' Lena reminded her encouragingly, despite the fact that she didn't want Lizzie to go.

Ned smiled at her. 'That's true, Lena.'

'And ... and when you're in Liverpool you can always come and visit us. You'll always be welcome,' Lena added hopefully.

'Thanks, Lena, I will.' Ned turned again to Lizzie. 'You have to think about what's best for you, Lizzie. If you do go, I promise I'll try to come and visit when I can.'

She nodded. 'Maybe I could come up to Liverpool – if I know when you're going to be home.'

He leaned back in his seat. 'You see, it's not all that difficult – travelling, I mean. Not with modern trains and ships. Now, I think we're pulling into the station. So let's go and enjoy what this place has got to offer us.'

Chapter Twenty-Three

Lizzie had enjoyed the day – indeed, they all had. They'd strolled along the length of the promenade, taking in the sea air and admiring the floral displays – although they were now past their best

215

– then sat for a while and watched the boats on the marine lake. They'd gone window-shopping along Lord Street and in the elegant Wayfarer's Arcade, with its decorative wrought-iron work, galleried balcony and glass roof. Then they'd crossed the road and admired the library, art gallery and town hall, and visited the equally elegant Cambridge Arcade before retracing their steps and having tea and sandwiches in a rather fancy tea room on Lord Street. After that, they'd walked to Victoria Park and sat and listened to the brass band playing in the bandstand before returning to the station. It had been a tired but happy trio who had returned to Olivia Street for supper, and nothing more had been said about Lizzie's trip to London.

After supper Lena thanked Eileen and reluctantly said good bye to Ned. Lizzie realised that she too would have to bid him farewell.

'We've had a wonderful day, Ned, but ... but I'm sad that you've got to go,' she confided as she stood on the doorstep with him.

'I know, Lizzie, and we *have* had a great day. But I'll be back again in a little over a fortnight. That's something to look forward to, isn't it?'

She managed a smile. 'Of course it is.'

'And the time will go quickly too. Don't forget, you've a big decision to make – and don't forget what I said to you about it, either,' he reminded her.

Lizzie hugged him and felt tears prick her eyes. 'I won't. Goodbye, Ned. Take care of yourself, and I'll see you soon.'

'You will, that's a promise,' he replied cheerfully as he turned to leave.

She stood on the step and watched him as he walked down the street. He turned to wave before he disappeared round the corner. She wished he could have stayed longer; she would miss him, and they had so much to catch up on still.

The letter came a week later, in the early evening post. She stood in the hall, turning the envelope over in her hands, trying to decide whether to open it now or wait until George got home.

'You'll never find out what they say if you don't open it, Lizzie,' Lena urged, finding her friend biting her lip and looking anxious. Lena had finished for the day and was about to go home.

Lizzie nodded. 'I know, but ... but I still haven't made up my mind.'

'Oh, just open it, Lizzie. The suspense is killing me!' Lena cried impatiently.

Lizzie opened it and scanned the typewritten lines. 'Well, they've offered me the position of an "in-house" designer. I ... I've to write back and either confirm it or ... decline it. Oh, Lena! What am I going to do?'

Lena frowned thoughtfully. 'Why don't you put your jacket and hat on? We'll go for a walk before I get my tram home. It won't be dark for a while yet,' she suggested. She always found that walking helped when she had something on her mind.

Lizzie went and got her things and then called to Eileen that she was going out but wouldn't be long.

'Just to the tram stop with me, Mrs Rutherford,' Lena called too.

It was still quite mild for the time of year and

217

there was a faint golden afterglow in the sky. The sun had already dropped below the roofs of the surrounding buildings, and the faint but distinct odour of the river and the sea beyond could be discerned wafting on the breeze. The lamps on the main road had already been lit, for it wouldn't be long before the autumnal evening dusk descended.

'You *must* have thought about everything and weighed it all up by now, Lizzie,' Lena said tentatively, determined not to try to influence her friend, no matter how she felt personally about Lizzie's decision. She was aware that finding Ned had had an impact on her friend, something Lizzie hadn't previously considered.

'I have, and I suppose I *know* that I'd be a complete fool to turn down this chance – George has told me so, often enough.'

'He's always believed in you, Lizzie. He could always see something ... different about you, something ... special. And he's always tried to help you, from the very first time he met you when you were out scouring the pubs for your da, if you remember.'

'I'll never forget, Lena. How could I? I was so grateful to him that night – and even more so, now. I'm so grateful to them both. They've been kindness itself to me, Lena, you know that. And I wouldn't be where I am now if George hadn't sat with me and helped me with my reading and writing. And he encouraged me to join the library, where I learned about design. Eileen has taught me so much too, and has virtually given up her business to help me get on. The last thing I want to do is disappoint them both, especially George. He has such high hopes for me, and I know he's proud of me – proud and pleased that he's been able to help me achieve so much."

'But?' Lena pressed.

'But if I'm really truthful, Lena, I'm afraid of so many things. Afraid to give up everything I have here; afraid I won't live up to Liberty's expectations. I'm scared that I won't be able to settle or to make friends, that I'll be lonely and miserable, and that it will affect my work. Afraid that I might then lose my position and have to come home. Think how *awful* that would be! How humiliating!'

Lena nodded thoughtfully; she could understand how Lizzie felt, and she hadn't half Lizzie's confidence.

'I know how much I will miss everyone too. And I won't see much of Ned. But he urged me to go ... those were his last words to me before he went back to sea.'

Lena sighed heavily. 'Well, you're going to have to make a decision – and soon, Lizzie. You can't keep them waiting too long, or they'll get fed up and give the position to someone else.'

'I know, but Lena, I'm so confused... I feel torn between everything!'

Despite her sense of loss at the thought of Lizzie leaving, Lena made up her mind. 'Give it a try, Lizzie. If you don't, you'll never know if you can settle down there and be successful.'

Lizzie looked at her friend intently, knowing Lena didn't really want her to go. She was telling her to have a stab at London, despite the fact she'd miss her. Didn't that say something?

'If you absolutely hate it and are as miserable as sin, you can always come back; no one will think the worse of you. At least you'll have tried,' Lena added.

Lizzie realised that her friend was right, although she also knew how bitterly disappointed George would be if she were to throw everything up and return home. She couldn't go on dithering like this. She had to make a decision – and the sooner the better. She squared her shoulders. 'You're right, Lena. I'll go. I have to at least *try*.'

Lena managed a wry smile. 'Thank goodness for that, Lizzie. Now, go back home and tell Eileen. Then sit down and write to Liberty's, telling them you'll be delighted to accept their offer.'

Lizzie smiled too, feeling a sense of relief now that she'd made up her mind, at last. 'I'll do that.'

'Did they tell you what they'll be paying you?' Lena enquired.

'They did – it's a very good salary. I ... I'm beginning to feel excited about being offered a job I'll love doing in such a prestigious store, but of course I'll have to find and pay for lodgings. Then there will be fares, food, toiletries – and I suppose things are more expensive there, as well. I'll have to give my notice in at Lewis's too. Oh, there seems to be such a lot to do, Lena. I hardly know where to start.'

'Well, it should all keep you occupied, then,' Lena replied briskly. 'Now, here's my tram. You get off home, Lizzie, and tell them you've made up your mind. I'll see you tomorrow,' Lena said, smiling, and quickened her steps towards the tram stop.

Eileen was a little perturbed when Lizzie told them about the letter, but George expressed his delight at the news, though with mixed emotions.

'You won't regret it, Lizzie. It's the only sensible decision to make. Now, there is a lot to do,' he said briskly.

She nodded. 'I know. Firstly, I'll have to write back – I can post it tomorrow morning – and then I'll have to give in my notice tomorrow...'

Eileen sighed as she got to her feet. She would just have to put her doubts and worries to the back of her mind. Lizzie had a whole new future ahead of her. 'I think this calls for a little celebration,' she announced as she poured three glasses of her best sherry and handed them around.

George smiled as he took the proffered glass and then became businesslike. 'We'll have to find you somewhere to live.'

'But somewhere that's decent and respectable,' Eileen put in hastily.

'That goes without saying. We'll want to make sure you're safe, Lizzie,' he agreed as he sipped his drink.

Lizzie also took a sip of the sweet wine; she supposed that her decision was a thing to celebrate. 'And then I'll have to find out about transport to work and back, and book my train ticket,' she added, beginning to feel some of her doubts slip away. 'At least by the time I've worked my notice, and we've sorted everything out, Ned will be back and I'll be able to see him before I go. Hopefully, I'll be able to give him an address where he can contact me.'

221

George looked at her enquiringly. 'Do you feel ... better now you've come to this decision, Lizzie?'

She nodded. 'I do, and although I'm still a bit apprehensive, I'm starting to feel ... excited too.'

'That's only natural; it's such a great opportunity for you, Lizzie. A whole new world is opening up for you – even if you are a little apprehensive to start with – and don't forget, you will always have a home here,' Eileen concurred. She would miss the girl. The house wouldn't be the same without her, but she wouldn't say anything to discourage Lizzie. 'And once you're settled, you must keep in touch and let us know all your news,' she added.

Lizzie smiled. 'I will. I'll write every week, I promise.'

'I know you will, Lizzie, and of course we'll keep you up to date with events here,' George promised, although there wouldn't be very much to tell her, he surmised. Life here would fall back into its routine – the routine that had existed before she'd come to live with them, four years ago. Somehow that prospect felt a little bleak, though George couldn't say why.

Chapter Twenty-Four

There was one thing still troubling Lizzie and, although it concerned her friend, she knew Lena hadn't yet thought about it. What would Lena do for a job, now that Lizzie was going to London?

It was she who had encouraged Lena to give up her job at the match factory and come and help her when her small business had begun to grow; she couldn't just leave and abandon her friend. Eileen had cut back on her dressmaking in recent years, but that was something she could easily return to, whereas she was certain Lena wouldn't want to return to Bryant & May's.

The following evening after supper, she went round to Nellie's to see her friend. Lena had left Olivia Street before Lizzie returned home from work.

'So, I hear we're losing you, Lizzie. Going off to London, no less,' Nellie greeted her affably. 'Well, I can't say I blame you, luv, for grasping such an opportunity with both hands. You've done very well for yourself, your mam would be so proud of you.'

Lizzie smiled at her. 'I know she would, Nellie. But I've come to have a chat with Lena. Has she gone out?'

'No, luv,' Nellie frowned. Then, as if she'd read Lizzie's mind, she went on, 'It's not occurred to her yet, what she's going to do for work now you're leaving, but I've thought about it.'

Lena came into the kitchen from the bedroom and seemed a little surprised to see Lizzie there. 'I'd have thought you'd be up to your eyes, getting organised ... doing things like ... writing letters.'

'No, George is insisting on doing that. Come and sit down, I want to talk to you,' Lizzie urged, patting the bench at the table beside her.

Lena raised her eyebrows and looked puzzled, but she sat down. 'What about?'

'You and what you'll do for work with me leaving.'

Understanding began to dawn in Lena's eyes. 'Oh, Lizzie, I'd not thought of that! With you gone, what'll happen? Oh, I can't go back to the match factory, I just *can't!*' She looked pleadingly at her mother. 'Our Peggy would never give me a minute's peace, Mam. She'd take great delight in tormenting me, you know she would! She hates the fact that I left and that I was doing so well with Lizzie and Mrs Rutherford.'

'Don't go getting upset, Lena. I've been thinking about it and, if Eileen agrees, you could both go on just as you are. It would be *your* business, yours and Eileen's, as I'll have my salary from Liberty's. You might lose the Lewis's contract, although I'll try and persuade them otherwise, but even without them there's still a living to be made.'

'But ... but neither of us can design the patterns, Lizzie! And it's the designs that people like and pay for.'

'I could still do that, Lena. I'll have time to myself, after work and at weekends. It will give me something to do. I'll make a template of each one and send it to Eileen; then all you have to do is pin it to the fabric and cut around it, the way you do now.'

Lena thought about it and slowly nodded. 'Yes, yes, that's more or less what we do now. We can still keep to the way we work.'

Lizzie smiled at her. 'Of course you can. I couldn't just go off and leave you in the lurch, without a job. What kind of a friend would I be then?'

'But won't Mrs Rutherford want to go back to her dressmaking?' Lena asked, thinking that the woman might want to resume her trade, with Lizzie gone. Then she could cut back on the hours she spent in the workroom, for she did get tired.

'I'll discuss it with her, Lena, but she knows you're a good worker, and she likes you. I don't think she'd be happy about you going back to being a matchgirl.'

Lena looked apprehensive; she just prayed that the woman would agree. She would sooner do anything, rather than have to go back to the factory and suffer the cutting remarks and jealous jibes of her sister and her friends.

When Lizzie explained everything, Eileen considered it and at last nodded her agreement. 'I wouldn't like her to have to go back to that factory either, Lizzie. I had hoped that I might be able to ... rest a bit more...'

'I know, but I'm sure Lena will more than pull her weight,' Lizzie reassured her.

Eileen nodded. 'She's a good little worker, and she's improved so much lately. I'll enjoy her company too, especially now you're leaving us. The house would be just too quiet without both of you. You are sure you won't find it too much to carry on designing for our little range of products? I mean, once you're settled and make friends, you'll want to go out with them. You're young and you should enjoy yourself.'

'I'll make sure I find time to keep sending you new designs,' Lizzie replied firmly. Just because she was going off to a new life, she had no intention of forgetting all about the people who had been so generous to her.

When she'd informed Mr MacDonald – the buyer at Lewis's who had encouraged her so much – he first expressed great disappointment at the fact that she was leaving. But then he admitted that the opportunity to design for Liberty's was one she simply couldn't turn down.

George, at his wife's urging, had taken it upon himself to find decent lodgings for Lizzie and had scoured the editions of the national newspapers in the library. Eventually, he'd spotted an advertisement that looked promising and had written asking for more details, enquiring if there was a vacancy for a young lady who would be coming to London to work at Liberty's. He'd then studied the street maps of London, trying to work out Lizzie's quickest route to work from the Pimlico address.

When the reply came, it was from a Mrs Braddan. She informed them that she was a widow and ran a small boarding establishment in a quiet area for what she termed 'people of a respectable and sober disposition with suitable employment'. She provided breakfast and an evening meal, should one be required. She expected her 'guests' not to keep late hours and did not allow visitors in their rooms, but they could be entertained in the parlour. She did have a room available at present but it would be advisable to let her know by return post, as the vacancy was sure to be filled very quickly.

'Well, it seems as if she runs a very suitable establishment, and her rates are not extortionate, particularly as she is providing meals,' George commented.

'That's something of a relief. You won't have to worry about buying meals, Lizzie, and it's good that she has sensible rules concerning "visitors",' Eileen added.

Lizzie nodded her agreement, although privately she thought Mrs Braddan's rules sounded rather restrictive. 'Shall I write and tell her I'll be happy to fill the ... vacancy?'

George nodded. 'I would, Lizzie. I suppose good lodgings are indeed quickly snapped up in London.'

So Lizzie had written, giving the date when she would be arriving, and the letter she received in reply seemed much less formal. It gave a brief description of the room she would occupy and the location of the nearest bus stops. Mrs Braddan also informed her that her other three 'guests' were gentlemen of middle age and unmarried.

Lizzie said nothing to either George or Eileen about that. But when she informed Lena, her friend grimaced. 'That sounds a bit stuffy, like. But at least you won't have to worry about where you're going to get a decent meal.'

'I know, but it does sound rather ... dull. But I don't suppose I'll see much of them; we'll all be at work during the day, and I'll be busy in the evenings after supper.'

Lena decided to change the subject. 'Do you think we could go and meet Ned when he gets back? Da's looked it up in the *Journal of Commerce*, and the *Ivernia's* due to dock about six o'clock on Tuesday evening.'

Lizzie brightened. 'That would be a surprise for him, and I'm sure Eileen would be happy to give him some supper.'

'Or we could all go and have something in one of the Lyon's tea rooms,' Lena suggested, knowing it would be unlikely that she too would be invited for supper. She intended to try to spend as much time as she possibly could with Lizzie and her brother.

The evening was chilly, and dusk was already deepening. The lights on the Birkenhead side of the river could be clearly seen, as could those of the ferries criss-crossing the dark, choppy waters of the Mersey. The two women stood waiting patiently, for the crew would not be paid off until all the passengers had disembarked.

Lena thrust her hands deeper into the pockets of her coat and shivered. 'I hope it's not going to take much longer, or we'll freeze to death; the dampness from the river seems to seep into your bones.'

Lizzie nodded, for she too was cold. 'He isn't expecting us to be waiting for him, so I hope he doesn't dawdle. Perhaps we shouldn't have got here this early?'

'Well, one thing's for sure, we'll need a cup of tea to warm us up,' Lena replied.

It was almost half an hour later when the crew started to disembark. They finally spotted Ned calling cheerfully to two of his departing mates.

'Ned! Ned, over here!' Lizzie cried, waving to attract his attention.

'Lizzie, this is a surprise, I didn't expect you! And Lena too! This is a great way to be welcomed home.'

Lizzie hugged him, smiling happily and slipping her arm through his. 'We thought you'd appreciate some company. We wondered if you'd like to walk into town and get something to eat at a Corner House.'

'That's if you've not got other plans,' Lena added.

He laughed. 'Well, I'd thought about going over to the Style House and having a pint or two – a lot of the lads make that their first port of call before going home – but how can I turn down tea with two gorgeous girls?'

They both laughed and began to walk towards James Street, which would lead them into the city centre.

'Did you have a good trip?' Lizzie asked.

He nodded. 'Not bad, much the same as usual. And how about you, Lizzie, what have you been up to while I've been away?'

'I'm going to London on Saturday, Ned.'

Her brother nodded approvingly. 'I don't think you'll regret it, Lizzie. And I'll get down to see you, like I promised. Have you got somewhere to stay?'

Lizzie informed him of her plans and promised to write her new address down for him. 'So you see, Ned, I'm so glad I could see you before I go,' she finished as they settled themselves in the café in Whitechapel.

'I know you've only just got off the ship, but when will you have to sail again?' Lena asked, hoping it would perhaps be a longer leave this time.

'Friday mid-morning, so I'll have to be back on-board either tomorrow night or Thursday night. Would you girls like to come to the Hippodrome with me after we've had tea? There's usually some good turns on there, and we should do something together before you go, Lizzie.'

'Oh, that would be great, Ned! I've only been to the music hall once before. Eileen doesn't really consider it suitable.'

He raised his eyebrows. 'I see. She won't object, will she?'

'Not this time, I'm sure,' Lizzie laughed. 'This time I'll be *suitably* accompanied.'

Lena poured the tea and smiled happily at Ned, delighted to have been asked to go along with them. And she was hoping he'd call and see her mam again before he sailed.

Chapter Twenty-Five

Eileen hadn't been very happy about the visit to the music hall when Lizzie told her where they'd been. But there had been little she could say about it, when all was said and done. And they'd all had a very enjoyable evening. Lena, in particular, had loved every minute. And when Ned had expressed his intention to visit Nellie, with Lizzie, on Thursday evening, she'd lit up with delight.

It would, of course, be the last time Nellie would see Lizzie and her brother together, which was a little sad, but she hoped Ned would continue to keep up his visits – she certainly didn't want to lose touch with him.

Those last few days were very busy for Lizzie as she packed her things and prepared for her departure on Saturday morning. She'd said goodbye to Ned on Thursday, after they'd left Nellie's, and given him her address on a piece of notepaper. She'd put it in an envelope – that way he was less likely to mislay it, she'd explained.

'As if I would, Lizzie!' he'd laughed before he'd hugged her and told her to take good care of herself.

She'd felt a little dart of sadness as she clung to him. 'Oh, I'll miss you, Ned. We've hardly had much time together, at all – and heaven knows when I'll see you again, or for how long.'

'It won't be all *that* long, Lizzie. You'll have so much to do and see; it'll be exciting and you'll be swept up in the whirl of it, so I bet you'll hardly think of me at all!'

'Of course I will, Ned Tempest!' she'd protested. 'You will visit Nellie when you're home?' she'd added.

'I've said I will. And I'll even pay the odd courtesy call on the Rutherfords, although not every trip,' he'd replied. They'd been good to Lizzie, but he had the distinct feeling that they really didn't want him turning up regularly on their doorstep.

'And Lena will be happy to see you, Ned. I think she's taken a liking to you,' Lizzie had confided.

'Has she really?' he'd replied. He was surprised but delighted. He'd wanted to ask her out, but he'd thought that with her being so pretty and vivacious, and him being away so much, he wouldn't stand a chance with a girl like Lena. 'She's a pleasant girl, and pretty too,' he'd added, thinking that maybe he should ask her out. It would be nice to have someone – other than a couple of his shipmates – to spend his short leave with.

On Saturday morning Lizzie was finally ready. Before she went downstairs she took a last look around the bedroom that had been her own for nearly five years, remembering how amazed and overjoyed she'd been when Eileen had first shown it to her. She'd little thought then that she would one day go to London, to live and work. She'd had no knowledge then of *anything*, she'd been virtually illiterate. She viewed the fact that she had achieved so much as a minor miracle. Now she was leaving with very mixed emotions.

She would miss everyone so much; she would miss the sights, sounds and even the smells of Bootle and Liverpool, for both were equally familiar to her now. But she was excited too, and looking forward to embracing a new city, a new life, a new job – and, hopefully, new friends. With a last glance around, and an affectionate little pat on the blue-and-white patchwork quilt, she picked up her reticule and went downstairs. George had already taken her case down and it stood in the hall beside the coat stand. The sight of it made her realise that these were her final moments in this house – for a long time, at least.

The Rutherfords were both waiting for her, dressed in their outdoor clothes, for they had insisted on accompanying her to the station. It only remained now for Lena to arrive, and they would be off.

'You've got your ticket, the address and the instructions of how to get to Mrs Braddan's house?' Eileen fussed. If she'd had a daughter, this is how she would have felt seeing her leaving home, she thought a little sadly.

'All safely in my bag,' Lizzie replied, smiling.

Further conversation was forestalled by Lena's arrival. They prepared to leave, George taking Lizzie's case.

Sitting in the hansom cab on the way to the station, no one seemed to have much appetite for small talk. Lizzie's new life in London meant that life for the friends she was leaving behind in Olivia Street would never be the same again. Yet each member of the little group kept that thought to themselves, putting on a brave face for the sake of the others.

When they arrived at the station, the concourse was crowded with passengers, friends and relations either awaiting arrivals or, like them, come to wave off a traveller. Porters pushing trolleys loaded with luggage moved between the crowds, railway officials bustled about, and everything was overseen by the watchful gaze of a police sergeant and a constable.

George looked up at the station clock and then the board on which departures were displayed, and guided them towards the appropriate platform.

'The train's already in, Lizzie,' Lena announced, pointing to where the huge black engine stood. Steam was issuing gently from it.

Lizzie took a deep breath; there was no turning back now. 'Then I'd better get on board and find a seat.'

Lena flung her arms around her. 'Oh, Lizzie, I'll really miss you! Promise you'll write very soon about ... everything?'

Lizzie hugged her tightly, swallowing hard and feeling tears begin to prick her eyes. The realisation that she was actually leaving was now beginning to hit her. 'I'll miss you too, Lena, and you'll have a letter by the end of the week, I promise.'

Eileen kissed her affectionately on the cheek. 'Take care, Lizzie, and good luck. I'm sure you'll settle in well with Mrs Braddan.'

Lizzie turned to George and reached up to kiss him on the cheek, her eyes bright with unshed tears. 'I'll never, ever forget everything you've done for me, and everything you've given me. If you hadn't gone out of your way to help me – a frightened, half-starved, frantic little slummy searching for my da – all those years ago, I'd not have such a future ahead of me now.'

George felt a lump constricting his throat as he too remembered when he'd first set eyes on her. She'd changed so much that she was unrecognisable as that young girl now. She was a beautiful, confident and talented young woman, and he'd miss her. 'Make the most of that future, Lizzie, but take care of yourself,' he urged.

She smiled up at him before she turned away. 'I will, I promise.'

She turned to wave after she'd gone through the barrier, and they all waved back. Lena was close to tears, while Eileen appeared resigned. George looked silent and thoughtful. Lizzie was going with his good wishes and prayers that no harm would come to her and that she'd be happy in her new life.

It was late afternoon when Lizzie finally walked up the quiet road in Pimlico, not far from the river. The houses were imposing stuccoed terraces from the last century and obviously well cared for. It hadn't really taken her long to find her way from Euston Station – that journey had been easier than she'd envisaged – and now she was standing on the doorstep of Mrs Braddan's boarding house. She took a deep breath and rang the doorbell.

The woman who opened the door reminded her of Nellie, at least in looks, but she was tidier and more reserved in her manner.

'You must be Miss Tempest?' she greeted Lizzie.

'I am, and I managed to find my way without getting lost,' Lizzie replied, smiling.

The older woman smiled back and held the door wide. 'Good, come on in, then. I'll show you your room and the other amenities.'

Lizzie followed her into the hall and up the stairs to a wide landing. She was shown a decent-sized room which looked out over the street. It was furnished comfortably, with mainly heavy Victorian pieces, but it contained everything she would need: a bed, wardrobe, chests of drawers, a washstand and even a small tub-like armchair.

'This is very nice, Mrs Braddan. I'll be most comfortable here.'

Her new landlady nodded. 'I aim to supply

everything that is needed; you'll see the bath-room is along the landing. Now, do you want to get unpacked? Or would you like a cup of tea while we discuss my terms and conditions?'

'Oh, I'd love a cup of tea. I've got the rest of the afternoon to unpack,' Lizzie replied.

She was ushered downstairs to the parlour and then the dining room, where breakfast and sup-per would be taken, and then Mrs Braddan told her to sit down and she would bring in a tray.

Lizzie did as she was bid and settled herself in a chair, wondering where the three gentlemen who also resided here were. She assumed they must be out, for she'd seen neither sight nor sound of them so far.

'Right then, let's get business out of the way first,' her landlady said briskly as she poured the tea. 'I require a month's board and lodging in advance, if you please, Miss Tempest.'

'Of course,' Lizzie said and duly handed over the money; she'd been aware that this would be expected.

'And you will require supper each evening, I take it?'

Lizzie nodded as she sipped her tea. 'Yes please, and I'm not a fussy eater,' she added, thinking of the times when she'd had nothing but bread and dripping to eat, if she was lucky.

'And you will be working for Liberty's? I have to say, I'm impressed by that, Miss Tempest. I've never had a "designer" lodging here before. I usually don't take lady guests, and I should make it clear that I am very strict about visitors.'

Lizzie smiled into the sharp grey eyes that were

taking in everything about her. She was already aware of most of the rules and regulations. 'To be honest with you, Mrs Braddan, I'm a bit apprehensive about it. Oh, I'm confident enough about my abilities, I'm just a bit anxious about ... fitting in, not coming from London or having been to any kind of art school. And I've not lived away from home before.'

The woman nodded and poured them both a second cup. 'I'm sure you'll be fine, Miss Tempest, and I hope I provide an "amicable" environment here.'

'The other gentlemen...?'

'Oh, you'll get along well with them. All three are bachelors and work as clerks in various offices in the City. You'll find them very ... personable and quiet. They are all out at present but you will meet them at supper. Have you any plans for tomorrow?' she enquired. Her three gentlemen boarders were all regular churchgoers.

'I thought I might go up to Regent Street, as a sort of "trial run", to get to know the area and the buildings a little better, find out which is the best way to travel to the store. Next month it will be dark in the mornings and the evenings when I'm travelling to and from work, so I'd like to be familiar with everything before then.'

'Very wise,' Mrs Braddan agreed. 'Why, before we know it we'll have Christmas upon us. I expect that will be a busy and exciting time for you at Liberty's?'

Lizzie hadn't thought of that, but of course her landlady was right. All stores were busy then. But as she finished her tea, she realised that this would be her first Christmas away from Olivia Street and her friends and her brother. She couldn't help feeling a little downhearted, but she was determined that she wasn't going to let it upset her. She had to make the best of things now.

Chapter Twenty-Six

She had worried needlessly about not fitting in, Lizzie thought as she walked home from the bus stop that November evening. She drew the collar of her coat higher up against the bitingly cold air; there would be a heavy frost tonight, she was almost certain. Her first two weeks here had been rather daunting. She'd got to know her landlady's three other boarders and her colleagues at work, at the same time finding her way around the imposing Tudor-style black-and-white department store and the area around it. The West End of London was full of fashionable shops patronised by equally fashionable customers, while Regent Street was always busy with cabs, horse-drawn carts, omnibuses and – increasingly – the new motor cars.

The three gentlemen at Mrs Braddan's boarding house – Mr Coates, Mr Harding and Mr Staunton – were all middle-aged, soberly dressed clerical types. They had welcomed her warmly and seemed genuinely interested in her work. Each evening, over supper, they regularly enquired how things had gone that day and what work she was presently engaged in. Sometimes she would sit in the parlour with them after supper had been cleared away, while she sketched out the designs she would send back to Eileen. They would all marvel that she could produce something so intricate and delicate, seemingly with ease.

At work she shared an office with three others – two girls and one young man – all older than herself and all of whom had been born and bred in the city and had also been to art college. When she'd told them of how she had come to be a designer, they'd expressed surprise but admiration too. Although they all got on reasonably well together, socially they didn't seem to mix, at all. Her colleagues had families and long-standing friendships with students they'd met at college, and while they talked about visits to the theatre, dances, art galleries and exhibitions, they didn't go together as she had thought they would. So there were none of the outings she'd hoped to be included in. But the lack of a social life didn't dismay her too much, for she had plenty to keep her busy. Apart from keeping her promise to send Eileen new designs, she also wrote regularly to Lena and Nellie – and, of course, to George and Eileen. At weekends she visited the galleries and museums on her own.

She'd had a couple of letters – notes, really – from Ned, one posted in Boston. She'd carefully cut the stamps off the envelopes to give to Mr Staunton, whose hobby was stamp collecting. Ned's handwriting had been scrawled, and the spelling was bad, but she was always delighted and a little relieved to hear from her brother, just the same. In his last note he'd promised to come and visit her before Christmas, and she was looking forward to that.

Sometimes, however, she thought as she walked briskly on, she felt lonely. She did miss both Lena and Eileen's company; she especially missed gossiping with Lena, for they'd more or less grown up together. She couldn't say she was unhappy here, but at the same time she felt there was something lacking in her life. Yes, she would like to go to the theatre and dances, or even the music hall, but she couldn't go alone. She brightened up as she thought of Ned's visit. Hopefully, they would have time to go the music hall here; there were so many to choose from, far more than in Liverpool.

Lizzie's route home had become familiar to her by now, and she was so wrapped up in her thoughts that she soon found herself walking along the streets of Pimlico, eager for the warmth of Mrs Braddan's cosy boarding house.

When she reached the front door, she had her key ready and turned it impatiently in the lock. She closed the door firmly behind her, shutting the cold night air outside. Before going up to her room, she paused to glance at the hall table. Her eyes lit up as she noticed two letters addressed to her – one in Lena's rather untidy scrawl, and the other in Eileen's neat hand. She would treat herself to a quiet half-hour with news from home – the perfect antidote to any lingering sense of loneliness – and then join the others in the dining room, as usual.

Mrs Braddan greeted her amiably when she came down for supper shortly afterwards. 'I was in town myself today, Miss Tempest, and I had a browse in Liberty's. I have to say, they do stock some very unusual and ... exotic things, though nothing in my price range, you understand.'

Lizzie nodded and smiled. 'And not in mine, either, I'm afraid. I'll be doing my Christmas shopping in the smaller stores, although I did see a very nice scarf that wasn't too expensive and which would suit Mrs Rutherford very well.'

'Take my advice, Miss Tempest, and stick to the cheaper places. Money isn't easily come by, not for the likes of you and I,' her landlady advised. 'Oh, there are two letters for you – both with a Liverpool postmark,' she added.

'Thank you, I picked them up from the table in the hall as I came in,' Lizzie replied, sitting down at the dining table. 'One was from my friend and the other from Mrs Rutherford. I had hoped there would be word from my brother, he's promised to come down to see me before Christmas. No doubt he'll stay in the seaman's hostel overnight.'

'That would be for the best. Hotels and board-ing houses can be very expensive,' Mrs Braddan replied, indicating that the subject was now closed.

The three gentlemen guests joined Lizzie, one by one, and supper was served.

The following evening, Lizzie left work and quickly made her way to the bus stop. The Novem-ber evening was blustery, and there was sleet on the wind. She'd got used to the crowds of people all hastening home, and wasn't surprised to find the bus crowded. At least it wasn't a very long journey, she thought, realising she would have to stand for most of it. There were a few people whose faces she recognised from her other journeys, and she nodded politely, but there wasn't the banter and joking that took place on public transport in Liverpool, and she missed that. They had been busier today, for the designs for Christmas had to be finalised. As the bus moved through the traffic, she wondered idly if there would be any post waiting for her. She smiled to herself, thinking of Lena's last letter. Her friend was looking forward to Christmas, but before that she was looking forward to Ned's next visit home.

Ever since Lizzie had come to London, Ned had kept his promise to visit Nellie and had taken Lena out each time too. On his last trip he'd brought Lena a gift – a little brooch – which had delighted her, and which she'd taken as a token of his deepening affection. However, when she'd confided this to her mother, Nellie had advised her not to read too much into it and explained it was a frequent custom amongst seafarers. Knowing her friend, Lizzie thought that wouldn't deter Lena.

She alighted from the bus on the main road and began to hasten towards home, the sleet stinging her cheeks, when she heard someone calling after her. Turning, she saw a young man hurrying towards her, his hat pulled down low over his eyes. She began to turn away, feeling a little uneasy.

'Miss! Miss, please wait! I think this is yours!'

Lizzie turned back, frowning, but then she recognised him as one of the passengers she'd noted regularly on the bus. He raised his hat politely as he caught up with her.

'You dropped this just before you got off the bus,' he said, holding out a glove.

Lizzie smiled; the glove was undoubtedly hers. 'Thank you.'

He smiled back. 'One glove is not much use on its own, is it?'

'No, and thank you again, er...?'

'Edwin Pierce. Glad to be of service, Miss...?'

'Elizabeth – Lizzie – Tempest.'

'It's a wild evening, Miss Tempest, so best not to linger. Do you live near here?'

'I do. I lodge with Mrs Braddan, in Brewster Road, just around the next corner.'

'Do you mind if I walk with you? I live further down. I've seen you before but, well ... I had no occasion to approach you, until now.'

Lizzie glanced sideways at him. He was, she judged, in his mid or late twenties, tall and well built, with reddish-brown hair – what she could see of it under his hat. And she noted that it was a hat, not a cap, and his overcoat was of a good material and cut. He obviously worked in the Regent Street area, and she wondered what he did for employment.

'You're not a Londoner, Miss Tempest, are you?' he asked as they walked on.

She laughed. 'Not with my accent, Mr Pierce. I'm from Liverpool,' she replied, thinking that there would be little use telling him she had lived in Bootle for years, as he'd probably never even heard of Bootle.

'I take it you came to London to work? Forgive me ... if you think I'm being too forward. I

243

wouldn't want to pry.'

She smiled up at him, thinking he was very handsome and very polite too. 'I did. I worked in a large department store in Liverpool, but then I was very fortunate to get a position at Liberty's, which I couldn't turn down, so here I am.'

'No, it would have been foolish to refuse that offer,' he replied, obviously impressed. 'Which department are you employed in, may I ask? I have a couple of acquaintances who work there.'

'Really? I work in the Art and Design department. I'm a designer.'

He turned to stare at her. She was a strikingly lovely girl; she had caught his eye the very first time he'd seen her on the bus, and he'd looked for her each evening since. 'Well, you must be very talented indeed, Miss Tempest,' he said, thinking that was probably why the two blokes he very occasionally had a pint with on a Friday night, and who worked at Liberty's, had not mentioned her. They both worked in the Stores and Warehousing department and knew nearly all the female assistants, but they wouldn't have come across Miss Tempest. If they had, they would surely have mentioned her, she being what they would term 'a looker'.

They had reached the corner of Brewster Road, and Lizzie held out her hand. 'Well, I'm nearly home now, Mr Pierce. Thank you for returning my glove and for walking with me. I've enjoyed your company.'

He took her hand and clasped it firmly. 'I've enjoyed it too, Miss Tempest. Perhaps I'll see you again tomorrow evening?'

Lizzie smiled at him, feeling for the first time as he gripped her hand the stirring of an emotion she didn't quite understand but had not experienced before. 'Yes, you probably will. I'm usually on that bus. Good night ... and thank you again.'

'It's been a pleasure,' he replied and stood for a few moments watching her before he resumed his journey, his head bent against the weather.

The following day, Lizzie found herself thinking about Edwin Pierce and wondering if she would see him again that evening. She hoped she would, for she'd liked him and it was nice to have someone to talk to on her way home. She'd wondered why she'd not really taken any notice of him before and had not been aware that he must have walked the same way home as her each night. There hadn't been time to ask him where he worked, but maybe she would find out this evening, if she saw him again. She'd never seen him waiting at the bus stop, so he must catch the bus elsewhere.

When she'd arrived home yesterday there had been a note from Ned, who had again promised to come and visit her next month. Everyone seemed to be getting ready for the Christmas season, and she was beginning to feel very optimistic, and even a little excited, about the prospect of her first Christmas in the capital.

As soon as she boarded the bus she scanned the faces of the passengers but was disappointed to find Mr Pierce wasn't amongst them. She paid her fare and, having managed to get a seat, sat staring blindly out of the window, not really seeing the other vehicles or the pedestrians hurrying home through the dark, busy streets. Oh well, maybe tomorrow, she thought, as she rose and made her way towards the platform as her stop approached, making sure that this time she had both her gloves.

To her surprise and mounting delight, he was standing on the platform, looking eagerly along the lower deck.

He smiled engagingly at her. 'When I got on, there was no room down here, I had to go up to the top deck. I wondered if I'd missed you.'

'I thought you'd missed this bus, that maybe you'd been delayed,' she replied, smiling back and feeling a little bubble of happiness and excitement rising up inside her.

Courteously he helped her alight, and they walked together along the road, neither of them hastening, even though it was again bitterly cold.

'Have you had a good day? I expect you are getting busy now.'

She nodded and smiled up at him. 'It's been busy, we finalised the designs for the Christmas decorations today. They'll be made up and put in place in three weeks' time – ready for the festive season. What about you? What kind of a day have you had?'

'Nothing nearly as interesting as yours, I'm afraid.'

'Where do you work, Mr Pierce?' Lizzie asked.

He smiled and shrugged. 'I work for Dickins & Jones. I'm a clerk in the accounts department – all rather boring, I confess.'

'But that's also a very prestigious store,' Lizzie replied, thinking of the imposing building, also on Regent Street.

'It is,' he agreed. 'But my job isn't nearly as exciting, interesting or ... glamorous as yours, Miss Tempest.'

Lizzie laughed. 'Oh, I certainly wouldn't call it "glamorous", although it is exciting to be part of the designs for Christmas. That's something I've not done before.'

He looked thoughtful. 'Is this your first Christmas in London?'

Lizzie nodded. 'It is, and I suppose it will feel ... different, but I'm looking forward to it.'

'So you won't be going back to Liverpool for the holiday?'

'No. I really won't have time. I'd have to travel up after work on Christmas Eve and then back again on the evening of Boxing Day – and I don't even know if there will be any trains running then,' Lizzie confided. It was something she had thought about doing, but realised it wasn't practical. 'I suppose you will be spending it with family?' she asked.

'I suppose I will,' he replied.

Lizzie thought he sounded a little offhand about it, but she didn't press the matter further. 'Well, here we are. Brewster Road – again.'

He stopped and turned to her. 'I wonder, Miss Tempest, I hope you won't think me too forward, but would you allow me to take you out one evening? I'd like to get to know you much better. Perhaps we could go for something to eat after work, say this Friday?'

Lizzie felt her heart flutter; she'd not expected this. She would like to get to know him better too. 'I'd like that very much,' she enthused.

He smiled delightedly down at her. 'Then shall I meet you outside Liberty's?'

Lizzie nodded. 'Yes, and I'll look forward to it.'

'So will I. But I'll see you tomorrow evening too, of course.'

'Good night, then,' Lizzie said, not really wanting to turn away and leave him – but, as he'd said, she would see him again tomorrow evening. And then she'd be spending the whole of Friday evening with him. The thought put a spring in her step as she walked the rest of the way home. She would have to let Mrs Braddan know she wouldn't be in for supper, and then – who knew? – if they enjoyed each other's company, he might ask her out again.

Chapter Twenty-Seven

Edwin Pierce was waiting for her, looking very smart and dapper, as Lizzie left the store on Friday evening. She too had taken more care than usual with her appearance, wearing a new pale blue blouse beneath her warm navy-blue winter coat and blue skirt. She'd tidied her hair before placing the navy-blue velour hat, trimmed with pale blue ribbon, over her thick, dark curls. She'd even splashed on a few drops of Yardley's Lavender Water, which made her feel fresher after a day's work.

'Good evening, Miss Tempest. You're very prompt,' he greeted her.

She smiled a little shyly. 'Well, I wouldn't want to keep you waiting, it's still very cold.'

'There's a little restaurant I know not far from here, I thought we could go there?'

Lizzie nodded her agreement as she walked beside him, thinking that she didn't know of many restaurants at all, for she'd never been asked to one before. She hadn't mentioned her outing to her colleagues but had explained to her land-lady that she would not be in for supper, as she had been asked out. Mrs Braddan hadn't asked any questions but had told her to be careful and not to be home too late.

It wasn't far, she thought, as they turned into a side street and she gazed with interest at the place he'd chosen. It looked smart yet inviting, and rather friendly, and as he ushered her in she looked around with interest. It was quite small but nicely decorated, she noted admiringly, in the Art Nouveau style, with tall potted palms placed tastefully in the corners of the room. Mr Pierce spoke to a man she took to be a head waiter or some such, while she was relieved of her coat and hat by a waitress.

They were duly ushered to a table for two, spread with a pristine white cloth and good china, and she smiled at her companion across the table.

'It is very nice here. I do like the way it's been decorated.'

He smiled at her. 'I thought it would suit you, being more "modern" than many I've been in. Would you like something to drink while we study the menu?'

'I'd like tea, please,' Lizzie replied, then wondered if she should have asked for something stronger. But she wasn't used to anything stronger than an occasional glass of Eileen's best sherry, and she knew wines were expensive.

He ordered tea for them both, and then they both finally settled on the lamb cutlets.

'I have to admit, I was a little ... nervous about tonight,' Lizzie confided.

'I don't blame you for that. I mean you barely know me, but I can assure you you'll be quite safe with me.'

She smiled at him. 'I know I will. If I hadn't thought so, I would have refused, Mr Pierce.'

'Do you think you could call me Edwin? "Mr Pierce" sounds very formal,' he asked, smiling engagingly at her.

'Only if you call me Lizzie,' she laughed. 'After all, we've become ... friends.'

'We have, and I'm so glad, Lizzie. And I hope you will agree to come out with me again.'

'How can I refuse when you're treating me to a lovely supper?'

'And I'll be seeing you safely home too,' he reminded her.

She began to relax. She *did* enjoy his company and she wasn't going to be inhibited by the fact that she'd never been asked out before – or been to a restaurant, either. She was dining with a handsome, attentive, pleasant young man; the evening was before them, and she was going to enjoy herself.

They chatted while they drank their tea. She learned that Edwin had always lived in London with his parents, and he still helped them out in

250

the house and the garden. He had two sisters; one had gone off to America to work, but the other was married with a young family and lived nearby. He didn't tell her a great deal more about his family, preferring to talk about his work at Dickins & Jones. He'd joined the store nearly five years ago, working his way up from a very junior clerk to his present position which, although it wasn't exactly an important one by any means, was steady and paid a reasonable wage. Something to be thankful for in this day and age, when there was high unemployment.

Over the meal they continued chatting easily together, and Edwin asked Lizzie about herself. She told him how she'd come to be a designer and how apprehensive she'd been about leaving everyone behind in Bootle and coming to London. She explained that she had been orphaned but that the Rutherfords had taken her in, and she'd been happy.

When they had finished the main course, Lizzie declared she was too full for pudding. She was enjoying Edwin's company but was also keeping an eye on the time; she didn't want to cause any awkwardness with Mrs Braddan by arriving home late after her first evening out. Edwin settled the bill discreetly and then helped her into her coat. They both made sure they were wrapped up warmly before heading out into the frosty night. The streets were sparkling under the lamp light as they made their way to the bus stop. At least they wouldn't have to jostle for room on the bus at this late hour.

Lizzie had enjoyed herself; the evening had

turned out to be everything she had hoped it would be. When they got off the bus Edwin offered her his arm and she willingly slipped her hand through.

He saw her right to the door of the house.

'Thank you for a really lovely evening, Edwin,' Lizzie said as she found her key.

'I've enjoyed it too, Lizzie. Can I take you out again?'

'Yes, please,' she said. She hoped she didn't sound too eager, but she did like him.

'Shall we say next Friday evening?'

She nodded. 'That will be something to look forward to, Edwin.'

'Well, goodnight then, Lizzie – no doubt I'll see you on the bus tomorrow evening.'

She smiled at him as she opened the front door. 'I do hope so. Goodnight, Edwin.'

She closed the front door and glanced at herself in the mirror in the hall, before heading upstairs to her room. She looked a little flushed, she thought, but that was probably due to the cold wind. Edwin had made no attempt to kiss her goodnight, but that wasn't unexpected. It was the first time they'd spent an evening together but she hoped it wouldn't be the last, and a frisson of excited anticipation ran through her as she looked forward to seeing him again. And perhaps on their next outing he might well kiss her.

They continued to see each other each evening after work and they returned to the same little restaurant a couple of times. The more Lizzie saw of Edwin the more she liked him. In fact, as she wrote to Lena, she was becoming very fond of him in a way she'd not experienced before. She sighed as she wrote that, wishing Lena was here to confide in. She chewed the end of her pen thoughtfully. Was she falling in love? she wondered. Edwin had never made any attempt to kiss her goodnight, but he always gave her his arm now, even when they were just walking the few hundred yards from the bus stop.

She was seriously thinking of asking him to call on her in Brewster Road next Friday, as she felt a little perturbed that he always insisted on paying for their supper and she was aware that he probably didn't earn all that much. Maybe she would buy some fancy cakes and Mrs Braddan would make them a pot of tea. After all, as Christmas approached he was bound to have gifts to buy, and she didn't want him spending money he could ill afford in taking her out. She resolved to mention it to her landlady in the morning.

Nora Braddan wasn't surprised by Lizzie's request; she had been expecting it.

'You see, what with Christmas approaching and everyone having gifts to buy, I don't think it's fair to let him pay for our evenings out together.'

The older woman nodded. 'That's very considerate of you, Miss Tempest, and I've no objection to him coming here or to making a pot of tea.'

So the next evening, Lizzie extended the invitation.

'You are sure she won't object?' Edwin asked.

'Not at all. I just hope the three gentlemen will make themselves scarce,' she added.

He nodded, thinking it wouldn't be much of a

fun evening with those three middle-aged bachelors sitting there – and no doubt he'd have to undergo the scrutiny of this Mrs Braddan too. These landladies could be dragons.

When Friday evening arrived, it was Mrs Braddan herself who opened the door to Lizzie's visitor and asked him to step inside. She took in everything about him; he appeared to be a decent young man.

'You look a bit familiar, Mr Pierce,' she stated as she took his hat and coat and directed him towards the parlour.

'I live locally,' he replied, looking a little uncomfortable, although any awkwardness quickly disappeared as he smiled at the older woman.

She nodded. 'That probably accounts for it, then. I'll put the kettle on while you join Lizzie in the parlour.'

Lizzie had been thankful that only Mr Staunton had stayed downstairs after supper, and once he'd glanced through the newspaper he'd taken himself up to his own room to peruse his stamp collection. She'd plumped up the cushions on the sofa, tidied the newspaper in the magazine rack, put more coal on the fire and then, catching sight of herself in the mirror above the mantel, she'd patted a few loose curls into place. She felt excited at the thought of entertaining Edwin, her first 'young man', and wondered if the friendship would flourish into something ... deeper. She hoped it would.

'This is very comfortable and cosy, and you look lovely, Lizzie,' he greeted her as he came into the parlour.

'Thank you, and I am very fortunate to have found such good lodgings. Do sit down,' she encouraged, ushering him toward the armchair nearest the fire.

He spread his hands gratefully towards the warmth. 'Do you know, Lizzie, this is really the first time we've actually been alone together? Even when we walk home together, there are always other people around.'

She smiled ruefully at him. 'I don't honestly think we're going to be alone for very much longer, Edwin.'

He laughed, hearing the rattling of china from the kitchen.

'I bought some cakes, and she's making a pot of tea,' Lizzie informed him.

'That's kind of you ... both.'

'I had some wonderful news when I got home today. There was a letter waiting for me from my brother, Ned. He posted it in Boston.'

He looked across at her, waiting for her to continue. She'd told him all about Ned Tempest.

'He's coming down to visit me on his next leave. He's been promising me he would, and I was beginning to doubt him, but he'll be here the weekend before Christmas. Of course that means he'll be away at sea for the holiday. But as he's not been around for Christmas for several years, I can't get upset. Although I'm sure Lena will,' she added.

She'd told him about her friendship with Lena Gibbons too. 'An occupational hazard, then. But I bet they get a slap-up meal, just the same.' He looked a little puzzled. 'Why will Lena be upset?'

Lizzie smiled. 'Because she's fond of Ned – I

think she's set her cap at him.'

'I see ... but him being away so often, and only home for a couple of days, doesn't make for an ideal relationship, Lizzie. I'd not be happy if I could only see you for a few hours at a time, in a matter of weeks.'

She felt herself beginning to blush. 'Would you not, Edwin?'

'Of course I wouldn't. It's great that we can see each other every day. I ... I have to say, I'm fond of you, Lizzie. Do you think we could consider ourselves to be "walking out"?'

She blushed even deeper and her heart began to beat oddly. 'I'm ... fond of you too, Edwin, and ... and I'd be delighted to be thought of as your "young lady".'

He got up and took her hands in his, drawing her to her feet, and she felt a surge of joy wash over her as he bent and kissed her gently on the mouth. She'd never felt like this before; the blood was singing in her ears, and she felt dizzy as she clung to him.

'You are so beautiful, Lizzie. How could any man not desire you?' he whispered, his lips caressing her neck.

The magic of that intimate moment was shattered by Mrs Braddan bringing in the tea tray. They drew apart hastily, and Edwin sat down as Lizzie rushed to help her landlady. The older woman gave her a sharp look as she set down her burden.

'There now, I've set the cakes out on a doily for you. Lizzie, have you told your young man your news?'

'About Ned? Yes, I have.'

Mrs Braddan addressed herself to Edwin. 'I expect you'll be looking forward to meeting him?'

'Of course. But I don't suppose I'll see much of him. After all, it's Lizzie he's coming to visit,' he replied a little tersely.

'Oh, but I'm sure we can all go out for the evening together. Ned won't mind, and it will be a special occasion. You'll like him, Edwin, and I'm sure you'll get on like a house on fire,' Lizzie enthused.

Now she really wanted Ned to meet Edwin Pierce, for he meant so much to her; she was sure she was falling in love.

Chapter Twenty-Eight

In the days that followed Lizzie became more certain that she was in love with Edwin Pierce. He was always in her thoughts; in fact, she'd been reprimanded at work for being so distracted. She counted the hours until she saw him – and when she did, her heart soared. He'd taken to waiting for her a few yards down Regent Street, towards the bus stop, and she looked eagerly for him as she left the store. They chatted as they walked along together amongst the crowds on the brightly lit and festively decorated street.

When they reached the quieter thoroughfares that led to Brewster Road he always put his arm around her and drew her closer, and when they reached the corner he kissed her. That was the highlight of her day, and she melted in his arms, clinging to his lips and wishing the moment would go on and on forever. The first time he'd told her that he loved her, she'd been breathless with joy, and tears of pure happiness had started in her eyes.

'Oh, Edwin! I think I've been falling in love with you from the first time we met,' she'd replied, clinging to him.

'Lizzie, you're such a ... delight! How could anyone not love you? I simply adore you, I mean that. There's no one else for me, Lizzie, and there never will be, I swear!'

'And there will never be anyone else for me either, Edwin,' she'd replied. She could never look at another man now; she was so much in love with him.

She hated leaving him each evening and walking the few yards home, but then she'd spend the rest of the night remembering his lips on hers and his strong arms embracing her, looking forward eagerly to the following evening.

Ten days before Christmas, she had exciting news to tell him as she hastened to meet him. 'Ned is arriving on Friday afternoon, Edwin.'

He smiled down at her. She looked even more beautiful with her eyes shining and her face aglow with happiness. 'That's great news, Lizzie.'

'He'll be coming to meet me from work, so I thought we could all go to that restaurant around the corner for the evening. He's staying at the seaman's hostel, near the East India Dock, so that's quite a way for him to go. But the best news is

258

that he'll be here until Sunday. Because of Christmas – and to make up for the fact that they'll be away – they've got some extra leave.'

She looked so animated, he thought. She must be really fond of her brother. 'Yes, that's a great idea; we'll go and have supper in our usual place. Are you not taking him to see where you live?' he added.

'Of course I am! I'm going to show him some of the sights, and then I'm going to bring him for tea on Saturday; I've already asked Mrs B and she's agreed. In fact, she said she is looking forward to meeting him.' She looked up at Edwin, a little shyly. 'Then I'm hoping we can all go to the music hall in the evening. Which one do you think would be best?'

He didn't reply, and she looked concerned. 'Edwin, is something wrong? Don't you think the music hall is very "respectable"? Should we go to a proper theatre instead?'

'No, no it's nothing like that, Lizzie. The "proper" theatres, as you call them, are expensive, but there are some really great music halls. I'm sure you and Ned will enjoy it, whichever show you decide on, but I'm afraid I'm not going to be ... free on Saturday night.'

'Oh,' she said in a small, hurt voice, feeling terribly disappointed. 'Why not?'

'I'm really sorry, Lizzie, but I've made other plans. I've promised to visit my sister and her family. Do you remember I told you all about our Violet and Ken, and the fact that I don't get to see them very often? I can't get out of it. I can't disappoint them – again. It's a Christmas visit – like

Ned's – but we'll have Friday evening together,' he added cheerfully.

Lizzie tried to push her disappointment away; perhaps she was being selfish. 'Of course you can't let your Violet down, Edwin, not at Christmas. Ned and I will have a great evening,' she said firmly, thinking that perhaps Edwin might take her to meet his sister after the holiday. After all, she was so pleased that he would be able to meet her brother when he arrived on Friday, and there would be plenty of time to get to know each other over supper. Christmas was a time for families – and at least she was going to see hers, in the shape of Ned. She couldn't wait to see her brother again.

The nearer Ned's visit drew the more excited Lizzie became. In truth, it was only a matter of months since he'd last been home. But remembering all the years they'd spent apart, any time with her brother was precious, and she wanted him to see how happy she was with her life now. He was all the family she had, for she knew she would never see or hear from Billy again. He could be back in jail; he could even be dead, for all she knew. She was aware that Lena too was looking forward to spending Sunday evening with Ned, before he sailed again the following afternoon. Her friend had written in her last letter that she had a special gift for Ned, which he must open on Christmas morning – wherever in the vast expanse of the Atlantic he would be. She wondered if Ned had bought anything for Lena? Maybe he would purchase something for her while he was here in London.

Eileen had written that it would be a very quiet

Christmas this year, with just herself and George, and Lizzie had frowned when she'd read that Eileen was a little worried about her husband, as apparently he had become quieter and more withdrawn lately. Of course he was always busy at the factory and tired when he got home, she'd written, so maybe she was reading too much into it, but Lizzie thought it was very unlike George. He was always so cheerful and optimistic. Eileen had concluded by saying that winter was such a long and depressing time that everyone needed Christmas to lift their spirits.

Everyone except herself, Lizzie thought happily. She was in love with a truly wonderful man who was always telling her that he adored her. She was certain that she'd see more of Edwin over the two-day holiday and she'd already bought his gift, a very smart pair of cufflinks set with small pieces of polished jet. She'd been drawn to them immediately when she'd spotted them in a small gentlemen's outfitters just off Regent Street. They were in a design well known to her – the same as the brooch George and Eileen had given her on her birthday, all those years ago. The very first birthday gift she'd ever had. Lizzie's gifts for the Rutherfords, and for Lena and Nellie, had also been bought; they were wrapped and ready for Ned to take back and give to Lena, who would duly distribute them.

When Lizzie emerged from the store into Regent Street on Friday evening, she was amused to see her brother standing staring in some amazement into one of the windows. Smiling, she hurried towards him and caught his arm. 'Here you are, Ned! Oh, it's so good to see you again!' He looked well, she thought. He was wearing a very stylish overcoat which, although the material was not expensive, nor the cut great, had narrow lapels of black velvet, making it look rather distinguished. No doubt he'd bought it in Boston.

He turned and hugged her, grinning broadly. 'It's great to see you too, Lizzie. There's some fancy stuff in there, it looks like an Eastern bazaar. I've seen lots of big shops in America, but nothing quite like this. I expect you're used to it all now, what with working there.'

She laughed. 'I suppose I am. You look very smart, Ned. Did you have a good journey?'

He nodded. 'And you're looking well too, Lizzie. Now, where's this young feller you've taken up with?'

'He'll be along any minute now. He always meets me, and we travel home together. But I slipped out a bit early tonight, I couldn't wait to see you again.'

Ned jerked his head in the direction of the ornate facade of Dickins & Jones. 'I take it that's the place he works? Very posh it looks too.'

Lizzie laughed again. 'Oh, Edwin's not at all "posh". You'll like him, I know you will.'

'Well, at least he's got a decent enough job, Lizzie. That's a good start.' He looked at her intently. 'Are you serious about him?'

'Oh honestly, Ned! Of course I am! I ... I've never met anyone like him, and he's always telling me how much he worships me.'

'So, how did you meet him?' he probed. After

she'd gone to live with the Rutherfords, Lizzie had led what Ned considered to be a rather sheltered life, and he realised that she was probably a bit naive where men were concerned.

'I dropped one of my gloves on the bus, and he returned it to me.'

Ned looked sceptical. He'd expected her to have met this Edwin through mutual friends, not just by chance. 'That's a bit trite, Lizzie!'

'Well, you see, we get the same bus and walk the same way home each night, so he'd seen me before – and I'd noticed him too – but of course we'd never had occasion to speak to each other. It's not like Liverpool, Ned; here complete strangers don't strike up conversations.'

He nodded his agreement, but before he had time to speak she cried out happily and waved, and he saw a smartly dressed fellow approaching. So, this must be Edwin Pierce, he mused. He was older than he'd imagined him to be, definitely older than himself.

Lizzie delightedly made the introductions and then Edwin took her arm and turned to Ned.

'I've booked a table at a restaurant we sometimes go to. I hope that's all right, Ned?'

'That's fine with me, although I hope it's not going to be too "posh".'

Edwin laughed. 'Not "posh" at all. Humble accounts clerks can't afford to eat in those kinds of places.'

'And neither can equally humble merchant seamen! But lead on, Edwin. I'm starving.'

Ned agreed that the place was just to his liking, and as they studied the menus Lizzie looked happily from her brother to the man she'd given her heart to. They seemed to be getting on quite well together. Ned looked very relaxed, but of course he'd probably eaten in restaurants before. In fact, when Edwin asked him about Boston and New York, he confided that there were some decent eating places not far from the docks in both cities, serving good food at reasonable prices.

To celebrate the occasion Edwin expansively ordered a bottle of wine. 'After all, Ned, it is a special evening. We won't be seeing you at Christmas, I'm sorry to say, and I'm afraid I won't be able to join you tomorrow evening.'

Lizzie smiled, although she determined only to have one glass; Mrs Braddan would not appreciate her coming home tipsy. Ned would have been quite happy with a bottle of beer, as he wasn't used to fancy wines, although a lot of passengers on the *Ivernia* were – those with money, or so a waiter in his mess had informed him. He looked enquiringly at Edwin. 'Made other plans?'

It was Lizzie who answered. 'Edwin has promised to visit his sister; he doesn't see her very often. It's a Christmas visit like yours, Ned, and he can't disappoint her.'

'Got to keep the family happy, eh, Edwin? Does she live far away?' Ned asked.

Edwin tasted the wine slowly and appreciatively, and then nodded. 'No, she lives in London too,' he replied at length.

Ned wondered why, if Edwin's sister lived fairly close, he didn't see more of her. But then he and Lizzie had only lived a few miles apart, and yet they hadn't seen each other for years.

Edwin became aware of Ned's scrutiny. 'I know I should make an effort to see my sister more often – but well, you know how it is? It's all work ... and now, of course ... well, now I try to spend as much time as I can with Lizzie. It's just unfortunate that I'd promised to go this Saturday.' He smiled ruefully at Lizzie.

'Oh, we understand Edwin,' she replied, smiling back.

'Maybe next time you're down, Ned, we could all go out?'

Their meal was served and while they ate Lizzie asked Edwin's advice on where she and Ned should go the following evening. He expounded the virtues of various music halls in the city, explaining their locations and the transport links for both Lizzie's lodgings and the seaman's hostel where Ned was staying. He stressed that he didn't go to any of the establishments very often himself. Ned sat quietly as Edwin talked on, but the more he heard and observed the more uneasy he became. The man seemed decent enough, quite plausible and affable. And of course Lizzie obviously was in love with him. But there was just something – *something* – Ned couldn't quite put his finger on. Maybe Edwin was just a bit too affable – suave, even?

'So, there you have it. You've quite a choice,' Edwin finished, topping up the wine glasses.

'We'll have a great night, wherever we decide to go – and don't worry about Lizzie, I'll see her safely home,' Ned said firmly.

'Just as I'll see her safely home tonight,' Edwin promised, smiling at Lizzie.

265

The evening came to an end all too soon, but Lizzie was buoyed up by the knowledge that she'd be seeing Ned again the following day. The two men shook hands amicably, before taking their leave of each other, and Lizzie felt sure that her brother approved of her 'feller'. If only Edwin hadn't promised to visit his sister on Saturday! But she knew it couldn't be helped. She respected Edwin's loyalty to his family and his desire to do the right thing. It only served to make him more lovable in her eyes.

This was the best evening she'd had for a long time, she thought, as she lay in bed that night. She was looking forward to spending the whole day and evening with Ned tomorrow. What more could she ask for? Although she couldn't help thinking, as she drifted off to sleep, that if Edwin had been able to accompany them too, everything would have been just perfect.

Chapter Twenty-Nine

They'd spent a wonderful day together, Ned thought, as he settled into his seat on the train on Sunday morning. Lizzie had taken him to see Buckingham Palace, the Tower of London and Westminster Abbey, and then they'd walked along the Embankment. It had been cold but bright and sunny, and many people were enjoying the crisp day, though he'd been glad to accompany his sister back to the warmth of Brewster Road for tea. He'd liked Mrs Braddan; she'd seemed a sensible woman, and he could see that Lizzie had decent lodgings. He'd been happy to sit in the comfortable warmth of the parlour and read the newspaper while his sister had got herself changed for the evening's outing.

They had enjoyed the music hall, but by the time he'd taken his sister home and then found his way back to the seaman's hostel, he'd been more than ready for his bed.

His sea bag, which now contained the gifts Lizzie had bought for everyone for Christmas, had been stowed carefully in the luggage rack above his seat. He'd been grateful for her advice on what he should get for Lena, to complete his tally of presents. He'd thought about buying something in one of the London shops but Lizzie had suggested he go to Lewis's tomorrow, which would be less expensive and with just as much choice.

He closed his eyes as the train slowly began to pull away from the platform; he was looking forward to seeing Lena again this evening. They got on well together, and she didn't seem to mind that he was away most of the time. She'd said that she had plenty to keep her occupied, with her work and helping Nellie, and she'd accepted his absences as part and parcel of who he was and the job he did.

He always enjoyed visiting Nellie, for there was a far easier atmosphere in her kitchen than he'd found in Eileen Rutherford's parlour. Nellie made him feel welcome, and it just felt more like ... home to him. Of course, Lizzie was used to much more comfortable and less cramped surroundings now – both the Rutherfords' home and Mrs Braddan's lodging house were a far cry from their childhood homes – but for himself, he was used to much simpler accommodation where he felt more at ease.

His thoughts turned to Edwin Pierce, and it still troubled him that he didn't altogether trust the man – didn't altogether *like* him and he didn't know why. He was usually good at judging people, and he wanted the best for Lizzie, didn't want to see her hurt. She obviously loved Edwin Pierce. So was it right to plant a seed of doubt in her mind that he was not all he seemed to be? Maybe he was just being overprotective. He pushed the matter out of his mind and fell into a doze as they travelled northwards.

When the train pulled into Lime Street Station, he was surprised but pleased to find Lena waiting on the platform for him.

'I thought I'd come to meet you. I looked at the timetable and hoped you'd be on this train. Did you have a good time? How is Lizzie? Has she changed?' Lena asked rather breathlessly.

He laughed as he took her arm. 'One thing at a time, girl! Yes, it was great, but I wouldn't like to live there. Like every big city it's a bit ... impersonal, everyone rushing here and there and totally engrossed in their own affairs. But I did enjoy seeing all the sights – well, a few of them.'

Lena smiled happily up at him. 'I don't think I'd like it much, either. I'm not confident like Lizzie.'

'Well, our Lizzie's looking fine, she's not changed. She's just the same, and the place she lodges in is very comfortable.'

'Did you get to meet her young man? What's he like?' Lizzie had written so much about him, but Lena wanted Ned's opinion. Lizzie was obviously rather biased, being in love for the first time.

'I did. We all went to a restaurant on Friday evening. He's got a decent, steady job, seems pleasant enough, and he certainly seems to be very fond of our Lizzie...'

'But?' Lena probed, noting the frown lines on Ned's forehead, and catching the doubtful note in the tone of his voice.

Ned shrugged and smiled at her. 'Oh, I think it's just me being over protective, but I just didn't really ... take to him, if you know what I mean.'

'Why not?' Lena persisted.

'Nothing I could put my finger on, Lena. Maybe it was because he's more middle class than working class like us.' He shrugged and smiled wryly. 'Or maybe it's because I think no one will be good enough for my sister. Oh, let's forget about him and get off home to Bootle. It's a raw afternoon, and you must be freezing standing around waiting on that platform. Lime Street is a draughty hole at the best of times.'

'Mam's got a pan of oxtail waiting on the hob, and I know she'll be as glad to see you as I am. Oh, and I've got a bit of news. Our Peggy's ... in the family way, so Mam's delighted she's going to be a granny, and I think Da's delighted too, although he doesn't say much. But I don't think our Peggy's too happy about having to give up work so soon,' she added.

'And then you'll be an aunty,' Ned reminded her.

'Well, I just hope that my niece or nephew will have a better temper than our Peggy – and without her wages she'll be even worse,' Lena replied flatly as they walked towards the tram stop.

Ned didn't reply; he was aware that Lena and her elder sister didn't get on, but then lots of sisters didn't. Families weren't exactly something he was an expert in. But whatever their ups and downs, he knew a family like Lena's was one he would have loved to belong to.

Ned spent a pleasant afternoon and evening at Nellie's, but as he left and got the tram back to his lodging house, he was again troubled by thoughts of Edwin Pierce. With Lizzie on his mind, he made a snap decision to get off at the next stop and call on the Rutherfords. His sister had begged him to go and see them. It wasn't too late for visiting, he thought. He wouldn't stay long, and his duty would have been done.

It was George who opened the door to him, and he looked surprised. 'Ned! I didn't know you were home. Has something happened? Is there something wrong?'

'No, not at all. I know it's a bit late, but I've just left Nellie's and thought I'd call as I'm away again tomorrow. And I promised our Lizzie I would.'

George ushered him into the hall. 'Come in, it's bitterly cold out there. I'm afraid Eileen has gone up to bed; she's not been feeling too well lately. I think she's tiring herself too much, with this

Lewis's contract as well as the other work.'

'I'm sorry to hear she's under the weather. Lena never mentioned that Mrs Rutherford wasn't well; all she said was they were doing a roaring trade now with Christmas approaching.'

George indicated that he should sit down. 'Oh, business is good – Lizzie sends templates regularly, as she promised. I take it you'll be away for the holiday? I have to say, it's going to be a very quiet one for us, without Lizzie.'

Ned nodded. 'I've been down to London to see her, as I said I would.'

George looked at him eagerly. 'How is Lizzie? Is she still happy, living and working there? Of course, she writes often.' Sometimes he didn't get to see her letters; Eileen just read bits out to him.

Ned smiled. He'd come to like and respect George Rutherford and was grateful for his concern for Lizzie, the very reason why he'd come. 'She seems to be. The boarding house you found her is very comfortable and the landlady is a respectable, sensible woman, you'll be glad to know. I met two of the gentlemen lodgers, and they seem to take a great interest in our Lizzie and her work. They're a bit ... staid, but pleasant enough.'

George nodded. 'If I had the time and could persuade Eileen, I'd like to visit Lizzie myself ... just to be sure in my mind she's happy.' He sighed heavily. 'But I'm concerned about Eileen's health; she's really quite frail, and so travelling is out of the question at the moment.'

'Oh, Lizzie would like to see you, I'm sure. But she understands that you're busy up here.' Ned twisted his cap between his hands. 'And has she

271

told you that she's got a young man?'

George nodded slowly. He'd felt a little concerned when Eileen had informed him of the fact, wondering what kind of person this Edwin Pierce was. Trustworthy, he hoped.

'Edwin Pierce. I met him when I was down there; we all had a meal together, and it was quite an occasion. He even bought wine, although I don't know if that was meant to impress me.'

'And she's ... happy with him? Is it serious?'

Ned nodded. 'She says so, and I know she loves him. You've only got to look at her face when she's with him, or even speaks of him, to see that.'

George nodded and rose and poured out two small glasses of whisky. He handed one to Ned.

'Thanks.' Ned took the glass gratefully and took a sip before he continued. 'But I just couldn't take to him, Mr Rutherford; that's part of the reason why I called. There was nothing I could put my finger on ... no definite fault I could see. It was just a feeling I got that maybe he was trying too hard to be liked, or trying to be ... something he wasn't. I know it sounds a bit mad, like, but I didn't really trust him. I don't want our Lizzie to get hurt, and I thought I should tell you about my ... doubts and see perhaps what you think.'

George took a good swig from his glass. He didn't want Lizzie to get hurt, either – and he didn't like the sound of this. Ned Tempest was a young man who had come across people from all walks of life in his time – the good, the bad, the trustworthy and the chancers – and his judgement was likely to be sound. 'Maybe I should *make* time to go and see her, Ned.'

Ned shrugged and frowned. 'Mr Rutherford, I don't know if that would be the right thing to do. If you go haring off down there, she might think you ... we ... are trying to interfere, and I could well be wrong about the man. I was only in his company for a few hours, after all.'

'Please, Ned, drop the formality. It's George. I can see your point about her thinking we're interfering – but what else can we do? God knows, I don't want Lizzie to make a mistake or get hurt ... we're very fond of her.'

Ned nodded. 'I know that. All I can think of is, should I go and see her again on my next trip home? We aren't in port long, and I won't be able to spend as much time with her, but–'

'I'd be grateful if you could do that, Ned,' George urged. He wanted to go and meet this Edwin Pierce so he could judge for himself. But how could he?

Ned finished his drink and got to his feet. 'Thanks for the drink, George. I'll go and see Lizzie again after my next trip to New York, I promise.'

'And you'll let me know how things go?' George urged.

Ned nodded. 'I will – I'm relieved that I've confided in you. I'll be off now. Goodnight, and give my regards to Mrs Rutherford. Oh, and a happy Christmas to you both.'

Chapter Thirty

The first week of January was bitterly cold and, Lizzie thought, quite depressing now that the Christmas season was over. It seemed a very long time to the warmer, lighter days of spring. But at least she had started work on her designs for the new season, and she had Ned's visit to look forward to. He was arriving on Tuesday and would meet her from work, but he would have to return to Liverpool the following day. It would indeed be a 'flying visit', she thought; he would be cutting it fine, for his train was due into Lime Street in the afternoon and the *Ivernia* sailed on the tide that evening. She had wondered if there was another purpose to his visit, other than just to see her, but as she could think of no other motive she'd put it out of her mind. It would just be good to see him. It being midweek, her landlady had agreed to give Ned some supper, and they could then spend the evening together in the parlour. She was grateful for Mrs Braddan's consideration.

Christmas had been a relatively quiet affair in Brewster Road, she mused, as she looked down with a critical eye at the half-finished design for a toast rack that lay on her desk. It was to be made up in both pewter and silver, and the silver version would be an expensive item. On Christmas Day Mrs Braddan had provided the traditional lunch and sat with her boarders at the dining-room table to eat. Afterwards, Lizzie had helped her clear away while the three gentlemen played cards in the parlour, fortified with a small glass of port each. She'd been very disappointed that Edwin had only been able to spend an hour or so with her in the evening, but she told herself firmly that she understood. It was only right that he was expected to be part of his family's Christmas, and no doubt it would have been taken greatly amiss if he had left them to spend most of the day with her. And their relationship had not yet reached the stage where she had expected to be invited to join them. But she'd been thrilled with the earrings he'd bought her. They were not expensive – that would not have been considered 'proper' at all – but they were very pretty, and she'd worn them frequently ever since. She smiled as she remembered how he'd admired the cufflinks, complimenting her on her excellent taste and promising to wear them the next time he took her out.

She'd had Christmas cards from George and Eileen, Lena, Nellie and Ernie, and then letters thanking her for her gifts, but she admitted to herself that it had been a much quieter and less convivial Christmas than usual, compared to the festivities she'd shared with Nellie and her family. She'd felt a little homesick too, particularly when she'd received Lena's letter in which her friend described in detail how she and her family had had the best Christmas she could recall – mainly due to the fact that, as she had more money to spend, they'd had a slap-up meal with all the trimmings. Peggy and Bertie had been invited and, for once, there had been no animosity between the two sisters. Of course, Nellie had insisted that they do their shopping late on Christmas Eve, when there were always bargains to be had, but the atmosphere in the market had been jovial and festive. Lizzie had pictured them all, squashed around Nellie's table, enjoying themselves, with Peggy the centre of attention now, for this time next year there would be an addition to the family. She sighed and pushed aside the thought that she might have been there, had she not been in London. She had work to do – and she'd promised Lena some new designs too, which she would work on this evening.

Ned was waiting for Lizzie when she left work on Tuesday, his hands thrust deep into the pockets of his overcoat, stamping his feet to keep the circulation moving, for it was bitingly cold and frost was already beginning to form on the glass of the street lights.

'You're coming home with me tonight, Ned. We're having supper in, and then an evening by the fire,' she informed him as she hugged him.

'That suits me fine, Lizzie. It's freezing already! Do we have to wait for Edwin?' he enquired, looking around.

She smiled. 'Of course. It's a shame we won't all be able to go out together, this time; but we never go out when we've work in the morning,' she explained.

To Ned's relief they didn't have to wait long for Edwin, and all three of them walked to the bus stop, Lizzie chatting happily away about her work and asking Ned if he'd seen any eye-catching designs in the shops in Boston.

'You're a bit quiet tonight, Edwin?' Ned remarked casually as they walked toward Brewster Road.

'I've had a difficult day, Ned. It takes a while to ... unwind, and I don't think it will be much better tomorrow. It's the time of year for ascertaining what profits were achieved over the Christmas season, and drawing up the customers' accounts – those that have accounts. Then there's the job of getting them to settle them.'

Ned nodded. It must be deadly dull, dealing with figures all day – and probably in a stuffy office too. 'That would give me a real headache, I have to admit,' he agreed.

They were approaching the corner of Brewster Road. 'Do you have much further to walk from here?' he asked.

'No, I live in Marlborough Street. It's only three streets down, on the right, but I'll be glad to get home and put my feet up,' Edwin replied. 'I'll see you tomorrow, Lizzie. And it's good to see you again, Ned,' he added, before kissing Lizzie on the cheek and shaking Ned's hand as they all parted company.

Lizzie and Ned hurried gratefully into the warmth of Mrs Braddan's boarding house. The fire was already lit in the cosy parlour and the dining-room table had been laid for supper. Ned helped Lizzie out of her heavy winter coat and bundled their overcoats, hats and scarves on to the coat stand in the hall, before joining the other guests in the dining room.

Lizzie's landlady had provided a substantial

winter supper of beef casserole with dumplings, followed by treacle tart and custard. Ned willingly answered the three gentlemen's questions about life at sea, the tribulations of crossing the Atlantic in all seasons, and the sights to be seen in Boston. Lizzie listened happily, thinking how much her brother seemed to enjoy his life. After supper Mr Coates and Mr Harding retired to their rooms, while Mr Staunton added some newly acquired purchases to his stamp collection – which Ned duly admired – before also retiring, leaving them alone in the parlour.

'You know, I could get used to all this, Lizzie,' Ned informed her, waving his hand to encompass the warm comfort of the room.

Lizzie laughed. 'It *is* nice to come home to on a winter's evening. It's such a pity Mrs Braddan doesn't have a spare room, or you could have stayed.'

'That wouldn't make good business sense for her, Lizzie, keeping a room empty when she could let it out with no trouble at all.'

Lizzie nodded. 'You're right – this house is how she makes her living.'

'I suppose the house Edwin lives in must be pretty much like this one,' Ned mused aloud.

Lizzie shrugged. 'I suppose so. I've not been to Marlborough Street.'

'He hasn't taken you home to meet his folks yet?' Ned probed, although he kept his tone light and casual.

Lizzie smiled at him. 'No, not yet – but I hope he will ... very soon.'

'Well, I've no one to take Lena to meet. She's

already your friend – you introduced us,' he reminded her, before turning the conversation to Lena and Nellie, and then Peggy and her news.

The evening seemed to have just flown by, Lizzie thought, as Ned rose to leave, with some reluctance. It would take him at least half an hour to get to his hostel, and he had an early start next morning.

'Next time, I'll try and time it so I'm here for longer,' he promised as she followed him into the hallway. 'But you know, Lizzie, you could go up to Liverpool for a weekend. They'd all be delighted to see you, and I think Eileen worries about you too.'

She frowned. 'I know, and I really do intend to make the trip soon, but there just seems so much to do here. And it's really only at the weekend that I can spend time with Edwin. Even then, quite often he has things to do for his parents, and so our time is limited,' she added.

Ned made no comment but gave her a hug before she opened the door and they made their farewells.

When he reached the corner of Brewster Road, he stopped and stared back down the street. He'd planned to do this earlier in the evening. It wouldn't take him long, and he hoped it would set his mind at rest. If he was later getting back to the hostel, it would be worth it; he could catch up on his sleep tomorrow on the train. He crossed over and began to walk back, heading for Marlborough Street.

The houses were very similar to those in Brewster Road, he thought, as he walked slowly along.

He'd concocted an excuse for calling, but he had no idea what number Edwin Pierce lived at. He stopped outside a house, walked up the path and knocked.

A middle-aged woman wearing a floral apron tied over her neat, plain grey dress, her greying hair scraped back in a bun, answered the door.

'I'm so sorry to trouble you, madam, but does Edwin Pierce live here? You see, I met him a while ago up north, and we got on really well. He said if I was ever in this area, I should look him up and be made very welcome. The thing is, I don't recall exactly what number Marlborough Street he lives at. Can you help?' he asked, hoping he sounded polite and sincere.

She smiled back. 'Why, of course I can. He lives just four doors down, at number eighteen, with his wife and two young kiddies. Lovely young family they are; they've lived here now for about ... four years, I'd say. They'll make you very welcome. I'm Mrs Shipton, do give them my regards.'

Ned was struggling to keep the shock from his expression, but he managed a smile.

'Thank you, Mrs Shipton, it's very ... good of you. Yes, yes, that's definitely him ... them.'

As he turned away and she closed the door, shock gave way to a flame of anger that started burning up inside him. He'd been right to have his doubts about Edwin Pierce, but he'd not expected *this*. Oh, he was definitely *not* what he purported to be. He was a married man, with two young children, and was now making a play for Lizzie, who had no experience of men and was so trusting as to believe everything he told her – including the fact that he *adored* her – and whom he no doubt hoped to be able to seduce, in time. The bastard wanted a wife and a mistress!

Ned closed the garden gate and walked purposefully on as his anger intensified. No wonder they spent little time together! No wonder she'd never been invited to his home – and never would be! No wonder the man had told a pack of lies about visiting his sister and helping his parents! Well, Pierce wasn't going to make a whore out of his sister, and Ned wasn't going to let him hurt Lizzie.

He knocked loudly on the door of number eighteen, shaking with the force of his anger and not caring who opened the door to him. Even if it were the poor deluded wife, he'd still demand to see Pierce – and say why.

It was Edwin himself who answered the door. The colour instantly drained from his face as he stepped outside and closed the door behind him. 'How the hell did you find me?'

'Never mind that!' Ned spat, grabbing him by the front of his waistcoat and shaking him roughly.

'You lying, cheating swine! You stay away from Lizzie, do you hear me? You see her again and I'll break your bloody neck – and that's a promise! Don't think I won't. I've beaten bigger rats than the likes of you to their knees! You tell her it's all over between you, and don't go near her again, or I'll make sure you suffer for it. I'll tell your wife, your neighbours, and your bosses too, just what you've been up to! That's *after* I've given you a bloody good hiding!'

Each threat had been accompanied by a violent shake but now Ned released his grip and Edwin

281

Pierce slumped back, his face a mask of terror that intensified when a female voice called to him from inside the house. Edwin failed to answer her – speechless and shaking with shock and fear – but Ned had turned away and was stalking down the path.

Edwin didn't doubt the truth of Ned Tempest's threats. The man was a merchant seaman who could look after himself and anyone else who wronged him. God knows how he'd found out and tracked Edwin down to this house, but it was all over now between himself and Lizzie. He'd have to tell her tomorrow, and that only added to his desperation.

Chapter Thirty-One

The following evening, it wasn't until they had alighted from the bus and had walked some way down the street towards Brewster Road that Lizzie noticed that Edwin was very quiet. In fact, he had been quiet for almost their entire journey, she thought. As usual, she had chatted on about the events of her day, but he'd said little about his day at work.

She looked up at him, frowning slightly. 'Edwin, is there something wrong? Are you not feeling well? Have you had a trying day at work?'

To her concern, he didn't reply but just kept on walking towards the junction. 'Edwin, what is it?' she pressed.

He stopped as they reached the corner of her road, and she was even more disconcerted when he removed her hand from his arm. 'Lizzie, there's something I have to ... say and ... and there's no easy way of doing it. I'm sorry, but I'm afraid that I won't be seeing you again. It ... it's all over between us.'

She stared up at him, utterly bewildered, unable to believe what he'd just said. 'Edwin! Edwin ... what ... do you mean?' she stammered.

He frowned. 'Don't you understand, Lizzie? It's over ... finished! From now on, I'll be getting a later bus and...'

She clutched at his arm as her heart lurched sickeningly. It couldn't be true! It just *couldn't!* 'Edwin ... why? What have I done? I love you, don't you understand that? You swore you loved me ... *adored* me!' she cried, too numb with shock even for tears.

Again he detached her hand from his arm and shook his head. 'It's nothing you've done or said, Lizzie. It's just ... it's just that I don't love you. So what is the point of dragging things on? It's better that we end it now.'

She'd begun to tremble and her throat felt so constricted that she couldn't speak. Shock, grief and pain were numbing her mind.

'Don't take it too hard, Lizzie, these things ... happen. You think you're in love and then you find you're not. It's part of life. You'll soon meet someone else, you're too beautiful to be on your own for long.'

'No! No! You can't ... mean it, Edwin! You *can't!*' she cried aloud, finding her voice. Waves of anguish and hurt washed over her. He didn't love her! He didn't want to see her ever again! How was she going to carry on without him? He'd said it was part of 'life', but what point was there to her life now?

'I'd better be going. Goodbye, Lizzie, and I'm sorry ... sorry it hasn't worked out for us. You're a lovely girl ... and I mean that.'

She stood rooted to the spot as she watched him turn and walk away from her. He was walking out of her life, and she was powerless to do anything about it. The cold wind stung her cheeks but it was nothing to the icy despair that filled her heart.

When he'd disappeared from her sight, Lizzie slowly turned into Brewster Road and, at last, the tears came. She was so blinded by them she could hardly see, but as she finally reached Mrs Braddan's house she knew that all she wanted to do was go up to her room and cry. She hadn't felt so utterly miserable and bereft since her mam died, and she'd been little more than a child then. This seemed far, far worse.

She went straight upstairs and, without bothering to take off her coat, collapsed on to the bed. Pulling the eiderdown around her, she sobbed into her pillow, ignoring the fact that the room was cold and dark. How could Edwin do this to her? How many times had he sworn he loved her, that she was the only girl for him? She'd had hopes of marriage, one day. Why had he suddenly stopped loving her, or maybe ... maybe he never really had? Maybe he'd been lying to her all this time? And he'd known how much she loved him. So how could he be so cruel as to just say it was all over and walk away? How was she going to face the days ahead without him? It was as if all the brightness – all the joy, happiness and hope – had disappeared from her life. How could she possibly go on now? She'd never cope with work, putting a brave face on her sorrow every day, amongst people she really didn't know. She wept uncontrollably into the pillow, broken and beaten down by the loss of him.

It was almost half an hour later when she finally became aware that someone was knocking on the door. She raised her aching head from the damp pillow, her eyes so swollen she could hardly see.

'Miss Tempest! Miss Tempest, are you all right? Will you be coming down to supper?' It was her landlady's voice.

Slowly Lizzie sat up and rubbed her eyes. 'I … I don't think so, Mrs Braddan. I … I'm not feeling very well, I … I'm so … tired,' she managed to reply, hoping the woman would go away and leave her to her misery.

'Dear me, Miss Tempest, I'm sorry to hear that. Well, you stay in bed and I'll bring you something up on a tray,' her landlady called back.

As her landlady's footsteps faded, she dragged herself to her feet and managed eventually to light the gas jet beneath the frosted mantel, despite her shaking hands. She took off her coat and hung it up, catching sight of herself in the mirror on the dressing table. She looked terrible; her hair had started to come loose from its pins, her face was blotched, and her eyes were little more than slits. She certainly didn't look well, nor did she feel it, and she was sure that any food would choke her.

She sank down in the little chair, trying, without much success, to control her emotions.

When Mrs Braddan returned, she got up and opened the door to her.

'I've brought you up some hot soup and a fresh roll, and a pot of tea to...' Nora Braddan's words died as she took in Lizzie's appearance. She set the tray down quickly on the bedside table. 'Miss Tempest! Lizzie! Whatever is the matter? What's happened?'

Lizzie couldn't hold back her feelings and began to sob incoherently. The older woman put her arms around her and guided her towards the bed, wondering if she should fetch her smelling salts, for the girl was distraught, even verging on the hysterical. Yet there had been no letters for Lizzie that day, so it wasn't bad news from home. Was it something to do with her job? She sincerely hoped not, for she liked the girl and would hate to have to tell her she must find other accommodation if she couldn't pay her rent. 'Now, try to calm down and tell me what has happened that has upset you so much, Lizzie?' she urged.

Between sobs Lizzie told her of Edwin's decision to end their relationship so unexpectedly, of how he'd stopped loving her, and how she now felt that her world had come crashing down around her.

'Oh, Lizzie, I'm so sorry, dear,' Nora Braddan soothed, thankful that it wasn't something far more serious. Obviously, Edwin Pierce had been the girl's first love, and she was devastated, but the older woman knew from experience that young hearts mend quickly. 'Try not to take it too hard. I know it's a terrible shock and that, right now, you feel you'll never get over it. But believe me, Lizzie, you will. You're very young, and men can be devils sometimes with the heartache they cause. Now, I'll pour you a cup of tea and you try and get some of this soup down you, and then get some sleep. That'll be the best thing for you, dear,' she urged sympathetically.

Lizzie sipped the tea half-heartedly, but felt she couldn't face the soup. How was she supposed to sleep when her heart was broken into little pieces? And how was she going to face tomorrow and all the endless tomorrows that stretched ahead of her? 'I ... I'll try and sleep now,' she managed to get out, at last.

Nora Braddan nodded. 'Good girl, for it won't do to go into work tomorrow in such a state. A good night's sleep will do you the world of good, and things never look quite so bad in the morning.'

Although she was certain she wouldn't sleep, Lizzie was so exhausted and drained that before long she had fallen into a deep slumber. But when she awoke next morning it was with a feeling of such loss and despair that she couldn't face either the journey to work or the day that stretched ahead of her.

She did what she could to repair the ravages of grief still evident on her face, but she barely touched her breakfast and walked to the bus stop in a daze. She didn't know how she got through the day, for she struggled to concentrate and was relieved when it was time for the store to close. But as she stepped out into the bitterly cold

January evening she knew that another ordeal lay ahead of her – the journey home, on her own, for the first time in months.

She tried to stop herself from looking for Edwin as she stood at the bus stop, and she kept her eyes fixed on the floor as she took her seat. As usual, the vehicle was crowded. But in her heart she knew he wasn't on this particular bus, and never would be again. *It's over. It's over.* These were the words that had filled her mind all day. But at least – somehow – she had got through the day, and she now clung to the hope that Nora Braddan was right; that in time, at least, she'd begin to feel better, for at this precise moment she couldn't envisage ever forgetting Edwin.

The journey passed in a blur, and Lizzie barely noticed when people jostled her as the bus filled up with more passengers at each stop. People started to alight once the bus had crossed the river, and the bus was half empty by the time it arrived in Pimlico. Lizzie walked dejectedly towards Brewster Road, trying not to think about how it had felt to walk with her arm through Edwin's, chatting about the events of the day.

When she arrived home, there was a letter waiting for her. 'Came only half an hour ago in the late post,' her landlady informed her.

Lizzie knew it was from George or Eileen, for it wasn't Lena's untidy scrawl, and Ned had sailed this very afternoon.

She opened it without much interest. It was from George, stating that Eileen hadn't been too well but was now on the mend. He hoped she hadn't succumbed to any of the winter ailments, that she was still enjoying her work and the company of her friend Edwin, and he asked her to write soon. She put the letter back into the envelope. She would have to reply, of course. But how could she tell him and Eileen that she was utterly devastated and was finding it hard to even think straight?

Suddenly, all she wanted to do was go home. Home to Bootle. Home to Olivia Street and Bennett Street, where there were people who really cared for her – and always would do – and where Ned would be returning after this trip. They all loved her, as Edwin Pierce did not. She knew she could always rely on them; they'd never just cast her aside the way he'd done. But with a deepening sense of sorrow she realised that she couldn't leave her life here and run back home – not when George and Eileen, and even Lena and Ned, were all so proud of what she had achieved. No, she would just have to stay and try to learn to live without Edwin and the hopes she'd been building in her mind of a future together. Somehow she would have to try to pick up the pieces of her life. But she knew she would never get over him, nor would she trust another man with her heart.

Chapter Thirty-Two

Throughout the entire trip Ned had worried about Lizzie, and whether Edwin Pierce had indeed ended the relationship, although he was confident he would have done. Poor Lizzie would be broken-hearted, he knew, and the fact that she was so far from home and everyone who really cared for her would only make matters worse. She'd be upset and miserable, living and working in a city of strangers, coming back each night to an impersonal house and the company of three middle-aged bachelors and Nora Braddan. He'd determined that as soon as he got back to Liverpool he would go and see George, and hopefully find out if his sister had written to them concerning Edwin Pierce.

It was well after six when, on the afternoon he arrived back from Boston, he turned up on the Rutherfords' doorstep, having come straight from the *Ivernia*.

'Ned, how nice of you to call. I'm sorry I missed you last time. I'm afraid Lena's already gone home,' Eileen greeted him pleasantly, ushering him inside.

'I'll go straight on to Bennett Street from here, but I called to see George. Is he home yet?' he enquired.

She nodded. 'Just about ten minutes ago,' she informed him.

George felt a sense of relief as his wife ushered Lizzie's brother into the parlour. So far, Lizzie hadn't replied to the last letter he'd sent her, but her brother might have news of her. 'Ned, it's good to see you.'

Eileen discreetly left and went to attend to the supper.

'I went down to see our Lizzie, George, before this last trip, like I promised I would.'

'How was she? We haven't heard from her while

you've been away. I did write her a short note, asking how she was, and posted it on the day you sailed. It's unlike her not to reply.'

Ned nodded grimly. That sounded ominous, for his sister wrote regularly and would surely have responded to George's letter. 'I was only there for one night, and she was fine when I left her. But I've been worrying about her all trip because ... because I found out that that bastard Pierce is a married man with two young kids!'

George stared at him, horrified. 'Lizzie...?'

'Lizzie didn't know, George. Pierce was just stringing her along, spinning her all kinds of lies, and I think we both know what for, so I put the frighteners on him. I was bloody furious, and I told him in no uncertain terms to leave her alone from now on, to end it, or I'd give him the hiding of his miserable life – and what's more, I'd tell his wife, his neighbours and his employers, if he didn't.' Ned sighed heavily. 'And it looks as if he *has* ended it, if Lizzie hasn't written.'

George could imagine what Lizzie would be going through. He felt upset, frustrated and angry. Upset for Lizzie; frustrated that he could do nothing to help ease her pain; and furious with Edwin Pierce. He stood up and began to pace up and down as he tried to think of some way to help Lizzie. 'I just wish I could go down to see her, Ned. She must be very, very upset, with no one to turn to.'

'I know, but it's just not possible for you to go, George, and I'm only sorry that I can't make it this time, either. We've got a quick turnaround, for some reason best known to the Cunard powers that be. Most likely, there's a strike in the offing, though I hope not.'

The thought of Lizzie down in London alone, and breaking her heart over that worthless bastard, was almost too much for George to contemplate. 'Would Lena go, Ned? They're close friends; surely she'd be a comfort to Lizzie. I'd be quite happy to pay her expenses, and I'm sure Eileen would agree.'

Ned frowned, knowing Lena didn't have his sister's self-confidence and had never been outside Liverpool in her life, never mind on her own. 'I can ask her, George.'

George nodded. 'I'm sure when you've explained things to her, Ned, she won't refuse. We just can't sit back and do ... nothing for Lizzie.'

Ned wondered just how much he should tell Lena. Would Lena knowing make it even harder for Lizzie to bear the pain of finding out the man she loved, and who'd sworn he loved her, was married with a family? He just didn't know.

Both Lena and Nellie listened with growing concern as Ned told them of Edwin Pierce's treatment of Lizzie, and of both his and George Rutherford's anxiety about how Lizzie would be coping. But Lena looked decidedly fearful when he suggested that she should go and visit his sister in London.

'Ned, I ... I don't know if I could! It's so far, and I'd be terrified I'd get lost–'

'In the name of God, Lena, you've a tongue in yer 'ead, girl! Just ask someone the way!' Nellie interrupted. Lizzie wasn't the first, nor the last, who'd be taken in by some silver-tongued charmer like this Pierce bloke. Thank God Ned had found out about him before Lizzie had succumbed to what she was in no doubt were his intentions. But she knew the girl would be broken-hearted just the same. 'She's yer friend and she's down there on her own, no doubt at her wits' end, with no one to turn to. Besides, it will do yer good to travel a bit,' she urged.

'George will pay your expenses, Lena, and I'll give you written directions of how to get to Brewster Road when you get off the train at Euston,' Ned encouraged her.

'And yer can write an' tell Lizzie that yer coming to visit. No need to say why, an' she might even be able to meet yer off the train,' Nellie added.

Lena nodded slowly. She couldn't bear to think of Lizzie upset, abandoned and bereft of a friendly shoulder to cry on. 'I'll go at the weekend. But what do I say to her? Ned, we don't know if that Pierce feller has told her he's married. Or if he just dumped her, like you told him to, without giving her any reason why.'

Ned looked perturbed, knowing she had a point.

It was Nellie who decided the matter. 'I think she'd better be told the truth. Oh, it will make her feel even worse at first, but it's better that yer don't keep something like that from her. At least she'll know *why* it all had to end, and she might well feel – in time – that she had a lucky escape. And in future she might be a bit more careful who she falls for.'

'She might well blame everything on me, Mrs

Gibbons,' Ned remarked gloomily. 'After all, it was me who found him out and put a stop to it.'

'She just might, lad, but she'll come ter see that you only had her best interests at heart. What kind of a brother would yer be if yer didn't care who she was mixed up with? And, she'd have got hurt in the end. That feller couldn't keep up the lies for ever. 'E'd trip 'imself up one day, they always do.'

'I'll point that out to her, Ned,' Lena promised, for she didn't want Ned blamed unfairly. But she really wasn't looking forward to this, her first trip to London, very much at all. However, she'd promised she'd go, so she couldn't back down now – and besides, poor Lizzie needed her.

It had been decided that Lena wouldn't leave it to the weekend, but would go on Thursday and stay until Sunday. To her profound relief and mild astonishment, she had found the journey not frightening or tedious at all. On the train to Euston she'd got chatting to another passenger, a young woman in her early thirties with whom she had quite a few things in common, and so before she knew it they had arrived in London. Her newfound friend had directed her to the right bus stop, and she'd gazed out of the window of the bus at the bustling streets of the capital with avid interest until the conductor obligingly called out her stop.

When she alighted, she glanced again at Ned's instructions and began to walk towards Brewster Road. It all looked much 'posher' than either Bennett Street or Olivia Street, and she wondered what this Mrs Braddan would be like. Lizzie would be at work today and tomorrow, and it had been decided that Lena would stay at Lizzie's lodgings for the three nights, having never been away from home before. Mrs Braddan had kindly agreed to put a camp bed in Lizzie's room – and of course Lena would take breakfast and supper with the other lodgers. She'd been rather relieved at these arrangements, for she'd felt very apprehensive about her visit and wanted to be able to spend as much time with her friend as she could.

Turning into Brewster Road, Lena noted with approval the imposing and well-kept frontage to each house. She continued down the street, checking until she found the right house number, then walked up the neat, polished front steps to Mrs Braddan's front door. She took a deep breath to settle her nerves before lifting the brass knocker.

'I'm Lena Gibbons, Lizzie's friend from Liverpool,' she introduced herself when Nora Braddan opened the door to her.

The woman looked relieved to see her. 'Well, I have to say, Miss Gibbons, I'm very glad you've come. She's really cut up over all this ... unpleasantness. She's hardly eaten enough to keep a bird alive, and she's going about in a sort of daze.'

'Oh, poor Lizzie!' Lena replied, wondering whether she should mention to Mrs Braddan that Edwin Pierce's conduct was worse than Lizzie thought it was. She decided against it, for the woman might view her friend in an altogether different light if she knew Edwin was married.

Lena had unpacked her few things in Lizzie's room, and had a welcome cup of tea, when Lizzie arrived home. Lena took one look at her friend's pale face, her haunted eyes, and rushed to hug her, the tears pricking her own eyes. 'Oh, Lizzie! I wish there was *something* I could do or say that would help! But at least I'm *here!*'

Lizzie clung to her, tears sliding down her cheeks, which were still cold from the wintry weather outside, but with relief flooding through her.

'Come on into the parlour. There's still tea in the pot ... and we can talk,' Lena urged.

Lizzie shook her head, dashing away her tears with the back of her hand. 'No, the others will be in soon. I ... I'd rather go upstairs.'

Lena nodded, thinking the sooner she got this over with the better they'd both feel. They sat on the bed, and Lena took Lizzie's hand.

'Oh, we've all been so worried about you, Lizzie. George and Eileen were really concerned that you haven't written.'

'I ... I couldn't, Lena. I just couldn't bring myself to tell them about ... it all.' She looked at her friend closely. 'He... Edwin just told me it was ... over! He just didn't love me.' It still hurt to utter his name, and in her dazed state it hadn't occurred to Lizzie that Lena already knew. She just thought Lena had, at last, decided to visit, and had been grateful for the fact.

'I ... we know, Lizzie. Ned told us. That's why I've come, because neither Ned nor George could get away – and besides, I wanted to try to help you get over ... him.'

Lizzie frowned, puzzled. 'Ned? How did Ned know? Everything was fine when he left here.'

Lena took a deep breath. 'Oh, Lizzie. I just don't know how to tell you this, but ... but Ned found out that Edwin Pierce is married. He found out where he lives and ... and was terribly shocked and furious when he discovered that *that* feller has a wife and two young kids. It was Ned who told him never to see you again or he'd do his best not only to ruin his life but he'd beat him up as well. Ned only wants the best for you, Lizzie; we all do. He couldn't just come back to Liverpool and sail off, knowing how that feller was stringing you along. He had to do something. Oh, Lizzie, luv, I'm so, so sorry.'

During this explanation Lizzie had stared at Lena, her eyes growing wider and wider with shock and horror. 'Married! And with ... with ... children! I ... I don't believe it, Lena! He couldn't be! I'd have known, I would! I ... I never even ... suspected.'

'Of course you didn't, Lizzie.' Lena put her arm around Lizzie's shoulders. 'How could you? He didn't want *you* to know!'

'It ... it makes it all so much ... worse, Lena! I feel such a *fool!* I feel so ... humiliated. He never loved me – how could he?'

Lena nodded sadly. 'That's why I've come, Lizzie. We couldn't let you go on believing ... even hoping he might change his mind. He needs horsewhipping for what he's put you through. But at least, luv, you know now that he didn't just drop you.'

Lizzie took a deep breath. Lena was right, for

297

she had begun to hope he'd come back to her, that one evening he'd be waiting for her at the bus stop. But knowing the truth didn't help. She felt even worse now; she felt she had just been *used*. How could he tell her such barefaced lies? How could she have been so blind and trusting? How could she ever trust another man again after this? Tears began to fall rapidly down her cheeks and, as Lena gathered her in her arms, she sobbed out the bitter hurt and humiliation that engulfed her.

By the time Lena was due to return to Liverpool Lizzie had begun to feel a little better, a little more resigned to her loss; she seemed less dazed and certainly less confused.

Lena had plucked up enough courage to come to meet her from work on the Friday evening, and Lizzie had shown her friend some of the fine shops on Regent Street. Nora Braddan and the three gentlemen lodgers had all liked Lena, and she had been made to feel very at home in Brewster Road. On Saturday she had persuaded Lizzie to show her some of the sights of London, and Lizzie had even raised a smile at her friend's obvious enjoyment of their sightseeing excursion. On Sunday, when Lizzie accompanied her to the station, Lena felt that her visit had been a partial success. Lizzie no longer had that lost look, and she seemed to have regained her appetite.

'I'll be able to tell them all that you're feeling – and looking – better, Lizzie,' Lena remarked as she hugged her friend on the station concourse.

Lizzie smiled sadly and nodded. 'I ... I think I'm over the worst now, Lena, but I'll never be able to forgive him for all the lies and deceit, and the hurt and utter humiliation.'

'Of course you won't, and I don't blame you. But you've got a great job, and a lovely place to live with nice people – and there's plenty more fish in the sea, Lizzie. And they're not all like *him!*'

'I'll write to George and Eileen this week, I promise. And, Lena ... tell Ned I'm ... glad he found out.'

'I will. He cares about you, Lizzie, you know.'

Lizzie managed a smile. 'You'd better be going, Lena, or the train will leave without you.'

Lena hugged her friend again before hastening towards the platform. She was glad she'd been talked into coming, and she was sure Lizzie was feeling better for her visit. And now that she'd actually made the effort, what was there to stop her from coming to London again?

Lizzie waved back as Lena turned to wave good-bye before disappearing into the clouds of steam issuing from the engine. Lena was right. She did have a pleasant place to live, and she did have a great job – things that made life seem brighter now.

Chapter Thirty-Three

The dark, miserable months of winter were finally over, Lizzie thought thankfully as she went into work that early May morning. The new buds on the trees were starting to unfurl, giving the appearance of a foaming wash of pale green, there were swathes of brightly coloured flowers in the many parks, and even the grey waters of the Thames glinted with gold spangles of reflected sunlight. She had to admit that London in the spring was an entirely different city and, judging by the expressions on the faces of her fellow travellers, she didn't think she was alone in this assumption. Of course there were still many problems facing the country, for unemployment and industrial unrest were causing grave concern – and downright hardship for many thousands. But she had never been interested in politics, and was profoundly thankful that the present troubles did not affect her directly, as they had when she'd been a child.

With the new season upon them, there was a decided air of anticipation in the store. She'd been working on the designs for summer, for picnic ware, and also linen and tableware for al fresco dining, which was becoming very popular with the advent of the warmer weather. Such 'decorative furnishing objects', as they were called, were displayed and sold in Liberty's famous Eastern Bazaar, situated in the basement of the store. Through the final weeks of the winter Lizzie had studied many books and illustrations on botany, to gain inspiration. It had also helped to take her mind – thankfully – off Edwin Pierce.

She'd caught a glimpse of him once, weeks ago now, walking along Regent Street at lunchtime, and to her surprise – and relief – all she'd felt was contempt. She'd known then that she was over him; any feelings of love, or even affection, that

300

she'd had for him were dead.

As usual, when she arrived at work she'd taken off her jacket and hat and then sat down at her desk, which faced a large window through which light streamed, to open her portfolio and scrutinise critically the work she'd done so far. These designs were not quite as elaborate as those she'd created in the past – they were devoid of the intricate, interlaced Celtic scrolls and knots that she'd produced for many decorative household items for last season – but the simple flowing lines of the leaves and flowers she'd used lent themselves more to the summer months, she thought, as she began to shade in the pastel colours she'd chosen.

'Lizzie, Mr Vernon would like to see you in his office,' Charlie Foster, one of her colleagues, informed her as he entered the large, sunny room.

She looked up, surprised. 'Now, Charlie?'

He nodded.

'Any idea what for?' she asked, putting down her pencil and closing her folio.

He shrugged. 'Search me, Lizzie but he didn't look annoyed or anything. In fact, I thought he looked a bit smug.'

She got to her feet, frowning. Edmund Vernon was in charge of the entire art and design department. It was a senior position, and a very important one too, and she was rather in awe of him. But up to now she'd had little direct contact with him, being such a recent addition to the department.

His office was further along the corridor. When she reached it, she patted her hair to ensure it was tidy before she knocked and waited for his instruction to enter.

She'd only been in here once before, she thought, glancing briefly around as she entered the office; it was when she'd been interviewed for her present position. It seemed as if a 'hushed', almost reverential, atmosphere prevailed in the ordered, airy room. Mr Vernon was a tall, slim man in his late fifties or early sixties, she surmised, with silvery hair worn slightly longer than was fashionable. His beard and moustache were neatly clipped, and he was always impeccably dressed. He had been with the company for years, she'd learned.

'You wished to see me, sir,' she said, a little hesitantly.

To her surprise, he smiled at her. 'I do, Miss Tempest. You have settled in well here, and although you've only been with us for a relatively short time, your work is excellent.'

She smiled back, feeling a glow of satisfaction at his praise. 'Thank you. I do try my best, even though I'm not formally trained.'

'Indeed, but you have a rare natural talent, Miss Tempest. I'm referring particularly to the design you produced before Christmas for a toast rack, the solid silver version of which sold remarkably well indeed.'

A flush crept over her cheeks, for this was high praise indeed.

He leaned forward and extracted what appeared to be a note from a folder on the desk. 'We are proud that a fair-sized order of that item, made to your design, was purchased on behalf of the royal household...'

Lizzie felt the flush deepen; she'd not known that.

'In the past, great interest has been shown by them for certain products we market, and so impressed were they by that particular item that I was asked to pass that praise on to the designer concerned – you, Miss Tempest.' He paused and held out the single sheet to her.

Lizzie took it hesitantly, for her hand was trembling. She just couldn't believe this! Had she heard him correctly? The words on the expensive cream vellum, edged with gold, seemed to blur as she read them. *Innovative, intricate, artistic* and *delightfully modern,* she managed to pick out, and there at the bottom was the signature: *Alexandra R.*

She gasped and held tightly on to the edge of Mr Vernon's desk, for she was so overwhelmed that she felt dizzy and unsteady on her feet. *The Queen!* The Queen herself was congratulating her on her design! Little Lizzie Tempest from Liverpool, the matchgirl who'd had no education, no training ... nothing! She'd never even dreamed that she had any kind of a talent when she'd wandered barefoot, hungry and ragged, following wherever her da had dragged them to, and now ... oh, how proud her poor mam would have been. How proud Ned would be – and George and Eileen, and everyone she knew. How proud and grateful that she had received such an accolade.

'Miss Tempest, are you quite well?' Edmund Vernon asked, with concern, for the girl's cheeks had drained of all colour and there were tears on her dark lashes. She looked stunned.

'Yes ... yes, I think so, Mr Vernon. It's ... it's

such a ... shock,' she stammered, still unable to quite believe it.

'And quite an honour too, Miss Tempest. I think you'd better sit down,' he urged, getting up and moving a chair closer for her to sit on.

Lizzie sat down gratefully, still clutching the precious letter in trembling fingers. 'Oh, it is, Mr Vernon. I never thought ... never imagined ... *me* of all people!'

He smiled at her. 'It doesn't happen very often, Miss Tempest, so I think I speak for everyone at Liberty's when I say we are very proud to have you on our team of designers.'

She was still stunned. 'May I ... keep this, Mr Vernon?'

'Of course. It's well known that Her Majesty has excellent taste and particularly likes the modern styles in preference to those favoured by the old Queen, God rest her, and she is refurnishing and refurbishing the royal residences to her own style.'

Lizzie nodded; she'd heard that too, and seen pictures in the papers of Queen Alexandra. She thought her a stunningly beautiful woman. So beautiful that she wondered how King Edward could even think about taking mistresses.

'And I think that now we can promote you to a senior designer, even though you've only been with us for a short time. It will mean an increase in your salary too, Miss Tempest.'

Lizzie was completely overwhelmed. In such a short time she'd achieved far more than she'd ever hoped she could. In her wildest dreams she'd never imagined she would obtain a senior position in such a prestigious store, or that her work would be singled out for praise by the Queen. Oh, she had so much to be grateful for.

'Thank you! Oh, Mr Vernon, this is a truly ... wonderful day for me! One I'll never forget.'

He smiled as he rose to indicate the interview was over. 'Indeed it is, Miss Tempest. Now, I think you'd better return to your work.'

Lizzie was still in a daze as she walked back down the corridor to her office. When she had left her desk, only moments earlier, she could never have imagined that Mr Vernon's summons would result in such a change in her fortunes.

Charlie Foster looked up when she walked into the room clutching the letter.

'Not your notice, Lizzie, I hope?'

She laughed with the sheer pride and joy that was filling her. 'Oh, Charlie, nothing at all like that!'

Everyone looked up from their work, for they'd never seen Lizzie look so happy or so animated.

'Don't keep us in suspense, Lizzie!' Alice Medway demanded.

Lizzie sat down before reporting the entire interview, her words interrupted with gasps and cries of surprise and delight. There was virtually no resentment at Lizzie being singled out for praise and promotion, and the approval of the royal household was deemed an endorsement of all their work.

'Maybe they'll order more "decorative items" from us now,' Alice enthused. Lizzie was popular, being quiet, hard-working and down to earth, without any airs and graces, and she was pleased

305

for her.

'I think it's just satisfying to know that our designs are appreciated and are in line with the really great designers, like Morris and Knox,' Charlie added.

'You should get that framed, Lizzie,' Martha Richards advised.

'I think I will. But how on earth am I going to come down to earth and get on with my work now?' Lizzie laughed.

'Working out the design for boring table napkins should do the trick,' Charlie remarked amiably.

'I'm going to have to do a lot of letter writing this evening,' Lizzie mused happily.

'Well, I think to celebrate we should go to a Lyon's Corner House at lunchtime,' Alice suggested, and it was very readily agreed upon as they all turned their attentions back to work.

Lizzie received fulsome praise from her landlady and all three gentlemen lodgers that evening. In fact, Mrs Braddan stated firmly that she'd always known Lizzie had great talent and would go far – you only had to look at the designs she sent back to Liverpool. But she'd never known anyone who had been praised by the Queen and had a letter to prove it. Her landlady seemed, Lizzie thought, a little overcome by the fact.

She'd written briefly to Lena and Nellie, and then to George and Eileen, reminding them that if it hadn't been for their generosity and encouragement, this would never have come about, and she hoped that they were proud of her. She only had the address of a shipping agent in Boston, so she decided that she'd write to Ned at Nellie's address, although she was sure Lena would tell him her news long before he could even open her letter.

Tired but happy, she at last tidied away the writing materials and stacked the letters for posting neatly on the table. She felt a huge sense of achievement and an increased enthusiasm for her future and her work. She'd been right not to go running back to Liverpool after she'd been dropped by Edwin Pierce, as she'd longed to do at first. How could she leave all this good fortune behind? She had begun to make a name for herself, she had a very promising career, and she'd just received an increase in her salary. 'What more could she ask for? She certainly had no need of the attentions or company of the likes of Edwin Pierce. Maybe one day, in the future, she'd meet someone she could love, although she'd be very, very wary of trusting her affections and her hopes. But for now she was happy with life just the way it was. She finally felt that she had 'arrived'.

Chapter Thirty-Four

The city seemed even more crowded than usual, Lizzie thought as she left work that warm, golden late June evening. Then she remembered why, for it had been in all the newspapers. Suffragettes from all parts of the country had answered Mrs Pankhurst's call to attend a huge rally in Trafalgar

Square, and women from Lancashire and Cheshire had also converged on Hyde Park. Emily Davies and Annie Kenney had at last been granted a meeting with Sir Henry Campbell-Bannerman, which the women appeared to think was a big step forward.

She made her way along the crowded road to her bus stop. As she waited for her bus, Lizzie contemplated the demands of the Suffrage Movement. Oh, she admired ladies such as Mrs Pankhurst and her daughters, and she'd found the newspaper reports of the treatment of women sent to jail for 'civil disobedience' really horrifying. She supposed that, at heart, she did believe in their demands, but she felt she wasn't educated enough to judge the rights and wrongs of all the arguments. If the right to vote would help the plight of poor women like her mam, then surely it could only be a good thing. Why shouldn't she and the thousands of women and girls like her, have a say in matters that affected them? After all, she worked; she paid her taxes; she looked after herself; she was an independent young woman. Maybe she should go to one of these demonstrations and learn more, she mused, as the bus came into sight and the queue began to move forward.

During the journey home Lizzie turned her attention away from politics and thought about the events of the day. She had been busy at work, with some important deadlines approaching, and her head was full of designs and templates when she alighted at her stop and walked the short distance to Brewster Road.

When she arrived home, it was to find Nora

Braddan waiting for her in the hall, a telegram in her hand.

'Is that for me?' Lizzie asked with some trepidation.

The woman nodded as she handed it over. 'The lad brought it about ten minutes ago. I hope it's nothing ... serious, Lizzie.'

'So do I,' she replied grimly. There had been no mention in the news of any ships in trouble, so it couldn't be Ned. She tore open the envelope and read the brief message: *Eileen very ill in hospital. Polio. George.*

'Oh, no! It's ... Eileen!' she cried.

'She's ... she's not...?' Nora asked tentatively.

'No, thank God! But she's in hospital with something he calls "polio". Is that serious, Mrs Braddan?' Lizzie begged.

Nora Braddan nodded gravely. 'It is, Lizzie. You'll know it as "infantile paralysis", and I'm afraid it can be ... fatal.'

Lizzie's eyes widened in shock. Eileen had never been robust, and lately George had written that she was tiring very easily. But how ... how had she contracted this disease? 'I'll have to go!' She dropped the telegram and pressed both hands to her cheeks. 'Where do I start? Should I send him a telegram? What about work? Is there a train?'

Her landlady took the situation in hand. 'Of course you must go, Lizzie. First, send a reply to that effect. Mr Staunton will take it to the telegraph office for you. Then write a note to your superior at Liberty's explaining ... everything and hoping they will allow you this brief leave of absence. Mr Coates works quite near, so I'm sure he'll take it in for you first thing in the morning.'

Lizzie nodded gratefully. She would be on the first train in the morning – unless, of course, there was one later tonight.

'Then pack a few things and, while you're doing all that, I'll get your supper and make you some sandwiches. You'll have time to get the overnight sleeper from Euston,' Nora informed her briskly.

The next hour seemed to pass in a blur as she wrote out the message for the telegram and then the letter for Mr Vernon, bolted her supper and hastily packed her things into a Gladstone bag. Oh, why hadn't George, or even Lena, written to say Eileen was ill long before this? she wondered as she hurried to get herself ready for the long journey home.

Mrs Braddan ordered a hansom cab to take Lizzie to the station. 'No sense in messing about waiting for a bus,' she said matter-of-factly. Lizzie was grateful for her landlady's calm, capable manner; it was just what she needed to help marshall her disordered thoughts. Mr Coates gave her a hand with her heavy bag and she was soon on her way, taking everyone's good wishes with her.

She arrived at Euston in time to purchase her ticket and find her way to the tiny compartment she'd paid almost a week's wage for, sinking down thankfully on the edge of the narrow bunk as the train shuddered and rattled in its efforts to move out of the station. Oh, please God, let Eileen get well, she prayed. She knew little about this disease but hoped against hope the doctors would be able to do something ... *anything* to make Eileen better. She had been so good to her, and Lizzie

310

was very fond of her. Then guilt assailed her. Oh, she shouldn't have kept on sending designs. Eileen had wanted to do less work, not more, but she hadn't wanted to let Lena down. And they had been earning a decent living. But now...

She took off her hat and her jacket and lay down on the bunk as the train gathered speed. She must try and get some sleep, for she didn't know what faced her on her arrival in Liverpool. She prayed it wouldn't be the news she feared most of all.

Lime Street Station was bathed in the early morning sunlight streaming in through the glass-domed roof when Lizzie alighted from the train. She blinked rapidly, shielding her eyes from the glare as she hastened toward the exit. George hadn't said which hospital Eileen had been taken to, so she'd decided to go straight to Olivia Street. She hoped Eileen wasn't in Bootle General, for that place held too many painful memories. She would rest easier in her mind once she'd seen Eileen for herself.

As she alighted from the tram and walked quickly towards her old home, she felt a sense of relief that she was back and surrounded by everything familiar, mingled with anxiety for Eileen – and for George, who must be frantic with worry.

When he opened the door to her, she flung her arms around him. He looked grey and haggard, his face lined with worry and lack of sleep. 'Oh, George! I came as quickly as I could. Why didn't you let me know sooner? How is she? Is she any better? What are they doing to help her?' All the

311

questions that had been circling round and round in her mind on the long journey burst forth.

'Lizzie, I'm so glad you're ... here!' His voice cracked with emotion as he drew her inside the house. He was haunted by his fears for his wife. But he was also relieved that Lizzie had come home, for he knew she was very fond of Eileen, and Eileen of her.

She left her bag in the hallway and went straight into the kitchen to put the kettle on. 'I think we both need a cup of tea. While I make it, you tell me what ... how...'

George nodded slowly. 'She hasn't been well for a while ... tired ... out of sorts. Then two days ago she ... she said she felt as if the influenza was returning. I begged her to go to see the doctor, and she said she would, but ... but then...' He shook his head.

'What? What, George?' Lizzie cried, fear clutching at her heart. She could see in his face that something was terribly wrong.

'She ... she couldn't move her arms and legs. She was ... paralysed. I sent immediately for the doctor and he sent for an ambulance. It's polio, and it's ... serious, Lizzie. They ... they don't know if she will get over it. She ... she can barely breathe!' His voice cracked and his shoulders slumped.

She felt so sorry for him that she went and put her arms around him. He was such a good, kind, generous man and he'd worked hard all his life to give Eileen a comfortable home and a secure life. Why oh why should this have happened to them?

George was worried sick about Eileen and couldn't envisage what lay ahead, but he'd missed

Lizzie. Missed her company, missed her laughter and enthusiasm, missed the support he knew she would have given unstintingly, these past few terrible days.

Lizzie raised her head and drew away from him, concern filling her eyes. 'Where did they take her?'

'To Liverpool. To the Royal Infirmary, they have more advanced ... facilities than the local hospitals.'

She nodded slowly, his words deepening her fears. 'Can we ... see her ... soon?'

He nodded. 'They have been very good ... very accommodating. We'll go as soon as we're ready.'

Her thoughts went back to her poor mam's last days and the way she and Nellie had been restricted by the visiting times, so she'd not been there when Florrie had passed away. 'Good. I'll make us both some breakfast, I'm sure you've not eaten in days, then I'll get tidied up and we ... we'll go.'

He nodded. 'They've been good at the factory too. I go in for a few hours between hospital visits, but I know that can't continue indefinitely.'

'Don't worry about that now, George. I sent a note into work, begging leave of absence, and I'm sure they'll understand. But of course I'll have to go back too.' She suddenly thought of Lena. 'Has Lena been coming to the house?'

George struggled to pull himself together. 'She has, but not to work. She ... she comes to ask about Eileen, and she's taken stuff home with her to work on. She'll probably be here shortly, as she knows when I'm about to leave.'

'I'll see her soon, then,' Lizzie replied, and busied herself with the tea and then getting together the ingredients for breakfast. She'd be relieved to see her friend, for the situation was grave and she knew she would need Lena's support.

Lena hugged her tightly when Lizzie opened the door to her. 'I'm glad you got here so quickly, Lizzie!'

'Come in. I got the overnight sleeper – not that I got much sleep, what with worrying and the noise and jolting of the train.'

Lena nodded. Lizzie looked pale and tired, but it was only to be expected. 'Oh, it's been terrible these last two days. It was such a shock ... and he's been going around in a daze ever since. After they took her into hospital, it was me who told him to send word to you. It all happened so fast, like. First she said she felt exhausted, weary to the bone, no energy. Then she developed a bad headache and a sore throat and said she ached all over ... we thought it was influenza, and then her neck was stiff, and then...'

Lizzie bit her lip. 'I don't know much about this "polio", Lena.'

'You do, Lizzie; Mam says it generally affects children, but it's something you can catch at any age, and it's ... serious.'

'I know. Mrs Braddan said it ... can be ... fatal.' Indeed, Lizzie thought, she recalled it was usually fatal in children. 'George says that now she can hardly breathe. Oh, Lena, why did this have to happen to someone like Eileen?'

Lena nodded seriously. 'I know, she's been

good to both of us.' She'd been shocked when she'd heard Eileen had suffered paralysis, but she hadn't known that Eileen was getting worse, struggling now to breathe, and she was appalled. It didn't look good. 'I take it you'll both be going to the Royal this morning?'

Lizzie nodded.

'Well, I hope there's some ... improvement. It's supposed to be a very good hospital, they'll do everything they can. I'll call again later this afternoon, Lizzie, to see how she is. I've enough stuff at home to keep me going.'

'Thanks, Lena. I think I'll need someone to talk to. George will probably go into work for a bit, he can't desert his job.' Lizzie frowned. 'Don't you need a sewing machine?' she enquired, trying to think practically.

'I took one, Lizzie. I asked, and he said I could. Me da and our Peggy's 'usband fetched it to our house on a handcart.'

Lizzie managed a smile. 'I bet that caused a bit of a stir in Bennett Street.'

Lena smiled back. 'Someone asked me mam if she'd come into money. I won't repeat what she said, but she agrees that me keeping busy is the best thing.'

'She's right,' Lizzie replied, sighing. She wished there was more she could do to help George, but if she could just make sure he ate and that he spent some time at the factory, that would be a start.

The green-and-white tiled walls of the hospital corridor and the smell of disinfectant mingled with ether brought the memories flooding back to Lizzie of Florrie's last days in Bootle General. With an effort she pushed them away as she and George followed the sister to the side ward where Eileen had been taken. She glanced hesitantly up at George, seeing the look of anguish on his face. She'd assumed that Eileen would be in a general ward – obviously this didn't bode well.

'Doctor thought it best she be isolated, as it's contagious,' the sister informed her, seeing the concern in Lizzie's eyes. 'But I'm afraid that I have to tell you that her condition has deteriorated overnight. Dr Harding will explain everything to you,' she added, before ushering them into the room.

Lizzie clutched George's arm tightly with shock as she caught sight of Eileen lying in the narrow bed. She hardly recognised her; she looked to be barely alive.

'Can ... can she speak to ... us?' she asked in a whisper.

Sister shook her head. 'It would be too ... taxing for her to try to speak.'

Lizzie still clung to his arm as they approached the bed. She didn't know what she had expected, how she would find Eileen, but ... but she'd never imagined this!

'Can she hear us?' she whispered to the sister.

The woman looked at her sympathetically. 'We assume so, but she does drift in and out of consciousness.'

George gently placed his hand on his wife's forehead. 'I ... I've brought someone to see you, Eileen. It's Lizzie, she's ... she's come from

London to be near you.' There was no response, and he looked appealingly at Lizzie.

She was desperately trying to hide her feelings and keep the tears from her eyes. 'I came straight away, Eileen. George sent me a ... telegram. I ... I got the first train, the overnight sleeper.'

Again there was no sign that Eileen had heard; her eyes remained closed, her breathing shallow and laboured. Lizzie looked despairingly at George. All they could do was wait and pray, something she could see George was doing silently, to himself. She bit her lip hard, to try to stop the tears, for there was really very little hope. In her heart she knew Eileen Rutherford was dying and, once again, she felt like the young, disbelieving, heartbroken girl she'd been when she'd been told of Florrie's death. Since then Eileen had been her mentor, her support, her friend – almost a second mother – and now ... now she too was going. This cruel disease would rob Eileen of her life long before anyone had expected her to die. She should have lived for years yet, for she wasn't old.

Lizzie would miss her terribly, and so would George. Gently she placed her hand over his as it rested on Eileen's forehead. 'I ... I'm so glad I'm here. I'd never have forgiven myself if I ... I'd been too late.'

He didn't reply, for the lump in his throat was too great, but he nodded slowly. Like Lizzie, he knew there was very little time left before his wife slipped slowly out of both their lives.

Chapter Thirty-Five

When Lena arrived at the house later that afternoon she was stunned to hear that Eileen had died. 'It ... it's so ... sudden!' she cried, tears springing to her eyes.

Lizzie nodded miserably and dabbed at her eyes with her handkerchief. 'I know, I'm finding it hard to believe. Oh, Lena, it was so ... pitiful! She ... she struggled so much, and there was nothing we could do to ... help her.'

Lena dashed away her tears and took Lizzie's hand. 'Well, she's at peace now, Lizzie. And at least you got here in time.'

'But she was too young to die!' Lizzie protested.

Lena nodded sadly. 'I know, but these ... terrible things happen. How is George taking it? Where is he?'

'I don't think it's really hit him yet, Lena, that she's ... gone. He's very shaken, but he's going to inform them at the factory and then ... see about the arrangements.'

Lena nodded. These things had to be done. 'So, I suppose we'll know more when he gets back?'

'Yes, although I just don't know what to say to him, how to help ease things for him. I wish I could find the right words.'

Lena could understand that; it was very difficult. 'How long will you be able to stay on for, Lizzie?'

Lizzie made an effort to think clearly. 'I'll have to go back after ... after the funeral. I don't want to, but ... but I'll have to write to Mr Vernon and explain what's happened, and hope they'll understand.'

'Well, I don't think they'll be handing you your notice, Lizzie – not after that letter an' all,' Lena said seriously. But she was already wondering what would now happen to her. Would she be able to continue working from this house in the future? There simply wasn't the room in Bennett Street, and she had to earn her living. There was no way on earth she would go back to that factory – any factory – but now wasn't the time to voice her worries. 'We are all so proud of you, Lizzie. We could hardly believe it, and she ... Eileen said she just couldn't get over you getting a letter from the Queen herself.'

Lizzie managed a wan smile; it didn't seem to matter so very much now, but she was glad Eileen had been pleased.

'Ned will be home in a couple of days, Lizzie, so that's one bit of good news at least.'

Lizzie hadn't seen her brother since that brief and fateful visit in January, and she felt relief at Lena's words; she'd be glad of Ned's support, especially at the funeral.

'Why don't you come and see Mam later on, Lizzie? It might help, like,' Lena urged, hoping to cheer her friend up a little.

'I ... I'll see how George is when he gets back. I'll make some supper and try to get him to eat something, although I don't much feel like eating myself. But I don't think he should be left alone

'– not tonight, Lena.'

Lena sighed; she could see Lizzie's point, but Lizzie would feel better when Ned got home. She was certain she'd feel better herself for having Ned around. They had grown closer, these last months, and she'd come to realise that she could depend on Ned's love and support, even though he wasn't home very often.

When George returned at last, Lizzie could see he was exhausted by the day's gruelling events. She'd spent the time waiting for him writing to both Nora Braddan and Mr Victor at Liberty's but she'd found concentrating difficult; everything seemed so *unreal*.

'George, is everything ... arranged?' she asked, as he sank wearily down on to the sofa and covered his face with his hands.

He felt numb and devastated, but he supposed that was with shock; he just hadn't expected Eileen to go ... like that. So quickly, so suddenly. She'd only been ill for a few days.

Lizzie sat down beside him. 'I've made some supper ... nothing elaborate. You ... we both have to try to eat, George.'

He nodded and looked up at her. 'I just can't believe it, Lizzie! I can't take it in, at all. It ... it's as though it's all happening to someone else.'

She reached for his hand. 'Neither can I, but at least she didn't ... linger for weeks. We should be thankful for small mercies.'

'I went to the funeral people and then to see the minister; it's arranged for Thursday morning. And then I had to go into the factory,' he informed her wearily. Everything had been an ordeal, although everyone had been kind and respectful.

'At least all that is done now. We ... we'll get through it, George, somehow.'

He squeezed her hand. 'I'm so glad you came home, Lizzie.'

She got to her feet, pulling him up with her. 'So am I. Now, let's try and eat some supper. Lena was telling me that Ned will be home in a couple of days, so that might ... help us both.'

George didn't reply but followed her into the kitchen. He couldn't bear to think about the next few days; he didn't dare let himself dwell on the fact that Lizzie would certainly be going back to London after the funeral, leaving him here alone in this house that seemed empty and desolate already without Eileen's presence.

Lizzie was very relieved to see her brother when he called, accompanied by Lena. She had gone to meet him at the landing stage and had brought him up to date with the tragic events.

'Oh, Ned! What a homecoming,' she greeted him as he hugged her.

'I know, Lizzie. God rest her, she was a good woman – it's a shock. How is George taking it?'

She ushered them into the parlour, where the curtains were closed out of respect for their loss, making the room shadowy and a little stuffy. 'Better than I expected he would. But I think he'll be glad to see you, Ned. At first he seemed dazed ... unable to take it in. But he's been going into work, which I think is helping, although I'm not really sure about that, either. I've been keeping busy too. I suppose it's different for me, for I've not been living in this house now for months.'

Ned nodded. 'You've your own life, Lizzie; and, despite everything, a man needs to keep his job – at least while George is there, it might take his mind off things.'

'The funeral is on Thursday morning at the Providence Baptist Chapel, and that's going to be an ordeal for him; they were married there,' Lizzie informed them both.

'At least Ned and I will be able to attend, Lizzie. Mam would like to, as well,' Lena informed her.

'I'll be sailing later that evening,' Ned reminded Lena, before turning to Lizzie. 'And when will you be going back? I don't suppose you can stay up here much longer, not now you're a senior designer?' he asked. She couldn't risk the position she now held by being absent for a long period of time, he was certain of that.

Lizzie frowned; she'd already been thinking about this. 'I'll go on Sunday, Ned. Then I can start work again on Monday. They've been very accommodating but, well...' She shrugged. 'I'm dreading telling George, though. I don't want him to feel as if I'm abandoning him. But I don't intend to say anything until we get Thursday over.'

'He'll understand, Lizzie, although I suppose he won't be looking forward to being here ... alone,' Ned agreed.

Lizzie twisted her hands helplessly together. 'I wish I could stay longer, Ned, really I do. I hate to think of him coming home from the factory to an empty house, with no one to talk to and cheer him up, and with no meal waiting for him. I just hope he's going to be able to manage.'

'What else can you do, Lizzie? You can't give up your job. You've done so well, everyone is so proud of you.'

'I wouldn't have the job but for the fact that George and Eileen took me in. George virtually taught me to read and write; he encouraged me to take up design; he encouraged me to go to London when I wasn't at all sure, and Eileen too...'

'I know, Lizzie, but she wouldn't want you to give everything up,' Lena urged.

'You can't, Lizzie!' Ned agreed.

Lizzie nodded slowly. Lena and Ned were right, but she wished she didn't feel so guilty about leaving George here alone.

'I'll look in on him whenever I'm home, maybe take him out for a pint,' Ned promised.

'And I'm sure I can do his shopping and cook him something he can warm up when he comes in from work,' Lena added.

Lizzie managed a smile. 'Have you thought what you will do about your work now, Lena?'

'I'll keep working from home, if I have to, but there's not much room, and Mam is starting to moan a bit about the added clutter. I ... I'll ask him if I can go on working here, if he doesn't mind. It won't disturb him, as I won't see much of him. I'm usually gone by the time he gets home from the factory, but at least I can make sure the place is kept clean and tidy for him and see there's food in the larder.'

Lizzie nodded. Before she went back she would quietly mention this to George; if he agreed, she would feel infinitely better about leaving. 'I'll keep sending you the templates, Lena.'

Lena smiled at her. 'Thanks, Lizzie. I'd still be stuck in that packing room, if it wasn't for you.'

Ned took Lena's hand and smiled at her. 'She's getting to be quite the little businesswoman. Did she tell you she's managed to get a new contract?'

'She did. It's with Blackler's, and I'm proud of her too,' Lizzie replied, smiling at them both and now feeling less stressed and anxious about leaving George.

Thursday arrived with a grim inevitability. It was a beautiful June day, and the chapel was bathed in pale summer sunshine. Lizzie could hardly believe that they were gathered here to say goodbye to a young woman whose future had been cruelly taken away from her when she'd still had so much to look forward to.

Somehow she had to get through the ordeal of Eileen's funeral; there would be time later to dwell on her own feelings, but now she had to support George on what must surely be the bleakest day of his life. He had asked her to accompany him at the head of the funeral cortège, saying it was what Eileen would have wanted. As they entered the chapel, Lizzie saw that every pew was filled with people who had come to pay their respects. Eileen Rutherford had been a much loved member of the congregation, and Lizzie hoped that the obvious affection in which she had been held would comfort George and be a source of consolation in the coming weeks.

It was a dignified service and the minister was very kind, speaking at length with George as they left the chapel. They proceeded to the cemetery, where Eileen's body was buried with respect and due ceremony; there would be a fine headstone placed on her grave, Lizzie thought sadly, as she stood beside George and murmured her private words of love and thanks to the woman who had been her friend and mentor.

Lizzie had been grateful for Ned's presence at the funeral. When they went back to Olivia Street for the funeral tea she noted with relief that he assumed the role of helping George with the formalities – greeting the mourners, shaking hands respectfully and accepting expressions of condolence – while Lizzie supervised the setting out of the tea.

It was a small gathering of close friends and neighbours at the house, many of whom expressed their shock at losing Eileen in such tragic circumstances. Lizzie knew they meant well, but their words only served to underline the huge effort that would be needed to get George to look at the future with some grain of hope.

When the last mourners had said their goodbyes, Lizzie closed the front door. At last, she and George were alone together. She dreaded telling him that she would be returning to London on Sunday. Ned had told her earlier that he'd already broached the subject with George and that George seemed resigned to her going and was determined that she shouldn't abandon her career.

Lizzie knew she had to speak up now; it would never be the right time to say what she had to say. 'I really do wish I could stay longer, George, but I'm afraid I have to be back in the office on Monday morning,' she explained. 'I feel awful ... leaving you,' she finished.

He smiled sadly, but nodded. 'You've worked so hard to get where you are, Lizzie, and you've excelled too. I ... we ... wouldn't want you to give it up now to come back here because of ... me.'

'I'll never forget that I couldn't have done it without you George ... without both of you.'

'I ... we're so proud of you, Lizzie.'

'I know, but I'll miss her and I *will* worry about you and how you are managing.'

'Life goes on, Lizzie. I'll cope,' he replied, but with a catch in his voice.

She went on to explain about the difficulty of Lena working from Nellie's kitchen, and George agreed that Lena should continue to use the workroom. He even managed a brief smile when Lizzie told him that her friend would be happy to do a bit of domestic work too, to help him out.

Lizzie felt a huge sense of relief that she'd finally told him and that, with Lena in and out of the house, at least he wouldn't be completely alone there.

Lizzie was surprised on Saturday afternoon when she answered the front door to find Mabel Woods standing on the doorstep. 'Miss Woods!'

'I just thought I would call to offer my condolences to Mr Rutherford,' Mabel explained, looking a little disconcerted. She'd assumed Lizzie had gone back to London the previous day.

'Thank you. I'll tell him, he's gone out for a bit of fresh air after being in the factory all morning,' Lizzie replied. She'd been getting her things ready to pack into the Gladstone bag when she'd heard the knock at the door.

'I expect you will be going back to London? We've all heard how well you are doing down there. Quite an achievement – an honour, in fact.'

Lizzie smiled at her. George had obviously told people about the Queen's letter. 'Yes, I'm going back tomorrow. I really would have liked to stay longer, but I can't.'

Mabel smiled back. 'Of course not. Well, I wish you well, Lizzie. You will tell him I called?'

'Of course I will; I'm sure he'll appreciate your thoughtfulness.'

As she closed the door, Lizzie thought it a little strange that Mabel Woods should feel that she had to call in person. She assumed she would have already offered her condolences to George. After all, he'd been into the factory a few times since Eileen had died – and, in fact, that very morning. Surely Mabel would have seen him there? She shrugged and pushed the thought aside, but she would mention to him that Mabel had called.

George insisted on accompanying Lizzie to the station, even though she'd said it wasn't necessary if he didn't feel up to it. 'I'll see you safely on to the train, Lizzie,' he'd said firmly.

As usual, the concourse was busy, but she didn't notice it so much now. Her train was already in. She was thankful, for she still felt awful leaving him and couldn't quite believe that it was barely a week since she'd arrived here. So much had happened; both their lives had changed in that short time.

'I'll write more regularly, George, I promise, and I *will* worry about you,' she said as she took her bag from him and reached up to kiss him on the cheek.

He held her briefly and returned the kiss. 'I know you will, Lizzie.'

'George, promise me you'll look after yourself?' she begged.

He smiled. 'I promise. Now, get on the train.'

She turned away and walked briskly towards the platform, still feeling anxious and upset.

George watched her until she disappeared from his sight. He couldn't ask her to stay. It would be selfish, and he felt he didn't have the right, but he wasn't looking forward to the days and months ahead.

He at last turned away and walked out of the station. There were numerous pubs on Lime Street, and he felt he needed a drink before he could face returning to a silent, empty house that no longer felt like a home.

Chapter Thirty-Six

As she had promised, Lizzie did write more often than she had in the past. She wasn't too concerned at first that George's replies were infrequent; she felt certain that he was doing his best to cope on his own. She heard regularly from Lena, who informed her that she kept the place tidy and did whatever shopping was required, although she saw very little of George. However, she did mention that he often left the food she'd prepared untouched, which then went in the bin. Lena thought this was a criminal waste, seeing as so many went hungry. That worried Lizzie – obviously George wasn't eating properly – and she'd written urging Lena to get Ned to visit George on his next leave and try to broach the subject.

They were all busy in the design department, for even though it was barely August, and the sun still beat down from a cloudless blue sky, they were already working on the Christmas and winter designs. True to her word, she continued sending designs for Lena to make up for the coming months and the festive season. She wished that either her friend or Ned would come and visit; she did miss them. But she knew Lena was busy herself, and she couldn't blame her brother for wanting to spend the short time he had at home with Lena. She was delighted when Lena had hinted in her last letter that she might be getting engaged at Christmas; Ned had proposed and, of course, she'd more than happily accepted, and mention of a ring had been made. The prospect of Lena as her sister-in-law was a very pleasant one. Her own weekends seemed to fly by, and there was enough in her life to keep her busy and occupied, but she did hope that George was coping; things wouldn't be easy for him.

Ned smiled as he caught sight of Lena waiting for him on the landing stage that late summer evening. It was still very warm and the Pier Head was busy with people making the most of the pleasant August evening. He was always glad to get home; he knew Nellie would have a good supper waiting and that Lena was bound to have news from Lizzie. He was saving hard so he would be able to buy Lena a decent ring at Christmas, and then they could plan their future together. Maybe they could get a place of their own, he'd often mused, but realised that, with him being away and Lena still working, no doubt she'd spend what free time she had at her mam's.

'Have you been waiting long, luv?' he asked after kissing her and putting his arm around her as they walked towards the waiting trams at the terminus.

'No, I've got used to what time you get paid off now – and I know you don't dawdle around,' she laughed happily. She was always glad to see him safely home.

'Business is still good?' he enquired.

She nodded. 'It is, and Lizzie's sent me designs for Christmas. I've actually got more work than I can manage; I've been wondering if I should look for a girl to help me – someone I could train, like Eileen did me – but then if things get slack... I've had to carry on working late into the evenings, just recently,' she confided.

'Don't go overdoing it, Lena,' he urged. 'Don't be wearing yourself out. Maybe you do need a bit of help, now and then.'

'I won't go "wearing myself out", I promise.' She frowned. 'Ned, I ... I'm a bit bothered about George.'

He looked down at her, with concern. 'Why?

What's wrong?'

'Well, more often than not, he doesn't eat what I leave him. It ends up either in the bin or, if I can salvage it, I take it home to Mam.'

Ned nodded. 'It can't be easy for him, Lena. He's not used to being on his own.'

'I know, but because I've been staying on later at the house, I've found out that he isn't coming straight home from work, Ned. Sometimes he's not back when I leave – and that's been as late as ten o'clock. I don't know where he goes and it's ... worrying.'

Ned frowned as he helped her on to the tram and they settled themselves into their seats. 'But he does get home ... eventually?'

She nodded. 'He's always gone off to work by the time I arrive, but his bed has been slept in; I've looked to see.'

Ned was thoughtful. 'Maybe he's going to see ... someone?'

Lena raised her eyebrows. 'Who? No, George wouldn't do anything like that, not with Eileen only being ... gone a couple of months.'

'It's not unknown, Lena. But maybe he's got mates, friends from school?'

Lena shrugged. She supposed it was possible, although in all the time she'd known him he'd never gone visiting mates. 'It's still a bit of a mystery, Ned. I just hope he ... he's all right.'

'I know I've only just got home, but would it put your mind at ease if I go round to see him after supper? Then I can see for myself, have a chat to him, try and find out?'

'I'd be glad if you would; it is worrying me,'

Lena confided.

'Have you mentioned it to our Lizzie?'

'No. I've told her he doesn't seem to be eating, but I've not said anything about him staying out – and I don't intend to, just yet. It would only upset her, you know that.'

He nodded. The times he'd seen George Rutherford lately he'd seemed to be coping well. He wasn't exactly what you'd call 'cheerful', but that was only natural. He hadn't seemed too down or depressed, either – but maybe that was just an act for his benefit. He supposed he lived a 'bed to work existence' himself, which also appeared to be George Rutherford's lot now. But in the evenings he didn't go back to an empty house; he had plenty of company around him – too much sometimes. He'd go and see if he could find out why George wasn't coming home from work until late. At least it would stop Lena worrying.

When they arrived at Bennett Street, Lena told Nellie about Ned's intention of popping round to see George. Nellie totally agreed with the proposed visit. 'The poor man must be eaten up with 'is loss. It's early days yet an' it must be awful going into that 'ouse an' just sitting there – alone an' with not a soul to talk to. Poor feller's not used to it. Go an' see iffen yer can cheer 'im up, like, Ned.'

'I wonder, Mam, if it's because he knows I'm still there working? Maybe he doesn't feel ... comfortable about it. Maybe that's why he's not coming home,' Lena put in.

Nellie frowned at her. 'I thought you said he's never 'ome when you leave? So, 'ow would he know you're still there?' she demanded. 'That doesn't make sense, girl. There's got to be more to it, Ned. You get on well with 'im.'

'I like him, Mrs Gibbons. He's a decent bloke, and he's going through a hard time now,' Ned replied and meant it, although he was a little disconcerted about the visit; he didn't want to appear to be prying into the man's life.

Ned waited until half past nine before he left for Olivia Street, for it would be pointless to go earlier and have to hang around. He'd make his way to his lodgings after he'd seen George.

It had been a wise decision, he mused, as he approached the house and saw the faint glow of a light in the parlour window. The evenings had started to draw in now and it was very nearly dark. He'd say he was calling in on his way to Great Howard Street, just to see how George was doing and find out the latest news – tactfully, of course.

When George finally opened the door, Ned was disconcerted by his appearance. He looked pale, his usually neatly combed hair was dishevelled, he was in his shirtsleeves and he looked a bit unsteady on his feet.

'I thought I'd just drop in on my way to the lodging house, George. See how you're getting on, like,' Ned said cheerfully, hiding his concern.

'Come in, Ned,' George urged, half-heartedly.

Ned did so, but he was now almost certain that George Rutherford had been drinking, probably for hours, and was on the verge of being blind drunk. He smelled like a brewery, and that concerned Ned deeply, for he knew George seldom took a drink. At least, he never had when Eileen had been alive. Was this where he was going after work – to the nearest pub?

'How are ... things, George?' he asked as he followed him into the parlour. He was quick to notice that there was a half-empty bottle of whisky on the sideboard and an empty glass on the floor beside an armchair. This didn't look good, but it often happened, he thought bitterly. George had taken to the drink to try to blot out the grief and loneliness in his life, but that wasn't the answer.

George picked up the empty glass. 'Drink, Ned?'

Ned shook his head. 'Thanks, but no.'

'You won't mind if I do?'

Ned shook his head. It wasn't his place to say he thought the man had already had more than enough, in his opinion.

George refilled his glass, took a hefty swig and sank heavily down in the chair.

'It doesn't work, George,' Ned said quietly.

'What? What...?'

'The drink,' Ned replied grimly.

'It ... it ... helps with the memories,' George slurred, taking another swig.

Ned took a deep breath, unsure how his next words would be received, but he had to try to get George to see sense. 'I can understand that, but in time you'll need more and more to be able to forget, George. Then you'll find reality slipping away ... everything will slip away, I've seen it happen. You'll lose your job, your home, your self-respect, all the things you valued in life. Is that what you want?'

George drained the glass and tried to get to his feet but sank back. He barely took in Ned's words; he didn't care any more about anything, and his head was spinning horribly.

Ned got to his feet and took the glass from George's hand. 'Is this why Lena never sees you, George? Is this why you're not eating or looking after yourself ... drinking yourself into oblivion every night?'

George nodded. 'What ... what's the point of coming back to ... this?' He made an attempt to gesture around the empty room.

'I'll get you to bed. God, man, you can hardly get up! Sleep it off, George. But you've *got* to make an effort to stop this, do you hear me?'

'Why? Life's empty ... useless,' George mumbled.

Ned heaved him to his feet and half dragged, half carried him towards the hall. He'd never manage the stairs; he'd have to more or less sling the man over his shoulder. This had to stop – and now, before it was too late. Before George lost everything.

But how could he do anything to help? He was away at sea most of the time, and he couldn't expect Lena or any of her family to try to stop George from sinking into a drink-fuelled pit of self-pity and despair; they were virtually strangers to him. As he struggled to get George up the stairs, he realised that there was only one person who could possibly help – and that was Lizzie.

Tomorrow he'd persuade Lena to go down to London and see his sister and explain just how bad things had become. Maybe she could come home and get George back on the straight and narrow – for if she didn't, Ned could see him ending up like his da, Art Tempest.

Both Lena and Nellie were horrified when Ned imparted the news to them.

'It's no use you just writing to her, Lena. That's not the answer. She's got to come and see for herself how bad things are. Maybe she can talk some sense into him. I hope so,' he'd urged.

Both women agreed and so, the following day, Lena undertook the journey to Lime Street, accompanied by her mother.

'You do yer best to bring 'er back 'ome, girl. That poor man needs 'er,' Nellie urged before Lena walked away towards the platform.

Her mam's words remained firmly lodged in Lena's mind during the journey south. Each mile nearer to London brought the certainty that Nellie Gibbons, as usual, had put her finger on what was wrong. Quite simply, George Rutherford needed Lizzie. But Lizzie was no longer the forlorn little waif he'd rescued all those years ago. She was now a successful designer whose creations had received the royal seal of approval. Would she be prepared to turn her back on her career, perhaps give up everything she'd worked so hard to achieve, in order to come home and rescue George Rutherford? Lena had to admit that she wasn't sure how Lizzie would react to this appeal for help.

She was still mulling all this over in her mind when she arrived at Euston. Having already visited Lizzie, she felt that London held no terrors for her now. She strode confidently towards the bus stop, remembering the route to Lizzie's boarding house, anxious to reach Brewster Street as quickly as possible.

Nora Braddan was both surprised and concerned when Lena arrived so unexpectedly on her doorstep.

'I know Lizzie is at work, Mrs Braddan, but I really do need to see her,' Lena explained. 'Things are not ... good, back home. Mr Rutherford is ... well, he's not himself at all, he's just not coping, and I think she should know.'

Nora nodded and ushered her in, realising that she would have to make up a bed for the girl. 'You often find, Lena, that men *don't* cope as well as women with their loss. It might take him some time.'

Lena nodded grimly. If George Rutherford didn't stop drinking like a fish, he wouldn't have the time.

When Lizzie arrived home from work and saw Lena, the first words she uttered were, 'Oh, Lena, what's wrong? Is it George?'

'Come on up to your room, Lizzie,' Lena urged, taking her friend's arm firmly, her demeanour grim.

Lizzie sat down on the edge of the bed as Lena explained, her expression becoming more and more horrified.

'It's been every night for God knows how long, Lizzie. I've only been staying late these past few weeks so I don't know if he'd taken to the drink before then. I know he's not eating, and if he goes on like this ... he'll lose his job for certain, and that's just the start of it. Ned said he was in a right state, he had to carry him upstairs.'

Lizzie pressed both hands to her cheeks. 'I ... I didn't think...! He barely used to touch a drop, Lena! Life must have become just too ... bad, too unbearable for him.'

'I had to come and tell you, Lizzie. We can't let him end up like your da – and he will. He's too good, too decent a man for that.'

Lizzie bit her lip as all the bitter memories of her childhood came flooding back. 'No! No, I won't let him get like ... Da! Lena, I'd be *nothing* ... have *nothing*, without George! I'll go back with you. I don't care if I lose my own job, I'll get something else. But I can't leave him to ruin his life. I *won't* let him do that! I'll make him understand ... somehow ... that he's got to stop drinking and try to look to the future.'

Lena nodded her agreement. She hoped Lizzie wouldn't lose her job, but she understood how her friend felt. Lizzie did owe everything to George and Eileen Rutherford, and she was sure that, given time, he would get his life back on a steady footing.

'Does anyone else know, Lena?'

Lena shrugged. 'Maybe the neighbours – and someone at the factory must have noticed.' She frowned, remembering a couple of incidents that she'd forgotten about but which now seemed to make some sense. 'I ... I think Mabel Woods might have done.'

'Why? Have you seen her? Has she said any-thing?'

'She called a couple of times, to the house. I don't think she expected me still to be there, and of course he wasn't home.'

'What did she want?' Lizzie felt a frisson of annoyance, remembering that Mabel Woods had called just before she'd left for London, two days after Eileen's funeral.

'The first time she said she wanted to discuss something with him, about work. Just what was so important about packing flaming matches, I don't know! And she'd had plenty of chances to speak to him at the factory. The second time she said she was a bit concerned about him. I told her there was nothing wrong with him, except that he'd recently lost his wife and was bound to be a bit ... down, like.'

Lena paused and frowned, thoughtfully. 'Now I think about it, perhaps she was trying to get her feet under the table. I think she's always had a soft spot for him.'

Lizzie didn't reply. Despite her shock and anxiety, she felt annoyed and strangely ... jealous.

They were both silent and thoughtful on the journey to Liverpool next morning. Lizzie hadn't slept well at all; she was so concerned for George, and she wondered if she did indeed have the power to help him overcome his grief and loss.

Nora Braddan had said she would deliver the letter Lizzie had written to Mr Vernon – in person, if that was possible. In it Lizzie had explained, as best she could, that she might have to take an extended leave of absence and that she would understand entirely if they couldn't keep her position open and had to terminate her employment with Liberty's. However, she hoped that could be avoided if things worked out better than she envisaged, although privately she didn't hold out much hope of that.

They'd agreed that Lizzie should go home with Lena first; it would be useless for Lizzie to go straight to Olivia Street, for George wasn't expecting her and probably would be late home – again.

'I'll go round there late afternoon, Lena. I'll get some shopping on the way and give the place a bit of a tidy and make some supper, just in case...'

Lena nodded her agreement, thinking it was a pity that Ned had sailed again. She was sure Lizzie would have been grateful for his support, particularly if George proved difficult or ... even worse ... incapable. Lizzie certainly couldn't get him up the stairs on her own, but Lena sincerely hoped he wouldn't be in as bad a state as that.

'You're sure you'll be able to manage, Lizzie? Da will come round later on, if I ask him to.'

Lizzie shook her head. 'I'll manage, Lena. Even if he ... he's in no state to hold a sensible conversation, he will be tomorrow morning. He's not going to go into that factory until I've made him promise to stop drinking,' she replied firmly.

Lena still looked anxious. Would George take any notice of Lizzie? She prayed he would. Oh, things were in a nice mess, she thought miserably. Her heart went out to her friend, for Lizzie knew at first hand what it was like to live with someone who existed in a haze of alcohol. Lena decided she'd work from home; she had no intention of going to Olivia Street for the next few days, she thought. She'd only be in the way.

It was the first time she'd been in this house since Eileen's death, Lizzie thought sadly, as she let herself in just after five o'clock that afternoon. The air seemed heavy and stale and the first thing she did was to open some windows. She put the groceries in the larder, removed half a loaf of stale bread and a piece of mouldy cheese, and tidied up the kitchen.

She then went upstairs and stood looking around the landing before going into her own bedroom to put away the few clothes she'd brought with her. She'd make something for supper that could be warmed up, even though she was dubious that it would be eaten. She felt dismayed, guilty, anxious and not a little uneasy as she wandered from room to room. She'd never seen George the worse for drink, and she found it hard to imagine. But how often had she seen her da in that state? All *too* often. She prayed George wouldn't be belligerent, or – what was utterly unthinkable – violent.

She'd made herself a sandwich at seven o'clock and sat watching the fingers of the clock on the mantel as they crawled towards the half-hour and then towards eight o'clock. Unable to settle, she got up and went to the window and looked out, hoping to see George walking towards the house, no matter how unsteadily, but the street was deserted.

She went back into the kitchen and put the kettle on, sighing heavily. This was going to be a long night, and she wished it was over, but there was nothing she could do except wait – and hope he would, at least, be sensible enough to listen to her.

Chapter Thirty-Seven

It was half an hour later when she heard the unmistakable sound of fumbling as a key was ineptly inserted into the lock on the front door. She got to her feet and walked into the hall. Her heart was hammering uncomfortably as, at last, the door opened and George Rutherford stood there, slightly dishevelled and bleary-eyed, but at least not swaying unsteadily.

'George... I ... I've come home,' she said, moving towards him.

He stared at her uncomprehendingly, in silence.

'Oh, George! Look at the state of you! Where have you been? I've been waiting...'

'Lizzie! Lizzie, is it ... you?' He couldn't quite believe it, wondering if it was the drink playing tricks on him.

She went and took his arm and pulled him into the hallway, closing the door behind him. 'It really is me, George! I got the train home this morning. I've been so worried about you, and it looks as if I was right to be concerned.'

He shook his head slowly, feeling for the first time in months stirrings of shame that she should see him in this condition. 'I ... I ... stopped off for a ... drink.'

She propelled him into the parlour and pushed him gently down on to the sofa; he reeked of spirits, and she'd never seen him like this before. 'George, you've had more than one. In fact, I'd say you've had far too much to drink. Oh, why are you doing this? You're ... destroying yourself, George!'

'I ... it's being ... alone here, Lizzie. I ... I ... can't face it ... day after day.' He covered his face with his hands, and his shoulders slumped.

'I know it must be hard,' she said tentatively, praying she could find the right words to help him, aware of the despair that filled him, 'but I can't ... won't let you do this to yourself.'

He looked up at her, his eyes full of misery and pain. 'Life ... life's so miserable, Lizzie. So ... empty, there's no ... purpose to anything.'

She took his hand. 'I know it must seem like that now, George, but you can't do this to yourself! You'll end up losing ... everything! Believe me, I know! Didn't I have the example of my da to show me that? Have you forgotten how you first met me, George? A half-starved waif, scouring the pubs looking for a man who cared for nothing except the drink!'

He stared at her, then shook his head slowly. 'Let it be, Lizzie. I'll manage. Go back to London...'

She shook her head vehemently. 'No! And I won't let it be, George! You've got to pull yourself together and stop this! You are a stronger man than my da was. You have a good job, a good reputation, and you're respected – or you were.

But if you carry on like this, you'll lose that, and your own self-respect too. Look at the state of you! Can't you see where all this drinking is leading? Do you really want to end up like my father? You *can* get through this, George, and I'm staying here to make sure you do. Eileen would be horrified to see what you are doing to yourself! We all are! Everyone who cares about you feels the same way. You've got to try, George!'

He groaned at the mention of his deceased wife. 'Don't ... Lizzie.'

Although her heart went out to him, she knew she had to be cruel to be kind. 'George, you know she would. She wouldn't want to see you behaving like this, destroying yourself, destroying everything you both worked so hard for.'

'Lizzie! Lizzie ... for God's sake ... stop!' he pleaded, although knowing she was right.

'Only if you'll stop drinking, George! I won't stand by and watch you ruin your life. I'm staying.'

'Your job ... so ... proud,' he muttered almost to himself.

She wasn't going to let him use this as an excuse. 'I'll sort something out. They've been very good to me in the past, so I hope they'll understand. I'll stay with Nellie; it wouldn't be right for me to stay here with you, without ... Eileen being here. People would talk.'

He seemed not to have heard her. He'd slumped back and closed his eyes, and she wondered if he had passed out. She shook him gently. 'George, did you hear me?'

He nodded slowly.

Lizzie sighed heavily, thankful he at least had understood. It would be a bit of a squeeze at Nellie's, but she couldn't stay here. She wasn't at all sure Liberty's would be as understanding as she hoped, but she wasn't going back until she was certain George was back on the straight and narrow, and off the drink.

'Get yourself to bed, George, you've work in the morning,' she urged him. 'I'll go back to Bennett Street,' she added before she left the room, closing the door quietly behind her.

Nellie was concerned when Lizzie arrived back. 'Hasn't 'e come 'ome, Lizzie?'

Lizzie took off her hat, placed it on the dresser and sat wearily down at the table. 'Oh, yes, and I'm afraid in the usual state!'

'What did you say to him, Lizzie?' Lena asked as she poured her friend a cup of tea.

'I told him off! Oh, I know it's so very hard for him ... being there alone, and still grieving ... but I just can't let him drink himself into an early grave, and I told him that Eileen wouldn't have wanted that, either. In fact, she'd be horrified at the state of him.'

Nellie nodded slowly. 'Do yer think 'e took it all in, Lizzie? Half the time when they've 'ad a skinful, they don't remember a thing next day.'

'He wasn't quite *that* bad, Nellie. And I told him I'm staying, that I'm not going back until I'm sure he's over all this.'

Lena frowned. 'What about your job, Lizzie?'

Lizzie smiled ruefully. 'I'll write to them and put in a formal request to take extended leave of absence, although I don't hold out much hope, and I wonder if it's even fair to ask. I'm part of a team, and my not being there will make extra work for them. But I just can't leave him, Lena, I just can't! If they say they can't do that, I ... I'll understand and I'll try and get something up here.' She turned to Nellie. 'I can't stay in that house with him, it wouldn't be "proper"–'

'Indeed it would not, my girl!' Nellie put in firmly. 'Folk would 'ave a field day gossipin' about both of yer. Yer reputations would be ruined. You'll 'ave ter stay 'ere, if yer can put up with us all, not used to bein' so cramped now.'

Lizzie smiled at her. 'Of course I can, thanks. I'm very grateful.'

Nellie nodded grimly. 'And if I were you, luv, I wouldn't be in any rush to be goin' back to Olivia Street. Let 'im stew for a day or two, it might bring 'im to 'is senses!'

Lizzie nodded her agreement, although she wasn't too sure if this was the right thing to do.

'I'll go round first thing and bring some of my work home here. I ... I ... don't want to be disturbing him in any way,' Lena added, thinking the whole affair was very sad.

Next morning, Lizzie did wonder if George had managed to get up and go into work. But then, she reasoned, somehow he had been managing to do just that for weeks. She hadn't slept well, for she was unused now to sleeping in the same bed as Lena, and she had been worrying about George and about her future. She really didn't want to have to give up such a prestigious position as the one she held at Liberty's. But what alternative did she have? It was because George had had such faith in her and her abilities, and both he and Eileen had encouraged her and been proud of her achievements, that she could not now leave him to try to cope on his own.

First thing, after she'd helped Nellie with the chores, she sat down to write to Edmund Vernon. It was a very difficult letter to compose, she thought. As clearly as she could, she set out her situation and that of George and again reiterated that if they had to terminate her employment, she would understand, but that she would always be grateful to them for the opportunities she had been afforded and hoped that, in the circumstances, they could see their way clear to help.

As Lena came in Lizzie looked up, enquiringly.

'Well, there was no sign of him, so he's obviously gone to work as usual,' she informed both her friend and her mother as she put her parcels down on the table.

Nellie just nodded.

'It's taken me ages to write this letter to Mr Vernon, and I'd better post it before I regret it,' Lizzie said, getting to her feet. She was thankful that at least George had made it into work.

'It's a lovely morning, so why don't we go for a walk, Lizzie?' Lena suggested.

Lizzie frowned but then smiled. 'Lena, you've got work to do, remember. We can't just go off on a jaunt at the drop of a hat because the sun's shining.'

Lena pulled a face. 'I suppose you're right.'

'I'll go and post this, and then I'll come back

and I'll give you a hand,' Lizzie said firmly.

Nellie sighed, thinking she'd have them both under her feet all day – and in such a cramped space too. But it couldn't be helped. Lena did have to work, and it might just keep Lizzie occupied too, for Nellie had no idea how this situation would turn out. She hoped Lizzie wouldn't lose her job and sincerely hoped that George Rutherford would pull himself together; he wasn't the first man to become a widower, and he wouldn't be the last.

It was three days later when Lizzie received a reply from Edmund Vernon. Despite her anxiety about George, she had taken Nellie's advice and not paid a visit to Olivia Street.

'Well, luv, what does 'e say?' Nellie asked, having noted the typed address and hoping it wasn't bad news.

Lizzie smiled. 'It's good news, Nellie. He says that under the circumstances, and taking into consideration the fact that I am a valued member of the design team, management are prepared to give me five weeks' leave of absence – without payment, naturally. But if I could see my way, circumstances permitting, to continue to work on my current designs here and forward them to him, it would be appreciated by the rest of the team – and some remuneration could, of course, be discussed. Oh, I never expected this, Nellie!'

'Nor did I, Lizzie, but yer 'ave ter admit, it's a godsend. They're bein' very good to yer, luv.'

Lizzie looked thoughtful. 'They are, indeed. And at least in five weeks I'll be able to see if

George has made an effort to get his life back on track. If he hasn't...' She shrugged helplessly.

'Well, if 'e 'asn't, Lizzie, and he won't take no heed of yer, there won't be much else yer can do. Yer'll just 'ave to go back to London and yer job. There's not many employers would be as understanding, an' they're goin' out on a limb for yer as it is,' Nellie pronounced firmly.

Lizzie bit her lip. 'I know,' she replied, praying that she wouldn't have to take that decision.

Lizzie was surprised and greatly relieved when, after supper that evening, George called at Nellie's house, quite obviously sober and his usual clean and tidy self.

'I hope I'm not disturbing you, Mrs Gibbons,' he said, a little self-consciously, as Nellie ushered him into the kitchen. He was obviously feeling rather uncomfortable.

That was only to be expected, she thought. 'Not at all. I take it you're 'ere to see Lizzie?'

George nodded and managed a smile as Lizzie got to her feet. 'I was hoping that we could perhaps go for a walk, Lizzie?'

She smiled back, relief evident in her eyes. 'I'd like that.'

As Lizzie quickly put on her hat and a jacket, Nellie busied herself with clearing the dishes, helped by Lena. Ernie retreated behind his newspaper, feeling embarrassed by the whole situation.

'I'll make sure she gets home safely, Mrs Gibbons,' George said, before ushering Lizzie into the hallway.

Lizzie had been outspoken in Olivia Street but

now, seeing George for the first time in three days, she felt an awkwardness between them and was unsure what to say. She decided to let George take the lead. When they had reached the end of Bennett Street and were walking slowly beside the canal, George turned to her.

'Lizzie, I ... I'm sorry for the ... condition you found me in the other night. I'd no idea you'd come home,' he said.

She looked up at him, with concern. 'I came because everyone was worried about you, George. Me most of all.'

He frowned. The past few days had been hell, but he'd been so ashamed of himself that he'd finally realised that she was right. He was destroying himself; he was throwing away everything that had always been important to him and to Eileen; and he knew that Lizzie cared about him. 'It was Ned who told you, I take it?'

She nodded. 'Lena had noticed that you were not coming home until late, and you weren't eating, and she confided in Ned and ... well...'

They both remained silent as they watched the last rays of the sun gilding the grey murky waters of the canal, but it was Lizzie who spoke first. 'It's not the most picturesque of views, is it – the Leeds to Liverpool canal?'

'Not here, it's not,' he agreed. 'What about your job, Lizzie? Have you heard anything? I take it you did write to them?'

'I did, and they've been so good, George. They've given me unpaid leave for five weeks.'

He stared at her in surprise. 'That is very generous of them, Lizzie. They obviously think highly of you, but it won't be necessary for you to stay away for so long,' he said firmly. 'I've come to my senses. I ... I'm fine now. All that ... is in the past. I won't slip back, I promise.'

She nodded and smiled and slipped her arm through his. She knew just how hard it must be for him to admit to his failings, but she had no intention of going back just yet. 'I'll stay for a while longer, George. It ... it really is something of a treat for me to be back home, and Ned will be docking in a couple of days,' she confided. She was enjoying being back now. And she was determined to stay, to make sure he kept to his word.

Chapter Thirty-Eight

As the weeks passed, Nellie noticed a change in Lizzie. Of course she'd been delighted to see her brother when he was home on leave, and they even went out to the music hall as a foursome: Ned and Lena and Lizzie and George. Lizzie was happier, relieved and somehow more settled in George's company, Nellie thought. And there was no sign of him taking to the bottle again.

Lizzie helped Lena during the day, and worked on her own designs for Liberty's. But every evening, after supper, George would come and they would go out, although Lizzie realised that the evenings were drawing in and soon she would either have to visit him in Olivia Street, or they would have to sit in Nellie's cramped kitchen.

Lena had noticed the change in her friend too. 'I am glad she came home, Mam,' she confided to her mother.

'Well, God knows what would 'ave 'appened to him, if she hadn't,' Nellie replied grimly. 'At least 'e's pulled 'imself tergether, but I just 'ope that when she goes back 'e doesn't fall off the wagon as quickly as 'e climbed on it!'

Lena looked thoughtful as she nodded. 'Do you think, Mam, that now ... Lizzie ... well, that she sort of likes him much more than she used to? In a more ... grown-up way?'

Nellie stared hard at her daughter. 'Has she said anything to you?'

Lena shook her head. 'No, Mam, she was upset and worried about him at first, and that was only natural, but I just thought that when we all went out – when Ned was home – that they both seemed ... closer, different somehow.'

Nellie nodded. She'd noticed a change in them both over the past weeks, although she'd said nothing. They did seem to have become much closer. Did they realise it? she wondered. 'Well, Lizzie's not a child now – far from it. She's a grown-up, independent young woman, and he ... well, he's not all that much older than her,' she mused aloud. She didn't know where this would end, but she hoped it wouldn't end badly.

The following Saturday afternoon, Lizzie decided that she would call at Olivia Street. After all, it had been her home for years, and the neighbours all knew her well enough, and as she had no intention of staying late into the evening there could be no gossip. She decided to go into Liverpool to Cooper's, the specialist grocers in Church Street, for George was very partial to freshly ground coffee. Eileen had occasionally bought it as a treat, and Cooper's was the only place she knew of that sold it; she felt that George more than deserved a treat.

She always enjoyed wandering around the big grocery store, with its displays of fruit and vegetables from all over the world and exotic food stuffs from the various parts of the country, the Continent and the Empire, and she loved the smell of fresh coffee that permeated the whole ground floor. She made her purchases and then took the tram home.

She got off the tram in Stanley Road, in Bootle, as she'd made up her mind to call at Olivia Street on her way home. That way George could enjoy the coffee after his supper, and before they went for their evening stroll. She was so thankful and relieved that George seemed to be keeping to his promise, and she really didn't have any serious doubts about him staying off the drink when she returned to London, as she must do fairly soon. She really would miss him and the time they spent together, she thought, as she let herself into the house.

She frowned as she heard voices coming from the parlour. She'd not expected him to have company; he'd said nothing to her about visitors, and she wondered who it was.

After taking off her hat and tidying her hair in front of the mirror on the hallstand, she went through into the sitting room.

'Hello, George, I've been into town and decided to call. I am sorry to interrupt, I had no idea you had guests–' she began. Her eyebrows rose sharply and she felt her quick intake of breath as she caught sight of Mabel Woods sitting on the sofa, looking quite at home and presiding over the tea tray.

'Mabel kindly dropped in to see how I was getting along,' George explained, looking a little embarrassed. He hadn't expected Lizzie to call today. 'She's sort of taken me under her wing lately,' he tried to explain.

'Really,' Lizzie replied curtly, sitting down in the armchair by the fireplace. 'I had no idea you were so friendly.' He had never mentioned Mabel before, although now she remembered that Lena had said the woman had taken to calling more regularly.

Neither George nor Mabel replied, so Lizzie sat down and placed the packet of coffee on the table. 'I was in town today, George, and knowing how partial you are to Cooper's coffee I brought you some as a treat.'

George smiled at her. 'That was kind of you, Lizzie, I *do* like it.'

Reluctantly, Mabel poured a cup of tea and handed it to her. Lizzie felt uneasy and suspicious, wondering how often Mabel had visited in the past. It wasn't as if the woman didn't see George almost every day at work, and had done for years. Just what did they find to talk about when they were here alone? she wondered. As far as she could see, George had nothing much in common with Mabel Woods.

They engaged in small talk until Lizzie, feeling annoyed and decidedly unwelcome in her former home, and noting that George did not appear to want to make arrangements for later that evening, decided she would go back to Nellie's. She rose and replaced her cup and saucer on the tray, determined she would not hand them to Mabel, thereby designating her the hostess. 'Well, I'd best be off, then.'

George frowned, disconcerted by Lizzie's abrupt departure and not really understanding why she appeared to feel uncomfortable – after all, she knew Mabel well enough. 'Must you rush off so soon, Lizzie?'

She turned to him, her eyebrows raised quizzically, but sensing Mabel's irritation. 'Will you be round later for a walk, then?'

George looked a little embarrassed. 'I think it might be a little too late tonight, Lizzie. I mean, it would be very churlish of me not to see Mabel home after she's so kindly called to see me and brought me cake and scones that she made herself, which I'm sure you'll agree is very kind of her.'

'Very thoughtful,' Lizzie replied, somewhat curtly, and feeling disgruntled as both George and Mabel rose.

To her surprise and annoyance, it was Mabel who accompanied her into the hall.

'I am quite capable of letting myself out, Mabel. In case you've forgotten, this was my home for years and, in fact, still is ... technically. It's only because I value both my own and George's reputations that I'm not staying here.'

Mabel seemed unperturbed. 'I'm quite aware of that, Lizzie. But I was wondering if you have any idea when you are going to go back to London?' she asked.

Lizzie glared at her, 'Why? Just what has it got to do with you when I return?'

Mabel managed a patient smile, as though dealing with a child – and a not very bright one, at that. 'I have to say this, Lizzie, I just feel that George's state of mind and his entire ... well-being and situation here would be vastly improved, become far more ... *settled*, if he was assured that you were back in London and back at work, where you belong. You know how proud he is of you, and you being away from Liberty's all this time must concern him greatly. How would it affect him if you were to lose such a good job, to throw such an opportunity away, and on the pretext of caring for *him?* You've admitted yourself it's not *practical* for you to stay here. So how can you care for him, Lizzie? The best thing you could do for George is to go back to London.'

Lizzie pressed her lips tightly together as anger surged through her. How *dare* she say such things! How dare Mabel Woods think she had the right to interfere in both her and George's lives? Oh, she could see clearly now just what the woman had in mind! 'I will go back to London when *I* see fit, and when I am sure that George is more settled and content, and coping well with his life!' she replied through gritted teeth. 'Which, believe me, *Miss Woods*, those of us who know him well will be far more able to ascertain than a mere acquaintance and workmate such as yourself!' Without

356

giving the older woman a chance to reply, Lizzie left without another word.

All the way back to Nellie's she fumed about the woman's sheer impertinence. What was the matter with George that he couldn't see just what Mabel Woods was up to under the guise of concern and consideration? Now she remembered the previous occasions when Mabel had called on some flimsy pretext. At least her motives were out in the open now, as far as Lizzie was concerned. Well, she had no intention of going back to London just to suit Mabel Woods! It was a long time since she'd felt so angry, and as she walked up Bennett Street, she began to wonder why – and, indeed, why she felt so jealous. The thought of Mabel Woods moving into that house with him made her blood boil. Yes, of course she did care for George – she cared for him a great deal – and he was vulnerable still. She certainly didn't want to see him succumb to the wiles of the likes of Mabel Woods. But was that all? Oh, she was becoming so confused, she thought. She wished she'd never bought the damned coffee or called in to give it to him.

She found Lena working patiently on one of her new designs. Of Ernie there was no sign, but Nellie was busily peeling potatoes for tea. 'You're back early,' the older woman greeted her laconically. 'Wasn't he in?' She wrapped the peelings in an old piece of newspaper and shoved them into the range before taking the big earthenware bowl over to the sink.

'Oh yes, he was in all right!' Lizzie replied grimly as she took off her hat, placed it on the dresser and sat down beside Lena on the bench at the table.

Lena and her mother exchanged glances.

'And?' Lena probed, aware that something had upset her friend a great deal.

'And guess what? He was entertaining Mabel Woods to tea!'

Both Lena and Nellie were astonished, but Nellie recovered first. 'Who the 'ell invited her fer tea?'

'I don't know,' Lizzie fumed.

'Probably invited 'erself!' Lena added tersely.

'Well, she looked entirely at home. And she'd brought him cake and scones, made with her own fair hands!'

Nellie sniffed. ''Ad she indeed! Pushy is that one, always 'as been, an' with an eye to the main chance. Intent on gettin' 'er feet under the table all right; he's a good catch is George Rutherford for the likes of 'er,' she added ominously. Nellie knew for a fact that it wasn't Mabel's first visit to George; she listened to local gossip, and Lena had told her too. But obviously Lizzie had had no idea of what was going on and was very upset, as well she might be. She'd been fond of Eileen and wouldn't take kindly to the likes of Mabel Woods taking her place.

'And she had the downright *cheek* to ask when I was going back to London, saying that *she* thought me staying on here wasn't doing him any good! Have you ever heard the like?' Lizzie had shredded a piece of tracing paper without even realising she had done so.

'Right 'ardfaced is that one! Well, I think we

could all do with a cup of tea. Lena, put that stuff away and put the kettle on. Did you say that you're going down to meet Ned tomorrow?' she queried, thinking Lizzie's brother might be able to pour some oil on the troubled waters that Lizzie was obviously envisaging in the future with George and Mabel Woods.

'No, Mam, not for three days yet,' Lena replied as she made the tea.

Lizzie had time to sit and brood on the situation as, later that evening, when she was usually out with George, Peggy came to visit her mother, bringing the baby and Bertie her husband, who promptly made an excuse to take his father-in-law for a pint. Lizzie was lost in thought for most of the evening, while Nellie exclaimed over her grandson's many and marvellous attributes and offered advice to both her girls on marriage and motherhood, all of which was greeted rather offhandedly.

At length, the men returned from the pub, Peggy gathered her little family together and departed, and Lizzie and Lena began to tidy up.

'Me da's retired for the night, so why don't you join him, Mam? We'll finish up here, you're worn out with our Peggy and the little feller,' Lena urged.

'I will in a minute or two, luv, but I can see there's been something botherin' Lizzie all night. What's up, luv?' Nellie sat down beside Lizzie at the table.

Lizzie managed a wry smile. 'I can't hide anything from you, Nellie, can I? Oh, it ... it's this business with Mabel Woods.'

'Don't let that get yer down, girl! I'm sure 'e's got more sense than ter get 'imself mixed up with that one!'

Lizzie bit her lip. 'I ... I hope so, Nellie. But the thing is, why do I feel so jealous? Angry, *that* I can understand, and I ... I've been thinking about it all night. I'd hate to see Mabel Woods living in that house, fawning over George, using all Eileen's possessions as if they were her own, but why am I so jealous? He ... he does deserve someone to look after him and care for him; he's still a young man. But ... but somehow I don't want that person to be anyone other than ... me! Even though I have my life in London...' She paused, twisting her hands together, confused by her sudden emotions. 'Oh, and I *am* jealous, Nellie! I don't want *anyone* else to live in that house with him and care for him, let alone Mabel Woods!'

Nellie nodded slowly. She'd begun to suspect that Lizzie's feelings for George Rutherford were far stronger than she realised. 'Maybe you're really fonder of him than you thought, Lizzie? That all sounds like some very strong emotions to me, even if yer 'aven't thought about them before now. Do yer think you've ... fallen in love with 'im?'

Now it was Lizzie's turn to stare as she pressed her hands to her cheeks. 'I don't know, Nellie, I just don't know! I've not thought about it before, but ... maybe, I have. Maybe I do ... love him. Oh, I just don't ... *know!*'

'Did George seem ... pleased that Mabel was there?' Nellie asked cautiously.

Lizzie nodded. 'I think so, and he did say he wouldn't be round later, as he couldn't let her walk home on her own – not after she'd brought him cake!' Lizzie frowned as a thought occurred to her. 'Maybe he really *was* pleased to see her?'

Nellie sighed grimly. 'He's that decent a bloke, he probably hasn't a clue what she's up to.'

'Oh, Nellie, what do I do? I'm so … confused! Should I go and talk to him?' Lizzie begged for advice.

'And tell him what, Lizzie? That you were spittin' feathers cos yer found that one sitting in 'is parlour takin' tea? That you think it's a disgrace that she can visit quite 'appily and you can't even spend an evenin' in yer own 'ome, but that yer don't want anyone else castin' their eyes in 'is direction, because yer jealous?'

Lizzie nodded unhappily.

Nellie's tone and expression softened. 'Lizzie, you've still got another three weeks before you 'ave to go back. That should give you time to make up yer mind about just what you feel for 'im, and then you can talk to 'im. Iffen yer want to, of course – yer might decide to say nothing and go back to your career.'

Lizzie nodded, even more confused now by Nellie's words. 'I'll just have to give it all a lot more thought, Nellie.'

On Sunday afternoon, she walked and walked through the streets of Bootle, streets familiar since childhood – and filled with such bitter-sweet memories – but at last she'd got a tram to the Pier Head. The afternoon was becoming increasingly warmer, and her head was beginning to ache, so she crossed to the church of St Nicholas and sat in the gardens there, thankful for the dense shade of some large shrubs. It was peaceful here, she thought, despite the hustle and bustle of the waterfront beyond, and the breeze from the river was cooling. She couldn't get out of her mind how at home Mabel Woods had appeared to be, and how comfortable George had seemed in her presence. She'd thought long and hard about it. Was she being unreasonable? Perhaps it would be better for George to seek out Mabel's company? She was more his age, and they did have quite a lot of things in common, after all. She was a decent, respectable woman who would no doubt make him a very good wife, although she could never aspire to the level of education, skill and manners that Eileen had possessed.

Should she go back to London? As everyone reminded her, she did have an excellent position, a promising career – and George *was* indeed so proud of her. She had become an accomplished young woman under his and his wife's guidance, and she knew he considered her now to be several steps higher up the ladder of success than Mabel Woods, who was still only a supervisor in a match factory. She would indeed be a fool to give up her prestigious career at Liberty's, but ahead of her stretched perhaps a life without the joy of loving someone, of getting married and of having a home and children of her own. But she really did not wish to see Mabel Woods taking Eileen's place at the altar in the Baptist Church beside George. Oh, there was so much to think about!

She'd thought she loved Edwin Pierce, but she hadn't; she'd been gullible, flattered, infatuated. When he'd kissed her it had been in an entirely different way, and he'd let her down.

He'd lied and deceived her and, when confronted, had cast her aside callously and without a second thought. George would never do anything like that; it wasn't in his nature. She'd vowed she would never give her heart as freely again, but had hoped that one day she would find someone to trust with her love.

The breeze moved the canopy of the leaves above her slightly and a bright ray of sunlight pierced the thick foliage. She'd been so *blind*, she thought suddenly, and with great clarity; there *was* someone she could trust and love; she didn't need to look any further. George had always been such a huge part of her life, and now ... now she realised that she wanted him to love her the way she loved him – but was that possible?

She sat there, examining her feelings, until the sun began to slip down in the sky, bathing the gardens in a reddish-gold light, and finally she got to her feet. She'd go home and tell George how she felt, and about the decision she'd made. How he would take it, she didn't know, for it was so sudden and so unexpected – even to herself – but she felt in her heart that her decision was the right one.

Chapter Thirty-Nine

Later that Sunday evening, when George finally sat down with his coffee, it reminded him how thoughtful Lizzie had been to purchase it, and he felt perturbed that she had seemed upset to find him entertaining Mabel yesterday afternoon, which was something he hadn't intended to do. She had just called and he'd been grateful to her for taking the trouble, and also for the cakes she'd brought. He'd felt obliged to invite her in, but that was as far as it went.

The last thing he had wanted to do was upset Lizzie, for he felt that the fact he could now move on with his life was due to her. He had to admit that she had made him see sense and that, in fact, his grief had lessened. He still hated coming home to an empty house, but at least he could now look forward to the future.

He sipped the coffee slowly, savouring the taste but frowning thoughtfully. What, in fact, did he want from the future? It was true that he was lonely and that he was still a relatively young man, and with a decent job. He missed Lizzie being around, even though of course she had been living and working in London for a while before he'd become a widower. He glanced thoughtfully across at the rather stiff, formal photograph of himself, Eileen and Lizzie that he'd insisted they have taken before Lizzie left for London, and which had pride of place on top of the upright piano. Lizzie's excitement and enthusiasm shone out, despite their serious expressions, he thought.

He smiled to himself and then sighed. More recently, it seemed as though he thought of her a great deal more than he used to. He really missed her chatter, her laughter, her sheer joy of life and her ability to make him look forward instead of back. But what kind of a future did he really have? He had come to realise lately that what he wanted from the future was, in fact, Lizzie. He had become aware that what he felt for her now was love, and that it was a feeling that was growing stronger by the day. A feeling for Lizzie that he'd never felt before. But what would Lizzie think, if he were to tell her? Could she possibly love him? Or would it ruin the close friendship they had, if he disclosed how he really felt about her?

He placed his cup and saucer down on the table and stood up, beginning to pace the room. In a couple of weeks she would be going back and Lord alone knew when she would be back. Should he have the courage of his convictions and tell her, and maybe lose that bond? Or should he say nothing – remain silent – and let her go back to London, to her career and her future and possibly a new love in her life, someone younger than himself, and not knowing how he felt about her? Oh, it was such a dilemma, and he was so unsure of himself. But if he said nothing...

He thrust his hands deep into the pockets of his jacket as he made up his mind. He would call round to Nellie's tonight. What was the point in waiting?

He was bitterly disappointed when Nellie informed him that Lizzie was still out. But she also said that she'd been out most of the afternoon and early evening, so she was sure she wouldn't be long now and that he was quite welcome to wait. He'd assumed Lizzie would be in and they could go for a walk, but if she'd been out so long... He shook his head, knowing they would have little or no privacy here.

'No, I won't impose on you. Will you just ... just tell her I called?' he asked Nellie as he left to return home, wondering if he would still have the courage tomorrow evening. By then would he think it was too late, or that he was too foolish, or find a dozen other reasons why he should say nothing to her? Indeed, perhaps this was Providence's way of pointing out that Lizzie was not for him.

He was very dispirited as he let himself into the house and went through into the parlour, and he almost wished he'd kept the half-bottle of whisky in the sideboard instead of pouring it down the sink. He sank down in an armchair, but as he did so he thought he heard a knock on the front door. He went to open it with some trepidation, and hoped it wasn't Mabel Woods again.

He was surprised to see Lizzie standing on the doorstep and realised his heart was hammering in his chest. 'Lizzie! Come in.'

Lizzie followed him inside. To George it seemed the most natural thing in the world that she should be back by his side, where she belonged, but did she feel the same?

'I thought perhaps you were annoyed with me about Mabel Woods being here yesterday,' he said quietly. 'I ... I called round to Nellie's, but you were out.'

'I was annoyed, George, and I was ... jealous too,' she confided, twisting her hands together. Now that the moment had arrived she felt tongue-tied and even a little afraid, but she plunged on before she lost her nerve. 'I've spent all afternoon and evening walking and ... thinking.'

George gently ushered her into the parlour and took her hands in his. 'Lizzie, I am sorry I upset you. There is nothing between Mabel and me; there never has been nor ever will be. You see, Lizzie, I ... it's you I really care about.'

Relief and joy washed over her 'No, George, *I'm* sorry! Sorry I've been such a fool not to realise how you've been suffering, not to realise that ... that my place is with you. Not realising that I love you, George.'

He couldn't help but draw her close to him, burying his face in her thick, dark curls, unable to believe what she had just said. 'Oh, Lizzie, don't ... pity me!'

She clung to him, feeling a surge of love, tenderness and happiness engulf her.

'I don't feel sorry for you, George! I love you. I realised it today, and I know now that I want to spend the rest of my life with you.'

He held her away from him so he could look into her eyes, and there he saw truth and love. 'Lizzie, do you mean that? I ... I couldn't stand it if...'

She pulled him towards her and kissed him for

a long moment before drawing away. 'Does that answer your question? I couldn't hurt you, George, just as I know you won't hurt me.'

George let the joy and relief wash over him as he kissed her forehead, her lips, her neck. 'Lizzie, my own darling, I never dreamed I would ever be able to say this but, will you marry me?'

'Oh, George, of course I will! You're still a young man and now we have a future together, but will you come to London? We ... can't ... it wouldn't be right to stay on in this house. You'll get work, I'm sure of that, and I'll be glad to see you leave that factory. It's a foul-smelling, dirty, noisy place ... and there would be too much gossip.'

Unable to let her out of his arms, George nodded his agreement. He didn't want to stay here now, either. 'We'll rent a place of our own and you can continue in your job. I really wouldn't want you to lose it or give it up, Lizzie. You're so talented, and I'm so proud of you.'

She smiled up at him. 'Then I'll go back, George. With your experience as a factory manager, you'll get a position before long. Promise me that you'll follow me as quickly as you can? As soon as you're able to work your notice and give the landlord warning that you're leaving.'

'I've some savings to tide us over, should we need them, until I get a job. Lizzie, I've had to live without you for so long that I'd follow you to the ends of the earth.'

She smiled at him, radiant with happiness. 'Just London will do, George. I'll start immediately to look for a place for us. I know from people at work there are some decent places to live in Holloway

– a girl I know has just found somewhere in Drayton Park.'

'Do I have to ask Ned's permission?' he asked, smiling back.

She laughed. 'No, although I think he'll be pleased. Do you think we should tell Lena and Nellie?'

He kissed her again. 'Lizzie, you can tell the whole world, if you like. I'm so happy that I feel as if I'm dreaming.'

'This is no dream, George. It's our life ... our future – together, at last.' She looked at him seriously. 'Do you think it was meant to be, George? That you would be the one I found to help me all those years ago?'

He nodded. 'I do, Lizzie. I really do. But I could never have imagined that in helping you I would bring into my life the one person who was also meant to help me. Your love has saved me, Lizzie. I love you, and I'm going to spend the rest of my life filling yours with the joy and happiness you deserve.'

The publishers hope that this book has given you enjoyable reading. Large Print Books are especially designed to be as easy to see and hold as possible. If you wish a catalogue please ask at your local library or write directly to:

Magna Large Print Books
Cawood House,
Asquith Industrial Estate,
Gargrave,
Nr Skipton, North Yorkshire.
BD23 3SE

This Large Print Book for the partially sighted, who cannot read normal print, is published under the auspices of

THE ULVERSCROFT FOUNDATION